MVFOL

HOT AND SMOLDERING NIGHT

"I wanted to make myself beautiful for you," Amelia said softly. "Did I manage well enough, Gray Wing?"

Gray Wing did not respond with words. He went to Amelia and drew her into his arms and stroked her cheek with his fingertips. She could see fire burning in his eyes, mesmerizing her into almost melting. She so hungered for his kiss . . . his lips.

He crushed her so hard she gasped, then moaned with ecstasy as his mouth scorched hers with a fiery intense kiss. His mouth was hot and demanding. One hand cupped her breast as the other began unfastening her dress from behind. A sensuous tremor soared along Amelia's flesh as the dress crept down her body.

She sighed as Gray Wing began to stroke her, setting fires along her flesh that were almost more than she could bear . . .

D0499163

Charter Books by Cassie Edwards

SAVAGE SURRENDER
SAVAGE EDEN
SAVAGE SPLENDOR
SAVAGE WHISPERS
SAVAGE BLISS
SAVAGE DREAM

SAVAGE BLISS

CASSIE EDWARDS

CHARTER BOOKS, NEW YORK

The poem by Blanche Shoemaker Wagstaff was published in *The Family of Best Loved Poems*, ed. David L. George (New York: Doubleday & Co., Inc., 1952).

SAVAGE BLISS

A Charter Book/published by arrangement with
the author

PRINTING HISTORY
Charter edition/April 1990

All rights reserved.
Copyright © 1990 by Cassie Edwards.
This book may not be reproduced in whole
or in part, by mimeograph or any other means,
without permission. For information address: The Berkley
Publishing Group, 200 Madison Avenue, New York, New York 10016

ISBN: 1-55773-285-X

Charter Books are published by The Berkley Publishing Group,
200 Madison Avenue, New York, New York 10016.
The name "CHARTER" and the "C" logo
are trademarks belonging to Charter Communications, Inc.

PRINTED IN THE UNITED STATES OF AMERICA

10 9 8 7 6 5 4 3 2

I lovingly dedicate *Savage Bliss* to the Suquamish Indian tribe of Washington State.

I also wish to dedicate this book to Jennifer McCord, a romance advocate in Seattle,

and to

Lynda Garcia, Mickey Brannan, and James Hanf, also of that beautiful state,

and to

Rochelle Wayne, a dear friend and a talented author.

Author's Note

While on a research trip in 1986, I met several members of the Suquamish Indian tribe; it was a heartwarming experience. After a forty-minute ride on the Winslow Ferry from downtown Seattle, Washington, I was given a glimpse of the history of the Pacific Northwest from the perspective of Chief Seattle and his descendants, the Suquamish people. In a forested setting on the shores of Agate Passage, the Suquamish Museum reveals the world of Puget Sound's original inhabitants. I spent time in the museum, feeling the texture of woven cedar strips, weighing the lightness of a carved grease bowl, and absorbing the beauty of the Suquamish canoes. The people were warm and friendly, the experience unforgettable. The Suquamish Indians welcome all visitors with the same vigor and warmth.

The Suquamish Indians of my book, *Savage Bliss*, were a special people. Their life was not so markedly different from that of other Indians who hunted seals and sea lions from open canoes, except that they hunted the whale, that huge and majestic mammal of the sea.

The Suquamish, or Canoe Indians, very rarely used horses as a means of transportation. These Indians were masters of handling canoes, building houses, and predicting weather. They did not make war with the white man. They saw that trading was much more profitable than bloodshed.

The city of Seattle was named for one of the greater Suquamish chiefs, Chief Seattle ("Sealth" in Suquamish) who, from the arrival of the first white men, became their friend.

All paths lead to you
  Where e'er I stray,
You are the evening star
  At the end of the day.

All paths lead to you
  Hilltop or low,
You are the white birch
  In the sun's glow.

All paths lead to you
  Where e'er I roam.
You are the lark-song
  Calling me home.

—*Blanche Shoemaker Wagstaff*

One

Puget Sound

Long ago . . .

Along the far horizon, the Olympic Mountains rose blue and crested with snow, like long seas breaking in the sky. Far beyond the opposite shore another peak, Mount Rainier, rose into the sky like a great white ghost, its cone tipped in snow. Steep hills and mountains and every part of the lowlands were covered with thick woods down to the margin of the sea. The silence was interrupted only now and then by the croak of a raven, the splash of a seal, the scream of an eagle.

Amelia Storm paced anxiously in her tiny cabin on her father's great sailing ship. Christopher Storm had left the ship to go ashore on Whale Island and sit in council with the Suquamish Indians and bargain for their valuable lustrous brown otter pelts. Amelia's father was a participant in the great fur quest, an adventurer from Boston who had learned of this land of treasure and who expected to become rich from his dealings with the Indians.

A captain's share from one extremely successful voyage to the Washington territorial waters could net him enough to set up a business ashore. Amelia knew that her father had the reputation of being scheming and greedy, with no interest in cultivating the goodwill of the natives. Nor would he hesitate to rob and cheat them to get what he wanted, for he did not expect to return or see them again.

Amelia's mother watched her daughter's pacing with weary eyes. "Amelia, will you *please* stop that? Come sit down and continue with your studies," Catherine Storm pleaded, exasperated. "Lordy, daughter, I would think you'd welcome *my* tutoring over your father's. You know how demanding he can be."

"It's just that I so wanted to go ashore with Father," Amelia said sourly. "I've never seen a Suquamish Indian. It's not fair that I can't *now*!"

Amelia put her nose to a porthole and tried to peer through the grime-coated glass. But because of the filth, she was denied even the slightest peek of what was transpiring on shore.

Her brilliant green eyes, moody beneath long silky lashes, and her rich, thick hair glowing with a lustrous red sheen as it bounced on her shoulders, Amelia whirled away from the grubby porthole and plopped down on a chair opposite her mother at the table. She arranged the skirt of her beautifully printed cotton dress about her legs, then resignedly picked up her mathematics book, eyed it, and placed it back on the table.

She looked at her mother, worried, never having seen such dark circles beneath her eyes before. "Mother, you surely don't feel like tutoring me today," she said softly. "You're so pale. Are you ill again? Is it the baby?"

Amelia studied her mother more intensely, seeing so much of herself in the older woman's features—the same green eyes, red hair, and petite form. The main difference of late was in her mother's waistline, which was beginning to thicken.

Shortly after the ship left Boston her mother had discovered that she was pregnant, and she was not faring well at all during these early months. Amelia was hoping finally to become a sister. She had waited thirteen long years for the sort of pleasure she heard one received from having such special kin.

Catherine Storm rose from her chair, placing a hand to her back as she softly groaned. "Yes, it's the baby. Nothing seems to be going right with this pregnancy. I'm not sure I'll be able to carry the baby full term. It's been so many years since I've had a child. Perhaps too long."

Going to Amelia, who sat watching, Catherine stepped behind her and circled her arms about her daughter's shoulders, hugging her affectionately. "Do you think you will feel close to a brother or sister?" she asked softly. "In just a few short years you'll be old enough to be wed and have children of your own."

Amelia leaned into her mother's embrace. "Mother, I shall love being a sister," she said, sighing. Then she laughed softly. "But I doubt if I shall ever marry. Thus far I've found boys utterly *boring*. They mean nothing at all to me. Nothing!"

Amelia grimaced when she felt her mother jerk away and heard her moan. Rising quickly from her chair, she turned with a start, stunned to see her mother doubled over in pain, even paler than before.

"Mother," she gasped, going to her, taking her by an elbow. "Lie down. Please lie down. I can tell that you're in pain."

Catherine forced herself to straighten and, laughing nervously, wiped away the beads of perspiration that had formed on her brow. "Darling, at times like this, when I have these fitful pains, I vividly recall being pregnant with you," she lied. She had seen how truly concerned Amelia was and saw no need to worry her further.

Softly patting Amelia's face, Catherine smiled at her. "The pains were worth it then; they'll be worth it now," she further reassured. "I can hardly wait to hold a baby in my arms again."

"But, Mother, I—" Amelia argued softly.

"I'll have none of your worries today," Catherine fussed, interrupting Amelia. "Girls your age aren't supposed to worry. Leave that for your elders."

"I can't help but worry, Mother."

"I know," Catherine sighed. "You've been a worrier since you were a mere child."

Catherine went to the table and closed the mathematics book. "That's all the tutoring for today, my dear," she said, smiling wearily. "I'd best go to my cabin and take a nap." She patted her stomach. "I must take care of your future brother or sister."

Amelia followed her mother to the door. "Which do you think it'll be, Mother?" she asked, her heart longing for a sister. "A boy or a girl?"

Catherine gave Amelia a sidewise glance. "It doesn't matter, only that it is as healthy and as beautiful as you," she said. She gave Amelia a quick hug, then left the cabin.

With worries of her mother replaced by renewed curiosity about the Suquamish, she reached for her embroidery hoop and needle, and began working the needle into the fabric, adding more stitches to the iris design already taking shape in a soft orchid color. When she pricked her finger, she groaned in frustration, tossed the embroidery aside, and rose from the bunk.

The floor-length skirt of her cotton dress tangled about her legs as she walked determinedly to the door and stepped outside into the dark, damp corridor. Only a dim light flickered from the whale oil lamps that hung on the bulkhead beside the many closed doors. Behind the closed door across from Amelia's cabin lay her mother, now surely in a sound sleep. If Amelia wished, she could go on deck and no one would be the wiser! Perhaps she could now see her father and the Indians involved in the transactions.

This was Amelia's first trip to Puget Sound. She longed for a glimpse of the Indians who were known to wear tattoos of all shapes on their bodies. How could she *not* seize this opportunity to take a quick look? Only the crew left aboard the ship would see her. They would have no reason to inform her father of her naughtiness in disobeying his strict orders. And if he had not wanted her to fully appreciate the experience of this sea journey, why had he even brought her?

But she truly knew why. Her father had left angry debt-ors behind and did not want to expose his wife and daughter to their hounding. When he returned to Boston with his valuable cargo, no one would ever again have cause to pester the Storm family over debts. Her father would have enough money not only to make his debtors happy but also to make his family comfortable forever.

Looking up and down the corridor, seeing no one, Amelia crept toward the companionway at the far end and scampered to the deck and to the rail. Amazed at the apparently deserted island, she was further surprised by the eerie silence. She hugged herself when the rustling of a breeze made her imagine she was hearing hideous monsters in the wilderness.

Yet when she let her eyes wander to the lovely setting, she realized it was nothing short of paradise. The land was shawled in the dark green cloak of cedar, hemlock and fir, dominated by the eternal white cone of Mount Rainier. Beneath the cathedral stands of virgin hemlock and fir, surely deer, fox, otter, and raccoons foraged, not monsters! she chided herself.

In the distance, a herd of harbor seals lay sunning on a ledge. Some were darting gracefully by in the water, their luminous brown eyes scouting kelp beds for a meal of bass and ling.

Her father's ship had found its way to Puget Sound, which covered some seven hundred square miles, encircled by mile upon mile of breathtaking wooded coastline, and dotted with islands. Amelia had read that it had been given its name by George Vancouver, who was the first British explorer to sail into the area in 1792 and who was courteously received by the Indians. Vancouver had marveled at this great natural basin and had named his discovery after a trusted lieutenant, Peter Puget.

Her gaze stopping, Amelia saw that the Suquamish village consisted of more than thirty cedar-plank houses strung along the beach facing the Sound. All were rectangular and supported by a framework of massive posts or planks. Her rapt attention was drawn to the massive totem poles—columns of carved animals, one above the other—that stood along the beach in front of the village. They were enormous!

On closer scrutiny, Amelia recognized the figures on the poles; they were whales. She admired the obvious skill that had been used in making the totems. The wood had been carved so that the entire animal was split down the front and opened out, to show both right and left sides, somehow hinged at the spine.

Forcing her eyes away from the totem, Amelia found her father, several of his crew, and the Suquamish quite a distance from the ship. They appeared to be having a cordial enough meeting.

Amelia smiled when she saw that her father and his officers were sitting on one side of a line drawn on the beach, facing the Indians seated on the other side. She had overheard conversations between her father and his first mate about how fearful the Indians were of the dreaded disease smallpox, which some other tribes had contracted from the white traders. The Indians believed they would be safe if a line separated them from the white men and their disease.

"So innocent," Amelia whispered to herself. "The Indians are *so* innocent to believe a line drawn in sand could protect them."

But she knew that the Indians were prepared to risk disease just to trade with those they called "Bostons," because so many of them came from that city. The coastal tribes were noted for their wealth. "Bostons" like her father could fill the holds of their ships with pelts worth a king's ransom in exchange for a few barrels of adze blades, roughly made knives, and cheap glass beads. Other Indians traded their pelts for "exotic" foods like molasses, rice, and rum.

The wind, filled with the sweet scent of cedar, whipped Amelia's loose and flowing hair about her face in wild red strands. Smoothing them away, running her slender fingers through her hair to encourage it to lie flat along the straight line of her back, she once again looked in the direction of the green mass of trees quite a distance from where her father continued to deal with the Indians. She had felt eyes on her and wondered why.

Then her breath was suddenly taken when she spied someone standing among the trees, indeed looking her way, obviously studying her, as if intrigued by her.

The intrigue was instantly mutual, for Amelia found herself looking at an Indian brave who appeared not to be all that much older than herself. Her breath and heartbeat quickened when she noted his handsomeness. Even from such a distance she could see the uniqueness of the Indian, who was tall and barefoot, wearing only a breech-cloth. His skin was a light shade of copper and appeared smooth, with youthful muscles that rippled beneath satin flesh. His hair was a dark brown and fell loose to his broad shoulders.

As he continued to watch her, Amelia could tell that his eyes were intense, dark, and observant. She wondered if he was looking at her because he saw something special in her or only because Indians were interested in all white men and women, fascinated by their fair skin, by what they ate, and how they lived.

Something deep within Amelia's stomach strangely stirred. Still being watched closely, she became warm from the wonder of the moment. This handsome Indian was fascinating. If only she could meet him face to face to talk with him. It would be so exciting!

As though some unseen force prevailed, guiding her movements, Amelia's eyes were drawn to the gangplank that reached from the ship to the dock that led to land. She glanced from her father, who was still deep in conversation with the Indians, back to the gangplank, then to a great cluster of madrona trees that grew to the edge of the beach close to the ship. If she could rush down to the dock and into the shadows of the trees, her father would not see her. And his back *was* turned to her. . . .

"And mother is quite asleep by now and would never miss me," she whispered, feeling her pulse quickening in the hollow of her throat.

Contemplating her daring desire to leave the ship, Amelia kneaded the side of her neck where the crisp white collar of her dress lay so neatly in place. Should she? What if she was caught? Her father was a strict disciplinarian. Whatever he ordered, she was forced to do. He was the voice of authority in her life and she respected him, for he was her father and usually knew what was best.

But this time Amelia wanted to follow her own feelings, her own intrigues. Life had become boring. Just a little bit of excitement now could perhaps sustain her during the long journey back to Boston!

"Yes, I *shall*," she whispered, nodding.

Cautiously looking over her shoulder at the activity on the ship behind her, she was pleased to find that the crewmen also understood who *their* voice of authority was: her father, Christopher Storm. Some men were pumping stale water from the ship's casks and refilling them with fresh, others were caulking the ship's sides. Some were preparing the sails for the departure from Puget Sound.

None were watching her, for they had all been warned by Amelia's father that they were never to confront her or they would be shot on the spot. Thus far, none had even come close to speaking to her, much less touching her. When she was around, they kept their eyes cast downward so as to avoid being accused of wrongful thoughts.

With a pounding heart, Amelia moved toward the gangplank. Once there she lifted the hem of her dress and hurried to the dock, and across it to the rocky shore. Scampering, she ran up the rugged slope from the beach. When she reached the forest edge, she stopped, startled, as the young brave of her fascination stepped into her path.

Never before had she seen such penetrating steel-gray eyes. They were hypnotic, making her feel suddenly more woman than child. . . .

Two

Gulls wheeled overhead on steady wings, turning their smooth heads slowly as they flew onward and scanned the water for prey. Amelia stood as though in a trance as she continued looking up into the mesmerizing eyes of the handsome young Indian brave, now wondering if she had made a mistake by coming to speak with him. Though he was making her insides quiver strangely, he had yet to change his expression or make anything resembling a friendly gesture toward her.

But she was there and she would not let the Indian dissuade her from her intention to befriend him. He had willed her there with his eyes, and she had come. She would not return to the ship without a civil hello first. Perhaps that would break his silence, encourage him to show his friendly side. Something about him and the way he was looking at her made her feel certain that he did not stare at her just because she was white. Perhaps he was greeting her with silence because he was full of wonder at having the same strange stirrings within himself at the sight of *her*.

Surely she was experiencing such feelings because of

the exotic setting and the forbidden elements one associated with a white girl being enamored of an Indian brave. Was he fascinated with her for the same reasons? Or could he have found something especially attractive in her even at her young age?

No matter the cause . . . Amelia only knew that she must make a sincere effort to get to know him better. And she would have to hurry. Her father must never know that she had left the ship for *any* reason!

"Hello," Amelia said, her voice unusually weak as she offered the Indian a handshake of friendship. "My name is Amelia Storm. What is yours?"

Her hand began to feel as heavy as lead when the Indian did not receive it as was intended for him to do, instead clasping his hands tightly behind him. Slowly Amelia lowered her hand and began fidgeting with the skirt of her dress as she shifted her feet nervously on the mossy ground.

"Surely you have a name," she said, a tentative smile quivering on her lips. "Or do you not even know what I am saying? Do you not speak English?"

Her eyes shifted, now focused on a tiny tattoo on the Indian's left shoulder; it was in the shape of a whale. Her eyes moved onward to a necklace of tusklike teeth that she had not noticed from afar.

She silently marveled over the smoothness of his light copper skin and the breadth of his shoulders, all of which made her heart flutter. He was the first young man ever to cause her to become a stranger to herself. Oh, she must discover why—if he would allow her to.

"*Nawitka*, yes," Gray Wing suddenly replied. "Gray Wing speaks some English. *Ik-tah*? Why have you come? What do you want on my father's Suquamish island? You are not among those who sit and trade."

Startled by the Indian finally speaking, and clearly enough so that she could understand him, Amelia was momentarily breathless. She wove her fingers through her hair, which fluttered in the breeze, and drew it back from her face, quite aware that this Indian's eyes had discovered its bright red color. He was looking at it even now, as though he had never seen red hair before. Amelia knew that it appeared even redder at this moment, for the sun was shining down upon it, highlighting it as though it were an extension of the sun itself.

"Why am I here?" she murmured. "I . . . I . . . wanted to come and meet you. You seemed to want the same. The way you were staring at me when I was on the ship? I thought it was because you wished to meet me, perhaps to become acquainted."

A slow smile played on his lips. His eyes lost their sharpness, becoming soft with pleasure. "Boston, you are different from the others I have seen on ships," he said, gesturing with his hand toward the vessel. "Most *la-dida*, women, do not so boldly stare back at Gray Wing from the enormous bird with wings that is the white man's great canoe. You are far different from the others, *nawitka*?"

A soft laugh trembled through Amelia as she noticed how he called her "Boston" and how he compared her father's ship to an enormous bird with wings. Oh, yes, it was going to be delightful becoming his friend! She looked forward to hearing his descriptions of other things of her world! If only she was given time to do so.

"I doubt if I am much different," she said, holding her skirt down as the saltwater breeze lifted it, revealing the tiny taper of her stockinged ankles to the Indian's studious eyes. "Perhaps more adventurous . . . more daring. But nothing more." She cocked her head. "You called yourself Gray Wing? That is your name?"

"*Ah-hah*, yes, Gray Wing is my name," he said, nodding.

"You called me 'Boston,'" Amelia said, her eyes shining. "I know that is the name given to most who trade with your people. But as I said before, my name is Amelia. Amelia Storm."

"Amelia." Gray Wing said the name slowly as though absorbing it one syllable at a time. "*Ah-hah, toketie*. Yes, that is a pretty enough name."

A frown creased his brow. He looked toward the ship.

"You will not be missed on the great canoe?" he asked thickly. "You are not watched by *na-ah*, mother, or *pa-pa*?"

Amelia looked across her shoulder at the ship, then slowly turned her eyes back to Gray Wing. "My mother is ailing and knows not that I am here," she said softly.

Her eyes shifted to the beach where, from her vantage point, she could barely see the council of traders on the shore through the trees. "My father is among those who are trading."

She smiled up at Gray Wing. "My father owns the ship that you call a great canoe. He is the one who trades with your people today. He seeks to take many otter pelts back to Boston."

Gray Wing folded his arms across his chest and nodded. "As does my father wish to trade for many things of *your* people," he said, smiling down at her. "My father is *tyee*, chief, among the Suquamish people. One day Gray Wing will be chief!"

In awe that he should suddenly be so open with her, so friendly, and that he would one day be a great Indian chief, Amelia was for a moment at a loss for words. "You will be chief?" she murmured. "How grand!"

"And you?" Gray Wing said, his eyes seeming to look into her soul, he was looking at her so boldly. "You will one day be a princess of your people?"

Amelia's heart frolicked. She giggled softly. "No," she said, casting her eyes downward. "I will not be a princess. There are no princesses among my people." Her eyes rose slowly. "Are there among yours?"

Gray Wing reached out to her hair and dared to touch it. He smiled warmly down at her from his six-foot height. "Yes, there are princesses," he said. "You would make a lovely princess. You are pretty enough to be a princess."

He moved his hand away, yet did not want to. He was fascinated by her hair, by its color and softness. He was fascinated with *her*. Though she was a girl just budding into a woman, he could not help but have feelings for her that drew him into wanting to embrace her. Perhaps later . . . ? At his age of sixteen he had already experienced the wonders of bodies touching in the darkness of the night. Had she?

"How many winters have you experienced in your lifetime?" he blurted, yet wondering if this was the proper way to ask her how old she was. He had learned the English language from his father, who had learned it from the traders. But he knew not of the white man's customs. And time would not allow him to know it from this intriguing white girl, either. Soon she would be aboard the great canoe, leaving Whale Island, and him, behind forever.

To Amelia his touch on her hair was pure golden. She was left a bit shaken inside by this and also by his words. He saw her as pretty? Pretty enough even to be a princess? How could she behave normally now, after he had so openly . . . so surprisingly . . . so suddenly confided his true thoughts to her. First he was stone silent. Then he was so open with her that it left her speechless!

Yet she did not want to spoil what had transpired between them. She must behave as though untouched by his words and actions, for later would be too late. Soon her father's ship would be sailing, with her aboard. She would never see this handsome Indian again. Never!

"Are you asking how old I am?" she blurted, tilting her head so she could look more directly into his eyes. He was so tall and masterful! Yes, one day he would be a great chief whom everyone would admire. If only she could be there to witness such a sight, to share in that moment when he would become chief.

But that was only what dreams—fantasies—were made of. Nothing more. This moment with him was stolen . . . only stolen, perhaps not even real. Would she soon awaken on her bunk in her cabin and realize that she had only been dreaming? If so, what a lovely, lovely dream!

"Yes. Your age is what I ask," Gray Wing said, his eyes touching her all over as he swept them up and down her, seeing so much that was different from the Suquamish women and girls in his village. Her eyes were as green as the moss on which she was standing. Her skin was almost as pale as the snow that capped the mountains. Her hair was the color of a sunrise.

These differences made her intriguing to him, yet he did not want to believe that she was special in any way, for he did not feel it was fair to compare her to his people. All Suquamish women were special! He must never forget that when in the presence of a mere white girl who would one day be a woman married to a white man!

Yet he could not stop wanting to know more about her any more than he could stop wanting to be with her.

Amelia looked away from him. Something compelled her not to be truthful about her age. Most had said that she looked and acted older than thirteen. Why not pretend for the moment that she *was*? In truth, her own father had worried aloud about her being mature beyond her years and way too independent for a girl her age! If this Indian knew that she was so young, he would look upon her as a mere child!

At this moment, she was anything but. He had stirred many new feelings within her . . . feelings that she would never forget once she left him behind.

"I am sixteen," she said in a rush of words. Her cheeks were hot with a blush as she locked her eyes with his. "And you are . . . ?"

"Why, that is my exact age," Gray Wing said, a soft smile touching his lips as he studied her, his gaze stopping at her breasts pressed against the cotton of her dress. She was as developed as the girls of sixteen winters whom he had been with intimately. She seemed even more mature in her behavior than most. He wished to have more time with her, to see how else she might differ from the Suquamish girls.

But time was passing too quickly. The talks between his people and the white traders never lasted long. He wanted time to walk and talk with this intriguing white girl!

A thrill coursed through Amelia's veins; this moment with Gray Wing was so precious to her. She was glad that he had not caught her in her lie and that she did look sixteen in his eyes.

Glancing toward his village, she chose a topic of conversation to lead them away from further talking about their ages. "I find your totem poles fascinating," she said, then slowly turned her eyes back to him, again looking at his tattoo. It was in the shape of a whale as were the figures on the totem poles. "Please tell me about them, Gray Wing."

"*Chah-ko*. Come. Let us walk while we talk," Gray Wing said, wanting to get her as far from the great canoe as possible. Perhaps if the great canoe left without her . . . ?

Amelia almost stumbled over her own feet as she began walking alongside him. She so wanted to do as he asked, yet knew that she must not. Soon she would have to return to the ship.

"Perhaps just a little way," she said, rearranging her thoughts to better fit her wants and needs. "But, mind you, I cannot go far. I must be back on board my father's ship when he returns. If I am not, I would hate to think what my punishment might be."

Gray Wing scowled as he looked down at her. "Your father punishes you often?" he asked angrily.

"No," Amelia murmured. "My father does not punish me all that often. I very rarely give him cause to."

Gray Wing nodded. His breechcloth flapped in the wind as he continued walking, leading Amelia deeper into the forest, away from the water. "That is good," he said, chuckling low. "That is good."

"Please tell me about your totem poles," Amelia said, again wanting to steer their conversation into other directions, away from subjects that were much too personal.

Never had she spoken so openly with a young man before, and this was not any young man, this was an Indian. Most would say she was taking a chance just by being friendly to him. If he chose to, he could abduct her and take her far away, so far that her father could never find her.

But there was too much about him that made her trust

him. And, after all, she was the one who had told the lie, not him.

The whisper of a stream as it flowed calmly across rocks met Amelia's ears. She stepped high over fallen tree limbs as Gray Wing led her to the curving shine of the freshwater stream where a deer had stopped to dip its head and take a leisurely drink. Its dark eyes suddenly turned to the approaching humans. Its ears pricked up and its muscles tensed; then it bounded away. Gray Wing took Amelia's hand and led her to the bank of the stream and urged her to sit down beside it.

Sitting next to her, Gray Wing sank his feet into the water. He looked at the long, flowing skirt of her dress and the toes of her shoes that were just barely revealed beneath it. "The water is as soft as a butterfly's wings," he said smiling. "Come. Join me. Place your feet in the water alongside mine. Then we shall talk while we enjoy ourselves."

Amelia was rattled first by his having held her hand, then by his request to remove her shoes. Would he expect her to remove more than her shoes? Could he truly be trusted? And dare she take the time to do this? If her father returned to the ship and found her gone . . .

Somehow not caring about anything but the moment and the pleasure of being with Gray Wing, Amelia laughed softly and slipped off her shoes, then her stockings. She placed her bare feet in the coldness of the water, then looked bashfully over at Gray Wing when she realized that his eyes were on her again, studying her as though she were a painting. What *could* she expect from him next . . . ?

Three

The cliffs, which could be seen in the distance through the trees, were golden in sunshine, crowned with madrona trees. Amelia wiggled her toes in the water, silken in its touch. She glanced tentatively at Gray Wing, feeling slightly more confident by the minute that his intentions toward her were pure. He had wanted a friend to talk with, the same as she. She was glad that he had looked to her as a friend; it could have so easily been just the opposite. She was lucky to have been given this rare chance to spend time with an Indian brave. It was something she would never forget.

"You asked about our totems," Gray Wing said, enjoying this time with the unusual girl. How wonderful it would be if she could stay on the island with him. If he could just draw her mind away from the great canoe, her father who would soon board it, perhaps . . . just perhaps . . .

"Oh, yes, please do tell me," Amelia said, her voice more that of a young girl in its pleading quality than of the woman she longed to be. "Though I read much about your customs after my father told me that we would be traveling to your great island, I would love to hear more about them.''

Gray Wing looked into the distance, staring blankly ahead, as though he was seeing more in his mind's eye than what was truly there in real life. When he began to talk, it was in a low monotone, as though he were meditating instead of talking to someone.

"The totem poles of Whale Island—of all Suquamish islands—are visual symbols of prestige," he said hoarsely. "The creatures carved on one's totem pole are associated with one's ancestral traditions. One is taught to feel respect and reverence. The totem, the crest that is tattooed on our bodies, is a brand of sorts, to establish legal ownership.''

Amelia looked at the tattoo on Gray Wing's left shoulder. Her fingers trembled as she raised them to trace the outline of the whale, her inner self shaken by a strange warmth at the mere touch of him.

"You wear a tattoo in the shape of a whale," she said softly. She eased her hand away. She feared these strange feelings invading her senses caused by touching his smooth, beautiful skin. "So this whale is your crest? Your mark? Even this island is called by the name of a whale. Why, Gray Wing?"

"The tattoo I wear represents a *wasgo*, a being that combines characteristics of the *eh-kol-i*, the whale, and the wolf," Gray Wing said proudly. "It is the greatest sign of nobility. You will find a crest only on persons of high rank in the village of the Suquamish. We who wear it are proud of our crest. We display it as often and in as many ways as possible.''

"But why the whale?" Amelia persisted, swinging her feet out of the water. She began drying them with the hem of her skirt, worrying about her father, and knowing that she should soon return to the ship. It saddened her to know that she could not stay with the Indian as long as she desired.

But any time with him was better than none. She *did* feel blessed to have been given this opportunity. It would even be worth a scolding if her father discovered that she had so openly disobeyed him. But she would do it again . . . and again and again if it meant time with the handsome Indian brave.

Gray Wing glanced down at Amelia, scowling when he saw that she was drying her feet. She most surely intended to leave him very soon, to return to her father's ship. Somehow he must continue to delay her. He would keep her attention by talking . . .

"Whale Island is an island of great *eh-kol-i*, whale hunters," he said, plucking a wild rose at his side. He gently placed it on Amelia's lap, drawing a slight sigh from deep within her. He smiled to himself, glad that he had thought to give her something she found special.

He glanced down at his necklace. If he gave it to her as a gift, would she see this as valuable and special, as it was to the Suquamish? Would she welcome such a gift?

Ah-hah, yes. He would give it to her. But later. It would be the last thing he would want her to remember before her return to the ship.

Toying with the necklace, but not removing it, Gray Wing smiled at Amelia. "Whaling is a most spectacular sea hunting venture," he said, squaring his shoulders proudly. "One day *I* shall be the greatest hunter of them all! I shall be a harpooner, a person of high rank. The secrets of success, practical and magical, which contribute to a good hunt, are cherished family secrets, handed down in noble lines only! Only a chief possesses the necessary wealth to have a whaling canoe built, to outfit it, and only he has the authority to assemble a crew. My father is a harpooner. Ah, yes, and so *I* shall be. Already I am preparing for the hunt. Tomorrow I will again practice with my father."

"It sounds so very exciting," Amelia said, lifting the rose to inhale its sweetness, loving his warm gesture of friendship. Her shoes and stockings lay beside her, forgotten. "Tell me more. Gray Wing, I would love to go on a whale hunt. Are girls . . . are women allowed?"

"Rarely," Gray Wing said, again locking her eyes with

his, holding her spellbound. "Only those who plan to marry a chief. The woman who is promised to a chief or future chief is required to accompany the man she is to marry on a whaling expedition. She is required to cast a harpoon into the body of a whale. If she fails to do so, she cannot become the chief's wife. *An-ah*, she would not be worthy of such a marriage."

Amelia's eyelashes fluttered nervously at the thought of being denied the opportunity to marry Gray Wing should she, in her wildest fantasies, ever be given the chance. To get so close to being his wife and then be refused because she could not throw a harpoon exactly as the Indians required? How horrible a thought!

"But, Gray Wing, surely you are jesting," she said in a rush of words. "Most women do not possess such skills. Some women are too weak even to throw a harpoon. And it is so dangerous. What if . . . if . . . the woman should lose her balance and fall into the open jaws of the whale?"

"If a woman falls into the open jaws of a whale, she is lost forever to her man," he teased. "It is as simple as that, Amelia."

"How horrible," Amelia gasped. She placed the rose on the ground and reached for her stockings and pulled them on, then slipped her shoes on. "I . . . I really must go. My father—"

Gray Wing interrupted her. "You have not yet heard all that is to be told about whaling," he said. He eased a hand about one of her wrists, urging her to stay beside him. "In the autumn both gray and humpback whales travel south. The grays stay fairly close to shore, while the humpbacks stay farther away."

His eyes sparkled as he slipped his fingers around hers, twining them together. "In the autumn, it is the time to challenge the whale, the biggest animal on earth. It is the time to witness the mating season of the whales," he said huskily. "It is the season of the mad moon."

Amelia's eyes were wide, her heart was thumping wildly as she looked down at their intertwined fingers. Never had she felt so wonderful inside. And this handsome Indian brave was causing it by his mere touch! She was feeling almost overwhelmed by troublesome feelings that were surely most wicked.

Yet it was dangerous to feel this way. She was not yet a woman. How could she be experiencing feelings of a woman?

She marveled as she raised her eyes slowly to meet the passion deep within his. She swallowed hard and jerked her hand away. Her knees were weak as she climbed to her feet. "I . . . I . . . truly must go," she said breathlessly, her heart pounding.

Gathering the hem of her dress into her arms, Amelia turned to hurry away, but a sudden low rumble and the earth strangely quivering beneath her feet caused her to lose her balance. When she felt strong arms about her waist catching her, she turned and found Gray Wing so close she could smell his wondrous woodsy scent.

She did not draw away when he lowered his lips and twined his fingers through her hair as he ever so gently kissed her. A dizziness began to slowly claim Amelia. It was her first kiss. It was her first time alone with a young man. It was her first experience of total rapture.

Another rumble, this time much louder, and the earth shaking like jelly in a jar drew Amelia and Gray Wing apart. Why was the earth shaking, and why was she so shaken by a kiss?

She touched her lips, still feeling his kiss, still tasting him.

Then she glanced down at the earth, wondering what had caused it to sway so strangely.

Gray Wing's heart was pounding. Though this girl's skin was white, she had stirred within him something hardly definable. Her lips had quivered so beneath his! Her taste reminded him of the scent of rose petals. Had it not been for the mountain of fire and ice sending off vibrations into the earth, he would have longed to explore more fully the experience of young love with this girl. Would she have allowed it? he wondered.

But perhaps the mountain had spoken its displeasure of

Gray Wing's being with the white girl. Was it sending a message that Gray Wing was wrong to be with her in such a way? Was it meant for him only to touch, only to love, women of his own color?

Turning his head away, he placed his back to Amelia. Gray Wing did not wish to believe the mountain could be so angered by a mere kiss. Yet perhaps the mountain could even read his thoughts. Yes, his thoughts had taken him far beyond a kiss.

"Gray Wing, I'm frightened," Amelia said, trembling from his kiss and what she now realized the earth tremblings had meant: They had experienced a small earthquake.

She went to Gray Wing and touched his arm, causing him to turn and look down at her from his great height. "Will . . . will you accompany me partway back to my father's ship? What if the earthquake gets worse?"

It was hard to stand so close to him, knowing that they had shared more than a kiss and that their feelings were mutual. And she knew that nothing could be done about such feelings. Soon she would be gone. From now on, he would only be in her dreams.

Gray Wing framed her face between his hands. His gray eyes were soft as he stared down at her, shaken by this experience. If he could not one day claim her as his own, he would only be half a man! She surely would only be half a woman; they belonged together. But the mountain had spoken. It was not best for Gray Wing to think any more of the white girl. It would not be best for his people since one day he was to be their chief.

"Do not be frightened," he said hoarsely. "It is only the spirits of Dahkobeed, Mount Rainier, the mountain of fire and ice, speaking. Sometimes the spirits voice their displeasure when they are displeased by something a Suquamish does. Sometimes the spirits withhold protection or good fortune, reviling or cursing our people. Perhaps it was not meant for Gray Wing and Amelia to become so fond of each other. It is best that I do accompany you back to your great canoe. We must say good-bye."

Amelia felt dazed, so caught up in feelings for him and knowing that the time *had* come to say good-bye. Perhaps it would have been best if she had never come ashore. Now, so involved in feelings for the Indian, she would always ache to be with him again! Sometimes life's twists were so cruel—so inhuman.

"Yes, I must return," she murmured. "We must say good-bye." Turning, she began to walk away, then stopped when he spoke from behind her.

"*Al-kil*, wait," he said, removing his necklace. He went to Amelia and, stepping in her line of vision, held the necklace out to her. "*Mesika*, yours. It is my gift to you. Please take."

Her whole body seeming to be centered on a heartbeat, Amelia looked up at Gray Wing adoringly as he slipped the Indian necklace about her slender neck. She had read of the value of such necklaces made from the tusklike teeth of animals; she was honored that he thought so much of her to give her this valued possession.

Reaching up to caress the necklace, she wished her dress did not have such a high collar so she might feel the trinket against her flesh. Forever it would mean so much to her. Whenever she touched it she would be touching Gray Wing. Whenever she looked at it, she would see Gray Wing. The necklace would be a substitute for the young man she most surely had fallen in love with. No feelings so dear to her heart could be anything less than love.

Choking with emotion, Amelia swallowed the knot that had formed in her throat, then smiled sweetly up at Gray Wing. "Thank you," she murmured. "I will always treasure the gift you have given me this day. Thank you so much."

Fearing that she might erupt into tears at any moment, Amelia rushed past Gray Wing. She ran beneath the umbrella of trees that hung lusciously on all sides of her. She hurried on toward the slight bluff that would lead her down to the beach.

When she finally arrived there, she stopped and gasped

loudly as she looked toward the spot where her father's ship had been anchored. The ship . . . was gone!

"No!" she cried softly. She shaded her eyes with a hand and looked into the distance, across the wide expanse of water. Flapping like large white wings, the sails on her father's ship were full blown and taking the ship farther and farther away from her. Her father had most surely been frightened by the earthquake tremors and had quickly boarded his ship and ordered it out to sea. Apparently believing that Amelia had obediently stayed in her cabin, he had not had cause to see if she was truly there before setting sail.

It would be quite some time before he discovered that she was not there. He would be busily logging his trades perhaps until the following morning! Her mother was already sleeping the day away and would probably do so even into the night, unaware that Amelia was not aboard the ship.

No one would notice—until it was too late. . . .

"*Hwah*!" Gray Wing said as he noticed the ship's departure. "*Kon-a-way*! The great canoe is gone! You have been left behind, Amelia?"

Amelia turned slowly to Gray Wing as he came to stand beside her. "Yes," she said faintly. "My father did not realize that I was not aboard the ship. He has left me and may not notice my absence for some time. Gray Wing, I am stranded! Stranded!"

Gray Wing smiled down at her, his heart soaring with happiness. No matter how much the mountain growled and roared, he was pleased that his plan had worked and that Amelia might now be his forever.

Ah-hah, yes, she would be his princess. When she grew to be a woman, she would be his wife.

"You will come to my village with me," he said, taking Amelia's hand. "My family will welcome you as though you are one of us."

Amelia felt an emptiness and fear over the loss of her parents, yet she felt strangely alive and safe in Gray Wing's company. She laced her fingers through his and moved beside him toward his village.

She grew cold inside as they drew closer to the totem poles. The statues seemed to be standing like sentinels guarding the village. To them and to Gray Wing's people, she would most surely be an intruder. . . .

Four

༄

Amelia walked warily past the totems, feeling as though they were alive and scrutinizing her. She shivered slightly when she recognized the long dorsal fin and flukes of the killer whale, and the large mouths displaying prominent teeth on each of the totems.

Without realizing it, Amelia locked her fingers more tightly with Gray Wing's. He was her only link to stability now. Since he was the son of the chief of this Suquamish village, surely he would make sure that nothing happened to her at the hands of the others.

But what if Gray Wing's father disapproved of her? Epidemics of smallpox, brought to them by the white man, had broken out among some other Indian tribes, making the Indians regard whites with suspicion, fearful of this evil "gift."

Amelia hoped her perfect health would persuade the Suquamish Indians to accept her into their village, at least until her father returned for her.

Lifting her eyes to Gray Wing, Amelia felt her heart tug at the thought of having to eventually leave him. Oh, that she could stay with him forever and be with her family also! But that could never, never be. They were from opposite worlds.

Now walking past crude gabled houses and leaving the totem poles behind, Amelia grew even more tense. Soon she would know whether or not she would be allowed to spend the night with Gray Wing's family. He was leading her toward a house that was much more elaborate than the rest. This, she knew, must be the house occupied by the chief of this village and his family.

The house had a portal totem pole built onto the front, rising high above the roof, with a large opening that served as a doorway. As Amelia was guided through, she felt for a moment as though she were being led into the large open mouth of a whale. She swallowed hard and closed her eyes as she walked beside Gray Wing into the house. When she heard voices whispering all about her, she slowly opened her eyes and found herself being closely observed by several people.

In one quick sweeping glance she saw them all. She saw a man who was most surely Gray Wing's father; his legs pulled up in a chair, squatting like a Turk, he wore a cloak of black sea otter that hung down to his knees and was belted at the waist. He had a massive head of graying, unbraided hair worn to his shoulders and a benevolent face, with bold features distinguished by a large Roman nose and intense dark gray eyes.

Powerfully built, he wore a headdress adorned with carved figures of whales, painted and inlaid with iridescent shells, spiked with sea-lion whiskers, and hung with ermine tails. His skin was painted, as were his breechcloth and leggings. Gleaming flakes of mica shone on his face, glittering in the glow of the blaze in the fire pit in the center of the room.

Moving her gaze, Amelia saw a beautiful middle-aged woman sitting beside the chief, spinning cedar bark, which looked like flax, with a distaff and spindle. She wore her hair in long braids that hung down her back, and she was garbed in a loosely fitted buckskin dress. Clusters of animal teeth adorned her ears. Squares cut from the irides-

cent shell of the abalone were sewn on her dress. She was
lovely, with tiny features and only a trace of gray hair at
her temples.

A frail young girl, dressed like the older woman, was
weaving flax with strips of sea otter skin on a loom placed
against the wall. Another young girl was preparing food
over the fire, while a young boy attired in only a breechcloth sat close by, carving what looked like the beginnings
of a bow.

Gray Wing ushered Amelia farther into the room. He
spread the skin of a big black bear on the floor beside the
fire and urged Amelia to sit down upon it. She scarcely
breathed while she watched Gray Wing move from person
to person, talking low in his Suquamish language. She
eagerly watched the expressions on his family's faces, hoping to catch some sign of acceptance in a smile or a gesture. She was at least grateful for one thing: Their eyes
did not hold hate within them . . . only puzzlement.

Feeling uncomfortable at being so closely scrutinized,
Amelia again let her gaze move about, studying the way
the Indians lived. The house was long and narrow, gabled,
with a gentle pitch to the roof. The walls were made of
vertical cedar planks, slotted, the crevices chinked with
moss. The small round doorway was set in the gable end,
where the mouth of the whale figure had been carved.
Gaps in the planks served as windows.

A fire pit had been dug in the earthen floor in the center
of the house. Fish racks hung over the fire as high as the
lower eaves. There the fish were drying for future use.

Amelia also saw platforms for sleep and storage next to
the walls, all of them covered with layers of bark and soft,
hairy pelts. Skin curtains had been rolled up, but would
be lowered when the family retired for the night. Wooden
chests, ornately carved with the crest of this family, were
tucked beneath the platform beds.

Checkerwork mats of red cedar bark seemed to be this
family's principal household furnishing, serving as uphol-
stery for the seats on which they were sitting, as mat-
tresses for the beds, and as a tablecloth, which was spread

on the floor and set with highly carved dishes filled with an assortment of foods.

She was finding that the Indian civilization was not primitive, as most would imagine, but instead sophisticated.

Amelia's eyes were drawn around when she felt a presence at her side. She smiled awkwardly at Gray Wing as he sat down beside her on the plush bear fur. She was glad when he scooted closer to her, making her feel less alone in the world.

"*Hwah*, Amelia, my family welcomes you," Gray Wing said. With a gesturing hand he told her the names of each. "My mother, Starflower, welcomes you. So does White Rose, my little sister. Sweet Water is my next to youngest sister, and High Hawk my younger brother. My father, Chief Bold Bear, also welcomes you to our dwelling. They request that you share not only a place to sleep this night but also the afternoon meal. My sister Sweet Water is a very fine cook."

Amelia clasped her hands tightly in her lap. Though she had just been accepted by Gray Wing's family, she was unable to quell her nervousness. But she would! She would not give them cause to change their minds about her!

She smiled from one Indian to the next, then lost her smile when she saw how they were now frowning, focusing their eyes on the necklace that hung about her neck. She did not like the way they were reacting to the gift that Gray Wing had given her. Did it show that she meant too much to him? Did they disapprove of the gift and of the fact that he cared so much for her? Amelia knew the value of the necklace made of animal teeth.

Self-consciously, she reached up to the necklace and covered it with her hand. She hoped that hiding it from their sight would be the same as erasing it from their minds.

And then she was drawn into another world, it seemed, as Gray Wing placed a bowl of food before her.

"*Kloshe*, good," Gray Wing said, smiling down at Amelia. "It is the popular sopalalli, a soapberry mixture that consists of berries whipped to a froth in cold water and *olachen*, grease. Eat. You will enjoy.''

Amelia smiled a thank-you to Gray Wing when he offered her an ornately carved flat wooden spoon with which she was to eat the strange mixture he was offering her. As she dipped the spoon into the sopalalli, she noticed that the carvings on the bowl in which the food was served represented a sea wolf, the crosshatching on the bowl. The carvings suggested reverence toward the whale.

Her first taste of the soapberry mixture was pleasurable. It was both sweet and tart, quite pleasing to her empty stomach. She proceeded to eat ravenously as the others joined her. She nodded a silent thank-you to Sweet Water when the girl handed her a cup of clam juice, which she drank in fast gulps.

Amelia jumped when she heard a low chuckle at her side. She turned her eyes slowly to Gray Wing. Her face grew hot with a blush when she realized that he had been watching her eat, and she now knew that she had been making a pig of herself. She lowered the wooden cup to the floor beside her and placed her hands in her lap. She had completely forgotten her manners. But it *had* been several hours since she had eaten, and the day's exciting activities had made her even hungrier than usual.

For a moment she had quite forgotten that she was stranded on an island with Indians. How could she have forgotten?

Her gaze moved slowly back to Gray Wing. *He* was the reason! Only he. . . .

''It is good that you enjoy the food of the Suquamish,'' Gray Wing said, now also eating. ''Later you will be introduced into many other ways of my people. Tomorrow I will have to leave you to learn the ways of whaling. But you will be with my mother and sisters. They will teach you how to dig for clams. Though it is work, it is also fun.''

''How long will you be gone?'' Amelia asked, shifting nervously on the fur beneath her, not wanting to be left without his protection. Somehow she felt that this was a threat to her. Without him she would feel totally alone. A chill shimmered across her flesh at the thought of being without family *and* Gray Wing, no matter how short a time!

Gray Wing set his bowl aside, having seen her suddenly engulfed in a chill. "You are cold?" he asked, forking an eyebrow. "The fire does not warm you enough? The lodge fire of the Suquamish is always a small one. Little fire— get close, cooking easy. Big fire—keep away, burn everything, cook nothing, no good."

Amelia fluttered her eyelashes as she laughed softly, loving the way he described things. "No, I am not cold," she murmured. "It just gave me a fright to know that you would be gone tomorrow for *any* length of time." She leaned closer to him, pleading with her eyes. "You did not say how long you would be gone. How long, Gray Wing?"

Gray Wing ignored the frowns of his family who were watching his communications with Amelia. He leaned closer to her, their breath mingling. "*Hwah*. Do you care so much that I will be gone?" he said beneath his breath so that only Amelia heard him. "Do you? *Kah-ta*, why?"

A blush heating her face again, Amelia looked away from Gray Wing. She refused to answer him, knowing that all eyes were on them, watching, observing two young lovers sharing admiring glances and words. It was embarrassing, knowing that she could care so much for a young man when she was so young herself. It wasn't fitting. Her mother would be alarmed to witness her daughter's shameful behavior!

"You do not answer me?" Gray Wing said, laughing softly. "*Hwah*, that is all right. Tonight you will answer me. When you are pretending to be asleep Gray Wing will come for you. We will sneak away from this dwelling of all eyes and ears and take a ride in my canoe. We will be alone. Alone."

Amelia turned bashful eyes back to him. Her insides were mushy warm, anticipating time alone with him again. . . .

• • •

The fire burned low in the pit, casting shadow images along the floor, ceiling, and walls of the gabled house. In an untailored wraparound garment loaned to her by Sweet Water, Amelia lay barefoot on a bunk not far from Gray Wing's, resting her head on a pillow of shredded bark. Although she was worried about her parents—how far had they traveled out to sea before discovering her absence from the ship?—she could not help but be eager for the moments ahead when she would once again be alone with Gray Wing. She had become breathless as she watched Gray Wing's family retire for the night to their own bunks. Soon . . . soon . . .

When a warm hand twined around hers, Amelia flinched as though shot, then smiled warmly at Gray Wing as he nodded toward the door. Her heart skipping several beats from her building excitement, Amelia scooted from the bunk and went hand in hand with Gray Wing from the house.

Rifted veils of fog wove their magic through the night air. A whippoorwill sang from somewhere in the distance as Gray Wing encouraged Amelia into a silent run through the village. Her bare feet stung from the cold, her eyes misted. Yet she ran onward, eager to share another stolen moment with Gray Wing. Perhaps this would make up for his absence the next day. She would take advantage of every moment they could be together, whenever . . . however. . . .

Five

❦ ❧

The canoe pushed its way through the cold sea of moonlight. The light from a jack-pine torch flickered in the breeze from where it was attached to one side of the canoe, shining on a face of radiance as Amelia sat behind Gray Wing, watching him draw the paddle through the dark abyss of water. They had yet to speak since he urged Amelia from his family's dwelling. He had led her to his canoe and had encouraged her to climb inside for a midnight ride.

Hugging herself in the sea-damp night chill, Amelia glanced away from Gray Wing, again admiring this sleek canoe hollowed out of cedar logs. It was adorned with the teeth of the sea otter and densely carved with depictions of many whales. Though it was quite large, Gray Wing labored hardly at all while guiding it through the waters of Puget Sound, staying close enough to Whale Island to see the outdoor fires of his village.

Strange as it seemed, Amelia was not at all afraid. Had it not been for her fears of possibly never seeing her parents again, she would have been totally at peace with herself. So much about Gray Wing made her comfortable with the situation in which she found herself.

Yet she could not put from her mind her curiosity about whether she would have a sister or a brother. Would fate cause her parents to once again have only one child to raise? If Amelia was not among them, how would their lives be changed?

She scoffed at her fear of never seeing them again. As soon as her father discovered her absence from her cabin, he would order his crew to turn the ship around and return as quickly as the wind would carry them.

Pressing her hand to the necklace of tusks, already feeling a bond with Gray Wing because of his special gift to her, Amelia once again looked at him. Though his back was to her, she saw enough of him to again feel the strange spiralings of feelings invading her senses. Never had a young man caused such sensations within her.

But none she had met before compared with the mystique, with the handsomeness, of this Indian who would one day be a great chief of his people. As his arms moved with the paddle, the moonlight caught the ripples of muscles beneath his satiny flesh. Under the moonlight sheen his bare and muscular torso possessed a sculptured quality. When a spray from a wave crest splashed upon him there was a slight, quick contraction of muscles, no more. The wind softly lifted his shoulder-length hair, the paddle he was drawing through the water hissed in its speed, as though snakes were hidden close by, making the sound.

Not understanding any of these feelings troubling her about Gray Wing, Amelia focused her thoughts and eyes elsewhere. Inhaling, she found the mixture of salt water and cedar sweet and refreshing. Her gaze swept across the land where in the darkness the tall pines and cedar trees were black against the horizon. Only their tops were silvered by the moonlight. . . .

Feeling the change of course in the canoe, Amelia glanced from Gray Wing back to the land. He was guiding the canoe toward shore. Within moments he was in the water himself, dragging the vessel onto a bed of rocks for mooring.

When he came to Amelia and gently placed his hands around her waist and lifted her from the canoe, she became breathless with his nearness, and yet she experienced shame for such feelings.

With her feet now on solid ground and Gray Wing leading the way through a thick stand of madrona trees, Amelia glanced nervously from side to side, wondering just how far he would lead her before finally deciding to stop and talk. The silence was unnerving her. It was as though Gray Wing had more in mind than to have a mere conversation to get further acquainted. Perhaps she had been wrong to come with him so eagerly. . . .

But had she had a choice? He was the only one in whom she could confide, the only one to share her trust. Though his family had been friendly enough, they had left her to Gray Wing for total companionship and communicating.

"Klat-a-wa," Gray Wing suddenly said, twining his fingers more securely through hers. "We will walk just a bit farther. Then we will sit and rest. It is late. Gray Wing knows you must be tired. It has been a long, troublesome day for you. But tomorrow will be better. Gray Wing will see to that!"

"Where are we? Where are you taking me?" Amelia asked, her bare feet paining her as she stepped first on a rock and then on the sharp end of a fallen tree limb. "Why are we now so far from . . . from your village, Gray Wing?"

She drew in her shoulders and looked cautiously about her, seeing total darkness on all sides. "Gray Wing, it is so *dark*. Are there . . . are there any wild animals to be wary of?"

She glanced down at the elaborately designed dagger sheathed at his waist. Though it was deadly in appearance, double-bladed, with one long and one short blade on either side of the central grip, and was eighteen inches long, it was surely not enough weapon to defend themselves against the attack of a bear or a wolf.

Yet Gray Wing had survived this long in this wilderness. He surely knew all the secrets of how to stay alive.

"*Al-hah!* Do not be afraid," Gray Wing said, smiling down at her. "Though I am not yet fully developed into a man, I think and act like a man. No harm will come to you. My arm and hand are swift. The dagger will move as lightning streaks through the heavens!"

Amelia looked slowly, bashfully, up at Gray Wing when he mentioned thinking and acting like a man. Did he notice that she possessed the feelings of a woman? Was it written on her face in each and every smile that she lent him? Should she fear this change in her? A part of her did. A part of her didn't.

"We are now where I always come when I desire to be totally alone," Gray Wing said, the moonlight bright on his face as he guided her into a clearing that stretched out onto a bluff that rose high over Puget Sound.

Amelia took cautious steps as Gray Wing urged her closer to the edge. She looked down at the steep precipice. She saw the waves washing up on the shore below them. She could hear their crash, repeated over and over again, like thunder echoing in the distance.

A shiver raced across Amelia's flesh as Gray Wing led her to sit on the edge of the bluff, then sat beside her with his feet dangling over the side.

"Do you not find this place peaceful in its solitude?" Gray Wing asked, looking across the moon-silvered water. "It is a place for communing with the Great Spirit."

"If this is a secret place for you . . . for the time you spend with your . . . your Great Spirit, should I even be here with you?" Amelia asked softly. She smoothed the skirt of her borrowed buckskin dress down over her knees, but the breeze soon tossed it back away from her bare feet and ankles.

"I share my secret place with whom I wish to share it," Gray Wing said, casually shrugging. "For now I wish to share it with you." He cast her a half-glance. "Are you happy that you are here with Gray Wing?"

Amelia felt a blush rising to her cheeks; she felt trou-

bled over whether or not she should confess her true feelings to Gray Wing. If he knew she cared so much, would
that change things between them? She always feared revealing her inner feelings to anyone.

Avoiding answering him for the moment, Amelia
crossed her ankles as they dangled over the edge of the
cliff. Caught up with Gray Wing's nearness as the moments passed, she felt her tension lessening. She gazed
across the breadth of the Sound, watching the moon's reflection rippling with the inward wash of the waves, and
was again reminded of her parents. Had they yet discovered that she was missing? Was the ship already headed
back to Puget Sound? Did she truly want them to hasten
their journey? Time spent with Gray Wing was becoming,
oh, so precious!

"*Na-ah*, you do not answer me," Gray Wing said, placing a finger under Amelia's chin, forcing her eyes to meet
the wonder in his. "You do not find my company distasteful, do you? I am Suquamish; you are white. To you, does
that make a difference?"

Understanding the meaning behind his question, she
knew the importance of making him understand that she
did not see his color or his background as anything but
beautiful!

Yet . . . she was afraid to open up so fully to him. Until
she knew him better, if she ever did, she must mark each
of her words . . . each of her confessions . . . with caution.

"Oh, but I am enjoying these stolen moments with
you," she blurted, surprised at herself for deciding so
quickly to forget her decision to be cautious with her
words. "That you are Suquamish and that I am white
makes not the least bit of difference to me."

Gray Wing's eyes softened as his lips lifted into a soft
smile. Even his shoulder muscles relaxed. He had heard
what he had wanted to hear. He felt that he could be open
with her now. The fact that she had accepted his gift of
friendship so readily and was even now wearing it around
her neck had made him think that surely she did not set

them apart as being so totally different just because of
their different cultures. She saw something special in him,
as he did in her.

Easing his hand from her face, he slipped it down beside her and took her hand in his. He smiled to himself
when he felt the tremor in her fingers, knowing that it was
because of feelings he was stirring inside her.

"Your family," he said thickly, again looking out to
sea. "Do you miss them very much?"

"Yes, very . . ." Amelia said, her throat constricting
at the thought of their absence. But she would not allow
herself to ruin this moment by becoming sad over her loss.
"Your family is very kind to accept me into their lives so
easily," she blurted, smiling over at Gray Wing. "They
are very nice."

Gray Wing nodded. His free hand brushed some loose
strands of his hair from his face where the wind had tossed
them. "*Ah-hah*, yes, they are good people," he said
hoarsely. "But you must excuse their silence while around
you. Many white people have brought the dreaded smallpox to the Suquamish. They have learned to be cautious
around all whites."

"Yet they took me in to your home and fed me . . .
even offered me a bed," Amelia said, sighing. "How can
I ever repay them?"

"No payment is required," Gray Wing said, again
shrugging.

The moonlight caught the movement of the whale tattoo
on Gray Wing's left shoulder as he shrugged. Amelia
reached out and traced its outline with her finger. "While
I was studying the Indians of this territory, I read that
tattoos were used, but I had expected you to have more
than one. Why don't you, Gray Wing?"

Gray Wing frowned. "Only the dreaded Haida Indians
of the North display a multitude of signs," he said mood-
ily. "They distort the meaning of the crest by using so
many on their bodies. But they distort the meaning of *life*.
They are violent and crazed more often than not."

"I know not of the Haida," Amelia said. She slipped

her bare feet beneath her, trying to make herself more comfortable on this seat made of rock.

"It is best that you never do," Gray Wing said, picking up a pebble, tossing it into the water. "They have many secret societies with rituals that are barbaric. The best known is the Kwakiutl, the cannibal society whose initiates are possessed by the Cannibal Spirit at the North End of the World. At their rituals a slave is killed and eaten."

Amelia paled. She clasped her hands over her mouth. "My word!" she gasped, her eyes wide. "How . . . how horrible!"

Gray Wing implored her with his eyes. "When white explorers first came to this land of the Suquamish, they offered my people what they called venison pie," he said guardedly. "My people thought it was made of human flesh and lectured them against cannibalism."

Amelia's eyes brightened and color returned to her cheeks when she saw the seriousness with which Gray Wing spoke of venison pie being mistaken for human flesh. She laughed softly and touched him gently on the arm. "But your people soon learned the truth, did they not?" she murmured. "Venison is the meat of the deer. Venison pie is delicious. Delicious!"

Gray Wing's lips lifted into a slow smile. "After a deer was slain and my people were shown how the pie was made, they knew the truth," he said, nodding. "I now, too, like venison pie."

Amelia moved closer to Gray Wing, shifting her skirt so that it was not lying twisted beneath her. "You spoke of slaves," she said breathlessly. "Do your people take slaves?"

"In both the Suquamish and the Haida culture it is the custom to take slaves as a result of tribal conflicts," Gray Wing said, tossing another pebble downward, watching its descent. "*Ah-hah*, even my father owns many slaves, but they are treated fairly . . . never eaten!"

Amelia looked in awe at Gray Wing, knowing that one day he, too, would take slaves. The thought made her uneasy, but she felt lucky to have been stranded among the Suquamish Indians instead of the Haida!

"But let us not talk about the Haida or slaves," Gray Wing said, squeezing her hand affectionately. "Let us speak of whales! Soon Gray Wing will know all that is to be known about harvesting the great animals from the sea! Tomorrow I will learn much that I yet do not know—"

A great rumbling and the shaking of the ledge of rock beneath Amelia and Gray Wing drew Gray Wing's words to an abrupt halt.

"The mountain . . . speaks angrily again," Gray Wing then whispered, scowling toward where Mount Rainier was hidden in the darkness.

The rock again shimmered beneath Amelia. Her throat went dry with fear, her spine became stiff. "Do you experience such tremors often?" she said in a rush of words. "Have you ever had a destructive earthquake on your island, Gray Wing?"

"At one time glacier-covered Mount Rainier was an active volcano, but now the mountain only occasionally speaks angrily," Gray Wing said, trying not to show disrespect to the spirits of the mountain in his tone of voice. "It has not erupted since Gray Wing has been a part of this land."

"What causes it to behave so . . . so badly now?" Amelia dared to ask.

Gray Wing did not want to confess that he felt the mountain was angry because of his being with her. He evaded her question. "Powerful spirits live on the tops of the highest peaks and must not be angered by anything or anyone," he said thickly. "The Suquamish never climb above the snow line on Mount Rainier. There is a lake of fire on top of the mountain. In the lake lives a mighty demon. If the Suquamish should reach the top, the demon would seize and kill them and throw them into the fiery lake."

A shudder racked Amelia. She squirmed uneasily on the hardness of the rock beneath her. Then she tensed when she felt Gray Wing's arm slipping about her waist. Slowly

she turned her eyes to him and saw within them something
she had never before been a witness to. The look of intensity caused her heart to frolic inside her chest and her
knees to become strangely weak.

"You have nothing to fear," Gray Wing said softly,
weaving his fingers through her hair as his other hand drew
her closer to him. "Gray Wing is here. Gray Wing will
always protect you."

Cast beneath his magnetic spell, Amelia did not fight
him when he lowered his lips to hers. She closed her eyes
and relished this moment of awakening sensations spinning inside her head. She had never felt anything so sweet,
so wonderful, as his kiss. She could feel his lips softly
tremble as he continued to kiss her, his hands now framing her face between them.

But when she felt one of his hands travel lower and
brush against the tender bud of her breast through the thin
buckskin of the dress she wore, her eyes flew wide open,
and she became aware of just what might transpire next,
if she did not stop him. She had been wrong to lie about
her age. He expected her to know what a girl of sixteen
knew. And though her body was revealing to her that perhaps she did know all she needed to know about loving a
young man, she could not allow him to continue. She had
been taught better. She must respect her mother's teachings! She must respect *herself*!

Placing the palms of her hands on Gray Wing's chest,
Amelia began to shove him away from her. When his lips
left hers, she could not deny that she hated the void left
behind, for she could still taste him, could still feel him,
even hungered for him.

Placing a hand over her lips, trying to seal his kiss there
for as long as possible, she scrambled to her feet. Soft
sobs surfaced from deep within her as she began inching
away from him, forgetting the steepness of the bluff behind her.

"No," she whispered harshly. "Don't—"

The crumbling of rock beneath her bare feet and the
sound of pebbles scattering over the edge of the cliff made

Amelia's heart jump as she suddenly became aware of the danger she was in. It was not from her feelings for Gray Wing! She was too close to the ledge!

Gray Wing saw the danger. He grabbed Amelia's arm and hauled her against him and held her there, his steel-gray eyes looking down into hers in a silent question. Never had he felt so torn . . . so in need, as now. But surely it was because she was denying this that he wanted! To be denied made the need even greater within his heart and soul! Surely this was the reason, for until now, Gray Wing had only let Suquamish women inside his heart!

"Gray Wing, please take me back to your village," Amelia said shallowly, her voice foreign to her in its weakness. "Please . . . ?"

"Why do you not like to be kissed by Gray Wing?" he said gruffly. "Was it unpleasant? Was not I gentle enough?"

"That is not why I want to return to your village," Amelia said, swallowing hard. She felt her pulse race as he again lowered his lips to hers. When he kissed her she again felt a strange mindlessness taking hold of her. Again she shoved at his chest. When he released her she wished to die, for never had anyone looked so hurt as Gray Wing was now looking!

Clutching her hands to her sides, Amelia stiffened her spine. She looked up into his eyes, blinking a tear from her own. "Gray Wing, I cannot let you kiss me again because . . . because I lied about my age," she sobbed. "Gray Wing, I . . . I am only thirteen. I am much too young to . . . to be kissed!"

Placing a fist against her mouth, Amelia spun around and began to run away from him. She ducked her head, crying. Now he would hate her! He knew she had deceived him by lying about her age. Never, never had she felt so sad and ashamed.

Gray Wing was momentarily stunned by this truth . . . that she was younger than she had admitted to. Her kiss was that of a more mature girl. But the age did not matter to him. Nor should it to her. She was a lucky one, one who knew the mysteries of love earlier than most! But he would not pursue her any longer, for he could tell that she was confused by her body speaking to her in ways that were unfamiliar to her.

Gray Wing ran after her. When he reached her, he stepped into her path and stopped her. Daring not to touch her again, he only smiled warmly down at her. Her face was awash with moonlight, blossoming in its loveliness. There was a radiance about her that stirred him clean to his soul. One day she would be his princess! Nothing and no one would stand in his way. Once she was able to accept her womanhood, she would also accept the fact that she, only she, could be his princess.

"Al-kil," he said thickly. "Gray Wing will not try to kiss you again. I will take you to my dwelling so that you can go to sleep. Will that make you happy?"

Amelia looked up at him, feeling dwarfed by his tall, powerful build and by his eyes, which were again mesmerizing her. She gulped hard. "Yes," she murmured. "That would make me happy. I am so tired. Rest is what I need."

Gray Wing nodded and began walking toward the Sound, this time not even trying to take Amelia's hand. She fell into step beside him, casting him an occasional troubled glance. She felt an emptiness surge through her when he did not return her looks. Had she ruined everything between them?

If so, she would forever hate herself. . . .

Six

❧ ❧

The Sound lay cobbled in a morning breeze as Amelia worked on her knees beside Sweet Water on the beach, digging clams. Close by, Amelia could see Gray Wing's mother and other sister on the edge of the forest. Star-flower was gathering wild blackberries, tart Oregon grapes, and fragile, grainy salmonberries. White Rose was digging the starchy bulbs of the blue-flowered camas plants.

On the beach in the distance Amelia could see Gray Wing's brother playing with other children his age. High Hawk was many years younger than Gray Wing and had been denied the opportunity to enter the great whaling canoes and accompany the whalers out to sea where they would teach their skills to the younger men.

Barefoot and attired in the Suquamish loose-flowing buckskin dress, Amelia raked her lean fingers through her windblown hair. She understood High Hawk's disappointment in not being allowed to go to sea in the whaling canoes. She had seen Gray Wing's anxiousness to leave this morning, to continue with his training.

It was the prime desire of all the young men to learn

the skills of whale hunting. The whale was their sole purpose for living, it seemed!

Amelia rose to her full height and stretched. She placed her hand at the small of her back as she looked out at the Sound. She could see nothing except the big swells rising out of the distance like shadows. *She* was as disappointed this morning as High Hawk, for the canoes had traveled far out to sea, way beyond the point where she could see them. Though she was being treated cordially enough by Gray Wing's kin, she still could not feel comfortable without him being near to protect her. As she saw it, until her father returned for her, Gray Wing was her protector.

Sighing, she gazed about her. It was a gray, overcast day. The firs and hemlocks on the nearby hills combed the bottom of the heavy clouds that pulsed in from the Pacific. This made her feel even more lonely . . . even more melancholy, for Amelia had never missed her mother and father as much as she did at this moment. Was her father's ship close by now? Would she soon see her loved ones?

Again raking her fingers through her hair, keeping its loose tendrils from blowing across her eyes, Amelia grew tense when she saw a sudden, unexpected movement out on the Sound. She took a step forward, straining her eyes to get a better look. Just beyond a bend in the shoreline several canoes had come into sight.

Amelia's heart skipped a beat when she saw that these were not Suquamish Indian vessels. The canoes were drawing close to shore so quickly she was soon able to see the Indians aboard them. Gray Wing's tale of the Haida Indians came to mind. She remembered that they raided villages and took slaves. The memory scorched Amelia's brain, for she knew that the approaching Indians were Haida: Their bodies were almost completely covered with hideous tattoos!

Amelia turned with a start, alarmed by the shrieks and shouts from the women and children of the village as they scattered in all directions. She watched, fear causing her legs to become too weak to respond as she should, as Gray Wing's sisters, mother, and brother ran wildly from the beach along with the rest of the people of this village. They knew they did not have sufficient protection from warriors, for all but the elderly Suquamish braves had gone to sea to observe the training of their sons for the whale hunt.

Amelia again looked toward the tattoo-covered raiders who were sweeping down the Sound in their swift seventy-foot war canoes while war chants rang out with their approach. Desperation seized her. She finally regained strength enough to run, to hide herself.

But she knew there was no escape. Hundreds of Haida warriors were already leaping from their canoes. Deadly weapons came into view as the Haida used spears, slings, clubs, and daggers to kill and maim whomever they caught. The women and children they did not kill were being carried off for slaves.

Amelia's heart sank and tears flooded her eyes when she saw High Hawk slain and then Gray Wing's mother and sisters. And when harsh, cold hands grabbed her from behind, she closed her eyes, awaiting the death blow to also claim her.

But she was somehow spared. She opened her eyes when she felt hands coil into her hair. She screamed and fought her abductor as he began dragging her by the hair across the beach. The more she fought the more her scalp pained her. Her insides recoiled when she looked into the face of her abductor. He had dark, cold eyes. His face was hideously distorted with tattoos, his mouth was set with a deep-seated hatred.

Powerful muscles rippled as he released his hold on her hair, then swept her up into his arms and ran with her toward a waiting canoe that did not yet have slaves as cargo. She had to surmise that she was a prisoner of the Haida chief and that this canoe was his, for the figures carved on its hull were bolder than the others, and fine furs were spread on the seats and the floor.

After dropping Amelia onto the floor of the canoe, the Indian stood over her, glaring down at her. "You are now Chief Dark Cloud's *elite*, slave," he growled. "Never before has Dark Cloud taken a white woman as slave. It will be good to use you for *huy-huy*, bartering. The Chinese should arrive even today. They will trade much for a woman with hair the color of the sun!''

Afraid to move, even to speak, Amelia inched as far away from the Indian as she could. Over the gunwale of the canoe she watched as other Haida Indians loaded the booty into their craft. Among the stolen goods were blankets of mountain goat wool, whale bladders, seal oil, and long strings of hiaqua shells, which served as money to the Indians of the Northwest.

Slowly her hands went to her necklace, the gift from Gray Wing. She wrapped her fingers about it, fearing that the Haida Indian would take it from her. When she looked up at him she could see a smile quiver on his lips. It was as though he had read her thoughts and knew that she did not want to part with the necklace. Now she would have to, most surely!

''Necklace will make you more valuable for trading,'' Dark Cloud said with a chuckle. ''Because you wear it, the Chinese will regard you as even more valuable. It is an object for barter in itself. *Hwah*. Yes. You can wear it, white one. You will be worth many silk fabrics brought to the Haida from the Chinese mainland!''

Trembling, huddling as close as possible to the side of the canoe, Amelia willed herself not to cry over what fate had handed her and this lovely Suquamish Indian tribe.

Her eyes sought the far reaches of the sea, hoping that the Suquamish warriors would return before the Haida swept their canoes from the land. She was recalling Gray Wing's tale of the slaves sacrificed during the Haida rituals. Though this Haida Indian had said she was going to be used as barter, she knew that his mind could be changed by others who might think differently.

But was one fate less gruesome than the next? To be sold to the Chinese and carried away to China to be a slave there might even be worse than death!

Hanging her head in her hands, Amelia rocked herself

back and forth, trying not to think of the upcoming hours, days, possibly even weeks.

"Oh, Mama . . . Papa . . ." she whispered as she felt the canoe lurching away from shore. She would not look upon the faces of the many Haida Indians who were now also in the chief's canoe, singing a victorious warring song as they maneuvered their massive paddles through the water. She willed herself to remember how sweet it had been to be kissed by Gray Wing. She would concentrate on Gray Wing . . . only Gray Wing.

Yet when she did, would she not be reminded of his losses?

Oh, what would he do when he discovered the death of his loved ones?

Tears silvered Amelia's cheeks at the thought. . . .

Bound to a stake in the center of the Haida village, her breasts bare, now only attired in the costume of the Haida women—a plant-fiber skirt—and proudly displaying the dentalia necklace about her neck, Amelia was in a state of shock from all that had happened to her. The twine used to secure her upraised hands to the wooden post was cutting into her wrists, sending messages of pain to her brain. The sun beating down upon her bare breasts was a constant reminder of the shame of being partially undressed so that all could see her.

Turning her head, momentarily closing her eyes, Amelia tried to block out all sounds and feelings. But it was impossible. In this village carved out of a coastline highly indented with bays and inlets, and marked by lines of grotesque totem poles, a celebration was taking place. Amelia and many Suquamish Indians, who were also bound to stakes on either side of her, were the cause. Many slaves had been taken from Gray Wing's village this day. One of these slaves would soon be sacrificed.

The steady rhythm of the Haida instruments accompanied by loud chants tore into Amelia's consciousness. Her body seemed to react involuntarily to the music, her pulse beating in almost the same rhythm at the base of her throat where she was so dry she could hardly swallow. The tambourine drum, having been made by stretching a piece of rawhide over a narrow frame bent into cylindrical form, thumped and thumped. Clusters of deer-hoof rattles, rings from which puffin beaks and animal teeth and claws were suspended, made a noise similar to the rush of rain. Long poles, distinctively carved and equipped with more clusters of deer hooves, thumped against the roof boards of some of the gabled houses, also keeping time with the music.

Feeling hands on her breasts caused Amelia's heart to skip a beat and her eyes to wildly open. A sick feeling invaded her senses. She grimaced and bit her lower lip, hardly able to bear this moment when foreign hands were becoming familiar with her body, as though she no longer owned it.

Hate raging inside her, she glared up at the one responsible. But it was hard not to show the fear that she was truly feeling, for it was not a face looking down at her, but instead a richly carved and ornamented mask worn by a Haida warrior. The imaginative design of the mask was in the shape of the mythical thunderbird, as though the Indian himself were the bird.

Willing herself not to feel the man's hands on her breasts, twisting the nipples painfully, Amelia looked beyond him. The Indian warriors were working up to a frenzy as they danced in time with the music. Huge beautifully fashioned blades of red obsidian were carried by some performers. Others carried the skins of the albino deer, the head stuffed and adorned with bright red woodpecker scalps. Those who were not masked wore headdresses made of wide bands of deerskin and the scarlet-feathered scalps of the pileated woodpecker. The barefoot Haida women who were standing, watching, wore only skirts of plant fiber.

Tears streaming down her face as the warrior's fingers continued to torment her body, Amelia focused on the dancers, wishing she were dead. . . .

The step of the dancers varied from a shuffle or a trot

to violent lifting of the knees and stamping of the feet upon the ground. Not only did the feet perform in these dances, but the body and arms as well. Some dancers were so vigorous there were pauses every two or three minutes during which time the drum tapped briskly until the singers and rattles began again.

Amelia's eyes burned with tears as she watched the Indians' feet as they were brought down with a resounding whack and then gave a softer hop or shove ahead. It was a bound and rebound accompanied by gestures of the arms and twisting of the body. The dum-doom-dum-doom of the tom-tom gave the rhythm.

The dancers became more frenzied, their eyes wild. They trotted ahead, striking the ball of the foot first and then scuffling it ahead until the heel struck. The song that went with their dance was lively and melodious.

But the warrior with the mask of the thunderbird turned with a start and momentarily forgot about her when great shouts from the beach resounded through the air. Amelia did not understand the language of these Haida who were shouting, for they did not speak in broken English as had her abductor.

She did realize why there was a sudden excitement unrelated to the celebration in progress. A great, two-masted ship was approaching.

The pit of Amelia's stomach rolled, for she knew that this was not just any ship. It was Chinese. The red-lacquered, scrambling dragons and centipedes carved into the hull of the vessel seemed almost alive, their bold black eyes shining in the afternoon sun. . . .

Seven

༄ ~ ༄

Amelia found it hard to breathe in her building fear as she watched a short, stout, sturdy Chinese man approach with many others following close behind him. He was brightly clad in embroidered silks, with decorative birds on his fur-lined brocade gown. He wore a sable-lined hat and was armed with a heavy cutlass at least two feet long, the back of the blade two inches thick. Its handle was of solid gold. The man's eyes were dark, bold, and almond-shaped. His skin was only a slightly lighter shade of bronze than that of the Indian he was now standing before.

Amelia's insides trembled as she watched the Chinese bow low with his pudgy fists together, his eyes now on her midst his bow. She did not know how to read his expression as he slowly scrutinized her. Did she even wish to? She knew the fate planned for her. She was to be bargained over, sold to the Asian, and taken to China!

But for what use? To be sold to the Chinese emperor for use as a concubine? Or to be used as a servant for the women of this man's family?

Not wanting to think further on her fate, Amelia cast her eyes downward, shamed by her half-nudity. Oh, where was Gray Wing? Had he not discovered her absence yet? Or even if he had, would he not tend to the woes of his people before he lent one thought to her welfare? She was nothing to him in comparison to those who had been a part of his life forever.

At this moment, she was worthless . . . nothing to anyone! If she had only been a dutiful daughter, none of this would have happened to her. She would be aboard her father's great ship even now, headed back to Boston. . . .

Amelia's eyes were drawn slowly upward when she heard Chief Dark Cloud and the other man, who seemed to be the leader of the other colorfully clothed Chinese, exchange soft murmurs. The Chinese knew many tongues. He was talking in Chinese one minute, Haida the next, and then in English.

Understanding enough of what he said made Amelia become less afraid, for he was telling Dark Cloud why he was willing to make a trade for her. He was saying something about a daughter aboard his ship who was lonesome and who would enjoy the company of another her age, even if the companion was white.

Amelia understood the man's English when he referred to her as a poor unfortunate and said that the fates had favored him, for many sons had been born into his family, yet only one daughter. The salvation of a man's soul depended upon his having at least one son to worship at his ancestral tablet. It did not matter how many daughters, for boys and *men* ruled the universe.

Listening even more intently, she heard the Chinese continue speaking to Dark Cloud.

"*Ai,*" Du-Fu Jin said in his gruff voice. "*Mei-ya-faza,* nothing to be done about having only one daughter except to buy her a companion!"

He smiled at Amelia, rubbing his finger and thumb together to indicate money. "Du-Fu will trade many silks to have this intriguing white child for daughter Mei-Ling's companion. Her face is beautiful in its difference. A woman's face casts her destiny. So does that of a child soon to be woman!"

His almond-shaped eyes moved to Amelia's hair. *"Tcha!* Her hair the color of the setting sun clearly indicates kinship to evil spirits! Soon it shall be another color! *Buh-yao-ching*, it does not matter. It will be good to fool the white woman's spirits by changing her hair coloring from red to black!"

Smiling weakly, Amelia met Jin's steady, friendly gaze. Though going with him meant being separated from her family and Gray Wing possibly for eternity, she now knew that going with the Chinese also meant that her life would be spared. If she stayed with the Haida, she could be a sacrifice to their gods!

Slight wisps of her hair fluttered about her face, enough for her to see its brilliant color. She had heard what Du-Fu Jin said about changing the color. That mortified her, for only whores dyed their hair.

But the thought of being taken prisoner on the Chinese ship to become a companion to another girl her age made the knowing of her fate somewhat bearable. Perhaps, eventually, the young girl might become a true friend in her life of sudden changes!

Oh, how badly Amelia needed a friend, someone to pour out her heart's mourning to!

Breathing harshly, her eyes wide, Amelia watched as the trading transactions began. She had never seen such beautiful silken fabrics as those being carried from the ship and placed at Dark Cloud's feet. Never had she seen so many fabulous otter pelts as those being placed at Du-Fu Jin's feet!

She was reminded of her father's eagerness for the otter pelts. Had he received as many in the Suquamish village? Had the pelts been worth losing his daughter over?

Amelia strained against the bonds on her wrists and ankles, wincing with the pain inflicted by her movements. Nervous perspiration beaded on her brow and streamed down her face. Her arms felt deadly numb from having been held over her head for such a long period of time. Her breasts seemed to be pulsing beneath the beating rays of the sun.

She began to silently pray that the trading ritual would soon be over. It was apparent that Gray Wing was not going to come to rescue her. If she must travel aboard the Chinese ship, then she wished it would happen soon. She was, oh, so tired . . . oh, so hungry. She felt dizzy from her long stay on the stake. . . .

Closing her eyes, Amelia dozed from her weakened state; then her eyes flew open when she heard the scraping of a knife on the bonds at her wrists. She looked up into the bold black eyes of a young Chinese, who was surely carrying out orders given by the older, more elaborately dressed Chinese trader who called himself Du-Fu Jin.

When Amelia's arms were finally set free, she cried out in pain as they dropped loosely, lifelessly, at her sides. As the blood began to return to the tips of her fingers, it was as though needles were poking into them.

But her pain and her fears were slowly ebbing away when Du-Fu Jin himself placed a luxuriant otter pelt about her shoulders, hiding her nudity beneath it. His hands were gentle as he led her away from the gawking, hideously tattooed Indians and toward his ship of strange design of gilt scrolls and yawning dragons with big popping eyes on the bow.

When she was aboard the big two-masted ship, she found it alive with colorful paint. The banisters and rails were gilded. The ropes along the deck were of silk. And as she was led down the companionway ladder, she heard the sweet song of a bird coming from somewhere close by.

When she was led into a brightly decorated cabin that was almost entirely occupied by an eight-foot-long highly carved bed from which hung flowered blue silk curtains, she saw the caged canary on the far side of the room, its warbles causing the moment not to be so strained for Amelia.

And then a movement from across the way caught Amelia's fullest attention. She gasped softly when a tiny, pretty thing stepped from behind a folding screen decorated with an elaborate bird design. Amelia's gaze swept over the young Chinese girl. She had almond-shaped brilliant eyes, black and proud. Amber-skinned, she was a round-faced beauty with a beautiful nose that hugged her face prettily.

Her hair was parted into strands, built up and drawn through and over an intricate frame. Stylized black satin bows decorated the headdress, and jade ornaments bounced and wobbled engagingly on gold wire springs as the girl moved in smooth, quiet steps toward Amelia. She was dressed in a long gown of heavy silk under a short jacket of a darker shade of medallion red satin. The skirt of the gown touched the toes of her embroidered shoes set high on white soles and center heels. Her hands were hidden in her sleeves, her eyes cast downward.

Standing stiffly, Amelia listened to Du-Fu Jin address his daughter, Mei-Ling, explaining in English why Amelia was there. Amelia glanced from daughter to father as they conversed fluently in English, but she grew cold inside when she saw the look of dislike deep within Mei-Ling's dark eyes. If Mei-Ling did not wish to have a companion whose skin and culture so differed from hers, would Amelia then be cast aside, left to the Haida, after all?

Amelia's breath was shallow as Du-Fu suddenly left the cabin, leaving her alone with Mei-Ling. Nervously, she shifted her bare feet on the plush carpet beneath them, waiting for Mei-Ling to say something. Instead, Mei-Ling went to an intricately carved chest and opened it, gesturing with a hand toward Amelia.

"What do you want me to do?" Amelia asked, her voice weak. She waited for what seemed an eternity for Mei-Ling to respond, then drew in a deep breath of relief when she did.

"*Zien*, common person," Mei-Ling said in a tiny voice. "My father wishes for you to choose a gown from among my many, to wear. *Tcha! Ou-nah-nay*, oh, fortunate one, my father chooses to make you special in our people's eyes. To me, Mei-Ling, you are no more than a horrible barbarian foreign dog, an outcast." Her eyes flashed and a defiant smile touched her lips as she looked at Amelia's hair. "Your hair reflects what you are. You are kin to evil spirits!"

A coldness touched Amelia all over. She shivered involuntarily. "If you dislike me so much, why didn't you tell your father how you feel?" she murmured, fearing to hear the answer.

"A woman obeys her father," Mei-Ling snapped, boldly tilting her chin. "It is the law! One must obey!"

"Oh, I see," Amelia said, swallowing hard. She now wondered if she would have been better off with the Haida. There had been a chance that she would have been spared. As soon as Mei-Ling's feelings for her were discovered by her father, would he not perhaps even chop off her head with his great, sharp cutlass?

"Choose!" Mei-Ling said, again gesturing toward the chest. "Now!"

Amelia stepped gingerly up to the chest. She lowered her gaze and her breath was completely stolen when she saw that the chest was filled with beautiful robes, ribbons, and jewels. As though she were a puppet, her movements being guided by invisible strings, she knelt down before the chest and let her fingers become familiar with the silken fabrics. Then she chose one gown in particular. Somehow it did not seem all that wrong to hold it in her arms. She could hardly wait to feel its softness against her body. . . .

Bold, heavy footsteps suddenly close by in the room drew Amelia's wondering eyes upward. Everything inside her grew numb when she found a young Chinese in the doorway, looking her slowly up and down. He had flashing almond-shaped eyes, a big nose with a proud arch, and a tall, strong Manchu physique beneath his intricately designed silk gown. His smooth lips lifted into a slow smile as he seemingly undressed her with his eyes.

"My elder brother, Bai-Hua Jin," Mei-Ling said curtly. "Bai-Hua, I am sure father told you about my foreign dog companion. Is not she strange in looks as well as coloring?"

Amelia's back stiffened as she heard Mei-Ling's mocking laughter hidden behind a hand and saw a look of possession in the young man's dark eyes. She hoped that sons were also taught to totally obey the wishes of their father, for Amelia saw Du-Fu and his gentle ways as her only hope for survival. . . .

Gray Wing was dressed in a war shirt ornamented to represent his life story. On the breast was embroidered a prayer for protection, and on the back was a beaded tapestry into which the symbols of victory were woven. On his head he wore a war bonnet with a crown of golden eagle feathers. Silently he prayed to Poushaman, the Great Spirit, as he led his swift fleet of war canoes north.

Eyes narrowed in his hurt and anger, he had not needed much time to know which Indian had slain his sisters, brother, and mother. He even had the enemy of the north, the Haida Chief Dark Cloud, to blame for his father's death!

Upon his arrival at the scene of massacre in their Suquamish village, Gray Wing's father had been downed by a sudden seizure, clutching at his heart. Only moments later he, too, had died.

Gray Wing was now the chief of his people! His duty was to revenge the losses of his people. He meant to revenge his own losses as well!

After proper burial rites had been seen to, Gray Wing only then let himself think on another loss. Amelia, who in the future was to be his princess, had been stolen away by the Haida. If Gray Wing did not arrive in the Haida village in time . . .

The long line of totem poles in the distance made Gray Wing's insides coil into a tight knot. He shouted to his warriors who paddled alongside him in their own canoes. War chants began to resound through the air as he led the singing loud and clear! And when their canoes were beached and their spears readied, they ran up the steep incline and killed and maimed as they made their way into the heart of the Haida village.

After Chief Dark Cloud was taken prisoner and he was staked spread-legged to the ground, his warriors always defenseless against the most fierce of the Suquamish, Gray Wing stood victoriously over him, his spear raised, his eyes filled with fire.

"You killed my people! You took slaves!" Gray Wing growled. He looked around him, wondering about Amelia and what might have happened to her. His insides trembled when he saw the remains of some of his people on the ground where they had crumpled from stakes. He could see where portions of their bodies had been eaten. They lay even now in pools of their own blood.

"You tortured my people!" Gray Wing shouted, lowering the spear so that its point only barely sank into the flesh of Dark Cloud's neck, causing a small trickle of blood to crawl across his chest. "You die soon, but first you tell me what you have done with the white girl you took from my village!"

Dark Cloud's lips lifted into a smug smile. "She meant much to you, Gray Wing?" he tormented.

"Where is ... . she?" Gray Wing growled, sinking the tip of his spear farther into Dark Cloud's flesh. He smiled to himself when he heard the throaty gurgle of pain emerge from between his enemy's lips.

Dark Cloud gritted his teeth, then spoke shallowly through them. "This woman with the pale skin?" he said, smiling crookedly up at Gray Wing. "She . . . was . . . a beautiful sacrifice . . . to the Gods."

Gray Wing paled. His stomach lurched. "She was eaten?" he gulped.

"She was eaten," Dark Cloud said in a hiss.

Gray Wing's hand tightened about his spear. With a loud cry of grief, a shriek that split the heavens, he plunged the blade through Dark Cloud's neck. He then jerked the spear away and threw it into the wind, blood streaming from it.

"*Memaloost!*" he cried, the veins in his neck cording. "*Peshak! Peshak!*"

His fists doubled at his sides, Gray Wing looked slowly among the surviving Haida who were being held prisoner. He did not see Dark Cloud's son, Red Eagle, who was

Gray Wing's age. Somehow he had escaped the wrath of the Suquamish this day. But one day he would pay for the deeds of his father! He, personally, would pay for the death of Amelia!

Yet Gray Wing would not be hasty in this punishment. He could cause this son many torments before he, too, died.

. No, Gray Wing would not hunt him down just yet. He . . . would not kill him . . . just yet.

There was time. There was time. . . .

Eight

◈

Canton, China

Ten Years Later

Sunshine poured in all along the windowed upper walls of the south side of the great beamed room. The floor of black marble shone so that one could see a face in it. The walls were hung with scrolls of raw silk decorated with phoenixes and birds of paradise, and dragons in intricate design so minute that it hurt one's eyes to discover them.

The click of chopsticks around the rich, polished blackwood table made Amelia aware that this was her last meal with the Chinese family whom she had grown to love even though the circumstances under which she had come there had been less than desirable. Now called Vona-Lee, a name bestowed upon her by the lord of this family, Du-Fu Jin, Amelia had almost forgotten that she had ever been called anything else.

Vona-Lee, she thought.

Yes, she had grown used to the name and loved it as though it had been given to her by her very own parents, just as she had grown used to her hair having been dyed black. She now wore it built up on a framework decorated with tasseled flowers.

Vona-Lee had even begun to smooth almond milk over

her face for her complexion. The Chinese said that one would become a legend by doing so.

She had also grown used to the weight of silks, satins, heavy gold, and jewels. She was now more Chinese than American, yet she longed to return to the life she had left behind those ten long years ago when she was bought and paid for by Du-Fu Jin.

Excitement was building to extreme proportions inside Vona-Lee. She had spoken of her desire to return to America so many times now, to see her true family, that Du-Fu Jin had finally given in. Because he had grown to love her as a daughter and wanted to see her happy, he had promised to take her to Boston the next time he traveled to America, but only after first transacting his usual trades with the Indians of the Puget Sound area.

The thought of perhaps seeing Gray Wing and her parents again made Vona-Lee's stomach flutter as though many butterflies had been set free inside her.

Could it truly be real that she was going to return home? Soon she would know whether she had a brother or a sister.

Oh! She was so anxious to see which it truly was!

"Vona-Lee, it is *buh-hao-eesa*, not good form, to look so starry-eyed while at the dinner table," Mei-Ling Jin softly teased at Vona-Lee's side. She motioned with her head. "Do you not enjoy the candied watermelon rind this evening? Or do you think of food you will soon eat when back in America?"

Vona-Lee picked at her food daintily with her chopsticks made of bamboo, silver, and ivory. She was recalling the time when she had just arrived in China and knew nothing of chopsticks or how to use them. Mei-Ling had said the way she ate was disgusting because she had asked for something with which to spear her meat instead of using civilized chopsticks.

Vona-Lee cast a soft smile at her best friend in the world, yet more a sister now than a friend. It had taken some time for Mei-Ling Jin to accept Amelia into the family, but when she had, it had been Mei-Ling who suggested the beautiful Chinese name that Amelia had been given. She said that the name Vona-Lee was quite appropriate, because it was as beautiful as Amelia!

From that point on, Vona-Lee and Mei-Ling had been inseparable. . . .

At moments like this, when Mei-Ling was flashing her tiny almond-shaped eyes, Vona-Lee felt torn by her decision to return to America. She so loved Mei-Ling! How could she exist without her? They had shared thoughts . . . dreams . . . the transformation from girl into woman!

But the fact that Mei-Ling was going to accompany Vona-Lee on the long journey made the decision again acceptable.

"Please understand why I must return to America," Vona-Lee said in a low whisper. She leaned closer to Mei-Ling and let her gaze move over her very slowly, as though memorizing her round-faced, amber-skinned friend's black and proud eyes, and her Chinese nose, which hugged her face prettily. "Though I have been treated so very kindly while in the House of Jin, I do hunger to see my family again. Your father allows it. So I must go."

Mei-Ling laid her chopsticks aside, casting her father troubled glances, for it was not polite to speak at the dinner table. She cringed beneath the heated gaze from his bold, dark eyes, yet knew that this time he would not scold her, for he surely understood that the time would soon come when Mei-Ling and Vona-Lee would never speak to each other again, once they said their good-byes in America.

She studied her father more closely. Though he looked important in his brightly embroidered silk robe embellished with decorative birds, she could see something else in his eyes tonight. She sighed. She knew that he had been taking time alone with his opium pipe. It showed in the flush of his cheeks. His personality changed so when he was under the influence of the dreaded opium! Perhaps he *would* soon scold her and Vona-Lee for disobedience to the rules that had been taught to them by the lord of the house!

Mei-Ling turned a slow eye toward her mother. Even in her mother's beautiful eyes she could see a glassiness. *Aie-yah!* Even her mother loved the opium too much. It was well known that her mother took her serving woman everywhere with her to carry her opium pipe, from which she took an occasional puff.

Ai, it would be good to take a long sea voyage away from the unfortunate habits of her mother. But she would not be getting away from her father. He would be the one in charge of the great dragon ship that would move from the China Sea into waters that stretched out to America!

But surely while commanding the ship he would not let himself be under the influence of a drug that would distort his decisions, which could mean life or death for those on board his beautiful ship!

Ai, she thought. She was being foolish for worrying about such things on this day that should be only Mei-Ling's and Vona-Lee's!

"You could marry my brother Bai-Hua!" Mei-Ling whispered anxiously. "Do you not understand that he is a young Manchu lord who is the heir of centuries of civilization? Vona-Lee, he has spoken of his love for you. He would treat you like a princess if you married him and remained in China."

Mei-Ling's pleas did not fall on deaf ears. Vona-Lee moved her eyes slowly to Bai-Hua who sat across from her at the massive table. A coldness touched her insides when she caught him staring openly at her. Though he was a splendid-looking young lord with flashing almond-shaped eyes and a tall, strong Manchu physique, and boasted a *ta-biza*, a big nose with a proud arch, an inheritance from his Manchu ancestors, she did not trust him. The most scholarly of the family, he had been away at school these past four years. But now that he had returned and was a part of the daily family affairs again, he made Vona-Lee uncomfortable with his watchful eyes. Once he heard of her return to America, she had even begun to feel like his prey. She had been watching and waiting for him to corner her . . . even try to seduce her. He did not approve of her trip to America. He wanted her—if not one way, then in another. . . .

Bai-Hua's dark hair was drawn back into a man's queue, and his satin robe hugged his muscled body, but Vona-Lee was nothing but repelled by his presence. While being observed by him she would force her thoughts elsewhere . . . to another man, another time. . . .

Deeply embedded inside her heart was the memory of Gray Wing. Oh, how many nights had she lain awake fantasizing over how it would be to see him again? If fate granted her the chance, would he even remember her? In ten years she had grown from a girl into a fully blossomed woman, he into a fully developed man, perhaps even a chief of his people!

Or had the Haida Indians . . . killed . . . *him*, too?

Shaking her head to clear her wandering thoughts, having had many nightmares of the massacre in Gray Wing's village, Vona-Lee tore her eyes away from Bai-Hua and again looked into Mei-Ling's beautiful face.

"Please do not speak of my marriage to your brother so openly," she softly scolded. "You know that it is not proper. And you also know that I have refused him. I must return to America. For many reasons I . . . must return."

Vona-Lee did not mention the fact that Du-Fu Jin did not approve of his son's choice of a woman to love. It was Du-Fu's desire that his son choose a beautiful Chinese maiden, one to carry on the tradition of the House of Jin.

This, also, was the reason Du-Fu had so readily agreed to return Vona-Lee to her family. Though he loved her, he saw her as a threat to his son's future. He was going to remove her entirely from his son's life!

"You have spoken of an Indian often while we have been speaking of the past. Is it because of him that you are so anxious to return?" Mei-Ling persisted. "Surely he is not as handsome as my brother! Vona-Lee, stay. Marry Bai-Hua. We would be true sisters then!"

"*Bi-ni-di-zueh!*" Du-Fu Jin suddenly said, frightening the two whispering women into attention. "If you two must chat, do it away from the table. Do you forget the manners taught by your elders?''

Vona-Lee and Mei-Ling exchanged downcast glances and pushed their chairs back from the table in unison. With their heads bowed and their hands tucked inside the heavy cuffs of their silken gowns, they inched their way backwards until they reached the screen that led around to the door. They then fled into the long corridor, giggling like schoolgirls instead of the women they were.

"*Wei*, father's voice carries so much authority, does it not?'' Mei-Ling said, slowing her pace, shuffling along the flagged floors rubbed smooth and clean. "We are, as you say, lucky he did not order a suitable punishment for talking at the table.''

Vona-Lee's giggle softened into a low laugh. She slipped her hands from their cuffs and took one of Mei-Ling's and held on to it. She again studied her friend. In her long gown of heavy silk under a short jacket in a darker shade of medallion red satin, she was a vision of petite loveliness.

Yes, Vona-Lee knew that she would miss Mei-Ling but she would be replaced by *family*. The hope of ever seeing Gray Wing again was surely farfetched! She must concentrate on family. Only family . . .

Vona-Lee's spine stiffened when she heard loud voices carrying from the room she had just left. She knew that Bai-Hua rarely showed even a trace of disobedience to his father but at this moment he was most definitely arguing.

Vona-Lee placed a hand on Mei-Ling's arm, stopping her. She leaned an ear in the direction of the continuing arguing voices. "Mei-Ling, why does Bai-Hua persist so?'' she sighed. "Why does he not just understand that your father is returning me to my home because it is best for me? Why can't he see that I do not wish to stay and marry him? There are so many lovely Chinese women just waiting for such a proposal from your handsome brother!''

Mei-Ling's face twisted into a grimace when she heard her brother's voice continue in its monotone as he still spoke of Vona-Lee and what he felt was best for her. "My

brother sees you as the special person you are,'' she said,
blinking her dark eyes nervously, awaiting her father's explosion. But perhaps the opium had numbed Du-Fu Jin's
brain so much that he did not realize when his son was
beyond that range of being respectful to him. "He has not
seen another woman he wishes to bear his children!''

Vona-Lee was taken aback by this statement. Her eyes
widened. "But I . . . would bear him a child who would
not be full-blooded Chinese,'' she said in a gasp. "How
could he want that?''

"Do you not know how vain my brother is?'' Mei-Ling
said, laughing softly. "He feels that the child would be
Chinese in appearance and attitude because he is such a
splendid, virile lord whose woman would bear him no less
than an exact replica of himself!''

"*Ai*, he is truly that conceited,'' Vona-Lee stated flatly.
She would not voice aloud her stronger feelings about Bai-
Hua—that she had, from the very beginning, thought he
was a cad!

"Conceited?'' Mei-Ling said, pinching her tiny face
into a frown. "Sometimes you speak in riddles, Vona-
Lee. But of course that is an American foreign dog word.
Is it not?''

"Mei-Ling, you still call me a foreign dog?'' Vona-Lee
teased, knowing how Mei-Ling had despised the American "barbarians'' before she met Vona-Lee only because
she did not understand American habits. Mei-Ling had
said Americans did not know the simplest customs that
even a poor coolie knew, and that Americans did everything backwards, just as they read books from left to right!

Mei-Ling giggled. "Should I call you a *zien*, a common
person instead?'' she said, grabbing Vona-Lee's hand and
again walking with her down the long corridor, which
glowed with gemlike paintings. "*Tcha!* You know that I
enjoy teasing you, my best friend in all the world.''

Tall pewter floor lamps lined the wall, bearing the character *shou*, which stood for good luck. Vona-Lee and Mei-
Ling passed a window with glass panes in the center of a
wooden trellis covered with a tough silk paper. Beyond it,

in the main courtyard, a lotus pool had been cleared and stocked with the rare white lotus. Goldfish with pop-eyes and butterfly tails swam among the lotus leaves.

"No, I do not wish to be called a common person," Vona-Lee said, laughing softly. "Nor do I wish to be called a *tai-tai*, a lady of a Chinese household whose problem is boredom and whose dearest desire is to kill time. I wish to experience things. *Do* things. In America I shall have that opportunity once again."

"*Ai.*" Mei-Ling sighed, nodding. "The most important actions of the day for Chinese wives is getting dressed up and having their hair coiffed. They have no daily chores whatsoever."

"And do you wish to live that way yourself, Mei-Ling?" Vona-Lee asked, entering a bedroom of beautiful silk tapestries and burning candles. "Or have I talked too much of the ways of American women to change your mind? Though most American wives have household chores to do, some, like myself, seek out adventure. Just like the time I left the ship to go and speak to Gray Wing. What fun it was to be alone, away from my family, for that length of time to do such a daring thing as that. I have always been that way. I love new experiences!"

Mei-Ling's eyes lit up with a smile. She watched Vona-Lee's movements as she crossed the room toward the eight-foot-square bed with its carved frame upon which hung flowered blue silk curtains. "You do not have the appearance of one who would boldly dare fate," she teased. "*Ou-nah-nay*, O fortunate one, do you not know that you have been gifted with the walk of one who needs only to motion to a man with your finger and he is yours? You would never want for anything with such a walk as that. All men would fall over themselves to be your servant."

Vona-Lee sat down on the bed and rested her back against the many folded silk *beiwu*, covers, piled along the side against the wall. The curtains of the room were also made of silk and bore the stylized bat motif, which symbolized luck. "You have never mentioned such a walk before to me," she said, reaching up to replace a strand of hair into the framework atop her head. "What is it called?"

Mei-Ling eased down on the edge of the bed. Her back was straight; the framework on her head looked top-heavy, with its jewels and flowers woven into it. "It is the lotus lily walk," she murmured. "It means that you sway voluptuously, the way the lotus blossom sways on its stem when the water of the lake laps against it."

"My word," Vona-Lee said, laughing softly. "I didn't know that I had any special way of walking. Now I will feel self-conscious when I do!"

"Self-conscious?" Mei-Ling said, squinting her eyes in wonder. "What does that mean?"

"When one is too conscious of everything one does," Vona-Lee said, reaching out to touch Mei-Ling's smooth whitened face. Then she drew her into her arms. "Oh, how I shall miss you and your beautiful way of describing things."

Mei-Ling's eyes stung with the need to cry; she already missed Vona-Lee. First her father gave her a sister! Then he took her away! Fates were unkind more oft than not!

Drawing away from Vona-Lee, Mei-Ling left the bed and went to the door and turned and smiled softly at her, then fled with tears streaming down her cheeks.

Vona-Lee swallowed hard, forcing a knot to leave her throat. Then she rose slowly from the bed and undressed down to her thin silk underthings and removed her headdress so that her long, flowing hair hung down her back to her waist in shimmering black. She combed her fingers through it, picking up the scent of the jasmine oil that had been combed into it earlier in the day.

Outdoor courtyard lanterns cast shadows in various light, and red bamboos and flowers waved back and forth across the windowpanes as Vona-Lee lit a precious stick of incense. She carried it to her private altar in one corner of the room and set it deep in ashes, then knelt down on a mat before Qwan Yin the merciful and began murmuring a soft prayer. This, also, she had grown to accept as a normal part of her life, yet never forgetting her own religion taught her by her parents. She felt blessed to have two gods to worship.

Slowly her hands moved to a velvet-lined box that she always left at the altar. Her eyes grew misty when she raised the lid and peered down at the tusk necklace that was so dear to her heart. Gently picking it up, she pressed it to her heaving chest and let memories so sweet of Gray Wing invade her senses. Her prayers were filled with a deep desire to see him again. In her dreams she had treasured remembrances of his kiss . . . his touch. . . .

A hand on her shoulder made Vona-Lee gasp and pale with alarm. Turning her head in jerks, she gazed up into the dark eyes of Bai-Hua Jin. His robe was a mass of superb embroidery from collar to hem. Realizing how scantily attired she was, knowing that her breasts were quite revealed beneath the thin garment of silk, Vona-Lee dropped the precious Indian necklace to the floor and quickly folded her arms across her chest as she rose slowly to her feet.

"What are you doing in the privacy of my bedroom?" she asked weakly, having never before been so boldly confronted by Mei-Ling's brother. "Bai-Hua, you must leave. It is less than proper that you should be here. I am . . . only partially clad."

His eyes now boldly raking over her, Bai-Hua was glad that Vona-Lee had not accepted the custom of binding her breasts, which all Chinese maidens practiced. His eyes feasted upon the round satin sheen of her breasts through the thin silken material that encased her like the petals of a rose not yet opened to the rays of the sun.

His loins ached with the need to touch . . . to devour her breasts with his lips.

But because of his scheming father, who did not approve of Vona-Lee for the chosen wife of his youngest son, Bai-Hua, this would never be.

Not unless Bai-Hua took advantage of the moment!

"Tomorrow you will be gone," he said. "I could not let you go without a private good-bye, Vona-Lee."

"But you could travel on your father's ship to America

with me and say good-bye to me then,'' Vona-Lee said in a scarcely audible whisper, her heart pounding in her fear of being alone with a man who loved her not so much with passion as with lust. "I still don't understand why you refuse to go.''

"It is because I do not approve of the journey and the reason it has been arranged,'' Bai-Hua growled, clenching his hands into fists at his sides. "You should not return to America. You should stay in China. You are now Chinese, not American!''

Vona-Lee took a step backwards, almost stumbling over the statue of Qwan Yin. "I was born American,'' she said stubbornly. "I shall always be American!''

"You now worship Buddha! You now dress Chinese! You live Chinese! In my eyes . . . in my heart . . . you are Chinese,'' Bai-Hua said huskily, reaching out and grabbing Vona-Lee by the arms. He drew her close and crushed her against him, reveling in the feel of her breasts pressed hard into his chest. "You are the only woman I have ever wanted. Why must you leave me?''

Vona-Lee's heartbeats almost swallowed her whole when his lips bore down upon hers so suddenly, stealing her breath away. Only one other man had ever kissed her. And Bai-Hua's kiss did not compare in the least with Gray Wing's! She felt nothing but fear with each mounting moment, for Bai-Hua's hands were now on her breasts, caressing them.

Squirming, trying to protest through pressed, bruised lips, Vona-Lee finally broke free of Bai-Hua. She ran across the room and grabbed a robe and wrapped it around her. Her pulse was wild, her face was hot with anger.

"Bai-Hua, how—how dare you! Get out of my room,'' she stormed, pointing toward the door. "If you don't, I shall call for your father. From the beginning you planned to . . . seduce me!''

Bai-Hua interrupted her by rushing to her and wrestling her over to the bed. "I will make you want me,'' he said thickly. "You will not want to return to the Indian who gave you that worthless necklace! Bai-Hua will give you gold necklaces and bracelets! How could you want less?''

One of Bai-Hua's hands probed beneath Vona-Lee's petticoat while the other held her immobile on the bed. Vona-Lee was trembling with fear as he touched the forbidden triangle at the juncture of her thighs. When he began to caress her there, where no man had touched before, she panicked and drew up a knee and thrust it into Bai-Hua's loins.

When he jumped from the bed, howling, she covered her mouth with her hands and watched, now afraid he might harm her for what she had done.

"Mei-ya-faza," Bai-Hua said as the pain cooled in his loins. *"Buh-yao-ching. Go* to America! You are only a *zien*, a common person, anyway! You would be a bad wife for Bai-Hua, the *hao-hanza*, the brave, lusty one!''

Vona-Lee breathed a sigh of relief as he stormed from the room, leaving her in peace.

Returning to the statue, kneeling down before it, Vona-Lee picked up the necklace and hugged it to her chest. "Oh, Gray Wing, if it had only been you kissing me . . . caressing me," she whispered. "I would not have stopped you. I want to be loved by you. *Totally.*''

The shore went up rapidly to high hills, and beyond the forest, on the hills, the morning was breaking gray and somber. Gray Wing was standing in the tabernacle of the mighty forest in the sublime silence of the stately pines, listening to the voice of nature, his ears trained to hear sounds ordinarily inaudible. He was beginning the months of preparation before the great whale hunt, fasting and praying to Poushaman, the Great Spirit. He would bathe in the icy streams; he would talk to the spirits. Soon he would be ready to go in search of the whales that would be offshore among the sheltered coves and winding channels. Pods of killer whales would endlessly be protecting the kelp forests in search of salmon, escorted overhead by whirling canopies of puffins, cormorants, and gulls.

But something else besides the hunt kept coming to

mind. He could not forget Amelia! She was a part of almost his every waking hour. No matter how many women he chose to feed the desires of his flesh, none had reached into his soul like the young girl-woman with the green eyes and flaming red hair.

Yet she was dead! He must forget!

Or was it her spirit that was always there, staying with him, touching him with Amelia's pure sweetness?

Attired in a brief breechcloth, his brown hair hanging long and loose across his broad shoulders, Gray Wing raised his eyes to the heavens. He inhaled a sweet scent from the nearby roses that brought memories of Amelia even closer. It was as though she was there, trying to communicate with him!

"*An-ah*," Gray Wing groaned aloud. "I must learn *mah-lie*, to forget! Yet how can I totally?"

Amelia's father was a constant reminder, if her haunting memories were not. After discovering the death of his daughter upon his return to Whale Island to get her, and not wanting to believe that it was true, her father had chosen to take a joint partnership with the owners of the Russian-American Fur Company, not far from Whale Island in Puget Sound, enabling him not to be far from where he had last seen his daughter.

Gray Wing had learned to hate the man who treated him like dirt beneath his feet. Gray Wing did not tolerate him except to trade with him, which was always most profitable to Gray Wing's Suquamish people. Aside from that, Gray Wing kept his distance from the intolerable Bostonian!

Stretching out on his back on a thick bed of moss, Gray Wing watched the grayness leave the sky, replaced by puffy clouds floating by. He let himself get lost in thoughts of Amelia, envisioning her as she might be at her present age of twenty-three. Her fiery red hair would be long and drifting as she came to him. She would then embrace him. Her lips would be as soft as the kiss of the sea, her breasts would fill his hands, the nipples taut against his palms.

Gray Wing became totally lost in the fantasy as his thoughts wandered, becoming real to him. Amelia's every secret place became his as his lips began to taste and worship her. After she seductively removed her clothes, Gray Wing trailed kisses down her slim, sinuous body and silken thighs, and long, tapering calves. She responded with hot, pulsing desire as their bodies tangled and melted into each other.

Groaning, he could feel the pressure building . . . building . . . then exploding, dissolving into a tingling heat, spreading . . . spreading . . . searing him, heart and soul. . . .

The cry of a hawk overhead drew Gray Wing from his reverie. He could feel his heart thudding wildly inside him, realizing what he had just experienced in his fantasies, oh, missing Amelia so much more than ever before! Would . . . it . . . ever end?

Now truly losing himself in his prayers to the Great Spirit, Gray Wing did not even realize when day had been replaced by night until he looked into the heavens and saw the bright radiance of the stars. His eyes sought out the Milky Way. In its path he could see the footprints of the departed Suquamish warriors.

And then suddenly he saw something else! Amelia was there, among the stars. . . .

Nine

❧ ❧

The big two-masted Chinese schooner, whose oars were manned by seventy men, continued to cut its way through the waters of Puget Sound. Vona-Lee stood at the rail, her heart beating in a steady rhythm of anxiousness about what lay ahead, perhaps only a few hours away. Vona-Lee had left China—that fairylike place of many courtyards filled with plants, pine trees, and red-lacquered colonnades enclosed by gray, high walls—and was now in the waters that stretched out to the wilderness of Washington Territory.

Everything was becoming familiar to Vona-Lee now— the wind, sharp with salt and sweet with the scent of red cedar, and in the east the mighty Cascade Range shawled in the dark green weave of cedar, hemlock, and fir, dominated by the eternal white cone of Mount Rainier.

Soon the great Chinese schooner would move to shore. Soon, perhaps, Vona-Lee would even get to see Gray Wing again! It had been voiced aloud by Du-Fu Jin that he preferred trading with the Suquamish this voyage instead of the Haida, fearing the fiendish ways of the Haida now that he had become familiar with their customs. He would not take a chance that Mei-Ling or Vona-Lee would be stolen from the ship while he transacted business on land!

Oh, how pleased Vona-Lee was about Du-Fu's wise decision! Oh, the hope that she might see Gray Wing again so thrilled her heart! She would have returned earlier had there not been so many obstacles in the way! The wide expanse of the ocean, the dangers of the ships' lusty crews, had she even found a ship on which to escape from China! The risks had been too many at age thirteen. But now at age twenty-three, no risks were even required! She was being returned willingly!

Her eyes slowly shifted downward, seeing how she was dressed, and doubt suddenly seized her. Would Gray Wing even recognize her in such Chinese attire? She was wearing a golden-green brocade gown that had been made by the Jin resident tailor. The brocade flowers with which it was covered had tiny crystal buttons sewn in their centers. The long gown was girdled at the waist with a length of green silk.

Vona-Lee had watched her reflection in the mirror as she moved about in her private room in the House of Jin while trying on this new gown, and she had noticed that she actually glittered like a dragon with every move she made.

She studied herself further now, wishing she had a mirror in which to see herself as Gray Wing would see her, if the fates granted her the chance that this ship would dock close by Gray Wing's village.

She held her hands before her eyes. She wore a ring on the second finger of each hand, having been taught that unpaired jewelry was unthinkable.

Her fingers went to her hair in sudden remembrance. She softly gasped to herself. It was no longer its lustrous color of red. It had been dyed black. Surely neither her parents nor Gray Wing would understand or recognize her because of this!

But considering this earlier she had refused to wear the usual intricate framework this day and, instead, was wearing her hair long and loose about her shoulders with a shell-pink camellia pinned above her ear on either side.

"The color of my hair must not make the difference!" she whispered to herself, her scalp aching even now from her incessant scrubbings in attempts to remove the dye before arriving in America. "That I am older may, though! I now have the look of a mature woman, not a mere child of thirteen."

For luck, having had so many frustrated worries to trouble her, Vona-Lee had applied a dot of rouge in the center of her forehead and on the bridge of her nose. She had rouge flecked fingertips and palms.

"Wei!" Mei-Ling said suddenly from behind Vona-Lee. "I see land. We are nearing America again, Vona-Lee. But this time it makes me so sad. America means one thing to me. Losing *you*."

Vona-Lee turned with a start, then smiled warmly at Mei-Ling, who was approaching her in her lovely embroidered silk gown. She was seeing, even now, sleep still heavy in her best friend's lovely eyes.

She embraced Mei-Ling softly, then stepped away from her, again grasping the rail of the ship as it pitched in the deep waves of the water. "You are finally awake, I see," she said, tossing her windswept hair back from her crisp green eyes. "Mei-Ling, I did not sleep a wink all night. Nor shall I until . . . until I see him again, now that I am so close to where he lives!"

Vona-Lee looked across the Sound in the pearl dawn, trembling with excitement as she once again saw the crescendo of forested hills rolling up like organ music from the margin of the sea. The breeze of dawn was fresh and stinging cold. The water danced as if every little sharp wave were tingling with life.

"You speak of the Indian again," Mei-Ling said in a disgusted tone. Her hair woven around its framework and sparkling with assorted gems, her face not yet decorated with color, she shuffled her feet until she was beside Vona-Lee. Her tiny fingers circled the rail as she held on against the powerful gusts of wind. "This Indian, this Gray Wing you have dreamed of for so long, will now surely have a wife at his side. You waste your time and energies dwelling on memories of the past, Vona-Lee. If you had only married my brother, you and I would never have to say good-bye!''

Only half hearing what Mei-Ling was saying, instead focusing on movement far in the distance in the water, Vona-Lee felt her heart skip a beat. She leaned closer to the rail and placed a hand above her eyes, shielding them from the rising sun, studying the movement.

Could it be . . . ?

Was it a massive canoe? Was it like the one in which Gray Wing patrolled the waters, looking for whales?

''You do not answer me, Vona-Lee,'' Mei-Ling fussed. She followed the direction of Vona-Lee's vision, now also seeing movement way ahead. She watched intently, then recognized a massive canoe filled with Indians. She turned her eyes slowly to Vona-Lee. ''It is Indians. Surely it isn't . . .''

Vona-Lee pressed her hands to her cheeks, feeling how even thinking of possibly seeing Gray Wing caused them to warm so.

Then she dropped her hands back to the rail and clutched it, scoffing at the possibility of coming across Gray Wing so soon after arriving back in the waters of Puget Sound.

''I dare not wish that it is.'' She sighed, now distracted by the *heang-kun*, the ship's priest, as he came walking behind her, carrying a censer filled with burning joss sticks and incense, blessing the ship.

Vona-Lee watched the priest as he ambled by. It was his duty to burn incense and gold and silver paper in front of Ma-tsoo-poo, the rather portly and round-faced sea goddess. The priest kept a lamp burning in front of her image day and night. Each morning the priest made his rounds, blessing all parts of the ship, even the galley.

This morning his presence was an annoyance to Vona-Lee. She wanted only to concentrate on who might be in the distant canoe. She wanted only to concentrate on Gray Wing!

Trying to ignore the intrusion of the priest, Vona-Lee turned back around, and it was then that she got the first sight of an island in the distance, opposite to where the large canoe was traveling.

"Whale Island!" she whispered, her pulse racing. "It is. I know that . . . is . . . Whale Island!"

Pinnacles of cumulus clouds streaked with gold and orange, with purple valleys in between, lay over the island in the morning sun. The slopes were glazed in a haze of pastel shades, the trees shone like dark metal. Vona-Lee was still too far away to actually see the Indians' dwellings.

But surely the totem poles would soon pick up the rays of the sun and reflect back into her anxious eyes.

Vona-Lee's stomach lurched when a powerful growl of a voice erupted from behind her. She turned and eyed Du-Fu Jin speculatively. In his heavy silk garment decorated with embroidery he swayed as he walked to the ship's rail. The flush of his cheeks and the redness of his eyes revealed that his body and mind were being controlled by opium. His personality changed when his body was consumed by the dreaded drug!

"Tcha!" Du-Fu growled, doubling a fist in the air as he saw the approach of the large canoe. "If that vessel dares to cross in the path of my great ship, run it over!" Du-Fu shouted to his crew.

His drunken laugh and his order to the crew made Vona-Lee's insides grow cold. She glanced from the canoe to Du-Fu, then back to the canoe, praying that Du-Fu would change his mind or that the canoe would not have Gray Wing as a passenger. Her heart beat out her fear as she watched the canoe and its occupants. Now that it was closer she could tell that it was a whaling canoe. She could see the shine of the harpoons. . . .

Ignoring the great colorful ship in the distance, only vaguely aware that it was drawing too close to the whaling grounds, Gray Wing stood tensely in the bow of his canoe, his twelve-foot harpoon in hand. The steersman crouched in the canoe's stern, using his paddle to guide the craft toward the twenty-ton whale that the Suquamish had been stalking as it dived and surfaced.

But now they were close. Gray Wing and his braves, all dressed in loincloths, did not need the steersman's signal for quiet. The long, narrow cedar paddles slipped in and out of the water soundlessly. Each paddle blade ended in a point, allowing water to drain off silently in a tiny stream.

The steersman maneuvered the silent canoe alongside the resting whale, slightly behind it, to remain out of its sight. Then just as the whale pushed its huge tail flukes downward to begin a dive, Gray Wing broke the eerie silence with a wild yell to tense his diaphragm and strengthen his upper body. He then thrust the harpoon, aiming just behind the whale's flipper. His entire weight and determination born of his long preparation for this hunt drove the point deep into the whale.

Gushing blood, the stricken whale dived, its fluke towering above the canoe. Paddlers hurriedly backed the canoe away and tossed baskets overboard, which held coils of rope attached to the harpoon head. Half a dozen inflated sealskin floats, attached to the rope, bobbed briefly on the bloody water and then were pulled under by the diving whale. Hauling the floats would tire the whale, forcing it up again.

Whooping, Gray Wing, with his canoe of braves, closed in. As the whale rose again for air, Gray Wing drove two more harpoons into its massive body. After a few more short dives, the exhausted whale lay quietly on the surface, its blowhole pulsing with short gasps.

Gray Wing's canoe pulled alongside the whale. He leaned out and, using a shaft edged with mussel shell, made a few strokes to cut the tendons of the flukes.

Then the final stroke. He thrust a spear into the whale's heart. A red froth erupted from the blowhole. The whale rolled and died.

Gray Wing felt victorious. His high status among his people was ensured. He had provided food for the village.

But more important, he had carried on the whale-hunting tradition of his ancestors.

Dropping over the side of the canoe into the water, Gray Wing swam to the dead whale's mouth, cut holes in the lips and used leather thongs to sew the mouth shut to prevent the carcass from filling with water. Others were pulling in the sealskin floats and tying them to the whale to buoy it.

His deed done, Gray Wing pulled himself back into the canoe, his thoughts of home warm in his heart. His people would have a feast this night. In his canoe, a crewman was already opening matched clam shells containing glowing coals from the home fire. Another was arranging cedar-bark tinder and kindling in a box full of beach sand. When they arrived home they would wait inside a protective reef but well offshore for a high tide that would allow them to pull the whale high on the beach for butchering. But while waiting, they would already be feasting on the great whale, cooked over the fire in the canoe.

Gray Wing continued thinking about these things as he took care of his whaling tools, the heavy wood harpoon shaft he had fished out of the sea after the whale had dived, and his spare harpoon point, a sharp mussel shell. The shell was backed by an elk-bone toggle designed to turn sideways and prevent the harpoon head from pulling out. For safekeeping, Gray Wing returned his spare blade and toggle to his cedar-bark envelope.

"*Hwah!*" a crewman shouted. "A ship! It is fast approaching! *Howh!* Hurry! We must get the canoe out of the ship's way!"

Gray Wing's head turned in jerks as he looked in the direction of the ship. His insides grew numbly cold when he caught sight of the colorful dragons carved into the sides of the ship. The dragons seemed alive, as though crawling atop the water in his canoe's direction, their beaded eyes wild and threatening!

Gray Wing's gaze went upward and saw two Chinese ladies peering anxiously down at him from the ship, and then a short, squatty man laughing boisterously and shouting something in Chinese as he flung his pudgy hands in the air.

Du-Fu Jin shouted for the canoe to clear the way. *"Wei! Wei!"* he said. When the canoe did not move quickly enough, he again commanded his crew to run it over.

Vona-Lee's heart beat erratically as she gazed down upon the handsome face of the lead Indian. Oh, Lord, it *was* Gray Wing! He had not changed. He still looked the same, except that he was more mature, which made him even more handsome. And Du-Fu was prepared to kill him!

Turning to Du-Fu, grabbing him desperately by an arm, Vona-Lee pleaded with him. "No!" she shrieked loudly. "Do not do this thing! It is wrong!"

But the wild look in Du-Fu's bloodshot eyes told Vona-Lee that she was speaking to someone who did not even hear. His brain and his logic were opium-soaked!

Vona-Lee turned back to the rail and clutched it, afraid to watch as the horrible deed was done, which would mean that she would never be with Gray Wing again, after all. He would . . . be dead. . . .

Gray Wing made momentary eye contact with Vona-Lee as he rose to his feet in the canoe, a harpoon in hand. Just as the Chinese ship ran into the bow of the canoe, Gray Wing launched the harpoon, laughing as it pierced the bulbous eye of one of the ship's dragons.

But then he lost his balance. Along with the rest of his crew he plunged into the gray waters of the Sound. As he fell, he saw the whale break loose from his canoe and drift slowly out to sea. In his heart he was cursing the fat Chinese trader. But not the lady whose eyes had stirred something strangely familiar within his heart. There had been something about those eyes. Somewhere in time he had seen them before. . . .

His lungs began to fill with water as he plummeted deeper; then he pushed himself back to the surface. He looked anxiously about him, worrying about his crew. His eyes brightened with gladness when one by one they began to swim to him. None had died.

Turning in the water, Gray Wing watched the Chinese ship move smoothly away toward the horizon. Hate was throbbing within his heart for the crazed man who for no reason had caused the wreck of his canoe and the loss of Gray Wing's prize whale. Vengeance became a strong drive inside him. If ever he got the chance . . .

Vona-Lee strained her neck to see whether or not Gray Wing was all right. But the ship was moving too quickly away from the scene of the tragedy. Her eyes heavy with tears, she watched Du-Fu saunter away, seemingly pleased with himself over what he had done.

"Father must believe the whale hunters are dead or he would not plan to go on to a Suquamish Indian village to trade with them," Mei-Ling said softly, interrupting Vona-Lee's troubled thoughts. "In his state of mind he does not know the danger in which he has placed us all!"

"I shall never understand him," Vona-Lee said, wiping a tear from her cheek. "First he is so kind, then . . . then . . . so heartless."

She watched Du-Fu go below deck, then turned with a start when several great blasts of air sounded from somewhere close by at sea. Her eyes following the sounds, she peered down into the ocean. Gasping, she quickly counted five massive whales beginning to circle the ship, the whipping of their flukes dangerously disturbing the water.

"Mei-Ling, look!" Vona-Lee cried. The creaking of the ship as it began thrashing in the water suddenly threw her off her feet. All that she could hear was shouts and screams, and then the splash of sails as they came crashing down into the water.

"Vona-Lee!" Mei-Ling screamed.

Vona-Lee reached for Mei-Ling's hand and desperately attempted to cling to it. Together they were washed into the ocean while the ship capsized behind them. . . .

Ten

The slap of the waves upon the rocky beach was rhythmic in its beat. Vona-Lee lay somewhere in between being conscious and unconscious, hearing the sound of water battering the shore close beside her. Slowly she was remembering the incident of only a few moments ago—the massive whales circling the Chinese sailing ship, the creak of the ship's sides as it capsized, the screams and shouts of the crew. . . .

Her eyes flying wildly open, Vona-Lee was now quite aware of her surroundings and what had happened to her. Thick fog embraced her, making it possible to see only the wet walls of rock behind her. The air was cold and gripping on her flesh where her wet clothes clung to her. Her hair was wet wisps of black, encircling her face, which was white with fear and dread.

Rising up on an elbow, rocks pressing on her flesh, paining her, Vona-Lee tried to peer through the dense fog, her heart crying out for those who had surely perished.

"Mei-Ling," she said, her voice crackling with emotion. She could recall clinging to Mei-Ling's hand as they were swept overboard.

But they had not been able to cling to each other for long. Slowly they had parted, both being thrashed about in the sea. Vona-Lee had felt unconsciousness claiming her as she became too tired to tread water, sinking slowly into the abyss of Puget Sound's waters. She could only barely recall grabbing on to a barrel as she felt a void of black claim her consciousness. . . .

Dizziness sweeping through her from weakness, Vona-Lee stretched out on the rocky beach and breathed hard. Because of the veil of fog she could not tell whether or not she was the only survivor. There was no human sounds within the reach of her ears. Only the beat of the waves . . .

And then Vona-Lee tensed, hearing movement close by. She moved to a sitting position and looked through the fog, hope springing forth inside her that it might be Mei-Ling! Her friend could have been washed ashore the same as Vona-Lee. Oh, pray that she had!

Combing her fingers through her hair, smoothing it back from her face and eyes, Vona-Lee pushed herself to her feet. Wobbling, feeling chilled clean through to the bone, she began to walk toward the sound of someone approaching on the beach.

"Mei-Ling? Is . . . that . . . you?" she said in a weak voice. "Oh, Mei-Ling, please . . . let it be you."

Had Du-Fu survived the shipwreck? How many of the crew had managed to come through it alive? Vona-Lee's thoughts were becoming scrambled from the worry and wonder of it all. . . .

Then her footsteps faltered when through the fog she got her first glimpse of the person who was approaching. He was so proud and tall. In his breechcloth, his muscular torso revealed its sculptured quality; his intense eyes were now locked with hers as his shoulder-length hair softly fluttered in the breeze.

"Gray Wing!" Vona-Lee gasped, placing her hands to her cheeks. "It *is*. It . . . is Gray Wing. He didn't die after all! He's . . . alive."

Forgetting for the moment that ten years had passed

since they had last seen each other and that she was now
a woman instead of a mere girl, *and* that her hair was no
longer a brilliant red, but instead, dyed black, Vona-Lee
began to run in a half-stumble toward Gray Wing, sobbing.

"Thank God you are here. Thank God you are all
right," Vona-Lee cried. "It's so horrible. The ship. It . . .
sank. Everyone surely is . . . dead. Tell me, oh, please
tell me that you have at least seen Mei-Ling!"

Hate was bubbling inside Gray Wing, only moments
ago having lost the great whale and his prized canoe because of the Chinese trading ship. He had vowed to himself to somehow seek vengeance for the deed done by the
fat Chinese, and it seemed that the Great Spirit had done
the deed for him. The trading ship no longer sailed the
waters of Puget Sound. The Chinese trader was now dead,
washed up on the shore and then back out to sea again,
and several of the ship's crew had already been taken prisoner and were now awaiting their fate.

But Gray Wing had recalled the lovely lady aboard the
ship and had not given up the search for her. And now
that he had found her, what *now*? He did not wish to make
her a slave. She was not responsible for what the ugly
Chinese trader had done. Gray Wing had seen her plead
with the man before the ship plunged into Gray Wing's
whaling canoe. . . .

Now seeing her so close, her loveliness enhanced by the
clinging, wet clothes, Gray Wing was disturbed by earlier
thoughts. There was so much about her that reminded him
of Amelia!

But Amelia was dead! The Haida had killed her . . .
had sacrificed her to their Gods!

"Please . . . say something," Vona-Lee said in a voice
too weak for him to hear, for dizziness was once again
overwhelming her. As he stopped before her, so many
familiar feelings that he had aroused in her before whispered through her body, telling her that she had been right
not to let herself love another. Forever there would only
be Gray Wing! As a younger man he had touched her heart

with such a sweetness! Now as a man, he caused her to be full of strange, wondrous desires!

Yet this was not the time for such feelings. Too much had just happened. . . .

"No. I have not seen anyone by the name of Mei-Ling," Gray Wing finally said, his eyes intensely studying Vona-Lee.

"No," Vona-Lee softly cried, yet having been raised in a different culture these past ten years, she had been taught a different way to approach death. It had been taught to her by her Chinese family that when people passed away, they were not dead, but had merely ascended, properly escorted, to the spirit world where they continued much the same as on earth.

She had been taught not to grieve over those who were no longer of this earth. Why grieve too deeply over death, which is only a portal? She must remember that. She must remember that when she thought of the loss of Mei-Ling and Du-Fu!

Her knees buckling beneath her, Vona-Lee was glad when Gray Wing caught her and drew her fully up into his arms and began carrying her away from the sound of the thrashing of the waves. It was so peaceful in his arms. She placed her cheek on his bare chest, only vaguely seeing his tattoo in the shape of a whale on his left shoulder. She clung to him, her arms wrapped about his neck, so strangely at peace in his embrace. It seemed that she had come home . . . rightfully home. . . .

Feeling the warmth of the fire upon her nude body, and the softness of a fur beneath her, Vona-Lee blinked her eyes as she slowly awakened. She emitted a low gasp when she saw Gray Wing there at her side, now drying her body with handfuls of pine needles. As she edged herself backwards, now embarrassed by her nudity in his presence and how his hands on her flesh were making her skin quiver so, Vona-Lee's heart seemed to be beating in her throat.

"Where . . . are my clothes?" she said in a shallow whisper, trying to hide the most vulnerable spot on her body behind the screen of her hands. "Gray Wing, will you please give me something with which to hide my nudity?"

Gray Wing's insides rolled strangely, hearing the familiarity with which she spoke his name. How did she even know it?

He ignored her request and continued to dry her body with the pine needles, yet by doing so, was becoming awakened inside as only one other time in his life—when Amelia had been in his arms, when their lips had met in an innocent, much too short kiss! Perhaps being denied her had made him want her more! No matter, he would never want her less. Unless this woman took her place inside his heart.

"You call me by my name," he said, his fingers brushing against the swell of her breast, causing desire to shoot through him. "*Kah-ta?* How is it that you know my name? You are Chinese . . . from China. Or is it the fat Chinese man who has been on Whale Island before and knew me by my name? Is that how you know my name, Chinese lady?"

He called her Chinese, but he had seen many Chinese ladies before and he knew the shape of their eyes was much different from this one who lay before him in her innocence. He had even seen the color of their eyes and skin. This lady's eyes were green; her skin was white!

A remembrance so keen inside Gray Wing's mind caused him to flinch and draw away from Vona-Lee. His breathing grew shallow as he studied the color of Vona-Lee's eyes more intently. They were the same as Amelia's. He studied the shape of her face, its similarity to Amelia's so keen, only now a woman's face, not that of a girl of thirteen.

Yet, it could not be! Amelia was dead now ten winters. He had mourned for her for ten winters.

"Do you not recognize me, Gray Wing?" Vona-Lee said, forgetting her nudity when she saw the puzzlement in Gray Wing's eyes. "Gray Wing, it is *I*. It is Vona-Lee.

Do you not recognize me? Have I changed so much in appearance since you last saw me?''

Gray Wing would not let himself get caught up in games this lady with the strange name of Vona-Lee seemed to be playing with his mind. He had brought her to his dwelling for only one reason. He wanted her to warm his bed this night, perhaps even many nights, before returning her to the first Chinese ship that came to Whale Island. She would be released. But never the Chinese crew! They would pay with their lives!

Her skin gleamed like warm satin in the glow of the fire, and Gray Wing smoothed the pine needles away from Vona-Lee's body. His heart was beating rapidly as he stretched out above her and pinned her wrists to the bear pelt beneath them.

''Does it matter that you are a stranger to me?'' he said huskily, brushing a kiss along the delicate lines of her face. ''We will be strangers no more after tonight. You will be Gray Wing's woman tonight. We will make love. Many times . . . we will make love.''

Panic flashed through Vona-Lee's mind the way lurid lightning streaked the sky on the darkest of midnights. Gray Wing did not recognize her. And it did not matter to him that he didn't. He had only one thing on his mind. He was going to rape her!

Oh, the nights she had dreamed of being in his arms and now to be there in such a way! She could not allow it. The first time with a man was supposed to be a sweet, unforgettable experience! And that man in her heart had always been Gray Wing.

But this was . . . different. He did not even know her! It would not be the same!

''No,'' she softly cried. ''Please don't. Gray Wing, do not do this. Do not force—''

His mouth bore down upon her lips in a fiery kiss, stealing her breath and her words clean away. He surrounded her with his hard, strong arms, pressing her against him.

Then his hands were no longer holding her in bondage, but instead one was gently caressing a breast while the other was stroking her tender flesh at the soft triangle of hair between her thighs, awakening a frantic passion inside her.

Vona-Lee sighed from the strange, pleasurable sensations his fingers were evoking. She now knew that she was not being raped. She was fully participating. She . . . could not help herself. She had dreamed of Gray Wing for too long not to revel in this moment of paradise with him.

Vona-Lee trembled as she became further alive beneath Gray Wing's caresses. She writhed. She closed her eyes with the pure ecstasy of the moment. She was forgetting everything but the pleasure of his kiss . . . of his touch. . . .

"Chinese woman, your body responds? You do not fight any longer?" Gray Wing said as he momentarily drew away from her, letting his eyes sweep over her with hungry intensity. He took in the liquid curves of her vibrant, glowing body, and her night-black hair, which was spilling over her shoulders. "It is best this way, is it not, Chinese woman? You also enjoy!"

Gray Wing once again calling her Chinese drew Vona-Lee from her magical trance induced by the masterful strokes of his hands. She tried to inch away from him, but his body held her prisoner beneath it.

"I am not Chinese," she cried, now knowing full well that he did not recognize her. And she realized why. Her hair was not the color he would remember. And she was now a woman with a woman's face . . . no longer a mere girl. "I am American, Gray Wing. When you knew me before I was not with the Chinese. I was with my American mother and father. I—"

Gray Wing placed a hand over Vona-Lee's mouth, stifling any further comments. He had grown cold, again believing this woman was trying to involve him in some sort of mind game, perhaps something the Chinese knew well. It could disarm him in mind and body if he let her succeed. He gave her a stern, commanding look.

"You talk too much," he scolded. "You confuse Gray

Wing's body and mind. Say no more or I will place you with my slaves.''

Vona-Lee scarcely breathed as he jerked away from her, his eyes dark with anger. She crept to her knees and drew a blanket snugly about her shoulders as Gray Wing placed a cloak of costly sea otter furs about his own shoulders and settled down before the fire. She was relieved that he had chosen not to rape her, but that he had even planned to . . . that he had needed woman companionship for the night . . . made her wonder whether he was married. Had he kept true to her in his heart these past ten years . . . ?

''You are not married?'' she blurted, drawing the blanket closer as she gave him a curious stare. He had just ordered her to be quiet. If she didn't, would he truly place her with his slaves? Would he lend her to the other Suquamish warriors of this village to use? She knew the danger of questioning him further, but she *must*!

She looked slowly about her, seeing the magnificence of his carved boxes and eating utensils.

He lived like one who was the head of a family. She could see the white deerskin clothes, his great flint blades, and many strings of animals' teeth. She could see his harpooning equipment and his weapons. She could see a skin curtain behind which he must usually sleep upon a bunk. Did he live alone? Was his father no longer alive? Was Gray Wing now chief?

When he chose not to answer her question, instead sat staring angrily into the fire, Vona-Lee felt desperate to find a way to prove to him who she was. If words did not reach into his heart, then perhaps showing him would be the answer!

Her thoughts went to the necklace he had given her. Surely he would recognize it and recall exactly when he had!

''Did you possibly find trunks of clothing washed upon the shore after the shipwreck?'' she asked cautiously.

''Yes. Such trunks were found,'' he said icily. ''There were many.''

''Where are the trunks?'' Vona-Lee said, hope rising

inside her. "May I go to them? Perhaps mine is among those that were found."

"They are just outside my dwelling," Gray Wing said flatly, gesturing with a hand toward the door. "Feel free to look. Perhaps that will silence you for at least a little while if you busy yourself by searching for your personal belongings!"

Vona-Lee was stung by his cold harshness. But determined to make things right between them, strength having returned to her legs, Vona-Lee held the blanket securely around her shoulders and went beneath the massively carved entranceway of his dwelling. Searching with her eyes, she could not believe it when she did see her trunk standing among those others fished out of the sea.

With trembling fingers she went to the trunk and raised the lid. To her surprise, nothing was wet, only the outside! Reaching between the soft folds of her silk dresses she felt the sharp points of the necklace softly pierce the tips of her fingers. Meditatively, she lifted the necklace from the trunk, and clutching it to her chest, she turned and looked at Gray Wing's dwelling. She had positive proof of who she was!

The necklace!

It was her lifeline at this moment. . . .

Eleven

❧ ～ ❧

Grasping the blanket around her shoulders, the necklace in her other hand, Vona-Lee started to walk back to Gray Wing's house, which as she now remembered had also been his as a young man when he lived with his family. Tormenting thoughts suddenly swirled through her head of that day when she had witnessed the death of his mother, sisters, and brother.

It tore at her memory, as it had in many nightmares of her troubled nights since the fateful day it had happened. Only wondrous thoughts of Gray Wing had been able to wash such terrible dreams away. She had begun to live for those dreams of being with him.

That she was truly with him now, in reality, still only seemed like part of a dream. Except that in this dream there was sadness. He did not even recognize her, and Mei-Ling! Oh, where was she . . . ?

Her gaze was drawn elsewhere, causing her to suddenly stop only a few steps from the massive totem archway that led into Gray Wing's house. Another totem had been erected close to the house, separate from the one that was attached. Carvings of whales adorned the pole, as they did all the other poles in the village.

But these were more intricately designed, more color-ful. The pole itself was many feet taller than the others in the village. The whales looked alive, almost comparable in size to the whale that Gray Wing had killed from his canoe only a few short hours ago; they were so large and real in design!

"*Newhah.* This is the memorial totem pole erected in memory of my deceased father," Gray Wing said as he appeared in the door of his house, having seen Vona-Lee's interest in it. He moved toward her, his eyelids heavy as he continued gazing at the pole that overlooked the grave of his father.

"Your father is dead?" Vona-Lee asked, a tremor coursing through her as she again recalled the death of the rest of his family.

"*Ah-hah*, yes. Ten winters ago he died from the shock of discovering the death of my brother, sisters, and mother," Gray Wing said in a low hiss. "I lost *hy-uh*, much, on that same day ten winters ago."

Vona-Lee's gaze turned slowly to him. She knew of which day he spoke. Was he also including her when he spoke of his losses? Had he truly missed her so much?

"I . . . I am sorry about your losses," Vona-Lee said softly, her eyes widening when she saw a strange sort of look lock on Gray Wing's face as he continued to stare at her as he had since she had returned to Whale Island. Was he finally recognizing her? Oh, had she changed all that much that it was so hard for him to recognize her?

"*De-late*, the Suquamish accept losses not so easily," Gray Wing said, stirred by remembrances of a voice in his past . . . Amelia's voice. This lady who had arrived on a Chinese ship had such a voice . . . so delicate . . . so sweet.

But it could not be. Amelia was *dead*. She had been among those losses that day those ten winters ago! The Haida had killed her!

"*Kla-how-yum*, compassion, is a big word in the Suquamish culture,'' he said hoarsely. ''We feel much for everyone, for every living thing. We feel deeply for those loved ones who have departed from this life.''

His eyes shifted to five other totem poles not so far from this memorial to his father. Four were for the other members of his family; one was for . . . Amelia. . . .

Vona-Lee's eyes were drawn back to the memorial totem pole. ''This pole. It is so *large*, Gray Wing,'' Vona-Lee said, shaking her hair to hang long and free down her back. ''But of course it would be. Your father was a chief.''

Her gaze switched quickly back to Gray Wing. A pink flush suffused her cheeks as she smiled slowly at him. ''Gray Wing, that means that *you* are now chief,'' she murmured, recalling his possessions in his house, which she now knew had at one time been his father's. They had been handed down from father to son, Gray Wing's inheritance!

''*Ah-hah*, that is so,'' Gray Wing said, folding his arms across his chest, squaring his shoulders proudly. He nodded toward the larger totem pole. ''A memorial totem pole is erected by a deceased chief's heir as part of the process of assuming his predecessor's title and prerogatives. Not only did the tribe become my responsibility but so did my father's personal belongings.''

He nodded his head, traces of sadness in his eyes. ''*Ah-hah*, Gray Wing is now *tyee*, chief. I am now a rich man, a man whose opinion carries more weight than that of my fellow tribesmen,'' he said, then squinted his eyes in questioning. ''But how would you know my father was chief? I have never told you this before this moment.''

He lowered his gaze, seeing what was clutched in Vona-Lee's right hand. His face became pinched with a puzzled look. ''You have in your possession a necklace of animals' teeth,'' he said thickly. ''Was it exchanged by your father for something of value when he was among the Suquamish another time he traveled from China? Is that also how you know so much about my father? About me?''

He looked slowly up into her eyes, then back down at what she held. ''You said you were getting something special from your trunk. I see nothing but the necklace. Is that what you speak of? The necklace? It is special to the Suquamish. Is it the same for the Chinese?''

Vona-Lee's heart plummeted. He did not recognize the necklace as the one he had given to her personally! And why would he? She now recalled that this sort of necklace was given in exchange often because it was of so much value. When one traded for such a necklace, the Indians got much in return!

Vona-Lee brushed past him and went inside his house and dropped down onto her knees before the fire. Her eyes misted with tears as she still clutched the necklace. All these years it had been so special to her. It had been the same as being with Gray Wing when she had worn it beneath her silken finery. Now she realized that it had not been special to him at all, for he did not see it as so!

Gray Wing moved back into his house and knelt down beside Vona-Lee, studying her. He saw tears silvering the corners of her eyes. He saw her sadness and he did not understand. What had he said? Why had she seen the necklace as so special in her eyes? Why did she not answer him about how she knew that his father had been chief?

Reaching for the necklace now held limply within Vona-Lee's hands, Gray Wing eased it away, into his own. He studied it, seeing it as most valuable, but no more so than the others used for bartering with the white man and the Chinese!

Vona-Lee turned her sorrowful eyes to Gray Wing, sniffling. ''Gray Wing, do you not recall the very moment you gave me the necklace?'' she said softly. ''I shall never forget it! Please say that you have not forgotten. That necklace was all that I had left of you those ten years we were apart. Now that we are together again, seeing you makes me so happy. But you do not recognize me! You do not remember me at all!''

Leaning her face in her hands, Vona-Lee began to quietly weep. ''Today I lost not only my beloved Mei-Ling and my adopted father, Du-Fu, but also in a sense *you*. I don't know if I can bear it!'' she softly cried. ''Though I have been taught by my Chinese family that when people pass away, they are not dead but merely ascended, it is different with you! You are here, yet not here at all!''

She looked wide-eyed over at him, wiping tears away with the back of a hand. "Even when you attempted to make love to me it meant nothing," she cried. "I was only a body, nothing more!''

Gray Wing shook his head, not understanding anything about this woman or about what she was saying. "*Hwah!* You speak in circles," he said thickly, placing the necklace on the floor beside Vona-Lee. "How can you speak of knowing me . . . of receiving this necklace from me? Gray Wing has never before seen you . . . been with you.''

The fact that she had mentioned having known him ten years ago stung his heart, again reminding him of when he had known and loved Amelia. Though they had been together such a short time, it had been the same with her. She had loved him as suddenly . . . as fully!   •

He looked deep into Vona-Lee's eyes, seeing their pleading. Then something deep within him made him see more than he had originally.

Those eyes!

His gaze moved slowly over her delicate facial features. That face!

His fingers went to her hair and stroked its utter softness, making him recall how soft Amelia's hair had been. But it was not this color. And Amelia was dead!

"*Hwah!* No! It cannot be!'' Gray Wing shouted, rising swiftly to his feet. He went to the back of his house and stretched out on his bunk, dropping the skin curtain down, placing a shield of sorts between him and this woman who was confusing his mind and heart.

Vona-Lee looked numbly at the closed curtain. She tried to understand Gray Wing's reluctance to admit who she was. It was in his eyes and expression that he was seeing her as she had been at age thirteen, now grown into a woman. Why was he finding it so hard to acknowledge it? Or did he just not want to?

Too stubborn to let this go any further, wiping her tears

from her eyes and face, Vona-Lee rose to her feet and went
to the skin curtain and threw it aside. "Gray Wing, you
must explain why you are treating me this way," she said
dryly. "Surely you recognize me. Though my hair was
dyed black by the Chinese, everything else about me is
the same . . . except that I am now ten years older and
have grown from a child into a woman. Now you tell me
you do not know me! Tell me!"

Confused even more by her erratic behavior and persis-
tence, Gray Wing rose up on an elbow and eyed her speculatively. "So much about you does resemble someone I
once loved," he said thickly. "But she is dead. She has
been dead ten winters now."

"Dead?" Vona-Lee gasped. "What do you mean,
dead? If it is I whom you speak of, can you not see that
I am very much alive?" She fell to her knees beside the
bunk. "And, Gray Wing, I love you as much now as I did
then. I love you even more."

Gray Wing inched back away from her, suddenly fearing what was happening here. Was she an apparition? Or
was she real? How could she know enough about Amelia
to pretend that she was his lost love?

"The Haida killed my Amelia those ten winters ago,"
he said thickly. "You pretend to know . . . to *be* her.
Cultus-kopa-nika! Why, your name is not even the same!"

Finally fully understanding why he had felt he did not
know her, why he was confused by her, Vona-Lee laughed
softly, then bounced to her feet and almost shouted from
her gladness. He had not known who she was, would not
accept who she was, because he had thought all along that
she had died those ten years ago. The Haida had told him
they had killed her!

And she had forgotten about her name change, that the
Chinese had given her a different name. To Gray Wing,
she was a different person with different hair coloring and
a different name. She was someone he had thought was
dead!

Gray Wing jumped with a start at Vona-Lee's reaction
to what he had said. He tensed when she fell back to her

knees and grabbed him around the neck and gave him a hug.

But her words began to touch his heart . . . his soul. . . .

"Oh, Gray Wing, do you not know that it is I, Amelia?" she softly cried, now framing his sculpted face between her hands. "The Haida did not kill me. They sold me to the Chinese! I have been with the Chinese these past ten years. They dyed my hair black because they considered red hair an evil omen. They even gave me a Chinese name! Don't you understand? It is I. I am Amelia Storm. It is I who love you with all my heart! No one could ever love you as much!"

Gray Wing was struck numb by these many confessions. His heart thundered wildly inside him, knowing now that what she said was true! His Amelia *was* alive. She had returned to him, to be with him. It was true! All of it was true! The many nights he had spent dreaming of her had not been in vain. She was real. She was *alive*!

Taking her hands, grasping hard onto them, Gray Wing let his eyes devour Amelia's face. He never wanted to stop looking at her. He had lost her for so long, never could he again!

"It *is* you," he said hoarsely. "Amelia, it is you."

He drew her roughly into his arms, causing her blanket to tumble down away from her, to lie about her knees. He whispered into her ear. "You are *klas-ka*, my woman," he whispered. "You are my *la-dida*."

Frantic lips met, hands sought out each other's bodies as Gray Wing urged Vona-Lee beneath him. His hands trembled as they sought and found her breasts. Stiffened peaks crushed into the palms of his hands.

Kissing Amelia with a fierce, possessive heat, Gray Wing felt her growing more limp within his arms and heard quivering moans surfacing from deep within her. He was giving pleasure, but not yet fully. With skills learned as a youth he slipped his breechcloth down his legs and away from him, then lowered his manhood toward her beckoning triangle. He drew a ragged breath as he eased her thighs apart and began to softly probe, all the while still kissing her, the power of his body preparing her for the upcoming brief moment of pain that would come with fully loving her.

Vona-Lee had not been prepared for this intense sort of passion being with Gray Wing was evoking. A flood of emotions filled her being. She laced her arms about his neck and responded to all his nuances of lovemaking, even the hardness of his manhood against her thigh. It seemed natural. It seemed right. She had waited an eternity for this moment. She would savor it. Every moment . . .

His hands sought the roundness of Vona-Lee's hips. Stroking their utter softness, he encouraged her to lift them closer to him as he sank himself slowly into her womanly depths.

Only a faint outcry of pain, and then Vona-Lee closed her eyes and let the euphoria swim through her. She clung to him. A feverish heat touched her insides as his lips now went from breast to breast while he moved within her with faster, quicker, surer movements.

She answered the call of his body with movements of her own, blotting out any feelings of shame for experiencing such lustful moments with the man she adored . . . with the man she would always love. He was sending her into a world of intense pleasure, a world that included only the two of them. All pain . . . all sorrow . . . was beyond that which one could reach. She welcomed this realm of reality that perhaps never could have been if she had never returned from China.

The thought of Mei-Ling stung her remembrances. But she cast the thought aside. Mei-Ling would want her to be happy. She would be glad that she had found the man her heart had searched for in all of her midnight dreams since she was last with Gray Wing.

The warmth blossomed inside Vona-Lee as Gray Wing continued his masterful strokes within her. His lips sought her mouth. His kisses bruised her lips. His fingers tweaked her crested nipples to hardness. His hard body against hers revealed that his passions were crested to match hers.

A tremor went through Vona-Lee's body and she cried out softly against his lips when something wonderful spread throughout her as his body lurched and he groaned. Together they had reached that peak of swimming senses and lethargic floatings.

Vona-Lee's insides were warmed and pleasant as Gray Wing looked down at her with passion-filled eyes. The dark droop of her lashes fell over her timid eyes and against her cheek as he looked at her with keen wonder, then began his slow strokes again.

"You could not forget me. You have returned just to be with me. Say you will never leave me again," he whispered, his breath now hot on her cheek. "Let us be together always. Let us live for making love. No woman has ever been able to take your place inside my heart. No woman ever shall."

With quick, eager fingers entwined in her hair, he forced her lips closer. His mouth urged her lips apart as his kiss grew more and more passionate. Vona-Lee was again being consumed with wondrous desire, spreading through her like wildfire. His hands were touching her all over with a fierce, possessive heat.

Gray Wing's lean, sinewy buttocks moved rhythmically. Vona-Lee lifted her legs and locked them at the ankles around him. Her body was growing more feverish; her lips were on fire with his continuing passionate kisses. The flood of emotions—of happiness, of joy, of love—filled her entire being again. Gray Wing had never forgotten her. He still loved her.

"My love . . ." Gray Wing groaned in a whisper against her cheek, his hips moving in fast, quick, sure movements. "My *la-dida*. It is autumn, the season of the mad moon. It is time for mating. . . ."

His tongue brushed Vona-Lee's lips lightly. "You taste as you did ten winters ago," he whispered. "Your taste is sweet, like the rare wild rose that grows thornless along the forest floor."

Vona-Lee giggled softly, her cheeks hot with a fever most consuming. "This is real, is it not?" she whispered as he cradled her close. Ecstatic waves splashed through her as he suckled on a nipple, drawing its taut tip between his teeth. "You are here. I am here. It is real, Gray Wing, is . . . it not . . . ?"

"Gray Wing will no longer have to live for mere dreams filled with moments with you," he said, brushing kisses along the gentle slope of her jaw. "Because you are here. I am here. Yes, what we share together is real, my *ladida*, my woman."

He paused and looked down at her with intense gray eyes. "But what does Gray Wing call you?" he said, cocking an eyebrow. "You now possess two names."

"In your heart I have always been Amelia to you, have I not?" she whispered, brushing a lock of hair back from his passion-heavy eyes. "From this day forth I shall again be called Amelia. I do not like it that for a while my other name caused confusion in our lives. Please do call me Amelia. It is my Christian name. I am glad to be able to claim it again."

"Amelia it is," Gray Wing said, smiling softly down at her.

An incredible sweetness swept through Amelia as Gray Wing's lips met hers in a gentle and lingering kiss while once again he began to move his body in unison with hers, almost hypnotizing her with the slow thrusting of his pelvis. She opened herself even wider, and her hips responded in a rhythmic movement all their own.

She clung and rocked with him. And once again she was beginning to feel the lethargic sensation of floating that she had experienced only a short while ago with Gray Wing. Never had she thought that being with a man in such a way could be so wonderful . . . so beautiful. The pulsing crest of her passion was drawing near, oh, so very near. . . .

Gray Wing could feel the pressure building within him, something so wild never experienced before. But he understood why. The woman in his arms was the woman of his dreams! He was able to let go, let his feelings for her fully consume him! And he could tell that he was transferring the same sort of feelings to her. It was there in the way she clung to him, in the way she breathed, in the way she sighed.

Drawing his lips from hers, he looked down into passion-filled eyes and smiled, then let his lips and tongue skillfully tease her taut breasts, holding off the moment of fulfillment until he could not wait any longer. The waiting always enhanced the pleasure. Especially now . . . especially now . . .

Bodies tangled, breaths mingled, as the wildest of passions soared between them. And then suddenly the eruption of heat combined into one explosion and their bodies quaked together, then grew still, then lay together in a lovers' embrace while they stared devotedly into each other's eyes.

"I do love you so," Amelia whispered, tracing Gray Wing's seductive lips with her forefinger. "Your kisses are electric. Your touch is like fire! Gray Wing, I am so glad that I found you again."

"That you cared enough to return just for Gray Wing lets Gray Wing know the extent of your love," he said huskily, his hand seeking a breast, flicking a thumb and forefinger over a rose-tipped nipple. "But how did you get the Chinese trader to return you? You said that he had bought and paid for you."

Amelia's insides tensed. How could she tell him that she had not returned only for him? She had been brought back to America to find her parents. She had only hoped that she might be lucky enough to see Gray Wing in the process. Deep inside, she had only hoped to one day get to be with him forever. But never had she thought it possible *now*. If the ship hadn't capsized, she would not be with him at all!

And being reminded of why she was there brought back much sadness into her heart. She had been wrong to be so intensely happy in Gray Wing's arms while she knew not of Mei-Ling or Du-Fu's welfare or that of the crew. Was she the only one who had survived? And how could she tell Gray Wing the true facts of why she was there? It would spoil what happiness they had just found together in each other's arms. This happiness could not be wrong! She could not spoil it with truths.

Yet she must question him about the other survivors of this shipwreck. She could hardly bear not knowing, now that her mind was back on the realities of what had just happened. Whether she wanted to accept it or not, there was more to life than Gray Wing!

Easing from his arms, drawing the fur cloak about her shoulders, Amelia looked sideways at Gray Wing. "Yes, I have returned. I am alive. I survived the Haida and the shipwreck," she murmured. "But, Gray Wing, what of everyone else who was aboard the Chinese ship? Was I the only survivor?"

Gray Wing's brow furrowed with a frown. He drew on his breechcloth, then removed the heavy cloak from around Amelia. He replaced it with a lightweight trade blanket with a dark blue and red border embellished with heraldic beasts outlined in pearl buttons.

"No, you are not the only survivor," he said thickly, placing a piece of wood on the flickering fire in the pit. He was troubled by something besides the talk of survivors. How could he tell her that her father now resided nearby on land occupied by the Russian-American Fur Company, where her father worked in joint partnership? Her father, the dreaded "Boston," had refused to believe that his daughter was dead and had stayed behind to search for her. And now he would find her.

And Amelia! Should she find out about her father being so close, he would be a threat to their newfound happiness! The telling would have to be delayed until she became his wife; then her father could do nothing about it!

Amelia watched Gray Wing's expression change from compassion to anger as he became lost in thought before telling her any more about the survivors. She became anxious, hoping that perhaps he had news about Mei-Ling!

Moving to her knees before Gray Wing, forgetting the blanket as it slid down and away from her, Amelia took Gray Wing's hands. She pleaded with her eyes. "Gray

Wing, tell me,'' she murmured. ''Did you find other survivors?''

Gray Wing blinked his eyes as he was drawn from his
troubled thoughts of Amelia's dreaded father. ''Survivors?''
he said, raising an eyebrow. ''Oh, yes. Survivors.''

Having seen the respect with which she voiced her concern about the fat Chinese trader, Gray Wing winced at
having to tell her that he was dead. Though Gray Wing
was glad that he was dead, Amelia would not be happy.
Yet she must be told.

''There are many survivors,'' he said thickly. ''But one
among them was not the fat Chinese who commanded that
my canoe be destroyed. He was found dead on the shore
just before he was washed back out to sea. Others are now
prisoners of Gray Wing and his people!''

Sadness stung Amelia's eyes with sudden tears at the
thought of Du-Fu's death, yet hope tugged at her heart
with the thought of finding Mei-Ling alive. ''Gray Wing,
among those prisoners did you find a beautiful Chinese
woman?'' she blurted. ''Oh, did you find my beloved Mei-
Ling?''

''You are the only woman among the survivors,'' Gray
Wing said, an air of caution in his words, knowing how
important it was to her that this Chinese woman be alive,
though he could not understand why she had love in her
heart for any Chinese, since she had been taken away by
force by them those ten years ago.

Yet she was the sort who made the best of any bad
situation. She loved so easily . . . so wonderfully!

Amelia turned her tear-filled eyes aside. ''No,'' she
whispered. ''No . . .''

Gray Wing placed a finger beneath her chin and turned
her eyes back to him. ''But that does not mean she did
not survive,'' he said hoarsely. ''I will send my men in
search of her. Perhaps she is farther down the beach quite
alive. Perhaps even the Haida—''

Amelia's insides grew cold. ''Please do not tell me you
think she was found by the Haida,'' she gasped. ''Do you
think that she might have—''

Gray Wing drew her into his arms and cradled her close. "Do not despair," he said. "The Haida of the past are not the same as those of today. The Haida chief who sold you to the Chinese is no longer alive. His son, Red Eagle, now rules as chief. By some ironic twist of fate we have become friends. He is not a demon like his father. If he finds your friend, he will not harm her."

Though Gray Wing spoke kindly of Red Eagle, Amelia could not find room in her heart to feel the same. She would never forget the gruesome scene when she had been held in bondage by the Haida. Never would she forget how they had consumed human flesh!

She closed her eyes to the thought and clung to Gray Wing, praying that Mei-Ling was alive and well, but not with the Haida. . . .

Twelve

Though she had been given dry clothes with which to replace her wet and clinging silk gown, Mei-Ling could not conquer the fierceness of the chill that was engulfing her. Her slanted eyes cast downward, she sat huddled beside the flickering warmth of a fire in the center of a Haida wigwam, not wanting to look the Indian's way again. The grotesque designs tattooed all over his body frightened her more each time she looked at them. And though Red Eagle's words had been soft and soothing, nothing could ease the mourning in Mei-Ling's heart. She was finding it hard to follow her teachings about death!

As far as she knew, her father and Vona-Lee were both dead. To her knowledge, she had been the only one rescued from the capsized ship. The last that Mei-Ling remembered, before being drawn into a black void of unconsciousness after swimming to shore, was losing touch with her friend, watching Vona-Lee float away from her in the vast realms of the ocean.

Ai, Vona-Lee and her father truly must be dead.

Red Eagle studied Mei-Ling, seeing her exotic loveliness. Though she would be worth much ransom, he al-

ready knew that he would not use her in such a way.
Somehow she would learn to accept that she was going to
be living with the Haida. She would accept that she was
going to be his.

But Red Eagle knew that it would take a while for her
to accept what fate had handed her. She was in a strange
land with people who did not have the same appearance
as her or the same customs. Even when she looked his
way, Red Eagle could see a disgusted, distasteful look in
her beautiful oblong eyes. He had seen her studying his
tattooed body and had decided it was because of his tattoos that she felt this disgust. Her body was smooth and
devoid of any sort of markings.

This, too, she would have to learn to accept.

Red Eagle moved closer to Mei-Ling's side and set a
wooden tray of food before her. "*Mesika*, yours," he said
thickly. "You must eat. The sea drained much strength
from your body. Eat. Become stronger."

Mei-Ling kept her eyes downcast, but she could not
help directing them toward the meal being offered her.
Though she did not recognize any of the food, the mere
sight and smell of it caused her stomach to growl unmercifully.

Yet how could she eat when she did not know the fate
of her loved ones? She did not even know the eventual fate
of herself!

Ai, she was so alone in the world! Food would not take
the place of loved ones!

"*Nay*," she murmured. "*Buh-yao-ching*. It does not
matter if I die. *Mei-ya-faza*, nothing to be done now except to let myself die!"

Fearing that she meant what she said, not knowing the
Chinese culture all that well, Red Eagle set the tray on his
lap and eyed each of his offerings, wondering which to try
to encourage her to eat first. His slave prostitute had
brought him fried bread, deer-bone soup, salmon-head
broth, camas roots, and foamberries. Which would someone from China be most tempted by?

Knowing the fried bread would be the simplest, least

messy food to offer first, Red Eagle took some from the platter, set the platter aside, then held the bread close to Mei-Ling's lips.

"*Klose-spose*, let me feed you if you do not want to feed yourself," he softly encouraged. "Eat. Eat *klahwa-wa*, slowly, if you must. But *eat*. You cannot want to die."

His dark eyes raked over her, seeing her tininess, her absolute loveliness. "You are too beautiful to die."

Mei-Ling's eyes wavered at his words, but she kept her lips pressed tightly together, refusing the food that was so temptingly close. She gave Red Eagle a sidewise glance, trembling again at the sight of his tattoos.

Yet this time she was able to see farther. She was looking into dark eyes warm with friendship.

Farther still, she could see the handsomeness of the man who had chosen to become her friend. His face displayed, besides the tattoos, a nose that was lovely in its boldness. His jaw was square and firm, his lips full and sculpted.

This Indian wore only a brief loincloth; his shoulders rippled with muscles, and his chest narrowed down into hips that were straight and well defined.

While she was in China, Mei-Ling had not wasted her time viewing the handsomeness of the Chinese men. Strange that she was viewing the handsomeness of a man now.

She looked quickly away, again looking downward. She must blot everything from her mind. She *must*. She would let herself just drift somewhere between living and dying! She wanted nothing more than to die at this moment! It would be much easier than living an unhappy existence without those she loved.

"If you do not eat willingly, I must force you," Red Eagle said, taking Mei-Ling by the wrist, holding her in place as she looked wild-eyed up at him.

"*Nay*," Mei-Ling cried. "Do not do this!"

"You will eat without further encouragement?" Red Eagle asked, his eyebrows forking.

"*Ai*, yes," Mei-Ling said, taking the fried bread in her

hands. She screwed her face up into a frown as she took her first bite.

She cast Red Eagle a frightened look when he held a bowl of foamberries before her and offered her a wooden ladle with which to eat them. "You are a barbarian!" she cried. "Only barbarians eat with utensils other than chopsticks!" She looked down at her dress made of woven plant fibers. "Only barbarians dress so crudely!"

Red Eagle scratched his brow idly. He ignored her reference to what she wore, confused by her mention of chopsticks. "Chopsticks?" he said, having difficulty with the word. "Not know of chopsticks."

"That is because you are a true barbarian," Mei-Ling repeated, pushing the foamberries away from her. "More bread, though. Mei-Ling enjoy the bread."

"Bread is all right now," Red Eagle said softly. "But you must eat something more substantial later. Bread alone will not give you back your strength!"

A commotion outside the wigwam, and voices recognized by Red Eagle to be those of his Suquamish friends, momentarily drew Red Eagle's attention from Mei-Ling. A broad smile crossed his face. It must be Gray Wing! He must show Gray Wing what had washed up from the sea!

Then he glanced over at Mei-Ling, recalling how Gray Wing had once loved a woman who was not of his tribe. Gray Wing might be just as intrigued by *another* woman with different features and skin coloring. It was best not to reveal Mei-Ling to him or any others of his tribe. Mei-Ling was his.

And he would not allow a challenge to grow between him and Gray Wing over Mei-Ling or anything else. Too much hatred had been exchanged between the tribes of the Haida and Suquamish in the past. It could never be allowed to happen again. Some time ago Gray Wing had rescued Red Eagle from the bowels of the sea after Red Eagle's canoe had capsized during a storm. That had been the beginning of a bond between them that was even stronger than the bond between brothers. Red Eagle at that moment would have let Gray Wing die if it had been Gray Wing who was caught in a fish net in the sea. Gray Wing had slain Red Eagle's father!

Yet had not Red Eagle's father killed Gray Wing's mother, sisters, and brother?

Ah-hah, they had reasons to hate each other, but they had chosen friendship instead. Their two tribes were better off because of it!

The continuing voices drawing closer to Red Eagle's wigwam caused him to scurry to his feet. He looked commandingly down at Mei-Ling, this time feeling the need to order her to do something, not ask like someone who begged! She did stir him so into behaving like a boy instead of a man!

"You stay," he said firmly, stiffening his arms at his sides when she did not look up at him to reply. Her downcast eyes irritated him! Would she ever look him directly in the eyes and confess that she saw him as a desirable man? He must make her *mah-lie*, forget, everyone else of her past. Her future would include only him!

"Red Eagle must see to friends who have come to call," he added. "Red Eagle is chief! No one enters the village of the Haida without first consulting Red Eagle!"

He set his lips in a firm, straight line and shook his head, disgusted with Mei-Ling's failure to respond.

Turning on a heel he left his wigwam made of sapling poles with skins draped over them, arriving outside just as several Suquamish warriors were directed to his dwelling.

Disappointment assailed Red Eagle when he discovered that his friend Gray Wing was not among those who had come to call. Spreading his legs and folding his arms across his powerful chest, Red Eagle nodded a welcome, then listened intently as one of the visiting warriors explained why they had come.

Red Eagle's spine stiffened when he heard their tale of a great Chinese ship capsizing close to the Suquamish village, too far from the Haida village for them to have witnessed it.

He listened warily when they talked about the survivors, one of whom was a white woman who was eager to find her Chinese friend. The Suquamish warrior then questioned Red Eagle about the Chinese woman.

Could the Haida possibly have found and rescued her?

Now knowing the danger of revealing to the Suquamish that Mei-Ling was alive, now knowing that she was being sought by Gray Wing, Red Eagle's eyes flamed with determination that they would not know of her rescue! It was quite evident that Gray Wing wanted her all to himself! Was it not enough that Gray Wing already had the white woman who was rescued? She could be Gray Wing's possession. Not Mei-Ling!

"Al-ah," he said, trying to voice an expression of surprise. "No Chinese lady is here. Sorry." He was glad that she was learned in his language. Trading between cultures gave rise to many advantages, it seemed!

When Red Eagle saw the eyes of the Suquamish warriors suddenly look on past him, his insides grew cold, for there would be only one reason for him to lose their devoted attention.

Slowly turning, fearing to find Mei-Ling there, revealing herself, Red Eagle felt his heart skip a beat when, *ah-hah*, yes, she was there, her eyes boldly returning the gazes of the Suquamish, instead of being downcast like one who was ashamed.

Rushing to her, Red Eagle grabbed her by a wrist and ushered her back inside the wigwam. "You stay inside the dwelling," he grumbled. "It is dangerous to let Suquamish see you. They are *masachie*, bad!"

"But did not they come to talk about Chinese wreckage?" Mei-Ling asked, wincing when his hold on her wrist pained her. "Mei-Ling did not hear all that was said. Let me go. I must hear! Is . . . is my father . . . ? Is my friend alive?"

"They are both alive and well," Red Eagle said, telling a half-truth, now knowing he had no choice but to talk of the survivors to her since she had heard some of the report.

But she was disturbed enough without him revealing the truth about her father. That would come later!

Mei-Ling's eyes widened. A smile blossomed in pinkish hues across her face. "The fates have been kind!" she sighed. Then she again tried to release Red Eagle's grip on her wrist. "I must go to them. Now!"

"No. That is not possible," Red Eagle said firmly. "You must stay and eat and get stronger. When your strength has returned, Red Eagle will then take you to your loved ones."

Again he told a nontruth.

But to have her to himself, he would do even worse. Mei-Ling could even become the cause of a rivalry between Red Eagle and Gray Wing. If need be, a challenge would be fought over possession of her!

Seeing the determination in Red Eagle's eyes and hearing it in his voice, Mei-Ling bowed her head. Again she looked downcast, having been taught from birth that men were the voice of authority. And this man was no different. He owned her, it seemed!

"*Ai*," she said in a near whisper. "Mei-Ling will do as she is told."

She raised her eyes slowly upward, a smile sweet on her face. "Mei-Ling is so happy," she softly cried. "My father and my best friend in the world are alive! That is enough for now, Red Eagle. That is enough for now." .

Red Eagle released her wrist. "Good," he said, nodding. He pointed to a pallet of furs. "Sit. Red Eagle will return soon to join you."

Her gaze obediently lowered, Mei-Ling eased down upon the pallet of furs. Her eyes were shining with radiance as Red Eagle returned to the Suquamish warriors to explain that he had at first lied about her presence there only to protect her, then encouraged the Suquamish to let her remain until she had become fully rested and had regained her strength.

Smiling smugly to himself, Red Eagle watched as the Suquamish warriors went to their intricately designed canoes, agreeing that Mei-Ling could stay and that they would return later to get her. It was enough to be able to return the glad tidings to the American woman who eagerly awaited the news. . . .

It thrilled Amelia so to know that her friend was alive and that as soon as Mei-Ling's strength returned they would again be together. Amelia did not trust the Haida. She would see to it that Mei-Ling would soon be in the Suquamish village! She would protect Mei-Ling from all sadnesses and wrongs. Having been brought up in a culture that catered only to the whims and desires of its men, Mei-Ling was not as strong in body or mind as Amelia. She would perhaps not even survive in an environment other than that in which she had been raised.

Not wanting to be troubled by Mei-Ling or by the question of how she might secure passage to Boston to see her parents and brother or sister, Amelia let herself get lost in the real-life fantasy of being with Gray Wing.

Laughing softly to herself, she knelt before her open trunk, which had been brought inside Gray Wing's house for her perusal. Her fingers savored the touch of the silken garments as she searched through them to find just the right one to wear. She wanted to look beautiful upon Gray Wing's return. He had left for only a moment to tend to some business in his village.

Since her arrival, they had not been parted except for brief moments. Being with him had been pure heaven. Could she even bear to leave him and go to Boston should she be given the opportunity?

After realizing paradise in Gray Wing's arms, could she ever leave him again? Would he allow it . . . ?

Choosing a heavily embroidered red silk gown, Amelia quickly slipped it over her head. As her heart beat out her excitement she placed golden earrings in her earlobes and matching gold bracelets on her wrists. With care she placed loops of golden combs in her hair, drawing her hair back from her face to hang in long lustrous ringlets down her back. She placed a dot of rouge on each cheek and rubbed some into her lips.

Amelia's eyes sparkled as she turned and found Gray Wing standing in the doorway looking at her, his eyes dark with passion and pride.

"You have returned," Amelia said, slowly moving forward on her bare feet, not yet having had time to slip into fancy shoes. She squared her shoulders to let her breasts become better defined beneath the clinging silk of her dress. She held her chin up and smiled seductively at Gray Wing. "I wanted to make myself beautiful for your return. Did I manage well enough, Gray Wing?"

Gray Wing did not respond with words. He went to Amelia and drew her into his arms and stroked her cheek with his fingertips. She could see fire burning in his eyes, mesmerizing her into almost melting. She so hungered for his kiss . . . his lips.

He crushed her to him so hard she gasped, then moaned with ecstasy as his mouth scorched hers with a fiery intense kiss. His mouth was hot and demanding. One hand cupped her breast as the other began unfastening her dress from behind. A sensuous tremor soared along Amelia's flesh as the dress crept down her body until she was again standing nude in Gray Wing's hungry arms.

Amelia sighed as Gray Wing lowered his lips to her breast while his hands were setting fires along her flesh. When he began to stroke the place where she so unmercifully ached between the thighs, a euphoria began to spread through her, almost more than she could bear.

And then he led her to the bunk where furs and blankets awaited. The softness of the furs pressed into her back as she stretched out atop them. Her eyes feasted on Gray Wing as he rid himself of his breechcloth. Though having never seen a man nude before Gray Wing, it seemed only natural now that Amelia should see him again in this way.

Her pulse raced as she admired the strength shown in his distended manhood. To her it was nothing less than lovely! And, oh, how it could pleasure her! That she could love a man so much, want him so much, did not astound her. She had always wanted Gray Wing.

Gray Wing gazed down upon Amelia, his heart thudding hard against his ribs. He had had many prostitute slaves since he had grown into manhood, but none disturbed his insides into wanting them as much as Amelia did. Before the day was over he would make her his wife. He must, before her father discovered that she was here!

Feeling a desperation seizing him at the thought of losing her, Gray Wing spread himself atop her and enfolded her within his steel arms. His thick lashes were heavy over his passion-dark eyes. *"Klas-ka,"* he said huskily, "you will become my wife? Today you will become my wife? You want this the same as Gray Wing?"

Amelia was taken aback by the question, yet did she not want this as much as he did? In her Christian upbringing she had been taught never to give herself to a man unless she was married to him. But she had not let this teaching cause her to deny Gray Wing's loving her so openly.

But marriage! She ached so to see her family! If she married Gray Wing, she would never, never leave him. But to see her parents, she *must!*

"Must we speak of marriage now?" she murmured, stroking his smooth copper cheek with her hand. "Gray Wing, such talk is not important. Just being with you is. Loving . . . making love . . . is. Please love me. Love me now."

Being so lost in the moment with her in his arms, Gray Wing did not grasp the importance of Amelia ignoring his question. The way she loved was proof enough that he did not have to concern himself with her evasive reply about marriage.

And wasn't she awesome in her beauty? Seeing her lying there, waiting to be loved, brought Gray Wing almost beyond coherent thought.

He bent his head to her lips, tasting her sweetness, inhaling the fragrance of her skin, as though jasmine-splashed. His fingers explored the softness of her body, moving from one pleasure point to another, eliciting tremulous sighs from deep within her.

In one movement of his hips he was finally inside her. His lips bore down harder upon hers as she wrapped her legs about him, responding in rhythmic movements to match his own. His fingers caressed her breasts. He tantalized her lips with his tongue.

A fire stirred within Gray Wing and was fanned to roaring flames as his strokes hastened deeper . . . deeper. . . .

The same drugged passion that Amelia had felt before while in passion's embrace in Gray Wing's arms overcame her, delighting her. The pleasure was spreading, searing her heart. She shuddered with desire as the feelings grew. The heat and excitement peaked inside her, almost alarming in its greatness!

And then she was aware of the familiar tingling that begun at the core of her womanhood when that peak was near that would momentarily send her spiraling to heaven and back.

She clung to Gray Wing. She became breathless as his kiss continued to mold them together like one being.

But too soon the rapture was over and they lay spent in each other's arms, breathing hard against the other's cheek.

Yet they were not allowed another moment's pleasure, for a familiar voice to both Amelia and Gray Wing boomed from outside the house, startling them both into consciousness of time and place. . . .

Amelia's heart skipped a beat. Her mouth became dry. She could not believe the voice she heard was actually that of her . . .

"Papa?" she blurted, jerking herself away from Gray Wing. She eyed him quizzically. "Gray Wing, that's my father! He's here! *How?*"

Panic seized her when she saw a sudden look of hate twist Gray Wing's usually handsome face into something ugly. . . .

Thirteen

When Gray Wing offered no response to her dismay other than the look of hate, Amelia scurried to her feet. Her eyes wild, she searched for her clothes, her knees almost too weak to stand while slipping the silken attire over her head.

Surprise . . . anxiety! She felt, oh, so many emotions it was hard to distinguish one from the other. She did not have to go to Boston at all to find her family. Somehow they were on Whale Island!

Questions flooded her consciousness. How? Why? Had they returned searching for her? Had they been told she was dead?

Not even considering that her father would see that she had been with Gray Wing and could suspect it had been in an intimate way since her face was so flushed and her hair was so tangled, Amelia rushed from the house, tears pooled in her eyes. She did not even pay heed to Gray Wing who was following close behind her, now also dressed.

But when he stepped before her and stopped her with

locked fingers on her shoulders, she froze inside at the determination and fire in his eyes.

"You cannot leave," Gray Wing said fiercely. "You have only returned. You must not leave!"

Amelia's heart was racing. She tried to understand Gray Wing's feelings, yet she could not. Her senses were too flooded with wanting to see her family!

"Gray Wing, I must see my *family*," she said, craning her neck so that she could see around him.

Her heart frolicked, for in the distance she could distinguish her father from the other traders sitting on the beach with the usual line drawn between them and the Indians. Her father's hair was carrot-colored, looking even brighter red in the splash of the sun. He was thinner, but still muscular and handsome for a man of fifty.

From this distance she could hear the boom of his voice, the authority that it always carried reaching Amelia in its familiar tone. Whenever he had spoken to her, it had been with authority. She had only disobeyed him once. And that had been the time she had crept from the ship, drawn by the eyes of a handsome Indian. . . .

Now looking toward the sea, searching for the ship on which her father had traveled, Amelia saw only a few canoes lining the shore, and surely those were the Indians'.

Her face became pinched with a quizzical frown. How had her father reached Whale Island? Where was his ship? Where was her mother? Where was her brother or sister?

Feeling Gray Wing's eyes bearing down upon her, still refusing to let her pass, Amelia moved her gaze slowly upward. "Gray Wing, I don't understand," she murmured. "Where is my father's ship? How did he arrive here?"

Gray Wing felt trapped, now knowing that he should have told Amelia about her father before she found out by other means. But he had thought that he had time. He had not expected her father to return this soon. He had only recently been there to trade.

"Your father," he said coldly. "He comes by canoe, not by ship."

Amelia took a step back, her face registering shock. "What do you mean, by canoe?" she gasped, placing a hand to her throat. "How *could* he have? Boston is too far to travel in only a canoe."

"Your father does not live in Boston now," Gray Wing said blandly. "He lives close by, on another island."

Amelia found it hard to grasp what he was saying. She looked blankly up into his gray, fathomless eyes, then on past him, at her father. "Why would my father make residence here instead of Boston?" she said, anxious to go to her father, yet feeling a need to know answers first.

Gray Wing's silence meant more to Amelia than words. Anger rose inside her. Gray Wing had known all along that her father was nearby, and had not informed her of such wonderful news. In a sense, he had deceived her.

She glared up at him, realizing that she did not know him at all.

Amelia's eyes burned with anger as she jerked from his grasp, cast him fiery glances over her shoulder, and stomped away from him. "How . . . could you. . . ?" she asked, a sob trying to surface. She bit her lower lip, trying to hide her tumultuous emotions from the man who had stolen her heart.

Now focusing on the familiar, wonderful figure of her father, who still communicated with the Indians across their drawn line in the sand, Amelia began to run toward him. "Papa!" she shouted, waving frantically. "Papa!"

She did not care that Gray Wing was watching her with sadness in his eyes. He had not been honest with her. He should not have kept the truth from her. If he was deceitful this time, would he not be another, if it suited his purpose? Why had he felt that he could not tell her about her family being so near?

Then her footsteps faltered as her heart whispered a small truth to her brain. Gray Wing would only do so because he had thought that he would lose her to her family. He was jealous!

Wisps of her silken black hair spun across her eyes as she momentarily turned and looked at Gray Wing. Brushing the hair away, she felt her insides melt as he gave her a look of longing that reached deep into her soul. He was fearing losing her! Oh, that he could love her so much made tears sting the corners of her eyes.

Amelia gave him her most winning smile. "Gray Wing, I shall return," she said silkily. "Oh, I shall, my love."

When he did not budge or change his facial expression, something stung Amelia's insides, yet she could wait no longer to see her father and her mother.

Spinning around, she resumed running toward her father who had not heard her call his name, for the wind had carried the softness of her voice in the other direction, away from him.

He did not even see her approaching. His head was averted from the brilliant rays of the sun, his fingers ambling through the many fine otter pelts laid out before him.

Anxiety caused Amelia's heart to beat wildly as, caught up in wonder of whether she had a brother or a sister, she lifted the skirt of her Chinese dress and ran barefoot along the beach, ignoring the piercing rocks that stung her tender feet. She was drawing close enough to her father now for him to hear . . . for him to see . . . her!

"Papa!" she once again cried. "Oh, Papa, it is I, Amelia! Oh, do hear me!"

She saw him turn his head and they made eye contact, but he did not appear to recognize her, and Amelia's insides grew cold. Had she changed so much?

But, yes, she had. Gray Wing had not recognized her, either.

Yet her father had known her for much longer than Gray Wing had. Her father had raised her from a baby! Surely there was much about her that would still be familiar to him!

"Papa!" Amelia said, her feet paining her as she ran harder on the rocky beach, on past the line of Indians, and then threw herself into her father's arms, weeping. "Papa, oh, how I have missed you!"

Feeling the tightened muscles of his arms slowly embrace her, she knew that he did not yet comprehend how this was happening, how she happened to be there.

Yes, he surely thought that she had died, the same as Gray Wing had thought these past ten years.

Tears wetting her father's fringed buckskin shirt, Amelia pressed her cheek hard against his heaving chest. "The Haida did not kill me," she sobbed. "They sold me to the Chinese, Papa. I have been in China ever since. But now I have returned. I am here."

"Amelia?" Christopher Storm said thickly, caressing her back, numb from the discovery. "Daughter, it *is* you."

He held her tight, never wanting to let her go. "Are you all right? Did they hurt you? Did the Chinese agree to return you home? If so, why did you come first to Whale Island? Do they know that I now live close by? Have they traded at my trading post?"

"Yes. They agreed to return me to you, but not here. They . . . *I* knew not of your presence here," she said, her voice carrying to Gray Wing as he moved toward her, intently listening. "We came to Whale Island to trade with the Indians. We then were going to travel to Boston. But there was a shipwreck. Again I was stranded on the island without family."

Her insides coiled with uneasiness when she realized that her confession had just reached Gray Wing's ears. All along he had thought that she had returned just to be with him. Now he knew. Now . . . he . . . knew! Now how would he feel about her? Would he love her less because she had played her own game of deceit with him?

Christopher eased Amelia from his arms and held her at arm's length. His green eyes raked over her. "Daughter, you've grown into a woman," he said hoarsely. His gaze stopped at her hair. "But your hair . . ."

Amelia sniffled, wiping tears from her cheeks as she smiled up at her father. She laughed softly. "The Chinese did not like the color of my hair," she murmured. "So they dyed it."

Christopher's insides twisted as he looked from Amelia to Gray Wing, who was now standing over her, looking at her with possession in his eyes. He again studied Amelia, seeing how disarrayed her dress and hair were. Had the damn Indian. . . ? Had she let him? Had she wanted him as a woman needs a man?

His arm about Amelia's waist, Christopher urged her to her feet. "Let's go home, Amelia," he said urgently, casting Gray Wing a troubled glance. "You need not stay in this Indian Village another moment. You are no longer stranded with savages. You will go home with me." He framed her face between his hands. "Daughter, I need you. You can help ease many of my burdens by being with me."

Amelia's eyes wavered as she saw so much sadness suddenly softening the green of her father's eyes. "Mama? Is she well?" she asked, something deep within her warning her that this question would bring an answer she did not want to hear. "And, Papa, do I have a brother or a sister?" She clutched his arm. "Papa, tell me about Mama . . . about the child you had while I was gone."

Amelia swallowed hard when he did not answer her all that quickly. She watched as one of the traders who had been sitting beside her father on the beach stepped to her side, his blue eyes piercing her with their kindness as he laced an arm about her waist, opposite the side on which her father was standing.

"Amelia, let me introduce you to my best friend and Russian trading partner, Joseph Beria," Christopher said, glad to see Joseph so sensitive to what was transpiring, offering assistance to a daughter who was soon to find out that her mother was dead. "Joseph, my daughter who I *knew* was not dead. You see, I was right not to give up on her all that easily!"

Joseph bowed low at the waist, his wavy blond hair rippling in the wind. His smile revealed sparkling white teeth where his face narrowed to a sharp point of chin, but this was somehow unnerving to Amelia, for she knew that the truth she had asked for was being purposely delayed.

"It is good to meet you," Joseph said in a mixed American and Russian accent. "Your father spoke of you often during your absence. It is good that you are all right."

"Papa," Amelia said, short of being rude to the man offering friendship. "Tell me of Mama. I can hardly bear not knowing!"

She flinched when Joseph's grasp about her waist strengthened. She cast him a sidewise glance. Did he expect her to faint? Was the news that terrible?

She jerked free of both Joseph and her father and turned to face them, angrily placing her hands on her hips. "Do not treat me like a child!" she stormed. "I am a grown woman. Do you not see? A grown woman!"

Feeling eyes of fire on her, knowing who had taught her all the ways of a woman, Amelia glanced over at Gray Wing. His jaw was set, his eyes were two narrow slits. She had given him reason to hate her!

But now was not the time to make wrongs right with him. She now sorely feared that her mother was no longer alive. Why else would her father hesitate to inform her of the welfare of her mother?

"Amelia, let's return home," Christopher said, attempting to take her hand, then wincing when she jerked it away from him. "It would be best to talk at home."

"Home?" she cried. "Just where *is* this home that you speak of? Papa, I am not sure I even want to go with you. Something tells me that I . . . I will be greeted with much sadness!"

Placing an arm firmly about Amelia's waist, Christopher was not to be dissuaded by her again. He began guiding her away from the throng of onlooking Indians and led her down the rocky shore to his beached canoe. Many traders accompanied him, each choosing his own canoe from among the many.

"As I have already mentioned, Amelia, home is no longer Boston," Christopher said. "Joseph and I are partners in a trading post adventure. It is Russian-run, with my blessings. I only planned to stay as long as it took to discover your true fate. But now that I am established here,

I am not so sure I want to leave. The Indians depend on me. I depend on *them*."

"I am surprised by such a confession," Amelia said, almost in a hiss. "Papa, I know how little you like the Indians. I am surprised that you have not been killed by them because they surely can tell that you despise them. Or have you changed?"

Christopher helped her into a canoe, then positioned himself at the helm as Joseph walked the canoe deeper into the waters of the Sound.

When Joseph was also in the canoe and it was weaving its way through the gray, splashing waves, Christopher turned to Amelia, eyeing her speculatively.

"Daughter, I do not carry love inside my heart for any Indian," he said solemnly. "And they know this. But trading keeps a civil tongue between us. Yet I do not turn my back to them as they do not turn theirs to me. It's not at all healthy, if you see what I mean."

He wanted to question her at length about her relationship with Gray Wing, but he feared the answers that he might receive. He now knew that it was imperative to get her married off to a fine gentleman, to ensure a future with a man who cared for her and who would treat her respectfully.

Joseph was the man.

Soon there would be a marriage, a marriage that would be witnessed by Gray Wing and his warriors. They would soon know that she was not a woman to be eyed like something they possessed! Gray Wing had made the mistake of showing his feelings too openly. He would learn that the mistake would cost him much; it would cost him Amelia!

Amelia clutched the sides of the canoe. Her gaze moved to the shore. Outlined against the horizon was Gray Wing, watching her departure. They had not even had the opportunity to say a good-bye at all. Amelia had been swept away much too quickly!

Amelia lifted a hand and waved at Gray Wing; her heart bled when he did not respond in kind. Somehow she would return really soon to make amends. She would not let him believe that she did not care for him. She was not a whore who lent her body to just any man! She had done so only because she sorely loved him!

Turning her tear-dampened eyes straight ahead, Amelia knew better than to question her father further about her mother. Soon she would know the answers. Soon enough she would know if her mother was alive or dead. . . .

The great Chinese ship forged through the waters of the South China Sea, Bai-Hua Jin at the rail, anxiously peering into the distance. His knuckles were white as he clutched the rail, now wishing that he had not waited so long to follow his father's ship and try to stop him from taking Vona-Lee to America! He had been wrong not to fight this decision with more strength!

But Bai-Hua's father was a *da-jen*, a great man, in the eyes of all Chinese people, and not one whose authority was to be questioned.

Yet Bai-Hua should have voiced his desire to have Vona-Lee as a wife much louder . . . much more determinedly!

"Aie-yah!" he exclaimed, his embroidered silk robe flapping in the wind as he shook his head in disgust. "Never have I made such a wrong decision in my life! I should have forced myself fully upon her to show that I would not let her leave so easily. Should she have gone to father to cry of my seduction, it would not have been shameful in his eyes. He would have seen that his son was strong, powerful, lusty! He would have approved!"

The wind carried his words away. The sea stretched out before him, a lonely blue. Bai-Hua had many weeks of travel before him. So much could happen that he had no control over!

"I will follow the trail of my father's great trading ship. I shall travel first to Whale Island," he whispered, doubling a fist in the air. "Then to Boston. I shall find Vona-Lee. Fates will be kind and grant me the chance to have her as my wife!"

In Bai-Hua's mind's eye he was already making love to Vona-Lee. . . .

Mei-Ling's unbound hair, long and silky, hung almost to her ankles without its headdress on which to wind it. She stood on a cliff overlooking the sea, watching . . . watching . . . watching . . .

Loneliness overwhelmed her, for she had been told of her father's death. She sobbed into the palm of her hand. Everything was different on this island of Indians. She no longer had a father, nor did she look Chinese any longer. She had nothing with which to make her face lovelier. She had no almond milk to apply to her skin. She had no fancy headdress, nor did she have beautiful silk dresses to drape over her body. She must look so ugly in the Indians' eyes!

Yet she had been treated in such a very special way! The Indian who was now more handsome than strange, with his many tattoos, made her days and nights lovely. She did not understand how she could even now pine to have his arms about her.

"It is surely because I hunger for the comfort of such arms . . . *any* arms," she whispered, yet deep within her she knew that her reason was more involved than that. She was falling in love. She was falling in love with the Indian!

Shaking her head, frowning, she did not want to accept this truth. She longed to leave this island, be with Vona-Lee again. She was strong enough. Why did Red Eagle not see that she was strong enough to travel to Vona-Lee, who was her only link to what was truly real in life! They both shared a love of China!

"Yet she so eagerly returned to America!" Mei-Ling wondered aloud. Again she shook her head. "I am so confused! *Wei*. I am so confused!"

Having been lost in thought, Mei-Ling had not heard approaching footsteps behind her. When strong arms slipped about her waist and drew her around, she smiled up into eyes dark and warm with passion.

She did not draw away when Red Eagle's lips moved slowly down toward hers.

She trembled sensually when she let him claim her lips with their first shared kiss.

Suddenly China . . . Vona-Lee . . . seemed so far away!

Fourteen

꧁ ꧂

Amelia's eyes were drawn to an island the convoy of canoes was approaching, not far from Whale Island. Along the north shore of the bay there was a sand spit with a long, sloping beach. A road led to a warehouse on the beach where also could be seen a mill, loft shops, launching ways, construction sheds, and piers. Several ships were moored to the pier, company vessels bringing supplies from Russia and picking up bales of furs for their return.

On the crest of the hill stood several houses, two of which were greater than the others, with hewed logs for walls and roofs of shakes. Amelia could even see an outside stairway on each house, which she presumed led to the lofts of the houses, and also chimneys of what had to be mammoth stone fireplaces.

Then something else caught her eye. Scattered among the wild bluegrass that grew waist deep across the vast island were Indian huts and overlapping cedar boards. Cattle grazed close by. Indian children ran and played with white children!

Amelia's insides tensed as she looked from child to child, wondering which one was related to her. Then her thoughts were interrupted by the lurching of the canoe as it became beached on the rocky shore and Joseph Beria helped her from the vessel, even carrying her through the water until he had her safely on the beach.

"Thank you," Amelia said, straightening the skirt of her silk dress, then combing her fingers through her tangled hair.

She smiled nervously at Joseph when he did not reply, but instead looked at her with the same toothy smile that he had given her since they had become acquainted. It was as though he had not seen a woman before. She did not like being singled out by him for such attention. She had no interest in any man other than Gray Wing!

She turned her gaze elsewhere, hoping to urge Joseph to do likewise. She focused on her father who was trudging through the depths of the water. She was not feeling any particular joy at being with him, as she should. So much about him had changed. He seemed distant, somehow. So cold and distant.

Perhaps it was because the news that he had to share with her was so tragic. She was anxious to get the telling over with.

Lifting the tail of her skirt, Amelia met her father's approach. She looked on past him, at the houses lined up on the hill, then back at her father.

"Which house is yours?" she asked, yet knowing she did not have to. He would have built one of the two largest houses for himself and his family. He would have brought all the comforts of Boston with him. He was not the sort to do without.

"I'll take you to it," Christopher said in a low rumble as he took Amelia by the arm and began guiding her up the steep road.

There was a strained silence between Amelia and her father as they walked past the many men who carried supplies to and from the ships. The warehouses were buzzing with activity. The laughter of children at play was a refreshing change as they left the warehouses behind.

Amelia stiffened when she saw a girl of about age nine,

attired in a printed cotton dress, running in her father's
direction. A strange sort of thrill then shot through Amelia
when she saw the green of the girl's eyes and the smile
that mirrored her own as a child nearing the age of ten.

Amelia choked with emotion as the child ran past her
and flung herself into her father's arms.

"Papa! You've returned!" Lorna Storm exclaimed, her
eyes dancing as she looked up at her father adoringly. "Did
you get some pretty things from the Indians? I love necklaces. Did you get me a necklace?"

Christopher's eyes shone with pride as he held Lorna at
arm's length. Then tidying her red hair back from her
cheeks, he gave her a kiss on the brow.

"Not much was traded for today," he said hoarsely. His
gaze moved slowly up at Amelia. "Except for . . . except
for perhaps a *sister*. Would you like to have a sister all
grown up and ready to take care of you as though she were
your mama?"

His words held many meanings within them, moving
Amelia's heart with joy *and* sadness. Her suspicion that
her mother was dead was confirmed. Also she had been
right to surmise this girl was her sister!

Tears burned at the corners of Amelia's eyes, and she
found it hard not to cry over the knowledge that her mother
was no longer alive.

Yet it was the sister she had never had the opportunity
to know who stole much of the grief from her heart, for
Lorna was like a breath of fresh air in her young and
beautiful innocence.

"Papa, this is. . . ?" Amelia managed to say through
a choked feeling invading her throat.

Christopher lifted his gaze, locking with Amelia's.
"Yes. This is your sister," he said thickly. Rising to his
full height, he gently eased Lorna toward Amelia. "She
needs you, Amelia. She has only you and me. Your
mother—"

"I know," Amelia said, interrupting her father. "I
know."

Christopher's eyes misted with tears as Amelia swept

Lorna into her arms and hugged her. "Lorna has never known a mother," he said, his voice cracking with emotion. "From the day she was born, Amelia, she has never had a mother."

Now understanding that her mother must have died in childbirth and that Lorna had not had the beautiful moments with her as had Amelia, she twined her fingers through her sister's soft red hair and looked adoringly down at her. "Lorna, I'm your sister Amelia," she said in a whisper. She devoured Lorna with her eyes. "Oh, how pretty you are."

Lorna's eyes were wide and green as she slowly scrutinized Amelia. Then, surprising all of them, she threw her arms about Amelia's neck and hugged her. "I'm happy that you are my sister," she said in a purr. "I'm glad you are *here*."

As she caressed Lorna's hair, Amelia's eyes flooded with tears. "I am, too," she said in a choked whisper. "I am, too, honey."

A firm hand on Amelia's arm drew her from the moment of sweet peace that being with her sister was giving her. "Let's go to the house," Christopher encouraged, guiding Amelia on up the steep road. "We can talk in private. You sisters can get to know each other. You should never have been apart." He paused and gave Amelia a sidewise glance. "Nothing is going to separate you again. Nothing."

Amelia jerked her eyes to her father, hearing the coldness with which he was speaking. Did he somehow know that deep within her heart she wanted to be with Gray Wing? If she voiced aloud her desire to go to him, would her father forbid it?

She was again reminded of how she had been taught obedience to her father as a child. Whatever he wished, she did. The fact that she had disobeyed him that day she left the ship had not yet even entered the conversation. Did her father have a reason for waiting to question her about that day?

A shiver ran up and down Amelia's spine. The homecoming was not at all what she had expected. Her father did not appear to be all that happy that she was there, alive. Had he become so used to the idea that she was not alive that he was not yet accepting the truth that she was? Had he wanted her to be alive for only one reason? To raise his other child, who was motherless?

In a sense, Amelia already felt that she was being used. It was as though her father was blaming her for something, but *what*. . . ?

Lorna eased away from Amelia when two Indian girls of her age came running down the road, their braids bouncing on their shoulders, their moccasined feet quiet. "I must go," she said softly. "My friends want me to join them."

Amelia glanced from Lorna to her father, then to the Indian children. Did he allow Lorna to play with Indians? Surely not! He looked upon Indians as savages. Yet even *children*?

Christopher waved a hand in the air. "Go on," he said, glancing from the Indian girls to Lorna. "Go on and play. But don't go down by the water. Do you hear?"

"Yes, Papa," Lorna said, then ran away, giggling, holding hands with the Indian girls.

"Come on," Christopher said, taking Amelia's elbow, guiding her on toward the house. "Perhaps it is best that we talk alone. We've got to get some things settled between us."

"Yes, I guess we do," Amelia said, her voice strained. She looked over at her father and smiled weakly. "I've missed you, Papa. I've missed you, oh, so very much."

Christopher nodded. His jaw firmed. "It's good that you have," he said. He gave her a squinted stare. "Yes, it's good that you have. It's been a damn hard ten years for me, also. Without you *and* your mother, it's been damn hard."

"I'm sorry, Papa," Amelia said, jerking her eyes away from him. Guilt was building inside her. Yes, he blamed her for something. But what. . . ?

Silence stretched between them like stiff branches on a

tree as they entered the sun-splashed rooms of the house.
Amelia's eyes shot around her, absorbing the grandness of
the decor and furnishings. Because of the steady ship traf-
fic traveling from Russia and surrounding areas, it was
apparent that her father enjoyed the refinements of civilized life in contrast to this community's wild surroundings.

As she was shown from room to room, she saw that the
spacious table in the dining room was set with linens,
silver, glassware, and fine China. The parlor furnishings
were plushly upholstered, the tables were carved from
cherrywood. A fire simmered on the grate of a massive
stone fireplace. A beautiful gilt clock ticked time away on
the mantel.

"I can show you the bedrooms later," Christopher said.
He gestured toward a chair before the fire. "Let's talk.
Before Lorna comes bouncing in here all full of life and
mischief, let's have us a talk about the way things are, and
should be."

"Whatever you say," Amelia said, smoothing the silk
dress across her legs as she eased down into the chair. Her
spine was stiff. She locked her fingers together on her lap
as her father poured himself a glass of vodka from the
assortment of bottles lined up in a liquor cabinet.

Settling down beside Amelia, Christopher leaned forward so that he was positioned almost directly before her
eyes. He sipped on the vodka as his eyes absorbed his
daughter who had changed into a woman since the last
time he had seen her. His gaze locked on her hair. He
tilted an eyebrow quizzically.

"So you've been in China," he said, now searching her
face for the daughter he had last seen at the age of thirteen.
"Tell me about it, Amelia. Tell me why you left the ship
that day and what has happened to you since."

Amelia swallowed hard, preparing herself for the scolding she should have received all those ten years ago. But
first, as best as she could recall, she began her tale sullenly.

Her father's reaction when she had finished caught her off guard and made her grow numb.

"It's your duty to see to Lorna now as though you were her mother," Christopher said, setting the empty glass on a table beside him. "It's because of you that your mother is dead. But of course you know that, don't you, Amelia?"

It took a few moments for the reality of what he was saying to sink in. Amelia now understood, fully understood, why her father had not been happier to see her. These past years he had grown to hate her because he felt it was her fault that her mother was dead! He had not stayed in these parts because of his love for a lost daughter, but to find this daughter and to punish her!

"Papa, why are you blaming me for Mother's death?" she gasped. Her fingernails dug into the palms of her hands as they tightened into fists on her lap. "How *could* you? What did I do? What?"

"Your mother grieved herself to death after hearing that you were dead," Christopher said hoarsely. "Through her entire pregnancy she grieved. She never left her bed! I had to wait on her hand and foot. She was not strong enough to live through childbirth. She left me burdened with a small child."

He cleared his throat nervously. "But now you are here. You can see to your sister. She will be your full responsibility, Amelia, for it is your duty to make all wrongs right for your father."

It was as though time had stopped and the world was crumbling at Amelia's feet, her father's words were so harshly cruel. She looked away from him, biting her lower lip to keep from speaking disobediently back to him. She would never believe she was guilty of that of which he was accusing her. She had only disobeyed him that one time and had gone to speak with Gray Wing.

Only that, and she would never be sorry for that. She loved Gray Wing with all her heart. Had she not ventured off the ship that day, she would have never known what true love *was*.

Amelia recalled that her mother was ill before she discovered her daughter's absence from the ship. It was not because of her absence that her mother had died! Her mother had not been a strong person physically, or mentally, for as far back as Amelia could remember!

But Amelia did have feelings for her sister. How could she make things right for Lorna, and for herself also? Amelia now knew that she could not live for long under the same roof with her father. She even felt a loathing for him that she did not enjoy admitting to!

Looking out the window of the house and beyond to the dark, beckoning trees that grew like giants across the bay on Whale Island, Amelia felt torn. She must somehow find a way to make things right with Gray Wing *and* with her sister.

But how?

Never had she felt so torn!

Recalling the many canoes at the quay, she knew that when darkness engulfed this mystical land of trees and water she would go to Gray Wing. Perhaps he could help her search for the right answers. . . .

Fifteen

※ ⁂ ※

With a knitted shawl draped snugly about her shoulders, and dressed in one of her mother's lovely, flowing cotton dresses with a sweeping neckline that revealed the soft upper lobes of her breasts to the moonlight, Amelia crept through the darkness toward the piers. She had talked to Lorna, telling her of her adventures in China, until her sister fell into a sweet sleep, and her father had drunk vodka until he fell across his bed in a drunken stupor. When loud snores reached Amelia's assigned loft bedroom, she knew it was safe enough to leave, to go to Gray Wing.

While in China, Amelia had dreamed of such rendezvous with the man she loved, but, alas, when oceans separated them, it had been impossible. But now when only a slight bay stretched between them, nothing would deter her decision to go to him, to attempt to make things right between them again.

Brushing wisps of windblown hair back from her eyes, encouraging it to hang lustrously long down her slender back, Amelia ignored the cabins on either side of her whose lights were still on. She began to run when a dog barked and came sniffing at her feet. She did not see Joseph Beria standing in the doorway of his grand house watching her hasty retreat down the steep dirt road. She was focusing on the canoes drawn up on the beach, already with her eyes choosing the one she would use to go to Gray Wing.

Pinpricks of fear raced across her scalp at the thought of possibly capsizing in the canoe, for she had never piloted such a vessel before. But to get to Gray Wing, she would chance anything!

Now farther down the road, falling into the shadows of madrona trees that stretched out from the beach like gnarled fingers of an aging woman, Amelia could breathe much more easily. She was beyond sight of the houses of the village. She was now moving among the shadows of the moored trading ships whose masts were ghostly in the moonlight.

The sounds of the waves slapping against the hulls of the ships were muted by a thick covering of fog smoothing its way in from the sea. The aroma that lay about her was a mixture of saltwater and fish, the touch of the air upon her face was stinging and cold.

Lifting the skirt of her dress away from the effervescent foam of the water slinking in from the sea onto the rocks at her feet, Amelia huffed and puffed as she continued to run, the canoe that would carry her to the man she loved only a few footsteps away. She weaved in and around the protective covering of the madrona trees, then felt a frightful light-headedness seize her when a figure in the darkness loomed suddenly before her, stopping her dead in her tracks. The fog was now too thick to discern who the nighttime intruder was. All that Amelia could see was darkness and shadow!

"Who's there?" Amelia asked, her voice trembling with fear. She took a backward step as the figure took a step closer.

Then a sweetness engulfed her when, through the break in the fog, the moonlight cast a velvet sheen on the face of a man she knew . . . the man she *loved*.

"Gray Wing, it's *you*," she sighed, a smile loosening the frown that had almost frozen on her face. Her gaze raked over him. He wore only his usual breechcloth. He was barefoot.

The fringes of her shawl blowing in the breeze, Amelia rushed to Gray Wing. Without hesitation she lunged into his arms, yet a cold aloofness radiating from him was transferring to her, causing her to draw away. She looked up at him, feeling the magnetic pull of his eyes. Seeing the fire in them made her wince and ease away from him.

"Why have you come?" she asked stiffly, shivering as a damp chill surged in from the bay, heightening the coldness she was already feeling from Gray Wing's continued strange aloofness.

She looked over her shoulder at the village lights, knowing that someone could come at any time and find them together. The dangers were many should this happen. Her father would be told when his alcohol-sedated mind became fresh and alert again. There was no imagining what his reaction might be!

Gray Wing reached behind him and removed a leather pouch that he had tied to the waistband of his loincloth. Without explanation he handed it to Amelia.

With trembling fingers and a question in her eyes, Amelia accepted the pouch, its softness like a butterfly's wings against the palm of her hand.

Yet she could feel the sharp points of something that lay inside the bag reaching out through the leather, digging into her flesh.

Her heart began to pound, for she had grown accustomed to the feel of something similar to that during those long ten years when she was separated from Gray Wing. Could it . . . be the same. . . ?

"Open," Gray Wing flatly ordered. "*Klas-ka*. Yours."

Gray Wing folded his arms across his chest as he watched Amelia fumbling with the drawstring of the pouch. Then a slow smile lifted his lips as she withdrew the Indian necklace from within it. It had been special to her once. Perhaps it would be again. . . ?

Amelia's eyes grew wide. She fingered the necklace, studying its intricate designs, recognizing it as, yes, *her* necklace. In her father's haste to remove her from Whale Island she had been forced to leave the necklace behind, in Gray Wing's house.

Oh, how could she not have missed it? It had been her link to Gray Wing for so long!

Yet her mind recaptured all the moments since she had left Gray Wing and his island, and the discoveries that had crowded, even overtaxed, her mind. Her father had brought many cruel realities to mind, even for a while erasing everything that had been good in her life.

Even Gray Wing . . . even the necklace . . .

"Oh, thank you, Gray Wing," Amelia said, almost in a whisper, looking adoringly up at him. "You *do* understand how special the necklace is to me. If not, you would not have returned it. It is the same as receiving it as a gift twice from you! I shall treasure it twofold now!"

Gray Wing eased the necklace from Amelia's hand and slipped it over her head, then positioned it about her neck. The fog swirled like ghosts trying to interfere with Gray Wing and Amelia's sudden meeting on the shore. Gray Wing then reached for Amelia and drew her closer to him. His eyes were fathomless as he looked down at her. He could not stay angry at her for long. The fact that she had chosen her father over him somehow no longer mattered! Just being with her did!

His fingers trembled as they clasped her arms. Though the moon was now hidden, he was close enough to Amelia to see the bold outline of her breasts, which swelled partially from the low-cut bodice of the dress. Gray Wing's loins ached as he recalled their utter softness, wanting even now to devour them with his lips.

But feeling the wonder in her eyes as she looked up at him, Gray Wing averted his attention upward. Her brilliant eyes with long, silky lashes spoke of so much yet unsaid between them this night. Her bright, curved mouth trembled as she softly smiled. He could not help but move his hands to her face where he meditatively moved his fingers along its delicate lines, then as though drawn there, lowered his hands to cup her breasts through her dress.

"Gray Wing, please don't . . ." Amelia whispered, fearing the dangers of such intimacy so close to the village . . . so close to her father's house.

Yet she could not deny the fires being stoked within her by his hands, his eyes, his aroma of muskiness as he bent his head to kiss the upper lobe of a breast.

"Not here, Gray Wing," Amelia softly persisted, wriggling away from him. "It is too . . . too dangerous."

Gray Wing's passion-filled eyes silently studied her. Then he swept her up into his arms and began to carry her toward the sea. Amelia's breath was stolen by the suddenness of his actions. She grabbed at her shawl as it rippled away from her to the ground.

But before she could speak an objection or rescue the shawl, she was in an intricately designed canoe, placed comfortably on a pad of otter furs, which stretched across the seat.

"Gray Wing, where. . . ?" she said, reaching out to him as he walked the canoe into deeper water. "I'm not sure if—"

He interrupted her. "We must be alone," he murmured, moving briskly into the canoe. "We must be alone *now*. We have much to say. We have much to *share*."

Having been on her way to him for those very reasons, Amelia sighed and accepted this change of plans. She clung to the sides of the canoe as it began sweeping down the long avenue of water, slicing a path through the dense, cottony fog. At this moment she loved Gray Wing so much her insides ached! That she was with him again seemed almost a miracle! And that he still cared despite the fact that she had left with her father thrilled her so much that she could hardly bear not going to him this very moment to throw herself into his arms. She hungered for his kiss, for the protective cocoon of his arms!

The fog thinned as the canoe traveled across the bay. The moonlight was now casting its soft rays down from the sky, illuminating the wide expanse of Gray Wing's sleekly muscled shoulders. When he lifted his paddle, his muscles stirred, sending ripples like waves down the length of his lean copper body. The wind lifted his hair from his shoulders; the salt water made a soft, wet sheen across his flesh.

And then they were there, beached on the shore of Whale Island. The light of jack-pine torches illuminated the path that led to Gray Wing's dwelling, also lighting the massive totem poles. As the reflections of the torch fires swayed along the poles, the figures on the poles seemed to come alive, dancing. Amelia recalled the first time she had seen them when she was thirteen. Had that truly been only ten years ago? To her it now seemed like an eternity!

With an arm about Amelia's waist, Gray Wing ushered her through the totem-pole archway that led inside his house. When fully inside, Gray Wing turned to Amelia and drew her to him, his eyes passion-heavy. "So much needs to be said," he said thickly. "It troubles my heart that you did not return to Whale Island solely to be with me. Your confession to your father revealed that truth to me. You practice deceit quite well, my *la-dida*."

Amelia was melting beneath his gaze, yet she held her chin firmly high, also recalling *his* deceit. "As do you practice deceit," she said softly, yet no longer angry at the deceit. Missing him so much had softened her feelings.

Also, she knew that he had kept the truth from her because he had feared losing her to her father, which, in a sense, he *had*—at least until she could figure out a way to be fair to both her father and Gray Wing at the same time.

And, then, too, there was her sister. . . .

"Sometimes deceit is necessary, as it was when I chose to use it," Gray Wing said, smoothing the palms of his hands across Amelia's cheeks to encourage some sea-dampened tendrils of her hair back in place. "Was it the same with you, my *la-dida*?"

That he still called her his *la-dida*, his woman, made

Amelia's blood soar warmly through her veins. That he had come to her thrilled her very soul!

"I truly did not wish to deceive you," she said, lifting a hand to clasp one of his. "Somehow it . . . just . . . happened. I'm sorry. I shall never deceive you again. I hope I shall never be given cause to."

Gray Wing took both her hands in his and guided her down on a pallet of furs before the smoldering fire in the firepit. He knelt beside her and began unfastening her dress, his eyes hypnotizing her into wanting him more and more by the moment.

"You are deceiving your father now?" he asked, his voice husky, the pulse beat throbbing at the base of his throat. "He would not want you to be with Gray Wing. He would not approve."

His fingers were eliciting fire along Amelia's flesh as he began inching her dress down away from her bosom. Her breathing was shallow; her heartbeat was erratic.

"No, he would not approve," she whispered, closing her eyes and gasping with passion as Gray Wing's lips covered a breast and began sucking the nipple into a tight peak. "Nor would he approve of what we are about to do. He would probably *kill* you, Gray Wing. He must never, never know. Not until I can tell him that I will be staying with you always."

Amelia's word, "always," struck a chord of happiness in Gray Wing's heart. She had just confessed to wanting to be his woman totally. It no longer mattered that she had returned to America for any reason other than to be with him. He knew that he was somewhere among her reasons. Her love for him was proof of that. She had missed him as much as he had missed her.

Somehow they would make all wrongs right between them.

But for now, he just wanted to make love with her. Those moments, when they were in each other's arms, could never be taken away from them by her father, or by time. Their love shared would be embedded inside their minds until the day they died!

Fully disrobing her, laying her out before him as though she were a rag doll, Gray Wing raked his eyes over her. He again saw her perfect breasts, her invitingly rounded hips, and her slim white thighs. Her eyes were dancing, golden, in the light of the fire as she beckoned for him to come to her.

Gray Wing straddled her, resting on his knees. He took one of her hands and placed it on the hardness that lay just beneath the buckskin breechcloth. He circled her fingers about his shaft and encouraged them to move on him.

Amelia was becoming breathless with desire. Her hand pulsed where she touched his hardened manhood. She shuddered sensuously as his body stiffened and he closed his eyes, reveling in the pleasure she was arousing inside him. Excitement lured her into boldly reaching beneath the breechcloth to touch his velvet shaft. Her other hand slipped the garment away from him, giving her freedom to tantalize him more with brisk movements of her fingers.

When she felt his hands entwine in her hair and gently urge her mouth where her hand so masterfully played, as though he were an instrument, she the musician, Amelia's eyes widened, not knowing what was expected of her.

"Make love to me with your lips . . . with your tongue . . . with your mouth," Gray Wing said huskily, his eyes dark pools. He positioned himself closer to her mouth and his insides flamed when her tongue touched him with its smooth wetness.

Knowing that she was not practiced in loving a man in such a way, Gray Wing taught her every movement in which she should move her mouth to pleasure him. And when he felt the peak almost reached that would fulfill his desperate needs, he eased himself gently away from her.

He now had to practice restraint if he was to pleasure her as she had just pleasured him. He would make her cry out, the pleasure would be so intense!

"Gray Wing, oh, Gray Wing," Amelia cried as his lips claimed hers in a fiery, lengthy kiss. She clung to him. She draped her legs about him, loving the feel of his manhood on her thigh. Recalling the wondrous joy he could give her with his masterful strokes inside her, she opened herself so that he could enter her. But he did not.

Instead, he eased slowly down away from her, kissing her taut breasts, her abdomen, and then lower.

It was as though electric shock waves splashed through Amelia when Gray Wing's tongue began to worship her where she so unmercifully throbbed, between her thighs. Closing her eyes, thrashing her head back and forth, Amelia cried out with the pleasure as it soared higher, higher, higher. . . .

She opened her eyes and smiled up at Gray Wing as he repositioned himself over her and entered her in one easy stroke. Desire shot through her as she clasped her legs about him and moved her hips with him, receiving him all the way inside her. He gathered her in his arms and molded her against him. Two bodies became one as the sexual excitement built to a frenzy.

With a fierceness Gray Wing held Amelia closer. His body moved faster, his thrusts awakening every nerve ending inside Amelia to pleasure never known before. She sighed, she moaned, she kissed him as his lips bore down upon hers. His fingers pressed urgently into her flesh as together they reached the peak sought and found.

When they lay spent, each breathing heaven against the other's cheek, Amelia could not help but sob softly, her joy was so immense and complete!

"You cry? Why?" Gray Wing questioned, cupping Amelia's face between his hands. "Did you not enjoy fully enough? It seemed that you did."

Amelia softly laughed, brushing foolish tears from her eyes. "I could never love as desperately, as fully, again," she said. "Surely never again could I enjoy it as much, Gray Wing."

"There will be other times?" he said, drawing away from her to sit before the fire. He stared into the flames, his eyes hauntingly fathomless. "You will come again to Gray Wing? Gray Wing can come for you? One day we will be together always?"

Placing an otter fur about her shoulders, Amelia moved

close to Gray Wing's side. She took his hand and snuggled it onto her lap with her own, then proceeded to explain about her mother's death, her sister who needed her, and her worry about Mei-Ling.

"It seems that I have the burden of the world upon my shoulders now that I have returned to America," Amelia said, sighing heavily. She placed a hand on Gray Wing's cheek. "And, my love, yes, there is *you*. You are my life . . . my very *soul*. We must be together. But first I must see what can be done about my sister. I feel so . . . so responsible."

Gray Wing took her hands and held them tightly. He glared down at her with eyes of fire. "You cannot blame yourself for your mother's death," he murmured. "It would be the same as Gray Wing blaming himself for the death of his father, sisters, brother, and mother. Life sometimes has ugly twists. It is no fault of yours!"

A low rumble and the shaking of the floor beneath them made Amelia lunge into Gray Wing's arms. "I forgot about the earth rumblings . . . about the mountain that frowns sometimes upon what people do," she gasped. "Surely one day there will be a terrible earthquake!"

"So you see? There are more things than family and friends to worry about," Gray Wing said solemnly, holding Amelia away from him, so their eyes could meet and lock. "The mountain . . . smallpox. Both curses trouble me and my people. One will claim many of my people one day, perhaps even *you*. We must grab life while we can, my *la-dida*. Remember that!"

His words reached Amelia's heart, filling it with dread. Throwing herself into Gray Wing's arms, she clung to him. "I know," she murmured. "I know."

But she still did not know *how* this was to be done!

And, oh, what of Mei-Ling? How was *she* faring? The Haida had promised that she would be returned as soon as she was able to travel. But would they keep their promise? And how soon? She would ask her father to go for Mei-Ling tomorrow!

"Hold me, Gray Wing, hold me," Amelia whispered,

knowing that in her next breath she must tell him that it was time for her to return to her father's island. If her father ever found out that she had left . . .

But she would chance this discovery over and over again. Again tomorrow night she would come to Gray Wing to be with him sensually again. She was like a moth attracted to flames . . . the flames stoked inside her by the wondrous passion found in Gray Wing's masterful arms!

"My *la-dida*, always you worry too much about everything," Gray Wing softly scolded. "Again I will show you ways to forget. . . ."

As he smoothed the furs from Amelia's shoulders, Gray Wing's lips were hot on her breast. The euphoria that swept through her was magical. All doubts and worries were erased from her troubled mind. Gray Wing knew her needs so well. . . .

Sixteen

Having hidden the Indian necklace beneath the mattress on her bed, Amelia took the indoor stairs from the loft down to the parlor. Something grabbed at her heart when she caught her father standing at the window looking from it as though he were a lost soul. In his dark suit, with his starched white shirt collar contrasting with his tanned face, he looked sad; his face was filled with troubled emotion.

Always as a child, Amelia had seen her father as a vibrant personality, not one who would get caught up easily in the burdens of the world. He had been a happy man who had made things happen with his charisma and voice of authority.

But now he was a tormented man. And he blamed *her*!

Swallowing back the urge to cry, not wanting to feel guilty about her father's new, most unlikable personality, Amelia swept on into the room.

"Papa, where is Lorna?" she asked, hating the fact that her weak voice revealed her emotions of only moments ago.

She went to her father and hugged him fiercely, trying to change his mood for the better. "Papa, I had such a wonderful night of sleep. I so love the loft bedroom,'' she said in a forced purr.

Christopher eased her away from him and let his gaze move over her. He saw so much of her mother in Amelia's expression this morning. Oh, such a wounded look in her eyes, and he was surely responsible, because of the disturbing talk they'd had the previous day. He should never have laid guilt heavy on her heart because of her mother's death.

But he had silently blamed her for so long that the words just had to be spoken aloud!

Amelia became unnerved beneath her father's solemn stare. She glanced down at what she wore. Did it disturb him to see her wear another one of her mother's dresses? It was all that she had.

She thought the dress was absolutely beautiful, with its gathered waist and the fabulous lace bordering the bodice, which perhaps dipped too low in front.

The dress was silk, reminding her of China, with a tiny yellow rosebud design on a white background.

Amelia's fingers went to her hair. Streaks of red were finally showing through the black dye that had been applied by her personal serving woman in China. Today she had used a yellow velveteen ribbon to draw her hair back from her face to hang in long, lustrous waves down her back.

Again she looked up at her father. "Papa, do you disapprove of the dress, or perhaps the way I have chosen to wear my hair?'' she blurted, her cheeks pink with embarrassment. "If it is the dress, perhaps you could get me some bolts of cloth. I could sew some new dresses if you like.''

Christopher shook his head as though drawn from a trance. He looked quickly away from her and motioned with a hand toward a window. "Isn't she lovely, just too lovely?'' he said thickly, his eyes now focusing on Lorna at play with her two Indian companions. "So much like you when you were a child. So . . . so full of spirit.''

"I feel no less spirited today as a woman," Amelia said, laughing softly.

Then she flinched when her father frowned over at her, as though he saw much hidden meaning behind her statement of fact. If he knew full well what her spirited nature had caused her to do the previous night, he would disown her. She must learn to choose her words much more carefully!

Wanting to change the subject, having thought of Mei-Ling most of her sleepless night, wondering just how she might ask her father to secure her release from the Haida, Amelia placed a hand on her father's arm and pleaded with her eyes as she spoke.

"Papa, I have a friend who traveled with me from China," she blurted. "She was among those who survived the shipwreck. But, Papa, she was rescued by the Haida Indians. She is at a Haida village even now. Papa, I fear for her safety. Could you . . . *would* you go to the Indians and ask them to release her into your custody? The Haida are cruel. They might hold Mei-Ling for ransom."

She turned her eyes away and shuddered with remembrances of those Suquamish Indians whose flesh had been consumed by the Haida.

"Or they might even do *worse* to her," she said fearfully.

Amelia again turned to her father. "Papa, please do something," she begged. "Please do it *today*."

Christopher squinted down at Amelia. "How could you want anything to do with any of the Chinese?" he asked solemnly. "They bought you just as though you were no better than an *animal*, to do with as they saw fit. They carried you from your homeland and took you to China. Because of this you lost ten years of your life!"

Anger flamed in Amelia's eyes and heart because of his cruel words about the Chinese. They had treated her like a daughter. They had *saved* her life by removing her from the Haida Indians!

"Do not speak so harshly about the Chinese," she said

in a more snappish tone than she intended. "They became my substitute family during those ten years."

She recoiled somewhat when she saw the surprised expression on her father's face. Perhaps this was the first time she had ever talked back to him like a disobedient child.

Then she squared her shoulders, feeling better for her loose tongue. Her father must learn now that she had a mind of her own, for very soon she would show him just how independent she was. When she left to stay with Gray Wing forever, her father would have to understand that it was a decision he could not change.

"Those ten years were *not* wasted," she blurted. "They were happy years . . . even a learning experience. I learned of a different, beautiful culture. I now speak Chinese quite fluently."

She cast her eyes downward, fidgeting nervously with the gathers of her dress. "But, yes, I did miss you and Mother terribly," she softly admitted, wanting to admit openly to her father how much she had missed Gray Wing.

She had felt guilty when at times she missed Gray Wing more than her family!

Heavy footsteps into the parlor made Amelia turn with a start. Her heart skipped a beat when she discovered that Joseph Beria had let himself into the house and was now walking toward her, carrying her mother's shawl.

Amelia was afraid to move or speak. Her fingers began to tremble at her sides, for she now recalled losing the shawl the previous night when Gray Wing swept her into his arms to carry her away.

Oh, Lord, had Joseph found it only now, or last evening? Had he seen her with Gray Wing? How was she to explain having lost the shawl?

"Joseph," Christopher said, going to greet him with a slap on the back, his eyes not having left the shawl. "What have you got there? Where'd you get it?"

Christopher's insides were knotting. He recognized the shawl. It was the one he had presented to his wife on their tenth wedding anniversary. Until now it had been among

his wife's belongings . . . belongings he had given to
Amelia for her own wardrobe now that she had no clothes
of her own.

If Joseph Beria had found the shawl, how had it gotten
outside? Amelia had been here only one night. He thought
she had spent that night in her loft room!

Joseph's blue eyes glinted as he smiled his toothy smile
at Amelia. So much in his expression revealed to her that,
yes, he had seen everything, even her escape with Gray
Wing!

Oh, what was she to do? What was *he* going to do?

Amelia wished she could escape now, for surely she
was about to get the scolding of her life.

"The shawl?" Joseph said in his deep voice thick with
his Russian accent. "Seems you lost it down by the sea
last evening." He eased away from Christopher and
walked determinedly to Amelia, offering the shawl to her.
"I hope you didn't catch a chill last evening after losing
the shawl. The fog carries within it much dampness as it
rolls in from the sea."

Amelia was torn with feelings—fear that her father now
knew that she had been restless enough to wander in the
night, and relief that Joseph did not feel a need to reveal
the full truth to her father.

But was this a trap? Was Joseph going to use for his
own purposes the knowledge that she had been with Gray
Wing? Would he use blackmail to get his way with her?

Amelia did not know whether to give Joseph a smile
with her thank-you, or a look of suspicion laced with hate!

"Thank you, Joseph," she finally said, forcing a light
laugh as she accepted the shawl into her arms. "I was
careless last evening, it seems. I did not even feel the
shawl flutter from my arms!"

"Then that must be proof that you did not catch a chill,"
Joseph said, returning the lighthearted laughter. He
smoothed his long, lean fingers through his golden hair,
then ran them nervously around the crisp white collar at
his throat. "That is good. That is good."

Amelia was puzzled by his kindness. He did not at all

seem to have devious intentions on his mind. The look he had given her earlier was surely only because of being in her presence. She did seem to unnerve him so!

Christopher went to Amelia and slipped the shawl from her arms. He studied it, then her, his green eyes squinting. "So you took a stroll down by the Sound last evening, eh?" he said, now placing the shawl over the back of a chair. "You could not sleep? Is that the reason?"

The glint in her father's eyes revealed to Amelia that he did not say all that he was feeling. She felt trapped. Nothing she could say would cover up the full truth. Her father was a man of many suspicions and doubts.

"Yes, I had a need to get away to . . . to think," Amelia blurted. "My heart . . . my mind was full of worry about . . . about Mei-Ling." Her pulse raced as she thanked the Lord for the words that had come when she so desperately needed them.

Yes! Wouldn't her worry about Mei-Ling sound valid? Only moments ago she had asked her father to see to Mei-Ling's rescue.

Kneading his chin, not knowing whether to believe Amelia, conjuring up the face of Gray Wing in his troubled mind, Christopher took long strides to the window and peered from it.

"Mei-Ling, you say," he murmured, clasping his hands tightly together behind him. "So your worry about Mei-Ling took you from your bed?"

Turning, he nodded at Amelia. "Mei-Ling it is," he said thickly. "If she is what you need to make you happy on this island with Lorna and me, then I shall go and get her for you."

A wicked smile lifted his lips. "Is she lovely, Amelia? Women from China are exotic, to say the least."

Having never seen this side of her father before, where he showed interest in other women besides her mother, Amelia was aghast. "Papa, she . . . she is even younger than I," she whispered harshly.

Then she returned his smile, not wanting to annoy him into not going to rescue Mei-ling from possible torture and death. "But of course she is lovely. And very, very timid and sweet," she quickly, very sweetly, added.

"Timid . . . sweet . . ." Christopher said, again kneading his chin. Then he laughed boisterously, going to hug Amelia. "Daughter, do not worry about this old man who speaks openly of a younger woman. My only interest is in making you happy. I shall gather together several men from this village and go for Mei-Ling tonight. We must travel by night to fool the damned Haida. We will steal Mei-Ling away before the Haida can even blink an eye!"

"Tonight? You will go tonight?" Amelia asked unguardedly, an anxiousness soaring through her not only to know that this night she would see not only Mei-Ling but also Gray Wing. While her father was on his mission, she would be on her own! She had promised Gray Wing she would return to be with him this night. The time it would take her father to travel to and from the Haida village would afford her the chance!

Casting Joseph a nervous glance, she wondered if he would travel with her father or remain in the village to spy for him. . . .

The moon was a full circle this night; the fog seemed to melt beneath its brilliant light. Her arms aching from paddling the canoe across the bay to Whale Island, Amelia puffed and wheezed as she dragged the vessel onto a spit of sand. She had removed her shoes, knowing that she would have to jump in the water to beach the canoe. She had tied her skirt up about her knees. Her hair was coiled into a tight bun atop her head.

The sea breeze cold and damp on her bare legs and feet, almost numbing the tip of her nose in its briskness, Amelia reached inside the canoe for her shoes. After putting them on and lowering her skirt to hang to her ankles, she began to walk away from the canoe when suddenly from behind her strong arms swept about her waist.

Gasping, she turned with a start, then smiled with relief when she found Gray Wing there, looking down at her with eyes heated with desire.

Amelia smiled up at him, touching his smooth cheek with her hand. "Must you always sneak up on me in such a way?" she asked, laughing nervously. "Gray Wing, you move so soundlessly, it is as though a cat were approaching!"

"Silence is needed when the Suquamish is on the hunt," he said, his eyes twinkling. "Tonight the hunt was for you instead of game."

He glanced at her beached canoe. "But my search has ended here."

His fingers went to her hair and loosened it from its tight confines. "My woman has come as promised."

His smile faded. "Your father? Is he again in the deep sleep induced by the firewater? Will you be with Gray Wing for long?"

He wove his fingers through her hair, encouraging it down across her shoulders. He frowned deeply. "It is not good that Gray Wing come second in your heart to your father! You should be here, not in the white man's village catering to drunken father! Gray Wing will not tolerate this much longer."

The anger, the threat, his voice carried, startled Amelia. She took a step away from him. "What do you mean?" she gasped, paling.

"Gray Wing only tolerates your absence now because of your concern for your sister," he said sullenly. "But for only a short while, my *la-dida*. Only for a short while longer."

A chill coursed through Amelia's veins. She not only had to grow used to her father's attitude toward women but to Gray Wing's as well. It seemed that neither man understood that she had a mind of her own and that she would do as *she* pleased, *when* she pleased.

Though she loved Gray Wing with all her heart, she would not let him run her life. She had witnessed too much of men demanding obedience of their women in China. She had thought it was wrong then. She thought it was wrong *now*. In her heart and soul she believed that men and women were equal!

Jerking her skirt around, Amelia began to stomp toward the canoe. "Perhaps I was wrong to come to you tonight," she said icily. "Perhaps I shall never return again!"

Gray Wing's insides recoiled at her reaction to what he had said. His eyebrows rose quizzically. In the Suquamish Indian village women did not turn away from the men.

Yet he must remember that Amelia was not Suquamish! She would not react like the Suquamish women to anything.

Ah, but her difference made her even more fascinating! He loved her more for her independent nature. This was why she had survived many traumas in her life. Her strength and courage would even enable her to thrust a harpoon into the body of a whale when the time came to prove her worth as the wife of a Suquamish chief! She would make him proud in the eyes of his people!

Determined not to let her go all that easily this night, having thought of her this entire day, Gray Wing took a wide step and blocked her way. He wove his fingers through her hair and drew her into his embrace. He pressed his lips softly, enticingly, against hers, glad that she was not struggling to be set free. She had spoken in anger only to prove that she was the spirited female that she was. She was not angry at all. . . .

Gray Wing's tongue brushed Amelia's lips lightly. "Ladida, let us not argue," he whispered, his hands trailing along the supple lines of her back, then lower to clasp her buttocks through the thinness of her silk dress. "Let us make love. Over and over again let us make love."

Amelia was becoming breathless as his hands now began creeping up the skirt of her dress, setting sparks of fire along her flesh wherever he touched her anew. Soon he would be touching that part of her that was already inflamed with wanting him.

Coiling her arms about his neck, she looked up at him, his face so keenly handsome in the glow of the moonlight. "You understand that I am doing everything possible to make things right in our life?'' she softly questioned, gasping as his fingers forged onward, now caressing her.

She closed her eyes when his tongue tasted her lips as he seductively moved it over them. ''Tomorrow, Gray Wing. I will speak to Father tomorrow. I will let him know of our feelings for each other. Even tonight he is traveling to rescue Mei-Ling from the Haida. When she is safely with me, we both shall travel to your island to stay!''

Gray Wing drew away from her, his pulse racing. He had to force himself not to smile devilishly down at her because of what she had said about her father and his foolish notion of going to the Haida village. If her father escaped unharmed, the Haida would come later to perhaps kill him.

The Haida would not tolerate interference by the white man. They now traded only with the Chinese. They did not need the white man's tools any longer. Soon the Suquamish, too, hoped to break all bonds with the white traders. It was something that needed to be done. Especially now. Once Amelia was no longer a part of that white community, bonds *would* be broken.

But perhaps the Haida would do Gray Wing a favor. If they *did* kill her father, would not things be so much simpler for Gray Wing?

''But what of your sister?'' he asked, his voice warm against her cheek.

''If I must, I shall bring Lorna with me,'' she said, her eyes suddenly flying open to see his reaction. ''My father does not have time for her. He would be glad to . . . to be rid of her, I am sure. A Mexican maid has taken care of her since my mother's death. She does not love Lorna as I do. Even you could love her as much, Gray Wing. You have much love in your heart. Wouldn't you share it with my sister?''

She could not believe that she was actually saying these things. She had tried and tried to come up with a suitable plan for her sister, a plan that would give Amelia the opportunity to be with Gray Wing.

Oh, yes. It was the perfect solution, if only he would—

agree and if only she could leave the trading community with Lorna without having to fight her father for the possession of her sister!

But this decision was the best. Her father's moods changed as quickly as a chameleon changed color. And he loved vodka too much. That even made it dangerous for him to be in charge of a nine-year-old daughter!

"She will be welcome," Gray Wing said thickly. "Your sister will be welcomed by Gray Wing and his people, just as you are welcomed, my *la-dida*."

Amelia melted into his embrace, sighing. "From the very beginning it was meant for you and me to be together," she murmured. "From that moment of our first eye contact I knew that it was our destiny to meet and love. I shall never regret leaving my father's ship that day to come to you. Never."

Sweeping her up into his arms, Gray Wing carried her from the beach, past many outdoor fires where meat turned on the spits. His people watched and for the moment accepted this decision of their chief to again take the white woman into his dwelling.

But in their hearts they awaited the day when she would have to truly prove herself worthy, the day when she would be given the harpoon, to test her ability to the fullest!

Having felt the many Indians' eyes on her, studying her, Amelia was glad to once again be inside Gray Wing's house. The fire burned low. Furs were spread on the floor beside it. Gray Wing deftly removed Amelia's clothes while she splayed her fingers across his powerful chest, awaiting the moment their bodies would once again fuse as one.

Gray Wing eased the last garment away from her, then stood before her with his arms folded across his chest.

"Now your turn," he said, his eyes lit with fire.

He smiled down at Amelia as her fingers went to the waistband of his breechcloth and began slowly lowering it, all the while smiling seductively up at him. When she sank to her knees to remove the garment from his ankles, she emitted a low gasp when she felt his hands reach around, to fully cup her breasts.

Tossing his breechcloth aside, Amelia let Gray Wing turn her and spread her out on the otter furs. She beckoned for him with outstretched arms, then trembled, flooded with emotions, as he leaned over her and kissed her with an easy sureness. Every secret place became his as his hands moved along her body. A soft cry of passion rose from deep within Amelia when he entered her with a gentle thrust.

Sweet currents of warmth swept through her as his lean, sinewy buttocks moved and he began moving within her with his masterful strokes. He cradled her within his arms now, kissing her hard . . . kissing her long. She clung to him, overcome with a feverish heat that seemed to match his own.

Gray Wing groaned huskily as the pleasure built within him. He smiled to himself as Amelia locked her legs about him, drawing him closer . . . closer. . . .

His fingers bit into her buttocks, clasping her to him so that they did not part for even that one second as she rode with him to that plateau of wondrous sensations only sought and found when in each other's arms.

Passions crested . . . passions peaked.

And then it was too soon over and again they were lying breathless in each other's arms.

"My *la-dida*," Gray Wing whispered into Amelia's ear, yet his thoughts were elsewhere. It would be so much simpler if Amelia's father did not return alive from the Haida village.

Perhaps . . . perhaps . . .

Seventeen

❧ ❧

Timidly Mei-Ling slipped the blouse of woven plant fibers off her shoulders, her eyes cast downward. Yet her insides revealed her true feelings of what being with Red Eagle truly meant to her. No longer did his tattoos make her cringe. No longer did she even notice them. His lips and hands had awakened her to feelings never experienced before. Red Eagle was instructing her in all ways of making love, and she welcomed his teachings.

In China the women did not share such maddening, sensual moments with a man. It was the woman's duty to only give pleasure, not to receive it. . . .

"Mei-Ling, my Mei-Ling," Red Eagle said huskily, lowering his lips to her brown-budded breast as the blouse dropped away from her.

His hands began smoothing the grass skirt down her slim and perfect body, glad that she was not as shy this time as times before. Though her eyes were still cast downward as though she felt timid and ashamed, her body would again speak to him of her intense passion while with him.

Mei-Ling was like a butterfly emerging from a protective cocoon, eager to experience all of life that had been denied her.

"Red Eagle love Mei-Ling?" she whispered, caressing his cheeks with her trembling fingers. "Mei-Ling good love partner? *Ai?*"

After removing his loincloth, Red Eagle urged Mei-Ling down beside the indoor fire onto a thick pallet of furs. He took her hand and rested it on his throbbing member.

"*Ah-hah,* you are everything to me," he said thickly. He held her hand in place on his shaft with his own. "Do you not feel how you fill my shaft with need of you? Do you not feel how it is almost alive with such need? It throbs so, Mei-Ling. It throbs so!"

Mei-Ling shivered with desire. She began to move her hand on him, smiling when he groaned out his pleasure against her cheek as he stretched out above her. With a boldness she did not believe she was capable of, she lifted her legs about his waist and guided his manhood inside her. She felt her breath catch in her throat, thrilled by how magnificently he filled her.

Slowly she moved her hips, encouraging him to do the same. It seemed that suddenly it was she doing the teaching! She could tell that he was happy with this change, for his lips trembled with the intensity of his feelings as his mouth closed hard upon hers.

His mouth seared her lips, their bodies tangled. Mei-Ling caressed his shoulders lightly with her fingertips while his fingers kneaded and pinched her nipples until the pain became sheer pleasure.

Reveling in this moment of wondrous sharing, when Mei-Ling did not have to wonder about Vona-Lee and whether or not she was all right, Mei-Ling let herself enjoy . . . fully enjoy. She gave in to all of the feelings mounting inside her as Red Eagle tantalized her with his hands and mouth. She moaned softly and continued to move with him.

Yet she began to find her mind drifting. No! She would fight it! She would not think of Vona-Lee *or* China! She would force herself to forget!

But at the back of her mind there were continued, constant flashes of remembrances of China and how she missed it and its people. Though she had found love in Red Eagle's protective arms, she did not know whether she could ever be fully content to stay with him.

Oh, somehow she must find a way back to China. It was truly where Mei-Ling belonged!

Red Eagle drew away from Mei-Ling, having felt her stiffening, her hesitation, within his arms, as though her thoughts were elsewhere. "Mei-Ling, where does your mind carry you?" he asked, his eyes devouring her innocent loveliness. The slant of her almond-shaped eyes, and her tiny facial features again almost stole his breath away.

But something *was* carrying her thoughts away from this moment of lovemaking. He did not like this. He feared her longing for her homeland of China! He had seen it too often in her eyes. He had tried to grow used to each night when she preferred to sit down by the sea, alone, to look across the wide breadth of water, lost in her thoughts of missing China. Perhaps she would forget one day. She must!

Yet even if she did, was there still another obstacle to overcome? Red Eagle lived in dread of the day when Gray Wing would arrive, demanding Mei-Ling's release. He hoped Mei-Ling would voice her decision to stay at the Haida Village!

Tears silvered down Mei-Ling's cheeks. She shimmered inside as Red Eagle's gentle fingers smoothed the tears away. "*Aie-yah,*" she murmured. "Mei-Ling sorry, my *hao-hanza,* my brave and lusty one. Yet my mind does stray to home more often than not."

"Even while making love?" Red Eagle said thickly, hurt dark in his eyes. "Is there nothing I can say or do to make you forget? Have you not found much love and happiness with the Haida? Do not my arms warm your very soul?"

He waved a hand in the air. "Life would now be *cultus-kopa-nika,* nothing to me, without you," he declared loudly. "Until you came, my life was guided by thrills only achieved by hunting and challenging my enemies!

And as for women! Neither thrills nor pleasures were ever as magnified with other women as with you. What thrilled your existence, Mei-Ling, before Red Eagle? Just being Chinese could not have been enough, and I know from that first time with you sexually that no man before me had yet pleasured you.''

A blush colored Mei-Ling's cheeks pink. She smiled timidly up at Red Eagle. "*Hao-hanza*, Mei-Ling does love you," she murmured. "But Mei-Ling has loved China and its people for so much longer! It will take time to erase its memory from my heart.''

Red Eagle held her lovely, delicate face between his hands. "*Hwah!* You will try?" he said huskily. "You will try to love only Red Eagle?''

Mei-Ling giggled softly. She cast her eyes downward. "*Ai*, Mei-Ling will try." Her lashes slowly lifted, feeling the command of Red Eagle's eyes drawing them open. "It surely should not be all that hard, for I already love you from the depths of my soul!''

"*Klas-ka,*" Red Eagle said, his eyes sweeping over her with a raging hunger.

His mouth touched her lips wonderingly, then showered heated kisses over her taut-tipped breasts, again taking his masterful strokes inside her. His hands took in the roundness of her breasts. He moved slowly within her with acute deliberation.

Then he moved faster with quicker, surer movements, feeling her hunger in the seeking pressure of her lips.

Mei-Ling's fingers bit into Red Eagle's shoulders as an incredible sweetness swept through her. She opened herself wider and her hips responded to his lovemaking in rhythmic movements that matched his. Her whole body quivered as her senses warmed, his tongue now exploring the inner edges of her lips.

Within Red Eagle's torrid embrace, Mei-Ling could feel the sensations building . . . building.

Together they shuddered with a rushing onslaught of passion, but still they could not part. Lips met, hot and hungry. Fingers explored, coaxing the senses again into a blaze of urgency. Again Red Eagle moved within her, finding it possible to prolong ecstasy and to find that peak of passion again so soon.

His mouth dipped down and fastened gently over Mei-Ling's breast, eliciting a quiet moan from deep within her. Her fingers dug into the tautness of his buttocks, reveling in this renewed moment of togetherness. There was only now. There was only Red Eagle.

Oh, China, it was . . . so very, very far away!

In the light of a jack-pine torch thrust into the ground at her side Mei-Ling's face was still flushed from the frenzied lovemaking, and yet she could not stay away from the sea. As she had every night since her rescue by Red Eagle, Mei-Ling sat on the beach alone, watching the hypnotic rise and fall of the waves, knowing that perhaps these waters could at one time have touched China's shores.

Oh, Mei-Ling was so envious of the sea because of this!

No matter how hard she tried, she could not erase the loneliness from her mind. She had been raised Chinese, something wondrous to behold, and she could not so easily cast it from her mind. Even though she had found passion in Red Eagle's arms, she knew that if she was given a choice, even tomorrow, between returning to China and staying with Red Eagle, she would choose China over him. The love of her country was thicker in her blood than the love of a man.

Longingly she looked from one avenue of the sea to another, thinking that perhaps a Chinese ship would arrive soon to trade with the Haida. She could request passage on the ship's return voyage to China!

Yet something fearful stirred within Mei-Ling's heart. She knew that Red Eagle would not give her up so easily. Determined to have her as his own, he might even hold her captive. What then would she do? Would she grow to hate him?

Sobbing, leaning her face into her hands, Mei-Ling was torn with feelings. Fate was not being kind or fair to her. She had lost so much. Yet she thanked Buddha for sparing

Vona-Lee's life. Perhaps they could see each other soon, to place sunshine in each other's hearts because of their devoted love.

The sound of paddles dipping in the water from somewhere close by made Mei-Ling's head jerk up. Her heart raced when she saw several canoes shadowed by moonlight quickly approaching.

Pushing herself to her feet, she looked desperately over her shoulder toward Red Eagle's village, hoping that someone was within yelling range, for danger was surely near!

Her heart fluttered, fear built inside her when she saw nothing but stoked fires burning outside the wigwams. Red Eagle had given orders to his people to leave Mei-Ling to her own private thoughts when she wished to go to the beach to meditate. His people were obedient, for all of them had retired into the privacy of their wigwams.

She was alone! Utterly alone!

Mei-Ling's head jerked around. Except for the approaching canoes she was alone.

Panic rose inside her. Her throat was so constricted from fear she could not even scream.

Then her gaze went to the torch beside her. *Wei!* It was casting its flickering golden light upon her. The men in the canoes had surely already seen her. She must run. She must go to Red Eagle, to seek shelter within his protective arms! He had assigned himself as her protector. At this moment she understood just how much she needed him. She had been wrong to wish to leave him!

Her knees weak, her heart pounding so hard she was rendered breathless, Mei-Ling turned and began to run up the rocky shore.

But her breath caught in her throat when she heard the thrust and then the drag of the canoes upon the beach much too close behind her. When she heard the scramble of feet approaching, she sobbed and stumbled, then felt a light-headedness overcome her when strong hands grabbed her.

One hand painfully covered her mouth to stifle her sobs

and screams. The other clasped hard onto a wrist. Her eyes were wide with fright as she was forced to turn and face her abductor. The light of the torch was behind the man, only illuminating the shape of his body, leaving only dark shadows on his face.

"Mei-Ling?" Christopher gruffly asked in a whisper, closely scrutinizing Mei-Ling. He glanced over at Joseph Beria who was beside him. "By God, Joseph, it *has* to be the Chinese lady Amelia was talking about. Just how many would be on the Haida island? Dammit, Joseph. I haven't ever heard of *any*."

Joseph nodded. His teeth were pearly white in the night as he smiled gently down at Mei-Ling. "Don't be afraid," he tried to reassure her. "We're friends. We've come to rescue you . . . to take you from this island of Haida Indians."

Mei-Ling's eyes were wild over Christopher's clasped hand. She struggled to get her wrist free. She did not trust these Americans. And she wanted to stay where ships journeyed to and from China! She did not want to be taken into the heart of America and never be heard of again. Surely a Chinese woman would be used as a slave. Mei-Ling was used to having her own serving woman. She would never withstand the grueling duties of being a slave.

"Goddammit, Christopher," Joseph growled. "You're hurting her. You're scaring the hell outta her. Explain who we are. Tell her about Amelia."

Just speaking Amelia's name sent a thrill through Joseph he did not want to feel. Though it was quite obvious that Christopher's intentions were that Amelia would become his wife, *she* would never allow it.

Damn. How could she have fallen in love with a savage?

But she had. Joseph had witnessed their torrid embrace . . . their torrid kiss. Amelia was probably with the damn savage now. She was a spitfire of a lady, daring and wonderful!

"All right, all right," Christopher said in a low grumble. He leaned down into Mei-Ling's face. His eyes narrowed. "Now listen here, Chinese miss, we aren't going to hurt

you. If I let you go, you must not run away or scream.
We've come to take you to Amelia. She asked us to. Don't
you want to go to her?''

Fear had stolen all of Mei-Ling's logic and reason; her
mind was a blank for a moment as she tried to sort out
who this Amelia was that he was talking about.

Then her eyes gleamed and she felt relief flooding her
when she was capable of recalling Vona-Lee's American
name. It was Amelia! These men knew Vona-Lee. Vona-
Lee had even sent for her!

Eagerly Mei-Ling began nodding her head. She mumbled
against Christopher's clasped hand, then spoke anxiously as
he eased his hand away.

''Vona-Lee! *Aie!* Mei-Ling wants to see Vona-Lee!''
she blurted. Her gaze swept over the two men who seemed
in charge of this mission. ''Are you . . . are you kin of
Vona-Lee's? Is this why you care so much?''

Joseph idly scratched his brow. ''Who is Vona-Lee?''
he asked, forking an eyebrow.

Christopher frowned at Joseph. ''Joseph, Mei-Ling is
referring to Amelia,'' he whispered harshly. ''Vona-Lee
was Amelia's Chinese name.''

''Well, I'll be damned,'' Joseph said, laughing.

Christopher's gaze swept up and down the beach. He
looked from silent wigwam to wigwam. Strange that no
warriors were guarding the village. But there had been no
warring between the Suquamish and Haida since Gray
Wing and Red Eagle had become chiefs of their respective
tribes. In peaceful times no guards were needed.

Laughing throatily, he placed an arm about Mei-Ling's
waist and began to guide her back to his canoe. ''Amelia
will be relieved to see you,'' he said. ''She was afraid you
might have been eaten as a sacrifice to the Haida gods.
They're known to do that, you know.''

Mei-Ling's insides grew numbly cold. During her wondrous moments while in Red Eagle's arms, she had forgotten Vona-Lee's tales of the Haida consuming the
Suquamish people's flesh before Vona-Lee's very eyes.

It was hard for Mei-Ling to comprehend . . . the fact

that the man she loved could be a cannibal! Perhaps she had been wrong to love so freely . . . so quickly . . .

Her head bowed, Mei-Ling welcomed Joseph's gentle arms as he drew her up into them to carry her to the canoe. . . .

Amelia's night-black hair spilled over her shoulders and tumbled down her back as she walked arm in arm with Gray Wing along the beach. Though she knew the hours were passing much too quickly and that her father could be returning to the small trading post across the bay from Whale Island, she did not want to hasten her farewell with Gray Wing. She would not always be as free to come to Gray Wing as she had been these past two nights. And she always carried fear around inside her heart that Joseph Beria knew more about her escapades than he had voiced aloud. Should he draw attention to her comings and goings to her father . . .

Casting all worries and doubts aside, Amelia looked up at Gray Wing. The moonlight was spilling its silvery beams across his face, allowing her to feast upon his finely chiseled features. A sensuous shiver traveled through her when his muscular arm drew her even closer to his side as the canoe in which she had traveled came into sight.

"Time has almost come for me to leave you again," she said, smiling up at him. Then her smile lightened. "I must arrive back at the trading post before my father." She turned to Gray Wing and squeezed his hands. "Just imagine! I soon will see Mei-Ling! How wonderful it will be, Gray Wing. I do so love her. She is like a sister to me."

Gray Wing's spine stiffened. What was happening on the Haida island? Who would be spared? Would the fight take long? Just when would Amelia know whether or not her father survived the battle?

The moonlight suddenly revealed more to Amelia than the handsomeness of the man she loved. On down the beach, only a bit beyond the spot where she had beached her canoe, she saw movement in the dark. She cringed when she recognized several of the Chinese crewmen bent low over the sand, digging clams by the light of the moon. With so much happening so fast in her life, with so much on her mind, she had forgotten the Chinese prisoners taken from the shipwreck. With Gray Wing, her father, her sister, and Mei-Ling so prominent on her mind, she had not thought to ask or wonder about the Chinese prisoners.

"Lord," she gasped, placing her hands to her throat. She glanced up at Gray Wing, then back to the laborers. Most of the Chinese men wore only torn shreds of clothing. They were gaunt! Had they even been fed?

"Gray Wing, those men!" Amelia said, gesturing with a hand. "They . . . they look so pitiful. Please do not treat them so unjustly. They meant no harm to you. It was Du-Fu Jin who gave the order to run you down. It was not the fault of the crew that they had to obey orders. They would have been beheaded had they not!"

"Someone must pay," Gray Wing grumbled, folding his arms stubbornly across his powerful chest. "Fat Chinese trader is dead! These men are not. They will be slaves forever."

Amelia's jaw tightened. She frowned up at Gray Wing. "I thought you were much gentler than this," she fumed. She turned and stomped away toward the canoe. She stopped abruptly when Gray Wing grabbed her by a wrist and swung her around to face him. "Let me go, Gray Wing. I have nothing else to say to you."

"The Chinese sailors mean this much to you?" he growled. "That you would turn your back on me?"

"It is not so much the men as it is my disappointment in *you*," Amelia said. "You could let the men go. Let them choose whether to stay or to leave."

Gray Wing looked over his shoulder at the laborers. They had become a nuisance more than a help. It would be easy to do as Amelia asked without seeming less of a man in her eyes by looking as though he did this only because she asked him to.

Shrugging, he turned his eyes back to her. "Gray Wing

will think about it," he said smugly. "Gray Wing will see."

Understanding more about him than he gave her credit for, knowing that he would not just suddenly release the men because she had asked him to, Amelia eased into his arms and hugged him. "That you will even consider it is enough, Gray Wing," she murmured. She raised her eyes, welcoming his lips as they came to her soft and sweet.

Then she fled from his arms to the canoe, excitement welling inside her over seeing Mei-Ling soon. It seemed that everything was falling into place; everything in life that would make her happy was suddenly there for the taking. . . .

The great Chinese ship with the writhing dragon designs along its sides moved at a steady pace. The wind fluttered its sails; the waters were dark as Bai-Hua Jin stood at the railing watching . . . watching. . . .

"*Hao, hao*, good! The waters of the Pacific will soon deliver me to America!" he whispered to himself, his crew obediently manning the ship. "Vona-Lee, this time I will not take no for an answer. No concubine will ever please me as you would. Vona-Lee, your *hao-hanza*—brave, lusty one—is drawing nearer . . . nearer. . . ."

His silk robe rustling in the wind, his dark hair drawn into a queue that hung down his back in shimmering black, Bai-Hua went to his private cabin. Taking a pipe filled with opium, he stretched out on a bed of many silk blankets and let himself get caught up in the rapture of visions of how it would feel to have Vona-Lee in his arms.

She would do everything he commanded. *Everything*. . . .

Eighteen

As her canoe swept to the shore in the shadow of the
trading post warehouse, Amelia's heart turned icy cold,
for her father's canoe was moored on the beach along with
the rest of those who had accompanied him to rescue Mei-
Ling. Though she was happy that her father had returned
unharmed from the Haida village, and hopefully with
sweet Mei-Ling, it was Amelia who was now in trouble.
There was no way to deny where she had been these past
hours. As she was the day she had left the ship at age
thirteen, she was, at age twenty-three, caught in another
disobedient act.

But this time her father would not have to guess with
whom she had been. He would have more than a suspicion
of what she shared with Gray Wing. She was now a woman
with a woman's needs. Gray Wing was a virile, handsome
man with the same needs!

A shiver raced up and down Amelia's spine when she
beached the canoe. Smoothing out the wrinkles in her silk
dress, she began walking up the dirt road to her father's
house where lamplight shone bright from all of the win-

dows, even the loft bedroom window, which was now her own private room.

What was she to do? What could she say?

She felt that she was walking into a trap set by her irate father! Surely he had known from the start that he would not be gone very long to the Haida village. Had he purposely taken Joseph Beria with him to give his older daughter free reign while they were both gone, to then return and catch her in her loose behavior? Had Joseph seen her with Gray Wing and told her father? Was Joseph to blame for what was soon to happen to her?

Hate swelled in her heart for the toothy Russian!

Anxious to see Mei-Ling regardless of any sort of punishment planned for herself, Amelia squared her shoulders and stomped on up the steep road. Sometimes she forgot her age. She was *not* a child. Her father would soon see just how much of a woman she was! When she left to stay with Gray Wing, her father would understand that she was not a child awaiting a scolding every time she did something he did not approve of!

Yet no amount of reassurance would make her dread confronting her father any less. He had always been a strict disciplinarian. She had been compelled, always, to do as he ordered. Even now she shuddered at the thought of him shouting at her when she arrived at his house after her daring escapade across the bay.

But she would not cower before him this time! She would not! Her pride would not allow it!

Her knees weak, Amelia climbed the steps to the porch that surrounded the house on three sides. Lamplight poured golden from the windows. Within she could hear voices . . . *male* voices. One was her father's; the other was Joseph Beria's. They were partners not only in business but in shaming her as well!

Amelia swallowed hard and combed her fingers nervously through her hair, then boldly opened the door and stepped inside. Her gaze swept around her, absorbing everyone in a flash of a second. Her heart swam with joy when she saw Mei-Ling standing at the far side of the room dressed in some sort of plant-fiber skirt and blouse, her almond-shaped eyes wide with anxiety. Oh, how happy Amelia was that her best friend in the world was unharmed by the Haida! She so wanted to run to her and embrace her, but the threat of her father and the fire in his eyes, and what he held in his hands, kept Amelia at bay.

Glancing from Joseph to her sister Lorna, whose eyes were filled with a strange sort of guilt, and then back to her father, Amelia paled. It was as though everything was closing in on her, for her father's eyes were on her, accusing.

Scarcely breathing, clasping her hands nervously behind her, Amelia once more looked at what her father held stretched out between his hands. Her insides ached, recalling the very moment Gray Wing had given her the necklace of animals' teeth. It had been her lifeline during those ten long years when she was apart from him. Now it meant everything bad, but only to her father!

"So you have returned, have you?" Christopher roared, the necklace now swaying from one hand. "Restless again, Amelia? Where did your restlessness take you this night? Canoe riding? One canoe was missing. Where did you take it, Amelia? Wasn't it enough that I went to fetch Mei-Ling for you? Or was that a ploy to get me off the island so you could go to Gray Wing?"

Amelia did not reply. She held her chin firmly in place, having already decided not to argue with him. He was her father. She must still show respect, though at this moment in time she felt close to hating him. To have found the necklace he would have had to ransack her bedroom. She had no rights in the eyes of her father. No rights at all. . . .

Christopher went to Amelia and stood over her, glaring. He shook the necklace in the air. "Where did this come from?" he shouted. "Lorna found it while playing in your room. Seems she likes playing hide-and-seek beneath your bed. She saw it dangling down from the springs. She thought it was pretty, so she showed it to me as soon as I arrived back from the Haida village."

His face grew red with anger. "You would have hidden

this necklace only if you did not want me to see it," he shouted. "It's an Indian necklace. Where did you get it? Who gave it to you? Did you get it last night? Did that damn savage Gray Wing give it to you? Were you with him again tonight? Did you have the audacity to go to him?"

Amelia was speechless, paling with his each and every word. She looked over at Joseph. He looked embarrassed for her instead of glad that she was being treated so unfairly by her father. That had to mean he did not approve. Also he had not told her father about having seen her and Gray Wing together even if he had, for her father was groping for facts. Her father was not sure at all of what truly had happened.

"Papa, you are—" Amelia finally managed to say, but her words were cut short when she became aghast at what her father was doing.

Pieces of her heart tore away as he began to jerk the Indian necklace apart and grind the broken pieces into the floor with the heel of his boot. So quickly Gray Wing's precious gift was taken away from her forever!

Oh, how badly she wanted to cry, but she would not give her father the pleasure of seeing her behave like a child, even though he treated her like one.

Instead, she squared her shoulders and glared at him, saying nothing.

"Joseph, you see a lot about my daughter that you like, don't you?" Christopher said, smiling crookedly at his partner. "Don't you think she'd make you a decent wife? You've been talking of being lonesome. Well, Joseph, you need not be lonesome any longer. Marry Amelia. She's just a mite too much for me to handle, with her liking savages so much. Marry her and make her respectable again, Joseph!"

"What . . . ?" Amelia gasped, taking a step backward. "Papa, you can't mean what you are saying. You can't treat me so . . . so unjustly. You are no better than the Haida, who traded me to the Chinese. I'm not just a thing to be bargained over. How can you?"

Joseph's eyes were wide, two pools of blue, as he looked from Christopher to Amelia, torn with feelings. It was his deepest desire to claim Amelia as his wife, but he did not like the way it was coming about. He had never liked Christopher's coldness, only having gone into partnership with him because of his good business sense, and tonight was proving just how dastardly the damn American could be!

He smiled awkwardly at Amelia, trying to reassure her that things were going to be all right, at the same time truly believing that she would be better off with him, instead of her father or the savage. It was in her best interest that he accept her father's offer. Joseph would then have a woman to grow old with. He would be so kind to Amelia that she could not help but learn to love him!

"If she'll have me I will gladly take her as my bride," he said thickly, his eyes heavy with passion as he raked them over Amelia, already seeing her as his wife, for he knew that once Christopher got his mind set on something, there was no changing it.

"No!" Amelia cried, doubling her hands into tight fists at her sides. "I won't have you. I . . . I'll have none of this." She went to her father and clutched his arm. "Papa, if you love me, truly love me, you will put a stop to this foolishness now. I won't marry Joseph or any man whom I do not love."

Christopher's eyes wavered beneath the pleading in Amelia's eyes, yet he had made a decision that he felt was best for his daughter. "Joseph," he said, never taking his eyes from Amelia's. "Go wake up the preacher. Tell him to meet us down by the piers when the sunshine breaks along the horizon. We will have us a wedding at the break of dawn. Tell the preacher we will be going by canoe to the banks of the Suquamish Indian village to perform the ceremony. We have a thing or two to prove to that savage Gray Wing. He'll see Amelia married off right before his eyes. He won't dare to touch her again."

Amelia's head was swimming, her father's words one confused jumble inside her brain. She eased away from him, unable to comprehend a father who would treat a daughter in such a way ever, for any reason. It was as though she had just stepped into a nightmare, one that was making her cold inside and out.

She shook her head, trying to clear her thoughts, but her father's words remained, haunting her. "You would do this?" she gasped. "You not only force me to marry someone I don't love, but also in front of Gray Wing and his people? You must hate me as much as you do the Indians, Papa!"

Flipping the skirt of her dress up, wrapping it in her arms, Amelia began to run toward the door but was stopped when her father's tight grip circled about her wrist. When she was forced to stop and turn to face him, she saw a trace of sadness in her father's eyes. But it was not enough to prove anything to her.

"Let me go," she demanded, no longer seeing him as her father. He was a man she had never known. "I will not marry Joseph. You will not shame me by forcing me to. And Gray Wing will not be forced to witness such shame and humiliation, either!"

With his free hand, Christopher withdrew a key from his breeches pocket. "Daughter, you were taught many years ago that when I said something I meant business," he grumbled. "This isn't any different except that this time I am stopping you from making a horrible mistake. If you marry a savage, your children will be savages! Did you ever think of that?"

He shook his head. "This is the only way, Amelia," he said hoarsely, guiding her toward the stairs that led to the loft bedroom. "I'll lock you in your room until morning. If I have to, I'll hold a gun on you until you speak the words of marriage with a decent, civilized man. Joseph is the man. Accept that and you'll be better off for it!"

Amelia grimaced with pain as she tried to break free of her father's grasp. "You plan to lock me in my room?" she cried. "Papa, what has happened to you? Did the death of Mama harden you so? Did it make you go crazy?" She looked wildly toward Lorna. "And what's to become of

Lorna if I marry Joseph? I thought you wanted me to look after her.''

"Lorna will be under your care,'' Christopher said sullenly. "Once you've had your wedding night with your husband, I'll send her over to you. She'll be much better off, Amelia. You'll make a proper mother for her once you are married and have a home of your own to raise her in. The older she's gotten the harder it's been for me to see to her properly. She needs a woman's gentle hand, and I'm not speaking of a damn Mexican maid. A sister's a good substitute for a mother, as I see it.''

Amelia stumbled up the first step, sobbing. "You're doing all of this to me because you still blame me for Mama's death, aren't you?'' she cried. "You're wrong, Papa. Wrong! Mama was sick all the time, way before I left that ship and got stranded on Gray Wing's island. You know she was frail and sick all the time. Having a baby was the worst thing she could have done. It wasn't my fault she got pregnant and then died having the child!''

Hearing Lorna's quiet gasp, Amelia looked quickly toward her. Oh, now what had she done? She had spoken too openly in front of Lorna. Now Lorna knew. She knew about a mother who had died too young. Lorna could now possibly carry the blame around inside her heart for as long as she lived. It seemed that Christopher Storm had struck two blows this night by forcing Amelia to say things that she should not have said.

Amelia winced as her father pushed her on up the stairs. When Mei-Ling spoke in a shocked whisper, revealing her fright at what was happening and what was to happen, Amelia turned with a start toward her.

"Mei-Ling,'' she said, beckoning with her free hand. "Oh, Mei-Ling, what will happen to you?''

"You can take Mei-Ling to your new home,'' Christopher growled. "Don't fret over her. She's yours to do with as you see fit. You'll need a maid, won't you?''

Amelia turned and looked at her father, numbness seizing her from head to toe. No. He was not a man she knew or even wished to know. Not only was her mother dead to her, but so was the father she had known as a child. . . .

"Papa, Mei-Ling will never serve in the capacity of a maid, and, Papa, no matter what you force me to do, you should know that, yes, I do love Gray Wing!" she hissed. "Now and forever. And somehow I *will* be with him. Somehow . . ."

Feeling that Mei-Ling had spent too much time alone, wondering about her welfare, Red Eagle threw an otter skin cape about his shoulders and left his wigwam. After lighting a torch, he walked toward the beach, looking for Mei-Ling's torch, which she always carried with her. When he saw a faint golden light pulsing in the darkness of the sky, he smiled and approached it, knowing that to find the light would be to find Mei-Ling.

His footsteps light, his heart merry, he hurried onward.

Then his footsteps faltered and his heart skipped a beat when he saw the torch thrust into the rocks on the shore, yet nowhere in sight could he see Mei-Ling.

Now running, his gaze sweeping the shore, up one side and down the other, Red Eagle began to grow cold with hate. He had trusted Gray Wing enough to let Mei-Ling sit by the sea alone, and Gray Wing had broken this trust, for it must be Gray Wing who was responsible for Mei-Ling's absence! Gray Wing's warriors had come once for Mei-Ling, and she had been denied them. This time they came and did not ask, but *took*!

Carrying his torch, brushing the cape from his shoulders, Red Eagle bent low and studied the signs on the beach where it was obvious that several canoes had only recently landed. "*Ah-hah*, yes," he whispered. "Gray Wing! He stole my Mei-Ling away!"

His eyes dark with despair and anger, Red Eagle looked across the bay. "Gray Wing, come sunrise Red Eagle will bring much into your life," he hissed. "Death most prominent of all!"

Nineteen

❧ ❧

The sea gulls' wings caught the orange light of the early morning sun as they wheeled overhead, their eyes dark as they watched two canoes move toward Gray Wing's village. Her silk dress clinging to her, its low-cut bodice revealing the upper lobes of her breasts, Amelia trembled in the morning dampness.

Drawing her mother's shawl more snugly about her shoulders, she clutched it hard. Her eyes were filled with fiery anger over what was about to take place. Her hair shimmering in its mixed shades of red and black, now more red than black, she jerked her head around and looked at the other canoe, where two of her father's men sat on either side of Mei-Ling. If Amelia did not go through with this farce of a marriage to Joseph, her father had threatened to return Mei-Ling to the Haida.

Her father had told her that he and his Russian cohorts had rescued Mei-Ling from a stake to which she had been bound and where she was being held to be the Haida's next sacrifice to their gods.

The two women had been kept apart since Mei-Ling's

rescue, so Amelia had not been able to question her friend as to whether her father had told the truth or a lie.

Amelia's gaze swept over Mei-Ling, seeing the woven plant-fiber skirt and blouse the Haida had given her to wear. Would she have been dressed in such a way to be offered to the gods? Wouldn't she have been nude?

Regardless of how Mei-Ling was dressed or how wildly frightened she looked at this moment, Amelia could take no chance that what her father had said was true. She knew very well the practices of the Haida. Though they now had peaceful relations with the Suquamish, that did not mean their customs had become more civilized.

Glowering over at her father, Amelia felt her insides tighten into a cold numbness. It was her father who had changed. He was less than civilized. Something had made him crazy these past years. Would losing a loved one—a wife—do such a terrible thing to a man?

Or had greed turned him into this thing that was less than human? He seemed to prize wealth over family now. Wasn't that the reason he had journeyed to these parts those ten years ago? To become wealthy?

He had achieved that wealth many times over while Amelia was in China, missing him!

"Ready your Bible, Preacher," Christopher said, rising to his feet in the massive canoe. He swept his coattails aside, revealing holstered pistols. "You've got a wedding to perform."

Amelia looked over her shoulder at the preacher cowering on the seat behind her, his white collar matching the paleness of his face and beady eyes. Joseph sat pale-faced beside him in his dark suit and neck scarf, with a diamond brooch thrust into its folds.

This was the first time she had not seen Joseph's teeth shining with a most unnerving smile. He seemed as uneasy about the wedding as Amelia. And he had good reason! Gray Wing was soon to be awakened, to discover what was about to happen in the waters close to his island.

Gray Wing would be ready to kill! Would not the bridegroom be one of Gray Wing's first choices?

Amelia's eyes took in other canoes silently approaching around the bend in the Sound. The shine of many rifles could be seen in the light of the rising sun. Her father had left no stone unturned. There were too many Russians already taking aim on the Indian village. Gray Wing could do nothing. Nothing! Or his people would be massacred!

Amelia flinched as though shot when her father lifted a pistol and fired it into the air to awaken and alert Gray Wing to what was about to take place. Tears burned at the corners of her eyes as she clung desperately to the canoe, watching for the first stirrings in the village.

Dogs scampered to the beach, barking and showing their teeth. Horses neighed in the distance. . . .

"All of you stand up, dammit," Christopher said, frowning at Amelia, then at the preacher and Joseph. "I said it's time to have a wedding, so let's have one. Gray Wing will soon stick his head out his door. Let him see what's happening. I've got a thing or two to prove to him. He'll know it's best not to toy with my daughter."

"Papa, please don't do this," Amelia said, pleading with her eyes as she moved slowly to her feet. "Don't you know how wrong you are? And, Papa, you'll not only never be able to trade again with the Suquamish, but you won't even be able to sleep at night. Gray Wing, he'll—"

Christopher smiled smugly down at Amelia. "Don't you know that I have that all figured out?" he said. He gestured with a wave of a hand toward Joseph. "Come on, Joseph. Time's a wasting!" His eyes gleamed down at Amelia. "Once that savage sees that you're legally married, he won't bother with you *or* with revenge. A savage at least understands ownership of women!"

Her father's crazed laugh sent gooseflesh crawling along Amelia's skin. She swallowed hard as Joseph stepped to her side, the preacher now facing them.

Movement out of the corner of her eye alerted her gaze elsewhere. She blanched as she watched Gray Wing walk stiffly to the bluff that overlooked the beach. His breechcloth rustled in the wind, the muscles of his copper body were taut and golden in the early morning light. His eyes were two points of fire as he shifted them from side to side, assessing the problem at hand. He was not sure, just yet, what was soon to transpire. He surely did not know the purpose of preachers!

Then his gaze locked with Amelia's: Though he was not yet sure about the reasons for this morning visit, he understood the threat of all the rifles pointed toward his village. It was obvious that not only he was being held hostage by the rifles, but also his woman!

Gray Wing could do nothing.

Not yet. . . .

The preacher looked from Amelia to Joseph. He opened his Bible where he had placed a purple velveteen marker. "Clasp your hands together, please," he said, clearing his throat nervously. He looked over his shoulder at the throng of Indians gathering along the shore, then back at the couple whose hands had not yet touched. He understood what was happening here and he did not like it.

But when Christopher Storm gave orders, everyone in his employ obeyed.

Even a man of God!

Joseph eased his hand toward Amelia's. He smiled awkwardly down at her, his golden hair fluttering in the breeze around his collar. "Let's make the best of this," he whispered. "Amelia, I plan to take care of you. You won't ever want for a thing. I've riches you wouldn't believe."

"To hell with your riches!" Amelia whispered back to him. "Joseph, you'll never have me as a true wife. Never!"

Joseph winced, but still seeing this as best for her, especially now after seeing the savage looking at her with eyes of fire, he took her hand and boldly held it. "We'll see," he whispered. "We'll see."

"Dearly beloved, we are gathered together this day . . ." the preacher began in his monotone, his every word tearing pieces of Amelia's heart away.

Focusing her eyes just over the preacher's shoulder, she saw nothing, felt nothing. . . .

• • •

Red Eagle's canoe moved ahead of the others manned
by his warriors. The muscles of his shoulders were taut as
he dipped the paddle in and out of the water; his eyes were
watching the rising of the sun in the morning sky. Soon
he would arrive in Gray Wing's village. Soon blood would
be spilled along the shore like an extension of the fire in
the sun! He had not wanted to fight, but Gray Wing had
left him no alternative. When Gray Wing had chosen to
steal Mei-Ling away, he had the same as signed a declaration of war with the Haida!

The tall Norway spruce shadowed the waters of the
Sound as Red Eagle guided his canoe closer to the land.
Great outcroppings of stone overhead echoed the lapping
of the paddle, the break of the waves. . . .

Raising a fist into the air, casting a warning look over
his shoulder at his warriors, Red Eagle let them know that
they only had to travel around a bend and they would be
at Gray Wing's village. Mei-Ling would soon be his once
again. He would never let her go again. He would kill
anyone who stood between him and his Chinese woman!

As he slowed the movement of his paddle, now only
inching his canoe along, Red Eagle's eyes were two slits
of hate as he guided his vessel around the bend.

Then his heart fluttered a warning inside his chest when
he saw the line of canoes just ahead, and within them,
Russians poised with rifles.

Quickly circling his canoe back around, Red Eagle motioned for his warriors to bank their canoes. With a thudding heartbeat he beached his own vessel, then crept along
the shore, staying hidden beneath the cover of madrona
trees, his warriors trailing stealthily along behind him.

Sliding a dagger from a sheath at his waist, Red Eagle
found a cover of jutting rocks on the beach and very slowly
crept around it to see why the Russians were armed and
obviously holding the Suquamish at bay.

Slowly his gaze moved about, seeing the Suquamish
lined up on a bluff above the shoreline. Then he looked at

the two canoes that floated some distance from the others
that were filled with armed Russians.

"Al-ah!" he gasped, seeing Mei-Ling in one of the canoes, obviously imprisoned between two men. She was
not with Gray Wing? Gray Wing had not stolen her?

His gaze then went to the other canoe. His eyebrows
forked as he wondered just what kind of ceremony was
being performed and why was it being celebrated in a
canoe so close to the Suquamish Indian island?

His insides strangely twisting, Red Eagle looked up at
Gray Wing, now knowing that he had been wrong to accuse his friend of stealing Mei-Ling. It was obvious that
Gray Wing was not pleased with what was being acted out
before his very eyes as he was held at gunpoint and forced
to watch.

"The white woman!" Red Eagle harshly whispered,
again looking toward the canoe where the ceremony was
being performed. "She is not with Gray Wing! Why?"

Red Eagle did not understand anything about this ceremony that he was a witness to, except that if Gray Wing
had not stolen Mei-Ling away, then the white men must
have done it!

Clenching one hand into a tight fist, his face twisted
with hate, Red Eagle now knew he had been ready to kill
the wrong person.

His gaze went to Christopher Storm and locked there.
If anyone was responsible for what was happening here,
he was. It was a known fact that this man hated Indians
and only traded with them to become wealthy by acquiring
the wonderful, rich otter furs from them.

This white man's daughter was the woman Gray Wing
had fallen in love with. She appeared to be speaking words
of forever with another man. And would not the evil
American be cruel enough to hold the wedding in front of
Gray Wing so as to torture him?

Hate swelling inside him, Red Eagle emitted a low growl
when he studied Christopher Storm's smug smile. *"Ah-
hah,"* he whispered. "He is the one whose blood will

soon be spilled. Tonight. Tonight! And I must do it before Gray Wing has a chance to do it first!''

The hours had been long since the wedding. Amelia dreaded having to go to bed with Joseph. Though he had treated her cordially enough, it was a man's privilege to demand much from a wife, even if the wife had been forced into marriage.

This was a mockery of a marriage, one that Amelia did not ever plan to consummate. If she had to thrust a knife into Joseph's heart to keep him from taking her sexually, she would! Then she would flee. She would go to Gray Wing. He would protect her from harm forever!

"I am so sorry," Mei-Ling said, hugging Amelia to her as they both climbed the staircase to the bedrooms. ''If it had not been for me, you would not be married to someone you do not love. If only I could have talked to you before the wedding, explained that I did not fear being returned to the Haida.''

Her eyes were suddenly downcast, her face flushed. ''Red Eagle was nothing but sweet to me,'' she murmured, holding up the skirt of the cotton dress Amelia had loaned her, as she crept on up the stairs. ''He would have never let anyone harm me.'' She raised her eyes, revealing the fear in their depths. The low-cut bodice of the dress accentuated Mei-Ling's frailty; her breasts were tiny buds in comparison to Amelia's. ''I still fear that he will come and . . . and do horrible things to your father for stealing me away!''

"As you have seen, my father fears nothing and no one," Amelia sighed. "Not even Gray Wing. He thinks Gray Wing will accept the fact that I now belong to another man." She smoothed her silken hair back from her shoulders. "Papa has much more to fear from Gray Wing than he does from Red Eagle. Gray Wing will not give me up easily."

Along with Mei-Ling, Amelia took the final step onto the landing that led to bedrooms in two directions. Mei-

Ling was to occupy a room at the far end of the hallway from the one Amelia was forced to share with Joseph.

"Mei-Ling, my worries about my father are behind me," she said, swinging around to take Mei-Ling's hands. She squeezed them fondly. "He does not deserve any worries I might have had for him. It is Lorna I am now worried about. If Gray Wing or Red Eagle should come tonight to seek vengeance, Lorna could be in danger."

Amelia's lashes swept over her eyes with frustration. "But it seems that there is nothing more I can do. Papa chose to keep Lorna with him this one last night." Her lashes rose slowly. She was ashen in color. "Papa did not want Lorna to disturb my . . . wedding night," she said, almost choking on the words.

Mei-Ling flew into Amelia's arms, sobbing. "I will pray to Buddha for you tonight," she whispered. "Things will be all right. You shall see, Vona-Lee. Oh, if only we had not left China! Nothing has been right since!" Her own words stung her heart, as she recalled the beautiful moments in Red Eagle's arms. *Ai*, loving him surely had been right. She had felt so wonderfully beautiful while with him. But that was in the past. So quickly . . . in the past.

"It was never meant for me to be in China," Amelia said, easing Mei-Ling from her arms. She swept her gaze over Mei-Ling's loveliness, her utter sweetness, a sister, yet not a sister. "But, no, I shall never regret having been there. For there was you."

She hugged Mei-Ling desperately, but when she heard a door creak open down the hall she knew what must be done. Yes, she would go to the room, but she would not let the terrible Russian touch her!

"*Mei-ya-faze,*" Mei-Ling said, hanging her head as she turned and walked to her bedroom. "Nothing to be done!"

Amelia moved determinedly to the bedroom where she found Joseph standing in the doorway, awaiting her arrival. His toothy smile almost sickened Amelia as she eased past him into the room.

But the plushness of the furnishings and the cozy blaze of the fire on the hearth somewhat eased the pain of being with him. She was bone-weary from this traumatic day. She needed rest, much . . . much rest.

Her gaze moved slowly about. A great bedstead filled one side of the room. A sofa and two matching chairs, upholstered in a bright flowered pattern, had been placed before the fireplace.

On a cherrywood table beside the fire two tall stemmed glasses were filled with clear vodka; the open bottle stood beside them.

Thick carpeting muffled Amelia's footsteps as she walked farther into the room. Her breath was stolen away when she saw a lacy chemise spread across the bed, so sheer and revealing that it would leave nothing to the imagination.

"You think I would be shameful enough to wear such . . . such a garment in your presence?" she said, tilting her chin stubbornly. "Joseph, you are fooling yourself by pretending that I am actually going to behave like a wife."

Half stumbling, Joseph went to the wardrobe and opened it, displaying to Amelia's feasting eyes an assortment of nighttime attire for her to choose from. His hands shuffled through the finery. "Wear what you will be most comfortable in, Amelia. I shall even turn my head while you dress. Even while you slip into bed."

Her emotions drained from remembrances of how Gray Wing had looked when she was forced to speak the words of marriage with Joseph, Amelia went to the wardrobe and grabbed the least revealing garment, then turned and eyed Joseph speculatively.

"I have no choice but to retire for the night because I am very, very tired," she said. "And, yes, please do turn your back so that I can undress."

Her eyes wavered as she glanced from the comfortable bed to the divan. "But I shall sleep on the divan tonight and *every* night, Joseph. You will not get the opportunity to grab me in my sleep and take advantage of me."

Joseph sauntered over to her. He placed a finger beneath her chin and tilted it up, so their eyes could meet and hold. "It is not my desire to ravage you," he said hoarsely. "I understand that you did not wish to be my wife. But in time, Amelia, this must change. You *are* my wife. A wife is expected to . . . to do her duty. You know that.''

"Never!" Amelia cried, jerking away from him. When Joseph grabbed her, clasping her hard in his arms, she screamed.

But soon the scream was muffled by his kiss, and his teeth tore into the flesh of her lips as though he was biting her. Amelia pushed and shoved at his chest. But nothing could stop Joseph's knee as he began to pry Amelia's legs apart, the skirt of her dress no deterrent to what he had in mind.

Her heart beating wildly, she feared what the next moments would bring her. Though Joseph had promised, it seemed that the passion that was building inside him had gotten the best of him. He had surely been without a woman for many months, for there were no desirable unwed women on this dreaded island.

Her fear was so great that Amelia did not hear any noises on the beach, nor would she, for Gray Wing was moving through the night swiftly, as stealthily, as a cat on the prowl. He was plunging his dagger into one Russian's chest, then another. . . .

Some distance out to sea, Red Eagle and his warriors were paddling their canoes soundlessly through the water. It would not be long now before they turned the Russian trading post red with blood!

He would make them pay . . . all of them!

Twenty

Everything inside Amelia rebelled against what was happening. She splayed her hands against Joseph's chest, pushing with all her might. But nothing could dissuade him from the madness that had suddenly seized him. His kiss was hot and wet on her lips as his one hand held her head in place, his other hand groping through the silk of her dress for a breast.

His knee probed harder between her thighs causing her to suddenly lose her balance. When she began to fall backwards, still Joseph did not give up. He followed Amelia to the floor, leering down at her, his teeth never whiter as the glow of the fire illuminated them.

"Amelia, you're my wife," Joseph said huskily, kneeling over her. He pinned her wrists to the floor and held her in place with the sheer force of his body. "How can I not take you on our wedding night? How can you expect me to wait? I'm human, Amelia. I'm a man with needs."

His lips brushed against Amelia's, his breath hot and almost stinging against her cheek as he now rested his lips there. "Love me, Amelia," he said, almost in a gurgle.

"I can make you feel good inside and out. My way of making love has to be better than any savage's."

The word "savage" and the implication of the word—that Gray Wing was less than human—fired Amelia's insides with renewed hate. She glared up at Joseph, then spat into his face.

"That is what I think of you and your opinions of Indians," she hissed.

She smiled smugly when Joseph's eyes widened with disbelief at what she had done. She saw a shudder course through him as he released one of her wrists to wipe at the spittle running down his lips.

This gave Amelia the opportunity she needed. With one hand free she could go far in defending herself. Reaching for his hair, she coiled her fingers through his golden locks and began to pull. His loud yowl filled the room. He grabbed her hand and tried to pull her fingers free, only causing her to hang on for dear life and pull harder.

"Dammit, Amelia, quit that!" Joseph said, then in a rush of words said something indiscernible to her in Russian as he eased his body away from hers, knowing that was the only way to make her let go of his hair. She had won this night. But tomorrow night he would have her if he had to tie her to the bed!

Amelia released his hair and eyed him dangerously as he slunk away from her, his face red with humiliation. Combing his fingers through his hair, he gulped down a glass of vodka, then climbed into bed in his loose cotton nightsack, turning his back to Amelia.

Sighing with relief, Amelia crept to the divan and stretched out atop it, yet did not take her eyes off Joseph. Something told her that she was safe enough this night to go to sleep. But first she would make sure Joseph was asleep.

She watched, scarcely breathing herself, as Joseph's breathing became more relaxed. When one of his hands dangled limply from the bed, she knew that he was asleep, and so she smoothed her skirt down over her legs and decided it was safe to catch a few fast winks herself. She had never been so tired. Wrestling with Joseph had been the last straw, it seemed.

Sleep. She . . . must . . . get some sleep.

Her lashes fluttering closed, long and thick over her pink cheeks, Amelia felt herself beginning to drift. But when she heard the squeaking of the door behind her, she tensed; her eyes flew wide open. Fear soared through her like wildfire. Were there other Russians who were just as woman-starved? Would one dare come and attempt to accost her with Joseph in the same room?

Amelia did not know what to expect, since so much was happening to her so quickly. Never would she have expected her father to force her into marriage.

Especially at gunpoint!

Would not his choice to use weapons so freely give any other man who might venture to have her think twice? Christopher Storm was not a man to be trifled with. He was a man Amelia would no longer call Father. From this night forth, he was nothing to her!

Slowly turning her head in the direction of the door, wishing that she had a weapon of her own with which to defend herself, Amelia watched the door inching open, farther . . . farther . . . farther. . . .

Then her insides splashed warm. Relief flooded her senses when she saw Gray Wing moving stealthily into the room, his breechcloth covering only a small portion of him, his eyes dark pools when he saw her lying there alone.

She could see his eyes sweep over her, looking for signs of having been harmed in any way, including sexually. He could not tell by looking at her that she had only moments ago fought hard for her virtue, had saved herself fully for him.

Rushing to Amelia, Gray Wing fell to a knee before her. As she pushed herself up on an elbow, his hands touched her face gently, his eyes still searching over her. "You are not harmed?" he harshly whispered. "The white man did not harm you?" His eyes narrowed into two angry slits. "You are still clothed. He did not force you sexually? You do not sleep in the white man's bed. He did not force you to behave like a wife?''

Amelia stifled a giggle behind her hand, afraid she might awaken Joseph. ''You ask too many questions at once,'' she returned in a whisper. ''But I think it would be safe to reply with one word: no. None of those things you feared happened.''

She was not going to tell him just how hard she had fought to occupy the divan alone this night. Perhaps if she did not anger Gray Wing any more than he already was, Joseph's life would be spared. She did not wish to see his blood spilled over something her father was truly responsible for!

Taking her breath away, Gray Wing swept her quickly up into his arms. She clung about his neck as he carried her from the room. She looked adoringly up at him, this man who risked everything to rescue her this night.

Her insides knotted as she wondered just how he had gained entrance to Joseph's house. Had he killed many Russians to save her from a fate worse than death? Had he killed her father after finding out in which house she could be found?

''My father—'' she gasped, paling. ''Did you . . . ?''

''If you ask if Gray Wing killed the man whose heart is made of stone, the answer is no,'' he said, carrying her cautiously down the long hallway.

''But how did you know which house I was in?''

''My scouts came before me. They watched through the day. They returned to the Suquamish village and told me which house they saw you coming and going from.''

''Then my father was not drawn into tonight's activities? You had no need to?''

''Only Russians who got in the way were killed,'' he said bluntly. ''More will get killed should they try to stop my escape with you!''

Shivering at the thought of Gray Wing doing anything violent, Amelia momentarily looked away from him. As he reached the staircase, her eyes were drawn elsewhere. Her heart frolicked inside her chest when she looked to-

ward the closed door of the bedroom in which Mei-Ling
lay sleeping.

Eyes wild, Amelia looked up at Gray Wing. "Mei-Ling
must go with us," she blurted, fearing what her father
might do with Mei-Ling should she be left behind to fend
for herself. "Gray Wing, we can't leave her here. She
would be in danger. That is why I allowed the marriage
to take place. Only for Mei-Ling! Only for Mei-Ling!"

Gray Wing heard the pleading, the sincere love for the
Chinese lady in Amelia's voice. He stopped abruptly and
looked in the direction of her gaze, seeing the closed door.
He glanced from Amelia to the door, then nodded.

"We will also take her," he said flatly. "But we must
hurry. More Russians might awaken at any moment and
make escape dangerous."

Easing Amelia to her feet, Gray Wing accompanied her
to Mei-Ling's room, which was golden from the light of a
fire burning bright in the fireplace close beside the bed on
which she lay. He watched as Amelia awakened Mei-Ling
and explained what was happening, all the while helping
Mei-Ling into her plant-fiber skirt and blouse.

After Mei-Ling was fully clothed, Gray Wing went to
her and smiled down at her, to reassure her. "It is good
to have a friend who cares so much," he said, gesturing
with a hand toward Amelia. "She treats you like a sister!"

Amelia's insides splashed cold when the word "sister"
reached her heart like a knife stabbing her there. She
turned and grabbed Gray Wing by the arm, her eyes wide.

"Lorna!" she gasped. "My sister, Gray Wing. What
will become of her if I leave her behind? My father seems
to have lost his mind. My sister will surely not be safe
with him any longer."

Gray Wing clasped her shoulders with his fingers. "Do
you wish for your father to die this night?" he asked solemnly.

Amelia was taken aback by his question . . . by the tone
of his voice in which the question was asked. "Why do
you ask that?" she asked, paling.

"The chances are that I would have to kill your father

to steal your sister away from his dwelling," Gray Wing
said, his dark eyes imploring her to make a wise decision.

"No!" Amelia said in a shocked whisper. "I do not
hate my father that much. I could never hate him enough
to want him dead. He *is* my father. I can never forget
that."

"Then you must forget your sister," Gray Wing said
flatly. "At least for tonight," he quickly added, his eyes
twinkling.

"Do you mean that . . . that you could come for her
later?" Amelia asked, hope rising inside her. "Could you?
Would you?"

"After tonight—after the slaughter of so many men who
take orders from your father—he will not have much to
say about anything," Gray Wing told her. "He will not
venture to further anger the Suquamish. He will know how
quietly, how swiftly, the Suquamish daggers kill."

A shudder embraced Amelia in its utter coldness at the
thought of so many dying. And all because of her?

No! She would not blame herself for this madness tonight. Her father was responsible. He had made all the
wrong decisions!

"All right." Amelia sighed, knowing that she had no
choice but to do as Gray Wing suggested. And surely
Lorna was in no true danger. She had been her father's
sole responsibility until now and had survived quite
healthily! So would she this one more night!

"We must leave," Gray Wing growled. "Now! We have
already taken too much time!"

Amelia and Mei-Ling clung to each other as Gray Wing
led the way down the stairs, then on outside where darkness shrouded them in its black cloak. But it was not too
dark for Amelia to see the many bodies lying in pools of
blood on the ground.

Covering her mouth with a hand, she emitted a choked
sob. Gray Wing placed an arm about her and ushered her
on toward the bay, with Mei-Ling clinging to Amelia's
other side.

Looking back over her shoulder at her father's house,

Amelia gazed at her sister's bedroom window. She prayed that she was not wrong to leave Lorna behind. When her father discovered the massacre, would he not become even more crazed than before?

Oh, that Gray Wing could come on the morrow and steal Lorna away before her life was in stark danger!

When Amelia was finally safe in Gray Wing's canoe, she was glad she was no longer in sight of the trading post as the canoe sped silently through the water across the bay. Covering her face with her hands, she silently prayed over and over again for her father's soul, then for Lorna's safety. . . .

The convoy of canoes moved effortlessly, silently, through the water. Red Eagle's muscles flexed as he drew his oars through the dark abyss of the Sound. His nostrils flared as he looked anxiously toward the trading post in the distance. Ships lay still in the midnight hour, their sails fully reefed. Nothing was stirring, only the beams of moonlight as it spread its silver glow over the land and the houses back from the bay.

Determinedly Red Eagle drove his paddle harder and more quickly through the water. He looked over his shoulder at his warriors, who were following his lead. Daggers and clubs were ready. Death would come to the Russians and the Bostonian this night. They would pay for stealing from the Haida! Stealing a woman who belonged to the chief was much worse than stealing precious furs and trade blankets!

After finally reaching the shore, Red Eagle beached the canoe, and when his warriors had done the same and were moving stealthily along behind him, he moved silently past the pier, then stopped short, stunned by what he saw. *"Al-ah!"* he whispered with surprise, his eyes scanning the land, seeing the Russians spread out, dead.

He gazed farther still, up the road, seeing many more dead Russians. "Who did this?" one of his lead men asked, glancing back at his warriors.

Chief Red Eagle stepped to his side. "It is the work of

the Suquamish," he said. "Only the Suquamish know the art of killing swiftly with the dagger as well as the Haida. Gray Wing and his warriors have been here before us!"

Red Eagle turned around, peering at the two tall houses in the distance, trying to distinguish between them, to know which of the two belonged to the Bostonian. "Mei-Ling!" he growled. "Did Gray Wing come for white woman and also take Mei-Ling?"

Anger scorching his insides at such a thought, Red Eagle began to run up the hill, his men behind him. He shouted out orders for his men to check the one large house for Mei-Ling, while he checked the other. If she was not in either house, he would have another decision to make!

Angrily tearing through the small village, killing any Russian who stepped from his doorstep to see who the newest intruders in the night were, Red Eagle finally reached Christopher's house. Rushing inside, he stopped only long enough to order a warrior to check the downstairs rooms. He assessed the stairs and the long hallways that ran along the center of the house.

His gaze moved up to where the staircase led to more hallways, and Red Eagle crept stealthily up the steps, nodding to a warrior to follow his lead. At the upstairs landing, the warrior turned left, Red Eagle turned right.

Room by room Red Eagle checked for Mei-Ling, finding her nowhere.

And then he came to the master bedroom. With anger he threw the door open, hurried inside, and stood over the bed, glaring down at Christopher Storm, who awakened from a sound sleep with a start just as another of Red Eagle's warriors came into the room, carrying Lorna.

Christopher began inching away from the threat of Red Eagle. He looked toward Lorna whose mouth was bound closed with a strip of buckskin and whose eyes were wild with fear above the gag. Her hands were tied behind her. In vain she wriggled and squirmed.

"What do you want?" Christopher asked, not recognizing his voice, which was so weak and strained. "Red

Eagle, hand over my daughter to me this instant. Do you hear?''

Red Eagle glanced over at Lorna, then looked down at Christopher and laughed hoarsely. ''Your daughter *is* still alive,'' he tormented. So quickly Christopher did not have a chance to draw away from him, Red Eagle was at his throat with the point of a dagger thrust against the tautness of his skin.

''If you want your daughter, give me Mei-Ling!'' Red Eagle growled, his eyes flashing.

Christopher dared to swallow, the knife·so sharp and piercing against his throat. ''Mei-Ling?'' he whispered harshly. ''You do all of this for Mei-Ling? Dammit, Red Eagle, you can have her. She . . . she is with my other daughter, Amelia, and her husband, Joseph. Go to Joseph's house.''

The scrambling of many feet into the room made Red Eagle whirl around, dropping the dagger from Christopher's throat. He looked from warrior to warrior. ''You found Mei-Ling?'' he questioned, forking an eyebrow. ''Where is she? Or was I right? Did Gray Wing take her away?''

Joseph Beria was pale and gaunt as he was shoved into the room, dressed in his long nightsack. He looked pleadingly from Christopher to Lorna and then to Red Eagle.

''Joseph?'' Christopher said, scrambling desperately to the far side of the bed away from Red Eagle. ''Dammit, *say* something! What's happened to Amelia? Why isn't she with you? Where's . . . where's Mei-Ling?''

''They're gone,'' Joseph said, wincing when the Indian who had half dragged him from his bed to Christopher's house dug his fingers painfully into his arm. ''You aren't aware of what has happened outside, are you?'' he said, his voice cracking in his fear.

''Happened?'' Christopher asked, looking from the curtained window back to Joseph. ''What *has* happened?''

"The damn Suquamish savages killed half the Russian population," Joseph dared to say, cowering as the Indians glowered at him for having used the word "savage" in their presence. "Amelia? Mei-Ling? They're gone. They've been taken. Gray Wing must have done his dirty business before Red Eagle and his warriors arrived to do *theirs*!"

Christopher's gaze moved slowly toward Red Eagle as the Haida chief, in turn, looked at him. His insides grew numbly cold, for he feared what the next moments would bring. Though it had been some time since he had prayed, something led him to begin reciting the Lord's Prayer to himself.

"You are responsible!" Red Eagle shouted, glaring down at Christopher. "Only you!"

As Red Eagle plunged the dagger into Christopher's heart, Lorna flinched as though the weapon had pierced her flesh instead of her father's. Her eyes flooded with tears. She felt a dizziness overtake her when she watched Red Eagle wrench the dagger from her father's body and wipe the blood from his weapon into a blanket spread across the bed.

Red Eagle looked at Lorna. A smile lifted the corners of his lips as he went to her. Thrusting the dagger back into its sheath at his waist, he grabbed Lorna into his arms and forced her tear-filled eyes to look up into his.

"Do not cry," he comforted. "You are not going to be hurt. Your father was bad. He deserved to die. Remember that, little one. He deserved to die!"

Lorna glanced at the lifeless form of her father, then at Red Eagle. She again wriggled and squirmed, trying to get free. When Red Eagle removed the gag from her mouth she screamed, "Papa! Papa!" Over and over again she screamed. . . .

Carrying Lorna against her will, ignoring her continued screams, Red Eagle went to Joseph. "Your life will be spared but for only one purpose," he said flatly.

"You are to go to Gray Wing and carry the message that I now have the white woman's sister. If she wishes to have her sister returned to her, there can be an equal exchange for her, with Mei-Ling's return to me. Go to Gray Wing on the morrow. Tell him, Russian. Then return to Russia. You and your kind are no longer wanted in these parts!"

Tears brimmed in Joseph's eyes; he was so relieved that his life had been spared. He ducked his head in order not to see Lorna, not wanting to think about her being taken as a hostage for bargaining. *He* was alive. That was all that mattered to him. He did not even care that he had lost a wife on his wedding night. She did not deserve any consideration, for she was a damn Indian-lover!

"Whatever you say, I'll do," he said hoarsely, flinching when the Indian who was still holding him tightened the grip on his arm. "Just let me go. I'll leave even now for the Suquamish Indian village if you want me to."

"No. That would not be wise," Red Eagle said, glad that Lorna had finally grown quiet. He ignored how she flinched when he began stroking the red curls that hung long and sleek down her back. "We must be given time to take the white girl to the village. Gray Wing can come to bargain for her tomorrow!"

Joseph nodded. "Whatever you say," he said thickly. "Tomorrow is just fine with me."

Chuckling, Red Eagle walked from the room, then shouted orders for his warriors to follow him. Carrying Lorna, he walked over the blood-drenched ground to his canoe. Forcing Lorna to lie on the floor of the canoe on a thick bed of furs, he smiled down at her.

"Tomorrow you will again be with your sister," he reassured her. "Close your eyes and sleep, little one. No one will harm you."

Lorna sniffled. She wiped her nose with the back of her hand, a shudder coursing through her when she glanced up at the house in which her father lay dead. Nothing that had happened this night seemed real to her. It was as though she was dreaming.

"Amelia," she whispered, closing her eyes as she snuggled down into the furs. "Amelia . . ."

She felt herself drifting . . . drifting. . . .

Twenty-One

꧁ ꧂

Light kisses upon her brow, then on her lips, caused Amelia to awaken with a slow, lazy smile. Gray Wing was looking down at her from where he was kneeling astride her, supporting himself with the palms of his hands on either side of her head. She knew she must look seductive to his dark, feasting eyes, for she now realized that she wore nothing at all, except a trade blanket that had slipped down away from her.

Yawning, stretching her arms above her head, oblivious of her nudity, Amelia felt free, and, oh, so alive. It was wondrous to awaken in Gray Wing's Suquamish home, so near to his comforting, loving arms. His kisses had sent a spiraling of warmth throughout her, warming her even more than the fire in the pit beside her.

Amelia's nose twitched as she recognized the aroma of salmon cooking over the fire. She realized that Gray Wing had been awake much longer than she to have kindled the fire and prepared the food for the early morning meal. She felt as though she had slept forever!

Once she had arrived at Gray Wing's home the previous night at such a late hour and had found rich blankets and

furs awaiting her beside the banked fire, it had been easy
to curl up beside Gray Wing and drift into a deep sleep,
blocking from her mind the deaths left behind at her father's trading post.

"Mei-Ling!" Amelia gasped, rising up on an elbow to
look desperately about her.

Then her shoulders relaxed and she smiled awkwardly
up at Gray Wing. "I forgot for the moment," she said,
almost in an apologetic tone. "You saw to Mei-Ling's welfare last night. She is probably sleeping soundly in the
house close beside yours."

Her smile faded when she recalled with whom Mei-Ling
would be staying—Gray Wing's prostitute slaves! He had
ordered the slaves to take Mei-Ling in and make her comfortable.

Amelia now knew that before Gray Wing learned that
she was still alive, these slaves, who lived nearby, were
the women he had sorted through each night to choose
one special lovely female to satisfy his lusty, fleshly needs.

Until last night Amelia had not been aware of this. The
slave prostitutes had remained hidden from her by Gray
Wing's orders, surely to save embarrassment on Amelia's
part.

But last night the prostitute slaves had been needed for
something besides pampering Gray Wing. They had been
assigned to care for Mei-Ling.

"Do not worry about the Chinese lady," Gray Wing
said, smoothing his fingers through Amelia's tangled hair,
straightening it back from her face. "My slaves will feed
and bathe her. She will be given Suquamish clothes to
wear. She will be happy she is no longer with your father
or the Haida. She will learn in time that this is her home."

His lips quivered into a smile as the fire's light captured
the red roots pushing the black dye farther away from
Amelia's scalp. "Perhaps in time she will even become
Suquamish at heart, just as the Chinese tried to train you
to be Chinese."

His gaze studied Amelia's long, lustrous hair, his fingers enjoying the soft texture of it, his nose savoring its

scent, so similar to that of the petals of a rose. There were full red strands now interwoven through the black, where the dye had washed completely away.

Day by day she was becoming more like the girl he recalled that first day he had seen her.

Yet now she was a woman. She was *his* woman. No white man who called himself a preacher could change Amelia's and Gray Wing's sincere feelings of love for each other. In Gray Wing's eyes and heart, the wedding between Amelia and Joseph Beria meant nothing at all.

"Today my warriors will go for your sister," he said, easing down beside Amelia, placing the soles of his feet close to the warmth of the fire. "Then, my *la-dida*, you will go with me in a canoe to practice hurling the harpoon. Soon you must prove your worth to my people. You will become my wife."

The word "wife" tore at Amelia's heart. She turned her eyes away from Gray Wing, recalling the forced wedding, the moments with Joseph when he had tried to force himself upon her sexually.

The words of the preacher haunted her. In the eyes of God, she was married! Oh, what was she to do? If she and Gray Wing made love, she would be committing an unpardonable sin!

Then her jaw tightened with stubborn determination. Though words were spoken over her and Joseph, it had been at gunpoint! The marriage could not be looked upon as a valid one. It was not fair to think that anyone would accuse her of adultery when in her heart, and in the eyes of the law, she truly was not married at all.

Gray Wing sensed that something was troubling Amelia. He turned to her, stretching the full length of his body against her back, the touch of her silken flesh against his own driving him almost insane with need.

Restraining himself from drawing her around to crush his mouth hard upon hers, to fully claim her as his, he instead gently turned her so that she was facing him.

Twining his fingers through her hair, he looked at her with passion-heavy eyelids. "My *la-dida*, why are you so quiet?'' he said huskily. ''Why do you turn your back to me? Are you not happy with my decision to steal you away from the man you were forced to marry? Do you not wish to be here with Gray Wing?''

His brow furrowed with a frown. ''Do you not look forward eagerly to the time when you will thrust a harpoon into the body of a massive whale? Does not the thought thrill and excite you?''

Amelia choked back a sob, seeing a sort of wounded look in Gray Wing's eyes. He deserved more from her than silence. He had risked much to rescue her from the clutches of a man she could hardly bear looking at, much less being married to. She owed Gray Wing, oh, so much.

Pressing herself fully against him, letting him cradle her close, she savored the feel of his sleek chest against her breasts. She sighed heavily. ''Gray Wing, never doubt my love for you,'' she murmured, clinging to him. ''But so much has happened that I do not know what to do about. Yesterday, the wedding—''

Gray Wing leaned partially away from her, his face a mask of determination. ''Wedding?'' he said, laughing throatily. ''Do not call what I was forced to witness a wedding. Your true wedding will be with Gray Wing!''

Amelia's eyelashes lowered, thickly feathered against her cheeks. ''Yes, you are right,'' she said, nodding. ''It was no true wedding yesterday. I shall never again think of it as such.''

Her eyes sparkled in emerald greens as she smiled slowly up at Gray Wing. ''And, my love, I do look forward to the day I will accompany you in a canoe to practice throwing a harpoon,'' she said, trying not to reveal a surge of chills charging through her at the thought, so truly fearing what was required of her.

She forced a soft laugh. ''But do not expect too much of me too quickly,'' she quickly added. ''Gray Wing, I only recently paddled my first canoe, and now I have to learn to throw a harpoon!''

''You will not disappoint Gray Wing,'' he said huskily, lowering a hand to gently cup one of her breasts. ''As now you won't disappoint me. In sharing sensual moments with you, I have never been disappointed.''

''Nor shall I ever disappoint you,'' Amelia whispered, twining her arms about his neck to draw his lips to her mouth. Gray Wing's mouth was hot and sweet as their lips met. Rapture blossomed within Amelia as his mouth forced her lips apart.

Gray Wing's kisses grew more and more passionate. His hands caressed Amelia's breasts as he eased himself above her, inflaming her senses more and more into fully wanting him. The palms of her hands moved seductively over him, touching his hardness through his breechcloth as it pressed into the flesh of her thigh. She dared to begin to lower the garment, but her eyes jolted open when he drew away from her.

But when she saw the reason, that he was disrobing, to match her own nudity, she shot him a look of passion, eagerly waiting.

Now stripped of his breechcloth, revealing his readiness to Amelia, Gray Wing leaned over her with burning eyes. She drifted toward him, his arms enfolding her with their solid strength.

Gray Wing's mouth then covered Amelia's with a savagery unknown to her before. It stole her breath away. It caused her pulse to race and her head to begin a slow reeling. With a moan of ecstasy she returned his kiss and clung to him, welcoming his hardness inside her as he entered her with acute deliberation.

Opening herself fully to him, Amelia met Gray Wing's thrusts with upraised hips, stroke by stroke. She leaned her breasts more fully into his hands, feeling the curl of heated desire growing within her, spreading. The world was melting, everything was beautiful . . . ah, so peaceful within Gray Wing's passionate embrace.

There was no sorrow, no unhappiness. . . .

Gray Wing continued to kiss her, a kiss that was all-consuming. He could feel the fire growing into an inferno within himself, his loins aching as never before. The need to reach fulfillment grew in his mind. It seared his heart. It scorched his soul!

He moved his hands from Amelia's breasts and let them travel over her, reveling in the warm pressure of her body as she clung to him, meeting him thrust by thrust. Burying his lips in the delicate, vulnerable line of her neck, he groaned out words of pleasure so that she could hear him, but only barely. He did not want to disturb this moment of magic within her arms. His body was near to exploding.

Trembling, his hands continued to move over her, from her thigh to her hip, from breast to breast. He looked down at her with eyes burning with passion, then once again kissed her, drugged by her presence . . . by her sweetness.

Amelia felt the wondrous pleasurable feelings mounting within her. She softly moaned, twining her fingers through Gray Wing's shoulder-length brown hair. Her lips were on fire with his kiss. Her body was floating, her senses dazzled.

Molding her closer to the contours of his lean, passion-filled body, Gray Wing felt the shimmering of her flesh against his at the moment of the explosion within that seemed to match her own moment of released passion.

They lay clinging, breathing hard. Amelia ran her fingers across Gray Wing's perspiration-laced shoulders, then down his spine. "I do so love you," she whispered. "Please love me forever, Gray Wing. Never . . . never feel the need to use your slave prostitutes while . . . while I am here to share my love so fully with you."

Gray Wing leaned partially away from her. His hand swept perspiration-dampened strands of her hair back from her face. He devoured her loveliness. As before, after making love, she was vibrant . . . she was glowing.

His gaze went to the tantalizing cleavage of her full breasts, causing his pulse to race, his loins to stir heatedly. "I need no other woman," he said thickly. "You are the only one who kindles my desire."

He leaned up away from her, still tempted by her sensual loveliness, so much that he felt the need to touch her breast, tease its nipple to tautness. He lowered his lips and swept his tongue around the nipple.

Searching and probing, his fingers arousing her, Gray Wing smiled to himself when he heard Amelia softly moan in response to his renewed lovemaking. He drew away from her and looked down into her green eyes, hazy with pleasure.

Again he drew her within his arms, his great shaft filled with renewed strength. He kissed her with a blaze of fury while he once again thrust his hardness inside her. Strokes began again, slowly at first, then quickly. Twining his fingers through Amelia's hair, Gray Wing held her closer to him, tasting the sweetness of her lips, feeling the responding rapture of her body.

But a sudden commotion outside the house caused his movements to stop, his eyes to fly wide open. . . .

Gray Wing looked down at Amelia with eyes of fire. "Do you hear the disturbance outside? Someone who is not welcomed by my people has arrived," he growled, easing himself away from her. "It is the chief's duty to see who causes such a stir in the village of the Suquamish!"

Amelia crept to her feet. She hurriedly slipped into the silk dress that she had worn not only to be married in but also to be rescued by Gray Wing. Wrinkles creased the front and sides. She attempted smoothing them away while Gray Wing, in his breechcloth, moved square-shouldered toward the door.

Once he was outside, out of her sight, and she could hear his voice booming in, she went to the door and inched on outside to see who had arrived.

Surprise lit her eyes and made her heart race. She took a quick step back, not wanting to be seen, for the morning caller was Joseph. If he had come for her, damned if she would go! Now that she was safely away from his clutching hands and wet, most dissatisfying kisses, she would never return to him. He was *not* her husband. He never would be!

Though she did not want him to see her, Amelia wanted

to hear him, for one glance at his face had revealed a man who was quite troubled. Something was not right. He would not be *that* disturbed over losing a woman who he knew would never willingly perform the duties of a wife.

Amelia looked cautiously from around the door, scrutinizing Joseph. Yes. There was something quite different about him this morning. There was a desperation in his eyes . . . a wildness that disturbed Amelia. And he had arrived *alone*! It would not be in Joseph's character to come alone to the Suquamish island to argue for her release. It was something else. Perhaps he had arrived with a tragic message!

Something grabbed at Amelia's heart; her throat went dry. If Joseph was not there to ask for her release, he was there for another purpose.

"No," Amelia whispered, her hands going to her throat. "Please, Lord, don't let it be Lorna . . . or Papa. Let them be all right!"

No longer caring if Joseph saw her, too concerned over her sister and father, Amelia walked boldly out into the open and to Gray Wing's side. She looked icily at Joseph who stood cowering, his clothes quite rumpled and his hair sprays of gold in its disarray, beneath Gray Wing's powerful stance. She squared her shoulders and tightened her jaw as she met his wavering gaze.

"Amelia, tell Gray Wing I have come in peace," Joseph said, his breath coming in short rasps. He glanced around at the circle of Indians with their daggers drawn, then back to Amelia. "Dammit, Amelia, I've come to relay a message to Gray Wing." He lowered his eyes and gulped hard. "And also to you."

"Well? What is it?" Amelia snapped, her insides becoming mushy with fear, now realizing that if none of her father's cohorts had accompanied Joseph, the news might be even worse than she expected. It was as though Joseph, only Joseph, had been assigned this mission. A mission of *what*, though? Would he ever speak his mind and get it over with?

Joseph clasped his hands together behind him. He

looked slowly up at Amelia, his eyes suddenly becoming bloodshot, tears so near. "Amelia, last night . . ." he began, then stopped to swallow hard. "Last night, I was awakened by the Haida Indians. Lord, Amelia, I found you gone. I thought they had come and . . . and stolen you away. But they said they had not and that they had come for someone else: Mei-Ling! They had come for Mei-Ling, but she was already gone."

His voice quavered as he frowned over at Gray Wing. "Amelia, it is obvious that you had already . . . already left with Gray Wing while I soundly slept," he said, then again implored her with his blue, tearful eyes.

"And? What then . . . ?" Amelia asked, her voice now weak with worry. She took a step toward Joseph and grabbed him by an arm. "My father. Lorna. Are they all right?"

Joseph emitted a choked sob. Again he lowered his eyes, unable to bear seeing Amelia's expression when she found out the truth. "No, neither is all right," he said in a whisper, a shudder coursing through him.

Amelia felt a light-headedness threatening to claim her. Her fingers tightened on Joseph's arm as she steadied herself. "What do you mean . . . neither is all right?" she asked, her voice trembling.

She was dying a slow death inside. Guilt was plaguing her. If she had not left last evening, nothing terrible would have happened to her sister and father. Had she never returned from China, oh, so much would still be the same as before! So often she seemed to make wrong decisions!

Yet she had to return to America! For so many reasons!

"Joseph, are they . . . are they . . . dead?" she blurted, casting her guilt aside, for deep within she knew she was not truly to blame for anything that had happened. If anyone was guilty, it was her father. "Did the Haida kill them?"

Joseph shook his head, claiming that no, both had not died. Then he spoke softly, painfully, admitting the truth of who *had* died. "Your sister is alive," he gulped. "She has been taken by the Haida. But your father . . ." His eyes lit up with anger. "He was killed by the vicious savages!"

Amelia flinched as though she had been hit. She dropped her hand from Joseph's arm and turned her eyes away, biting her lower lip to keep from screaming out. Though her father had become someone she did not even know, he was still her father, and memories of times long ago when she had worshiped him, as daughters do their fathers, made her know that she loved him even now!

Half stumbling, Amelia took several steps away from Joseph. She did not want him to see her sorrow. She did not want him to be a part of her sorrow! He was nothing to her, only a man who had brought her sad tidings that were tearing her heart into shreds.

Strong arms engulfed Amelia. Turning her, Gray Wing drew her fully into his embrace. He whispered into her ear. "You are strong," he said. "Let this strength show through now. And we will rescue your sister even from the Haida!" He could not envision Red Eagle stealing such an innocent girl, unless it was for . . .

He turned his eyes to Joseph. He cradled Amelia close, yet spoke over her shoulder. "And Amelia's sister?" he growled. "She is held for ransom? She is to be kept until Mei-Ling is taken to Red Eagle? Is that what you have come to deliver to my people? Words you were forced by Red Eagle to say to us?"

Joseph anxiously nodded. "You are right!" he exclaimed. "That is exactly why I am here. Red Eagle killed Christopher but spared my life so that I could carry this message to you today. Lorna is a hostage of the Haida. Only if you deliver Mei-Ling to the Haida will she be released!"

Amelia jerked her eyes up. She paled. "Hostage?" she gasped. "Lorna is being held for ransom?"

Gray Wing met her worried gaze. "Red Eagle sees Mei-Ling as his personal property," he grumbled.

Amelia shuddered. She closed her eyes and pressed her cheek hard against Gray Wing's powerful chest, not want-

ing to grasp the reality of the situation. Lorna. Sweet
Lorna! Hostage! And Mei-Ling? What of *her*?

Her insides rippled with a trace of hope. Mei-Ling had
spoken favorably of Red Eagle, of how sweet he had been
to her. It seemed that Red Eagle and Mei-Ling might even
have become more than friends!

"Mei-Ling will go willingly," Mei-Ling said suddenly
from behind Amelia. "Mei-Ling will go to Red Eagle.
Now, if you wish."

Amelia moved from Gray Wing's arms and turned with
a start. Her gaze traveled over Mei-Ling. She was dressed
in Chinese garments. The prostitute slaves must have taken
the highly embroidered red silk dress from Amelia's chest
during the night while Amelia was sleeping peacefully in
Gray Wing's arms.

Mei-Ling's dark almond-shaped eyes slowly became
downcast, showing the humility she had been taught from
childhood. Her hair was woven beautifully through framework atop her head where from its waves hung golden
jewelry in all shapes and designs. On Mei-Ling's cheeks
were dots of rouge, and her lips were red with the same.
She was nothing less than ravishingly beautiful, and, ah,
so innocent in her petiteness as she hid her hands inside
the wide cuffs of her dress.

"Mei-Ling," Amelia said, sobbing suddenly, again
fearing for her friend. She rushed to Mei-Ling and flung
herself into her arms. She hugged her fiercely. "Oh, Mei-
Ling, I cannot let you do this. You cannot return to the
Haida. No matter what you say about Red Eagle, about
how sweet he was to you, he killed my father last night,
Mei-Ling. He killed him in cold blood. He may even eventually kill *you*. I cannot let you go. I cannot!"

Amelia's words about Red Eagle killing her father made
Mei-Ling feel a deep sadness for the Indian she sorely
loved. That he could kill so easily made her not want to
still love him, yet such a sweet bond had formed so quickly
between them, how could she ever, ever *not* love him?
Surely he had killed for a valid reason! He would never,
never harm her.

No, she would not doubt his love or concern for her. In a sense, had he not killed for her? In China a man was treated grandly who killed for the sake of a woman his heart was lent to! In America was it not the same?

Mei-Ling slipped from Amelia's embrace. She looked boldly into Amelia's eyes as she grasped her hands. "Mei-Ling is sorry about your father," she murmured. "But, Vona-Lee, remember the teachings of the Chinese: Death is not death at all! It is only an extension of life!"

She squeezed Amelia's hands more tightly, reassuring her. "And, Vona-Lee," she whispered so that no one else would hear, "Red Eagle will not harm me. He . . . he loves me as Gray Wing loves you. And please do not think so badly of him for what he has done. He is a good man."

Amelia's eyes widened; she heard so much in Mei-Ling's voice that she did not speak aloud. Mei-Ling *did* love Red Eagle! Wasn't it plain to see? And Mei-Ling trusted Red Eagle, most likely because she knew that he, in turn, loved *her*. He did not want her returned to him for ugly reasons! He wanted her for loving!

"Mei-Ling, I don't . . . know what to say," Amelia said, her gaze studying Mei-Ling, wanting to be sure that Mei-Ling was telling the truth, not saying these things only to ensure Lorna's release from the Haida.

But, yes, it was there, the full truth of Mei-Ling's feelings in the depths of her eyes. She did love Red Eagle, perhaps with the same intensity that Amelia loved Gray Wing. It seemed that Mei-Ling even understood why Red Eagle had seen the . . . need . . . to kill!

"You need say nothing more," Mei-Ling said, bending to kiss Amelia's tear-streaked cheek. "Let us leave now. Let us go to Red Wing's island."

Joseph Beria was left behind, staring at the departure of everyone but him. Amelia cast him a glance across her shoulder, knowing that she would have to see him at least one more time. When she returned to the trading post to bury her father. . . .

Twenty-Two

❧ ❧

Sitting next to her friend in the canoe, Amelia clung to Mei-Ling's hand, hearing the sounds of musical instruments drifting seaward from the Haida Indian island just ahead. Amelia was now familiar with the instruments of the Northwest Indians. She could distinguish between the tambourine drum, which was made by stretching a piece of rawhide over a narrow frame bent into a cylindrical form, from those instruments made from long poles equipped with clusters of deer hooves, which were thumped against boards to make a loud clapping sound similar to thunder.

Rattles, made of mountain sheep horns and of baleen steamed and folded over and fastened to wooden handles, played their rhythmic sounds in time with the drumbeats. Whistles without reeds squeaked ominously through a fog that was just lifting from the bay.

Amelia smiled weakly at Mei-Ling, wondering about the many different musical instruments being played so merrily on Red Eagle's island. Usually such music was heard in an Indian village only during a great celebration. Gray Wing had sent word to Red Eagle of the arrival of the convoy of Suquamish canoes and the reason for their arrival. Was this why there was a celebration? Had Red Eagle received the message with this much enthusiasm? Did he want Mei-Ling with him that terribly? Was it because he loved her or only because he wanted to possess her as a thing he could use?

Again looking straight ahead, Amelia found herself torn with feelings. She was filled with dread of having to leave Mei-Ling with the Haida, yet anxious to remove Lorna from their clutches. Gray Wing had agreed that Amelia could accompany him and his warriors on this journey of exchange of woman for child.

She could never have stayed behind! She had to witness firsthand that Lorna was alive and well before the exchange was made, and she had to see if Mei-Ling went to Red Eagle enthusiastically, for Amelia would never sleep another restful night if she saw her friend left with Indians that Mei-Ling did not truly trust.

Amelia's vision shifted, and she felt a warmth of love surge through her when she looked at Gray Wing with such admiration and trust where he sat in front of her, deftly drawing the paddle through the water. Amelia let her gaze move slowly over him. This day, because he wanted to look like the proud Suquamish chief that he was, he had dressed much differently than Amelia had ever seen him before. He wore the same headdress that she had seen his father wear the day she was introduced to him at the age of thirteen. It bore carved figures, painted and inlaid with iridescent shells, spiked with sea lion whiskers, and was hung with ermine tails.

Around Gray Wing's powerful shoulders he wore a cloak of costly sea otter fur. His buckskin breechcloth and leggings were painted with intricate designs of whales and wolves, and he wore moccasins trimmed with colorful beads.

Never could she love Gray Wing as much as now. He continually proved his love and devotion to her! Though she was filled with sadness over her father's death, being with Gray Wing made her feel, oh, so grateful that he was hers, someone she could always trust and love. He was a man of inscrutable poise, triumphant courage, and stolid dignity. He was her lifeline, now and forever! She could hardly wait for the day she could prove herself worthy to be his wife!

The island was now so near that the waves crashing against the rocky shore sounded menacing, drowning out the sound of the music. The damp sea air brushed against Amelia's face, making her shudder.

Yet the aroma of food cooking somewhere close by made her feel a sudden, strange calm within, as though this was an extension of times in the past when she had awakened to her mother preparing breakfast, and how right it had seemed at the moment, as though nothing could ever break the spell of that time in space with family.

But now everything was changed. Everything . . .

Many Suquamish warriors were now in the water, pulling the canoe, beaching it. Amelia readied herself for the lurch of the canoe onto the shore. She glanced over at Mei-Ling whose eyes were showing a radiance from within, her eyes locked, looking up at a bluff overhead.

Amelia's eyes turned slowly upward. Her insides splashed cold when she saw a tall, lithe Indian, attired in only a loincloth, whose body was a massive display of tattoos. She could not help but shiver at the sight.

Yet when she looked at only his face, she could see his handsomeness. And the way he was looking at Mei-Ling! It was quite evident that he sincerely loved her with heart and soul, for Gray Wing always looked at Amelia in the same way!

She sighed with relief, her shoulders relaxing with the discovery. Everything was going to be all right.

Yes, very much all right . . .

His robe oppressive in the weight of its heavy silk, Bai-Hua paced the rocky beach, looking into the distance at the great white cone of Mount Rainier reaching through clouds in the sky. To get so close to the land of the Suquamish Indians and then to be delayed by repairs to his ship was almost too much to bear!

His hands folded into the wide cuffs of his robe, he glared at the workers who had already taken too much time applying pitch to the great crack inflicted by the incessant beating of the waves of the Pacific Ocean.

"Wei!" he shouted to his crew. "Do not rest between applications of pitch! Work! Work! It is *buh-hao-eesa*, not good form, to look lazy in my eyes. *Sha sha!* Kill, kill! That will be my next command if you do not put haste in your work!"

His dark eyes burning with restlessness, now believing that his father's great ship had left the Indian island and was perhaps even now heading for Boston, Bai-Hua was torn as to what to do. Once his ship was repaired, should he proceed to the Suquamish Indian island where his father had planned to trade for costly furs and whale oil?

Or should he make haste to travel to Boston where Vona-Lee's American parents made residence?

He did not want to waste time in getting to Vona-Lee. Though she had voiced aloud that she did not love him, he had decided he would steal her away and return her to China and make her his wife whether or not she approved! He could never love another woman as much as Vona-Lee!

It would make him look weak in the eyes of all other Chinese to take an American woman as a wife, but he would not let that dissuade him from having her!

Going to the rail, wrapping his fingers around it, Bai-Hua leaned his full weight against it as once again he peered at the mountain in the distance. In its shroud of white it appeared almost ghostly. The smoky mists rising from it looked like apparitions dancing, beckoning to him.

Something grabbed at Bai-Hua's insides when he heard a low rumble and then saw the madrona trees shuddering on the shore close beside the moored ship.

"An earthquake is imminent!" he gasped, once more looking at the fierceness of the mountain. He must make haste in getting Vona-Lee and returning to the safe shores of his homeland!

Yet he had said all that could be said to make his crew hurry with the repairs.

Trembling, he went to his cabin and lit his opium pipe. Stretching out on many cushions on the floor, he inhaled the drug that made him feel as though he was floating. He no longer concerned himself with anything of this mysterious northwest country of America. As always before, he let his mind conjure up all sorts of pleasures gained by being in Vona-Lee's arms.

She was his purpose for living . . . only Vona-Lee. . . .

Long feast mats had been unrolled to serve as a tablecloth. For napkins, bundles of softly shredded cedar bark had been prepared and distributed. Food was steam-cooking in large, shallow pits filled with hot stones, covered with leaves and mats. Fish and meat were being broiled over an open fire.

A low rumbling noise, then a slight shifting of the ground beneath where Amelia sat before the great outdoor fire in the Haida village, made her cringe and look toward the great mist-shrouded mountain in the distance. Surely one day there would be an earthquake. The signs of an earthquake were always there, making one aware of the danger of such an occurrence. . . .

The sound of the drums and whistles and the frenzy of excited Indians dancing about the outdoor fire, doing what Gray Wing called the Jumping Dance, drew Amelia's eyes back around to watch the entertainment.

She felt comfortably relaxed, for Lorna was at her left side, clutching her hand joyously, and Gray Wing was at her right side, sitting tall and proudly erect with his arms folded across his chest.

Across the way, Mei-Ling sat beside Red Eagle on a platform adorned with many otter furs, looking as though she belonged. Sitting proudly beside her, Chief Red Eagle wore a red cedar bark head ring filled with loose white down, and a stiff bark collar. A highly decorated loincloth was his only other attire, for he seemed proud to display all of the tattoos on the rest of his body.

Amelia's gaze moved back to Mei-Ling. Never had she seen Mei-Ling look so radiantly happy or so beautiful. Her embroidered red silk dress clung to every curve of her body; her hair was oiled with jasmine oil and coiled into a towering edifice atop her head. She had dabbed the red juice of the ripe pomegranate on the high points of her cheeks, tipped the end of her nose with the same, and had stained her small nails a bright red. Her almond-shaped dark eyes were shining as though waxed.

Amelia wove the fingers of her free hand through her own hair, positioning it to hang lustrously long and free down to her waist, glad that its original color was being restored. Though Mei-Ling looked beautiful as Chinese, Amelia was glad to look one hundred percent American! Never again did she wish to look Chinese, nor did she want to return to China. She was where she belonged. With Gray Wing!

Focusing her eyes on the dancers, Amelia could not help but admire their attire. The men's principal ornamentation consisted of wide buckskin bands tied across the forehead with the ends flapping loose, each decorated with a sort of feather mosaic made out of many bright red scalps of the pileated woodpecker, bordered by other feathers and white fur.

The women wore dance aprons of buckskin, and half-leggings painted and ornamented with porcupine quill embroidery.

Many of the dance steps consisted of springing into the air from a squatting position or turning fast on the heels in a narrow circle. Choral singing accompanied the dance.

Everything then became hushed. The dancers paused, then sat down in a wide circle around the fire, looking at their chief devotedly. Red Eagle lifted a large pipe filled with Indian tobacco. He lit it and passed it to Gray Wing.

"The curling smoke from the long-stemmed pipe breathes forth the pale quiet of peace," Red Eagle said, proudly lifting his chin. "Gray Wing, with this pipe let us pacify the elements on this festal occasion. It is good that we remain *sikhs*, friends!"

Gray Wing accepted the pipe. Placing it to his lips, he drew from its stem. As the smoke spiraled from between his lips, large amounts of *olachen*, oil, was poured on the fire, causing it to blaze up fiercely, celebrating with the Haida's own brand of fireworks.

"It is done. Gray Wing is *youtl*, proud," he said, passing the pipe back to Red Eagle. "*Sikhs!* Friends now . . . friends forever!"

Red Eagle piled food onto his tray and passed it around to Gray Wing. "As you know it is normal for up to six people to use one tray for eating, but a chief has his own," he said thickly. "*Muckamuck!* Eat from my tray, Gray Wing. Give the tray to your woman. It is a great mark of favor to be offered food from the Haida chief's tray."

"*Hy-uh*, it is," Gray Wing said, nodding. He accepted the tray of food and placed it before Amelia. "My *ladida*, eat. This will also seal your friendship with the Haida. As man and wife, you and I must seek the same friendships!"

Amelia looked guardedly at Red Eagle, then softened in mood as she once again looked at Mei-Ling, seeing her perfect contentment. Without hesitation she took a piece of smoked herring roe from the tray. As she ate, she felt as though she belonged in the Indian culture.

Oh, how good it was to be back in America. . . .

Amelia began unrolling the buckskin curtain, looking at Lorna sweetly sleeping behind it on Gray Wing's bunk. A strange nostalgic feeling surged through her, seeing in her sister so much of herself. Such trusting innocence was revealed in her peaceful breathing as she slept so soundly. She had been shifted from place to place these last couple of days, but she seemed to have accepted life as it was handed her, just as Amelia had when she was swept away to China to be raised by the Chinese.

But no longer did Amelia have to accept things as they were handed her. She now took . . . she now fought for what she believed in and wanted. And she had achieved the greatest of all her desires. She was now with Gray

Wing, and would be, forever. She would not allow anything or anyone to stand in the way of their happiness. . . .

Fully unrolling the curtain to the floor, giving her and Gray Wing the utmost privacy, Amelia turned to him and smiled. "Lorna's asleep," she whispered. "She loved the story I told her about China. Her questions about my adventures in China are never-ending!" A sadness crept into her eyes. "My papa used to sit at my bedside when I was a small child. He had some of the most fanciful tales to tell. He left me dreaming all night about queens and kings!"

A soft sob was stifled behind a hand, tears sparkled in her eyes as she recalled the brief burial of her father after they had arrived from the Haida island with Lorna. He was now gone from her life as though he had never existed. There was an emptiness assailing Amelia she did not want to feel. She lowered her face in her hands then melted inside when strong arms were there, embracing . . . reassuring her.

"Come over by the fire," Gray Wing said softly, nestling her close to his side. "I will help you forget all that is ugly in your heart and mind. Let us think of only now and our future."

"Yes. You are right," Amelia murmured, shaking her head. "I must forget what should have or what might have been. Papa is gone. Mama is gone. I must now make the best of the rest of my life."

"The rest of *our* lives," Gray Wing softly corrected. "Let me show you how easy it is to forget. Let my lips and hands remind you how to forget everything but you . . . and me. . . ."

Amelia's blood quickened as he spread her out beneath him. She began to sink into a chasm of desire as he kissed her passionately while his hands unfastened her dress and began to lower it. A peaceful languor washed through her and she felt her aching sadness being banished when he lowered his lips and his tongue began to circle a nipple while his other hand eased her dress on away from her, then her silken underthings. In one brief stroke he had his breechcloth off and for a moment let their bodies fully touch, flesh against flesh, her breasts pressed hard into his chest.

Then as Gray Wing resumed loving her with his mouth and tongue, Amelia abandoned herself to the torrents of feelings that were claiming her. He made love to her this way slowly, delighting every secret part of her body, pleasuring her.

Sweeping his tongue over Amelia's warm flesh, Gray Wing forgot his own sought pleasures. They would come later!

Amelia had never felt so desired, but she did not want to exclude Gray Wing. Her fingernails raked lightly down his spine, reveling in the exquisite feel of his smooth copper skin. Her fingers danced along his pantherish hips, then splayed over his firm buttocks.

Kneading him there, she was silently telling him that she was ready for that part of lovemaking that made them become as one.

Responding to her silent message, Gray Wing moved atop her. His hands cupped the rounded, soft flesh of her bottom and molded the shapely contours as with fire he kissed her, his mouth smothering her cry of passion as his loins thrust forward, his body plunging into her, his hard velvet sheath moving within her as she shuddered and gripped him tightly.

Gray Wing moved his lips to the slender curve of Amelia's throat. His warm breath stirred shivers of pleasure along her flesh. She moaned and clung to him as his hands cupped and kneaded a breast.

"Gray Wing . . ." she whispered. "My love . . . my love . . ."

"La-dida," he whispered, his lips now on a soft pink crest of her breast. His tongue flicked. His teeth nibbled.

Amelia ran her hand over the slope of his hard jaw, his searching fingers and lips igniting small fires along her spine. She was soaring with joy, for this day was the first day of their lives together.

Oh, tomorrow! How she would show him that she could

learn to throw a harpoon as well as any man! Then she could be his wife!

Tomorrow . . . tomorrow . . .

Mei-Ling was sitting nude in the shadows of the fire in Red Eagle's wigwam, the reflections of the flames causing her lovely skin to take on a golden glow. Her hands resting on her lap, she watched Red Eagle as his eyes branded her while he unfurled her hair from its framework atop her head. Red Eagle tossed the loosened framework aside. Mei-Ling's night-dark hair tumbled free and spilled over her bare shoulders and down her back.

A trail of fire was left by the touch of Red Eagle's eyes as they swept over Mei-Ling, causing her small buds of breasts to stiffly peak as though his hands were there, caressing her.

Breathing erratically from the building excitement, Mei-Ling watched Red Eagle drop to his knees before her, then raised her hands and acquainted herself again with his body. Ignoring the tattoos, she slid her fingers over his wide shoulders, the expanse of his sleekly muscled chest, and his hard, flat stomach. He was slim-hipped and well-muscled and fully aroused, his eyes charged with dark emotion.

"You could not have wanted to leave me," he said huskily, gently framing her tiny face between his powerful hands. "Tell me that you fought the American who came to steal you away, Mei-Ling."

"You know that I did," she murmured bashfully, humbly casting her eyes downward.

"Then you are glad Red Eagle bargained for your return," he said flatly. "No one will take you away ever again!"

Mei-Ling could not look up and let him see the wavering of her eyes, for he did not know the hunger growing inside her to see China again. She was so torn! She loved China! She loved Red Eagle! How was she ever to decide . . . ?

Red Eagle cupped her chin and forced her eyes to rise

and lock with his. "You are quiet," he said. "Why are you?"

Mei-Ling saw the growing passion in his face, so finely chiseled, so handsome, as he gazed down at her. His nose was so bold, his chin so strong! She shivered with ecstasy as his arms snaked around her waist and drew her close to him, crushing her breasts to his chest.

"Speak," he said huskily. "Do not be afraid to speak of your feelings to me."

"Feelings?" Mei-Ling murmured, her body pliant in his arms. Her eyes pooled with joyous tears. "*Aie!* Mei-Ling is overwhelmed with feelings of love for you. Kiss me, Red Eagle. Make love with me!"

Red Eagle kissed her hungrily, reveling in the sweet warm press of her body. His fingers sought the soft curves of her buttocks. Lifting her, he positioned her legs around his waist and buried his ready hardness deep inside her, almost stealing her breath away with the quickness of the action.

Showering kisses along the fragile line of her face, he began his eager strokes inside her. Her throat arched backwards; her hair tumbled to the floor. Red Eagle kissed the hollow of her throat, causing a soft moan to surface from between her delicate lips. His lips slipped down past her shoulder and fastened gently on her breast.

Mei-Ling felt a tremor deep within, beginning at her toes, then soaring wildly upward. She clung. She sighed. She rocked. Again he kissed her fully on the lips, molding her closer to him as he slowly lowered her to the pallet of furs beneath her.

Spreading himself out atop her, Red Eagle again plunged deep within her. His strokes quickened, their warm breath mingling, their bodies tangling. The silent euphoria of their need was shared while they torridly embraced; then they lay silent, spent, shaken by the wondrous sharing of incredible sweetness. . . .

A tremor went through Mei-Ling's body as Red Eagle gently caressed the damp valley at the juncture of her thighs, arousing her anew. She loved Red Eagle with such an intensity, and while she was in his arms, China did not seem important to her! It was during the moments away from him that loneliness for her homeland assailed her.

"Hold me," she softly cried. "Red Eagle, hold me and never stop telling me how much you need and love me."

She could not tell him how important that was to her. Surely after hearing it enough times, after sharing exquisite moments with him enough times, she would want only him! Only him . . .

Twenty-Three

༄ ⚭ ༄

The morning sun was melting the fog away over Whale Island. Amelia stood beside Gray Wing, listening obediently to him as he was teaching her about harpoons and whaling. His huge intricately carved canoe was being readied by several warriors. Within moments Amelia would be aboard this canoe, going out to sea, to practice throwing a harpoon.

Glancing down at her attire, which Gray Wing had said was best for her to wear while learning the art of harpooning, she felt only half dressed. The Indian blouse, made from finely woven twisted plant fibers, scarcely hid her breasts. Fringed buckskin leggings clung to her legs like another skin, revealing all of her dips and curves. She wore no shoes, and her hair was braided in one long plait down her back.

She felt primitive but knew that Gray Wing approved, for his eyes gleamed richly every time he raked them over her.

"The head of a harpoon is made of three pieces," Gray Wing instructed her, holding the harpoon out before him. "It's made of a sharp mussel-shell cutting blade, cemented with spruce gum between two heavy elk horn barbs.''

He moved behind Amelia and placed his arms around her, gently fitting the harpoon into place in her hands. ''This harpoon is only a replica of what you will be throwing when we go on a true hunt for a whale,'' he said, feeling Amelia grow tense within his arms as she stared down at the harpoon. ''You will practice with harpoons that are not as costly, for while practicing, you will be throwing into the body of the sea, not the body of a whale. The weapons will be lost to us forever.''

''But, Gray Wing, is it wise for me to practice with a harpoon of lighter weight than the one I will be using on the day my skills will be truly tested?'' Amelia asked, trying to familiarize herself with the feel of the harpoon as her fingers tightened about it. ''Gray Wing, it's important that I succeed in my trials to become your wife.''

''*La-dida*, you are such a worrier! Do not worry yourself so,'' Gray Wing reassured, chuckling low. ''Each day more weight will be added to the practice harpoons. In the end, on the day of your true test, you will be ready. Gray Wing will see to that.''

He clasped his hands over Amelia's and guided the motion, so that in slow movements he taught her how the harpoon should be held and thrown.

''It seems easy enough,'' Amelia murmured, confidence building inside her. ''But what *is* the difference between the practice harpoon and the true one? What can I expect?''

Gray Wing stepped away from her and went and got a harpoon that was ready for the true whale chase and kill. He laid it out between his hands, looking down at it as though he worshiped it as he began explaining its structure to Amelia.

''A heavy lanyard of sinew twisted into rope connects the harpoon to the end of a one-hundred-fathom-long line made up of cedar withes. Four sealskin buoys are attached to the line at intervals. A huge reinforced cedar bark bas-

ket in which the line is coiled is made fast to the bitter
end and serves as a drag,'' he said.

''The lanyard from the compound head of the harpoon is
attached to the shaft of the weapon at two points with a light
string so that the weight of the lanyard and the long line to
which it is attached will not pull the head of the harpoon
from the shaft before it is thrust into the whale,'' he added.

Gray Wing looked slowly up at Amelia. ''The craft of
whaling is both practical and magical,'' he said softly.
''What also contributes to the success of the hunt are cherished family secrets handed down in noble lines only.''

His eyes took on a faraway cast as he looked out to sea.
''One is always reminded that the whale is the world's
biggest source of meat,'' he said quietly. ''A whale kill
will provide a whole village with blubber and oil for a
year, as well as bone for tools and weapons.''

He thrust out his chest as he held the harpoon with only
one hand. ''That is why the whale hunter, the man who
stands in the bow of the canoe and thrusts a harpoon into
the whale, enjoys the highest prestige among the tribe,''
he boasted. ''Gray Wing is that man, Amelia. Only Gray
Wing!''

After placing the harpoon on the ground, he went to
Amelia and eased the smaller weapon from her grasp and
placed it beside the other. Drawing her into his arms, he
looked down at her with eyes of fire. ''And you will be
the woman who shares the highest prestige among Gray
Wing's tribe,'' he said huskily. ''For you, also, will have
the honor of thrusting the harpoon into the whale. Soon,
my *la-dida*. Soon.''

He pressed his lips to hers. With a moan of ecstasy,
Amelia gave him back his kiss, clinging to him. Yet deep
within the farthest recesses of her mind, she feared that
she would fail him.

What if she did . . . ?

The wind was brisk, the waves choppy, as Amelia stood
beside Gray Wing in the bow of the massive seaworthy
canoe. She knew that what she was attempting was stren-

uous and dangerous, but she was driven to succeed by her intense, devoted love for Gray Wing. If she failed, the chances were that she would lose not only his love but his respect as well.

She could chance losing neither, for he was her *life*, her *soul*. . . .

Gray Wing wrapped his muscled arms around her, holding her steady as the canoe pitched and wove through the waves. He gently placed the harpoon between her hands. "You just relax against me," he encouraged, knowing by the heaving of her bosom that she was afraid. "This first time you just let me guide your hands into the throw. You, then, will do it alone the next time."

"Whatever you say," Amelia said, hardly recognizing her voice, it was so strained. She gripped the harpoon between her hands, then sighed to herself when Gray Wing slipped his hands over hers, transferring their warmth to her, giving her more courage. The wind whipped seawater hard against her face, stinging it with salty spray. Her blouse was straining against her breasts, revealing their taut, cold nipples.

Glancing over her shoulder, she looked at the Suquamish warriors. She was relieved when she saw that they were fully occupied, busy paddling the canoe, working at keeping it afloat. She did not wish to have an audience for her practice harpooning *or* for the display of her body in her scanty, skintight attire.

It was enough that Gray Wing was there, feasting his eyes upon her, causing her blood to boil with desire for him. It seemed that she had more than one battle to win this day—the need to prove that she was worthy to be his wife, and the desire that always lay just beneath the surface when she was with Gray Wing!

How could anyone love anyone more than she did Gray Wing? To look into his eyes was to stir her senses into reeling!

Clearing her throat, shaking her head to clear her thoughts, Amelia focused once again on the sea and the harpoon in her hands. "I'm ready, Gray Wing," she shouted, trying to speak louder than the voice of the booming waves thrashing about in the ocean.

Slowly Gray Wing moved her hands and the harpoon, lifting it . . . lifting it . . . lifting it. Then he guided her arm back, then quickly forward. "When I release my hand, you release yours!" he shouted, his muscles rippling as he balanced himself and Amelia against the pitching of the canoe.

"Now!" he commanded, releasing his hands from Amelia's.

He watched as the harpoon sailed into the air, twirling, then made its plunge downward. . . .

A wide smile spread across his face. He grabbed Amelia by the waist and whirled her around to face him. "It was a perfect throw! You learn quickly, my woman!"

Amelia was numb, still looking out to sea, though she knew that Gray Wing's proud gray eyes were imploring her to look into them. She watched the ripples spread in the water where the harpoon had plunged and was now sinking. Had she truly thrown it so masterfully? Did that mean that it would not require all that much practice?

Perhaps even tomorrow . . .

Suddenly her attention was drawn elsewhere. Her insides quivered strangely when she saw the undeniable flutter of great white sails of a ship on the horizon, the strong winds carrying the vessel quickly in the direction of the whaling canoe.

But this was not just any ship. Amelia knew quite well the markings of a Chinese craft! The colorful, crawling dragon carved onto its sides made it quite distinguishable from the American or Russian ships that used the avenue of these northwest waters.

Amelia's thoughts went to Mei-Ling. If Mei-Ling had a chance to return to China, would she do so? Or would she choose to stay with Red Eagle?

This was the first Chinese ship in these waters since Du-Fu Jin's ship had traveled here and then capsized. . . .

Amelia felt Gray Wing stiffen as he held her within his arms. She looked slowly up at him, seeing hate distort his usually handsome face as he looked toward the approaching Chinese ship. She knew that he was recalling the one other fateful time that he had been as near a Chinese ship. He had lost a giant whale due to that ship's captain!

Amelia reached a hand to Gray Wing's cheek. "Do not upset yourself so about seeing a Chinese ship again," she tried to encourage. "Du-Fu Jin is not commanding this ship. This ship will pass on by us, unharmed!"

"No more Chinese ships are welcome on my island," he grumbled, his eyes dark with hate. "The Chinese are not to be trusted."

"Gray Wing, you must always remember that had it not been for the Chinese I might not even be *alive*," Amelia said sullenly, recalling her terrible ordeal with the Haida. It still did not seem possible that the Haida people could have changed so much. She would never forget the people whose flesh had been consumed by the Haida!

Yet it was most surely the chief who was responsible for the true difference. Red Eagle was not at all like his father, who enjoyed seeing others tortured, who even enjoyed tasting the flesh of other human beings.

Yes, Red Eagle was the cause of the change. Mei-Ling *was* safe with him. . . .

"If Du-Fu Jin hadn't swept me away from the Haida island years ago, who is to say what might have become of me?" she quickly added. "And, Gray Wing, as you have witnessed by Mei-Ling's utter sweetness, all Chinese are not the same. Even her father, Du-Fu, was more often kind than cruel. It was the opium that twisted his mind into doing what he did to you that day. Only the opium."

"Opium?" Gray Wing questioned, his eyebrows forking.

Amelia opened her mouth to explain about the dreaded drug, but suddenly she became aware of the closer approach of the ship when Gray Wing's crew began to shout and steer the canoe in the opposite direction.

With a jerk of the head, she turned and saw the closeness of the ship. She gasped and teetered, glad that Gray Wing was there to catch her when she was close enough to the ship to look up at the rail and see who was in command of it.

"Bai-Hua!" she whispered harshly, everything within her growing cold with wonder, then building dread. "Why? How?"

Something grabbed at Amelia's insides when Bai-Hua's eyes met hers, shock registering on his face as he stared openly at her.

"Aie yah! Vona-Lee?" Bai-Hua said, his senses reeling from wonder and shock at seeing her in a canoe with Indians, dressed as an Indian! Even her hair was in a long braid down her back like an Indian! How? Why? Had she asked to be left with the Indian she had talked of so often instead of being taken to her parents in Boston? Or had something else happened? Where was his father? Where was Mei-Ling?

His fingers grasped hard onto the rail; his jaw tightened. He would follow the canoe to the shore. He would demand to have answers. Then he would take Vona-Lee away. He would not let her stay with savage Indians, even if he had to force her to leave at the point of a cutlass!

Gray Wing looked with surprise at Amelia, having heard her whisper a Chinese name. "Al-ah! You know this man who looks down from the ship?" he said, now turning his eyes back to Bai-Hua, seeing so much familiar about him. It seemed there was a similarity between him and Mei-Ling. Could they be brother and sister? Had this Chinese traveler come to get Mei-Ling, perhaps even Amelia? Gray Wing had seen the look of utter surprise in the Chinese captain's eyes when he saw Amelia. It had been a look of recognition!

"I don't see how it is at all possible that Bai-Hua is here, but, yes, I do know him," Amelia said, still staring up at Bai-Hua as the ship began following Gray Wing's canoe that was now turned and headed for Whale Island. "He is the son of the man who gave orders to run down your canoe. Gray Wing, it is Mei-Ling's brother."

She shook her head, squinting as she felt Bai-Hua's eyes boring into hers. "I do not know why he has come. He could not have known what happened. No word has been sent. There hasn't even been enough *time*," she openly marveled.

Then everything within her became numb when she recalled how Bai-Hua had accosted her, had tried to rape her. He had said that he had loved her, wanted her. Only when she rejected him had he called her a *zien*, a common person. Deep within, where his desires were formed, he surely did still love her and had come to claim her as his. He never traveled alone to America! He had come for a purpose and Amelia had to believe that it was because of her. And if he had been determined enough to travel by ship this far because of her, he surely would fight to the end to have her. He had had enough time to think this through and knew that he would never let her say no again.

Amelia paled. What of . . . Mei-Ling? What were his true intentions for *her*?

As the canoe was beached Amelia heard a great splash behind her. She turned and saw that the anchor had been dropped and a longboat was being lowered from the ship's side. Attired in a rich, magnificently embroidered red silk garment, his hair drawn back in a queue, Bai-Hua sat in the longboat with his arms folded across his chest.

When the longboat splashed into the water and several of Bai-Hua's Chinese warriors began drawing massive paddles through it, he kept his hands hidden just inside the wide cuffs of his robe. His almond-shaped eyes were squinted in anger as again his gaze met and held Amelia's.

Gray Wing watched the looks being exchanged between Amelia and Bai-Hua and did not like it at all. He knew there was more there than met the eye. It looked as though the Chinese traveler bore some sort of grudge against Amelia.

Or was it . . . something else . . . ?

Wanting to prove to the Chinese that Amelia belonged to him, Gray Wing swept her fully up into his arms and lifted her from the canoe. He continued to carry her until he had her safely inside his house.

Amelia clung about his neck, looking adoringly up at

him, understanding how he felt. He had understood that
Bai-Hua was more than an adopted brother to her. Men
surely had ways to tell when another man was a rival! A
threat! Even if it was a man Amelia now despised!

"You can put me down now," Amelia said softly, feeling the complete calm that being in his house caused her.
It was soon to be *their* house. She already was familiar
with everything about it and accepted that it was nothing
at all to compare with the Chinese house in which she had
lived, with the lacquered walls, the bronze and gold wall
hangings, and tapestries that stole one's breath away. Gray
Wing's simple house with its simple furnishings was
enough, for she was sharing them with the man she loved.

Gray Wing placed Amelia on her feet. He cupped her
chin with a hand and lifted it so that their eyes could meet.
"You stay," he flatly ordered. "Gray Wing will see what
the Chinese visitor's business is here. If he has come for
you, he will be forced to leave again!"

Though Bai-Hua had forced himself on her, Amelia
could not help but feel a trace of loyalty to him. She suddenly recalled that he did not know about the death of his
father. Bai-Hua should at least know this, to take back
with him to China. The whole Jin family must have a
chance to mourn.

But Bai-Hua would become the lord of the family! Now
that Amelia knew him for what he really was, she did not
wish to see him have such an honor. She wished that he
could be sent back to China empty-handed of all things,
even news that would make him a man of wealth and position!

But she must tell him about his father. She could not
keep such a truth to herself. She knew what it was like to
have gone ten years without knowing of the fate of her
dearly departed mother!

Fair was fair.

Amelia grabbed Gray Wing's arm as he spun around to
leave. She stepped in his way, stopping him. "I must have
the opportunity to speak with Bai-Hua," she said. "I must
tell him of his father's death. He must be told that Mei-

Ling is safe. He could even collect Du-Fu Jin's Chinese crewmen who are now your slaves and take them home to China. You have voiced aloud that you are displeased with their labor, that they are useless to you.''

She implored him with a tilt of her head and twinkling of green eyes. ''Let me have a moment with Bai-Hua; then you can say what you must say to him yourself, Gray Wing,'' she said softly. ''It will be best this way. There will be fewer harsh feelings, perhaps less trouble, between you and Bai-Hua if you let me go to him first to clear the air.''

Gray Wing's face clouded with a frown as he glared down at Amelia. Then he nodded. ''Go to him,'' he said in a low growl. ''But speak quickly, for he will have to meet with Gray Wing, the chief of this village, soon, to save face for the chief in the eyes of his people!''

Tears burned at the corners of Amelia's eyes; she was touched by Gray Wing's generosity and understanding. Flinging herself into his arms she gave him a bear hug, then turned on a heel and walked barefoot from the house.

Her eyes wavered as she saw Bai-Hua walking toward her, his right hand solidly clasping the great cutlass at his side. . . .

Twenty-Four

Tense, Amelia stepped through the archway of totems at Gray Wing's door. Flashes of the day Bai-Hua had tried to rape her tore through her consciousness, sending a shiver of dread across her flesh as she made eye contact with him.

Two steps brought them only a few feet apart, close enough for Amelia to get the faint whiff of opium on his clothes and breath. He was carrying on from father to son, sharing Du-Fu's love of the dreaded drug that had probably contributed to Du-Fu's death. He was so drugged that he had not been able to free himself from the angry clutches of the sea the day his great ship had capsized. . . .

"So, Vona-Lee, it *was* you who shared a canoe with a savage!" Bai-Hua said, clasping his fingers more tightly about the hilt of his cutlass.

His gaze raked over her, seeing her attire, then moved back to her breasts. Through the thin, loosely woven plant fibers of her blouse he could see every curve of her breasts, even the taut, dark nipples. His loins began to ache heatedly, having desired her for so long, yet been denied her!

Tonight would be different. Once he had her aboard his ship, he would make her love him. There were ways. . . .

He lifted his almond-shaped eyes, dark with desire and determination. His jaw tightened. "How is it that you are here in this forsaken wilderness with savages?" he asked, gesturing with his free hand toward the Indian village.

Bai-Hua was ignoring the Suquamish warriors who were slowly circling around him, for he knew that he had enough men on his ship to slay all the warriors of this island, even the women and the children.

His warriors were even now lined up along the beach with cutlasses drawn, ready to rush the village at the slight flick of Bai-Hua's wrist, the command to do so.

Bai-Hua felt safe enough. *Aie*, he felt safe enough!

Amelia did not like the smug look of possession in Bai-Hua's eyes. It made her realize just why he was there! He *had* come to claim her.

She squared her shoulders and lifted her chin stubbornly. Bai-Hua did not know the danger he was in. Gray Wing would never allow her to leave, especially with a Chinese traveler!

Though she detested Bai-Hua, she cringed at the thought of telling him of Du-Fu's death. There was such dedication of son to father. Bai-Hua's attitude would change quickly when he heard of the tragedy of his father's ship and of his father's death!

Keeping this in mind, forcing herself not to see the desire for her in his dark eyes, Amelia took a step closer to him. She cleared her throat and implored him with her eyes. "Why am I here?" she said softly. "Bai-Hua, how can I tell you what has happened?"

Bai-Hua's insides coiled tightly, for he knew that Vona-Lee always spoke from the heart! And what she had just said made Bai-Hua's heart skip a beat! Had something happened to his father and sister? Was that why Vona-Lee was on the Indian island, dressed as Indian? Was it not as he had thought earlier? That she had chosen to stay with the Indian rather than to travel on to Boston to be with her parents? Would not Du-Fu Jin and Mei-Ling even now be safely on their return voyage to China? Or had fate been unkind to them?

Were . . . they . . . dead?

His gaze swept around the circle of Suquamish Indians. His eyes squinted with anger. Had the savages killed everyone aboard Du-Fu Jin's great and powerful ship except Vona-Lee?

Then his gaze moved slowly back to Amelia. No. She was too relaxed in the company of the Indians. She would not be so if she was being forced to stay with them.

"Tcha!" Bai-Hua exclaimed, not wanting to wait any longer for answers. "Tell me. What has happened?"

Amelia turned her eyes away. She swallowed back a lump growing in her throat, recalling the kindness of Du-Fu and how she had grown to love him. Only when he had begun partaking in the pleasure of opium had her loyalty and love wavered!

But at this moment she was recalling the moments when she had admired . . . had even loved him the most. Having to talk of his death would bring it all so close to her heart again.

But she must. She must!

Forcing herself to look squarely into Bai-Hua's troubled eyes, Amelia blurted out the terrible news, yet she was glad to be able to tell him that Mei-Ling was alive and well. She watched his expression become pained with the news of his father, then turn to hate when he discovered whom Mei-Ling was with, and why.

As he squared his shoulders, trying not to show his grief over his father's untimely death, or the pride of being the lord of the house of Jin now that his father was dead, Bai-Hua's eyes flashed angrily with determination to return to China not only with Vona-Lee but also with Mei-Ling! No sister of his would remain with an Indian, letting him touch her in all ways sexual. He would take her away! He would shame her as a brother had the right to do!

"Where is this island on which can be found my sister?" Bai-Hua growled, his fingers itching to draw the cutlass and use it on Red Eagle. *"Aie,* I must go to my sister and take her away. She will return to China with me.''

He took a step forward, his eyes snapping. ''Vona-Lee, *you* will return to China with me,'' he flatly ordered. ''You know you belong at my side. I now rule the House of Jin. You can rule beside me as my wife. Never will you want for a thing!''

He moved closer, his breath so close to Amelia's cheeks that she could feel its heat. ''My love for you is great,'' he whispered, leaning closer. ''How can you deny me this love? I have traveled far to prove how much I love you!''

He cast his eyes downward. ''If you will go willingly, my love will be gentle,'' he whispered harshly. ''Only gentle, Vona-Lee.''

Amelia paled, having never seen Bai-Hua humble himself in front of any woman with an audience. He had only humbled himself before his father! Only his father! This, and the fact that he had traveled from China just to get her, proved just how much he did love her.

But recalling how he had attempted to rape her made Amelia glad that she had made him humble himself so, for he would be shamed in the eyes of the Chinese warriors who stood watching Bai-Hua's demonstration!

''Bai-Hua, I cannot . . . I *will* not leave this island with you,'' she snapped. ''I have chosen to stay. I am going to become Gray Wing's wife.''

She jumped with a start when Bai-Hua jerked his head up so quickly to glare at her with disbelief in his eyes.

''Bai-Hua,'' she said, swallowing hard, ''I am no longer called by a Chinese name. When you address me, please call me by my original American name. Call me Amelia.''

''Gray Wing calls her his *la-dida*!'' Gray Wing said sternly, suddenly stepping to Amelia's side, placing his arm possessively about her waist. ''Now, Chinese traveler, if you have nothing further to say, leave this island.'' He turned and swept his free arm in a wide swing, revealing to Bai-Hua the Suquamish warriors Bai-Hua had not seen earlier as they stepped from their wigwams, clad in warring gear. ''My warriors will escort you and your men.''

Gray Wing's eyes twinkled amusedly when he saw fear enter Bai-Hua's eyes and his shoulders hunch as one by one he saw the many warriors, assessing the danger he was in. "Leave," he growled. "Your words of love to my woman were wasted words. Return to China. Use them on a Chinese woman!"

Amelia's eyes were wide, her spine stiff, as she watched and heard the exchange of words and looks of hate between Gray Wing and Bai-Hua. She glanced from Bai-Hua's strength to Gray Wing's. It was questionable which would win if they chose to fight, for there were many for both sides.

"My warriors' poison-tipped arrows move swiftly, if you are thinking of ordering your men to advance with their useless cutlasses," Gray Wing hissed, his hand on the sheathed dagger at his waist. "Leave, or die slowly as poison spreads through your veins to your heart!"

Bai-Hua glared from Amelia to Gray Wing. His silk robe rustling ominously, he spun around on a heel and began stomping in the direction of his anchored ship. He didn't look back at Amelia, for he knew that he would be returning for her. He had learned the art of moving quietly in the night quite well. He would go and get Mei-Ling from the Haida village, which he was now recalling from earlier voyages with his father. Then he would steal into the Suquamish village this night and get Vona-Lee!

Tcha! Soon she would call herself by her Chinese name again. The foreign dog name, Amelia, made her too much a *zien*, a common person! She was much more than that. She would soon be the mistress of the House of Jin!

Amelia sighed, yet something stirred within her as she watched Bai-Hua stomp angrily away. She knew him well enough to know that he did not give up on anything easily. . . .

"Come, my *la-dida*," Gray Wing said softly, urging Amelia back toward his house. "We will place all thoughts of what has just happened from our minds." He leaned to place a soft kiss on her cheek. "The sea journey and the sparring with the Chinese traveler have made me hungry.

Hungry for *you*. Let us make love. Let our souls spiral
heavenward with shared pleasure!''

Amelia smiled weakly up at him. Making love was the
furthest thing from her mind. She was worrying about
Mei-Ling. Bai-Hua would search and find her! What
then . . . ?

Wanting to belong, to adjust to being on the Haida island, Mei-Ling was on the beach on her knees, digging
clams with the rest of the women. Perspiration lacing her
brow, the skirt and blouse made of woven plant fibers
itching her tender olive flesh, she paused to brush strands
of damp hair back from her face.

As usual, her eyes were drawn to the sea, hungering for
China, grieving over the loss of her father. Soon her
mother and brother would be watching for the return of
her father's great ship with the decorative designs on its
sides. Soon they would know that the fates had not been
good to the Jin family! The lord of the house was now
dead, the sister and daughter gone forever!

The sea glistened beneath the rays of the afternoon sun.
Every wave had its own distinctive markings of whites and
blues, like precious diamonds, sparkling. Sea gulls dipped
and swayed over the water, fish flopped, porpoises bobbed.

Then Mei-Ling saw something else on the horizon. Her
mouth grew dry, her pulse raced. There was no denying
that she was seeing a great Chinese ship! The sun was
shining brilliantly down upon it, making everything about
it most identifiable! The crawling dragon design seemed
alive as the waves pitched the ship gently one way, then
another.

''*Aie!*'' Mei-Ling softly cried. She rose quickly to her
feet. She was a mass of tremors; she was so glad to see
something Chinese so near. Barefoot, she ran to the edge
of the beach, the effervescent foam of the water weaving
its way over her toes in its utter softness.

Bracing a hand over her eyes, she peered more intently
at the ship, her insides brimming with happiness when she
recognized it. It was the sister ship to her father's vessel

that had sunk. Bai-Hua was always in command of this craft.

"Hao, hao! Good, good," Mei-Ling whispered, smiling brightly. Bai-Hua was near! He had come . . . but why? He had not had time to hear of the shipwreck, much less to arrive in America after hearing!

Pressing her hands to her cheeks, Mei-Ling paled. "Vona-Lee!" she gasped. "My brother could not live without her! He has come searching for her!"

Her mind was swirling with questions. Had Bai-Hua already discovered that Vona-Lee was once again calling herself Amelia and had chosen an Indian for a husband? Did Bai-Hua know about the fate of their father? Was he coming to the Haida village knowing that Mei-Ling was there and in what capacity?

Bai-Hua would never approve of her loving an Indian. He looked upon Indians as savages. Especially the Haida. It was common knowledge among those traders in China that the Haida were called barbarous cannibals! Bai-Hua would see Red Eagle as nothing less!

"Hwah!" Red Eagle said, stepping up beside Mei-Ling. "A Chinese ship approaches!"

He swept Mei-Ling fully up into his arms and began running with her from the beach, toward his wigwam a short distance away.

"Red Eagle, what do you do?" Mei-Ling gasped, clinging about his neck as he ran so recklessly with her. "It is my brother's ship! I must see him when he arrives! My love is strong for my brother!"

"Kah-ta? Why do you wish to see him? Brother will take you away," Red Eagle said, frowning down at her. "You cannot leave me. My heart would cease beating. My life would be worthless!"

Mei-Ling's eyes misted with tears, hearing how very much Red Eagle loved her. She was suddenly torn between her feelings for the man she loved and her love for her brother. And also she was aware quite strongly all over again just how much she would like to return to China!

Oh, what was she to do? She could not have everything

she loved in her life at the same time. Too many miles separated these things that filled her heart first with joy, then with sadness!

"No," Red Eagle stormed, carrying Mei-Ling into the wigwam. He set her down beside the fire and threatened her with plant-fiber ropes. "You must promise not to leave my dwelling while your brother is here or I shall be forced to restrain you. Mei-Ling, you cannot be allowed to leave."

His eyes wavered. "Only if you insist that it is best for you to go, only then will I not restrain you," he said solemnly.

He knelt on one knee before her, his eyes dark with pleading. "Tell me you do not wish to go," he said thickly. "Your love for me is too strong. *Tell* me, Mei-Ling, *tell* me!"

Mei-Ling dropped her eyes humbly. Her heart was pounding so forcefully she felt almost swallowed whole by its thunderous beatings. She felt trapped. And she was! Trapped between two cultures . . . two loves . . . two commitments.

"I must see my brother," she murmured, slowly lifting her eyes. "It is my duty to inform my brother of my father's death. Fates were not kind then. They are not *now*. Please understand, Red Eagle. Families in China are devoted. I am very devoted to my brother!"

Feeling as though someone had splashed cold water into his face, having heard the determination in Mei-Ling's voice, knowing that restraints could cause her to love him less, perhaps not at *all*, Red Eagle saw no choice but to let her come face to face with her brother. He already knew the end result: She *would* leave him to return to China. She had been devoted to China long before she ever met him.

He would try to understand. . . .

"Then you shall see your brother," Red Eagle said, tossing the ropes aside. "I was wrong to even consider restraining you." He placed his hand on her elbow and helped her to her feet. "We shall meet the ship together."

Touched by his understanding and kindness, Mei-Ling threw herself into Red Eagle's arms, sobbing. "My darling, no matter what happens or what my choice is, oh, remember just how much I do love you," she softly cried, torn apart by the defeated look in his eyes. "Never could I love another as much as you. Never!"

Red Eagle brushed a gentle kiss on her lips, then placed an arm about her waist and led her outside. Together they watched the anchor drop into the sea. Then Bai-Hua was lowered in a longboat along with several other boats filled with Chinese warriors.

Hate swelling inside him, Red Eagle glared at Bai-Hua as he approached in the longboat, and then as he landed and climbed out onto the shore. Bai-Hua's long, flowing silk robe rustled as he walked, and his hand was guardedly on the handle of his cutlass. Red Eagle could already see in his mind's eye Bai-Hua suffering on a stake before he was killed.

But in reality he knew that would not be the way it would happen. Though his insides burned with the desire to kill the ugly Chinese, Red Eagle could not touch him. He would surely lose Mei-Ling's love if he did! He must let her make whatever choices she chose, then learn to live with them.

Bai-Hua's eyes had already found Mei-Ling, and then Red Eagle. He already knew how to get Mei-Ling to leave with him. He would *shame* her into going! She must be made to believe that she was wrong to love a savage Haida Indian. She must be encouraged to want to return to China, her beloved homeland!

Yes, shaming Mei-Ling would be the answer. She had been taught from childhood that obedience to the lord of the house was demanded of her. Bai-Hua was now lord of the House of Jin. Mei-Ling would listen to him, and then obey. . . .

Amelia lay snuggled beside Gray Wing, still warmed clear through from their lovemaking. For a moment he had transported her from this time and place. But now she was

again filled with wonder, staring into the dying embers of
the fire. She could not help but wonder about Mei-Ling.
Had Bai-Hua forced her to leave with him? Had Red Eagle
allowed it? Would Bai-Hua return to Whale Island for *her*?

A clap of thunder caused Amelia to flinch, the bright,
sun-drenched day having turned to night, filled with the
threat of a pending storm. It seemed the sort of night when
nothing could be at peace. She was becoming more and
more restless by the moment, yet Gray Wing was sleeping
soundly beside her, a soft fur blanket draped loosely over
his nude, muscled form.

The house became suddenly filled with light as a lurid
flash of lightning sent its jagged light through the small
cracks in the wall and down the smoke hole in the ceiling.
A great crash of thunder followed, and then the soft sobs
of Lorna who lay in her bunk behind a buckskin curtain.

"Papa, Papa!" Lorna cried softly. "I'm scared, Papa."

It was as though someone had pricked Amelia's heart
with many pins, the pain was so intense when she heard
her sister cry out for a father she would never see again.
Guilt washed through her as she recalled her father saying
that it was Amelia's fault that Lorna had no mother.
Strange how Amelia now felt such guilt because Lorna
had no father. Seems she owed her sister much more than
she could ever give her!

Scooting away from Gray Wing, drawing a chemise she
had taken from her trunk over her head, Amelia crept over
to the buckskin curtain and rolled it slowly upward. The
fire's glow across the room illuminated the tiny form of
her sister lying there, Lorna's green eyes beseeching her.

"Amelia, I don't like storms," Lorna whined. "I can't
help but be afraid. Please comfort me. Please?"

Amelia stretched out beside her sister. She drew Lorna
into her arms and held her tightly until Lorna was once
again lost in a deep, sweet sleep.

Amelia lay there awhile longer, looking up at a crack
in the roof. There was no more lightning or thunder. The
storm had passed on around Whale Island, but Amelia was
no less restless than before. She needed to be alone . . .

totally alone. She had the need to think. She wanted a private moment in which to worry about Mei-Ling and Bai-Hua. She must take a walk outside to ensure such total privacy!

Easing from the bunk, Amelia slipped a blanket around her and tiptoed past Gray Wing, then crept softly on outside where night engulfed her in its total blackness. She looked toward the sea, seeing nothing but a dark blot of black, the moon still hidden behind low, rolling clouds.

The damp, cold sea breeze stung Amelia's cheeks and bare arms. She shivered and changed her mind about the walk. It was too dark, even ominous, with everyone in bed and the village so quiet. Turning, she began to move through the whale totem archway that led back inside Gray Wing's house, but was stopped when strong, cutting fingers suddenly clasped her mouth, while others grabbed her painfully by a wrist. Her insides grew cold when she recognized the voice of her abductor.

"Bi-ni-di-zueh!" Bai-Hua growled. "You are coming with me, Vona-Lee. We are returning to China. You, Mei-Ling, and I, now the lord of the House of Jin."

Amelia's eyes were wild as she turned so that she could see Bai-Hua's shadow in the darkness. She squirmed, trying desperately to get free, for she was reeling from the strong smell of opium on Bai-Hua's breath.

But when he released her wrist and quickly held the blade of a cutlass to her throat, her struggles ceased. Would he . . . ?

"It is *buh-hao-eesa*, not good form, to argue with the lord of the House of Jin," Bai-Hua hissed against Amelia's cheek. "You see, I would rather kill you than leave you to share embraces with the savage."

His voice softened. "I will make this up to you, Vona-Lee," he said softly. "Once we are aboard my ship, you will see. Trust me, Vona-Lee. Trust me!"

Amelia dared not move. The point of the cutlass pained her throat. She did believe him capable of what he had threatened. He was crazed by opium again! She had no choice but to comply with his wishes!

As she glanced toward Gray Wing's house, her heart cried out to him, already missing him! Somehow she would return to him!

"Now just walk quietly beside me," Bai-Hua said, directing Amelia behind Gray Wing's house, moving along now in the shadows of the other houses that reached out to the beach. Amelia flinched when she saw stealthy figures of other Chinese warriors standing beside the houses, their cutlasses drawn.

Then her breath caught in her throat when she saw the Chinese who had been Gray Wing's slaves crouching, awaiting the right moment to enter the beached longboats. Gray Wing had refused earlier to hand over the slaves to Bai-Hua, so Bai-Hua had stolen them away, as well as her!

Amelia's eyes were adjusting to the darkness. As she neared the Chinese longboats she saw the tiny figure of Mei-Ling sitting in one. So it was true! Mei-Ling had been taken from the Haida village. Both factions of Indians had lost this night to the Chinese.

"Hurry!" Bai-Hua said to the waiting Chinese. "Should the savages awaken, they will be out for blood . . . Chinese blood!"

Amelia ran to the boat in which Mei-Ling sat. She climbed inside and they clung together as the boat was shoved out to sea. And as the longboat traveled closer and closer to the Chinese ship, Whale Island became only a slight blur on the horizon.

Amelia's eyes flooded with tears. She now wondered if these past days and nights were only a figment of her imagination. Strange how nothing at all seemed real to her anymore. Would it ever? Could it . . . ?

Twenty-Five

The gentle swaying of the Chinese ship finally lulled Amelia to sleep where she lay in her own private cabin, surrounded by beautiful silk tapestries and candles burning dimly, emitting wondrous scents. As she had lain there, fighting sleep, she had felt as though she had never been separated from the Chinese culture, for again she was shrouded in silks, perfumed with the finest colognes, and adorned with the most precious of jewels. Even now she lay curled between lavender silk sheets, her silk chemise clinging sensuously to her body. . . .

The creaking of the door stirred Amelia quickly from her sleep. Her gaze moved to the shadow moving across the room, only barely visible beneath the dim glow of the flickering candles.

Becoming breathless, feeling trapped, she began to inch backward until she could go no farther, her back now pressed hard against the wall.

"Bai-Hua, you don't want to do this," she said, not even seeing him, but smelling the vile opium on his clothes and on his breath as he moved closer. She pulled the sheet up to her chin. "Bai-Hua, leave me. You will be sorry tomorrow when your mind is clear. If you care about me as much as you say, you will not force me to do what you would not do if your mind were not opium-drugged!''

Bai-Hua chuckled low. He pulled his opium pipe from behind his back so that Amelia could see it now that he was standing over her, too close for her not to see his true intentions this night.

"You have never experienced the thrill of opium," he said hoarsely. "Tonight you will receive your first pleasure of the opium, and you will see how it enhances your need for me."

Amelia paled as she saw the long pipe, then gasped when Bai-Hua curled the fingers of his free hand through her hair and yanked her face toward the pipe. "No!" she screamed, pushing at his chest. "Please, Bai-Hua . . ."

The first taste of the opium stung Amelia's lips as the stem was thrust between her unwilling lips. A shudder coursed through her when the smoke of the pipe swept down her throat as she fought to speak and to force the pipe from between her lips with her tongue.

Choking, her lungs feeling as though they were on fire, Amelia pummeled Bai-Hua's chest with her fists, but felt herself weakening when a strange euphoria began to sweep through her. She had swallowed just enough smoke to cause the effect of the opium. She could even feel a strange tingling beginning between her thighs, as though she were experiencing a sexual encounter!

Afraid, fearing what even more opium might do to her, Amelia began to fight back more earnestly. But Bai-Hua held the pipe in place between her lips. She could not help but inhale more and more smoke. She was growing limper by the moment. She fell back onto the bed, her eyes closed. She felt as though she were floating, wonderfully floating. . . .

Bai-Hua laid the pipe aside, his eyes burning with desire as he threw the silk sheet away from Amelia. Moving a candle closer, dizzy from wanting her, he got a better look at her loveliness. His free hand went to a breast, freeing it from the thin garment. He laughed throatily when

Amelia softly moaned as his hand began to caress . . . to knead . . . to fondle. She was ready to respond. Fully!

Throwing open his silk robe, revealing his readiness, Bai-Hua stretched out atop Amelia. "Vona-Lee," he whispered huskily, then slid the chemise up past her knees so that he could have full access to her. "After tonight you will always want me, for now that you have been introduced to opium, you will hunger for it, and for the pleasure that is enhanced by being with me sexually. You will live for the moments we will share. You will want nothing more from life than this."

Crushing his mouth against hers, he pried her lips apart and plunged his tongue inside her mouth, tasting and sharing the taste of the opium with her. His hands could not get enough of her as they explored all of her curves, then teased and tormented her pleasure points.

Amelia's mind was screaming to be set free, but her drug-sated body was responding. She could not fight him *or* the feelings aroused by the opium in her system.

Tears silvered her eyes as he thrust himself hard inside her. Then suddenly Bai-Hua's body lurched and he howled with intense pain when a powerful blow to his head knocked him aside, away from Amelia.

Mei-Ling stood over Bai-Hua, weeping, clutching a broken vase. She had not seen her brother enter Amelia's cabin, but she had heard too much! This was the only thing she could have done to prevent the rape from becoming complete. Rape was not something she could accept a brother doing, even if he was her lord, her voice of authority, now that her father was dead.

Dropping the vase, letting it shatter into a thousand pieces at her feet, Mei-Ling first fell to her brother's side. "Oh, Bai-Hua, I had to!" she cried. "You could not do that ugly thing to Vona-Lee! You would hate yourself once you came to realize what you had done!"

Then she went to the bunk where Amelia lay in a crazed half-doze. Mei-Ling looked down at Amelia, her heart breaking when she saw Amelia's complete disarray, a crooked smile on her lips, and the limpness of her body.

She then looked down and saw the opium pipe and saw that she had been right to guess that this would have been Bai-Hua's tactic to finally get Amelia to display more than sisterly affection. The opium guided its victims into many ugly things!

But this?

Oh, how could Bai-Hua have done this?

"Oh, Vona-Lee, Mei-Ling is sorry that Bai-Hua treated you so unjustly!" Mei-Ling cried, dropping to her knees beside Amelia on the bunk. She eased Amelia's silk chemise down, to cover her nudity.

Then she caressed Amelia's brow. "Wake up, Vona-Lee," she cried. "Look up at me and see me. Your eyes are . . . so strange. The drug! It is evil!"

Amelia shook her head, hearing Mei-Ling, yet not hearing her. Her senses were reeling. Her head was beginning a slow ache; her stomach was feeling queasy. A bitter taste rising in her throat made her suddenly aware of what was real and what was drug-induced. She was going to retch!

Scrambling from the bunk, her knees weak, her heart pounding, Amelia rushed to a basin and hung her head over it. As her throat spasmed and she began to lose the bitter bile into the basin, her mind became clearer.

She then retched from remembrances of only moments ago. She clung to the basin, crying. She was recalling the moment Bai-Hua had entered her.

Yet deep within, where her desires were born, she knew that she had not wanted any of this. Her brain, which had been distorted by opium, had led her into false feelings of need . . . of desire. . . .

Panting hard, wiping her mouth, Amelia straightened her back and turned to look apologetically at her friend. "Mei-Ling, I am so sorry about this," she murmured, ashamed . . . embarrassed. She glanced from Bai-Hua to the opium pipe, then back to Mei-Ling. "That bastard brother of yours! He's the cause!" She hung her face in her hands, tearing apart inside. "How could he have done this. How?"

Mei-Ling moved cautiously about the quiet form of her

brother, afraid of what he was going to do when he awakened, yet more concerned for Amelia than for anything else. She embraced Amelia, cradling her close. "Vona-Lee, it is I who am sorry," she crooned. "I should have known not to trust Bai-Hua. I knew he was smoking the opium pipe. I knew how his mind was warped and twisted."

Amelia drew away from Mei-Ling and placed her hands on her cheeks. "Yet you left Red Eagle willingly to return to China with him?" she murmured. "Why did you, Mei-Ling? I was forced at knifepoint. Were you also?"

Mei-Ling's lashes lowered over her eyes. "He shamed me into coming with him," she said softly. "I had to obey. He . . . he is now lord of the House of Jin. He is *my* lord until . . . until I marry."

"Weren't you content with Red Eagle? Weren't you going to marry him?" Amelia insisted.

"It would not have been the same," Mei-Ling said, raising her lashes, again gazing into Amelia's eyes. "At heart I am Chinese. I must marry a Chinese lord to carry on the tradition of my family!"

"Not if you love Red Eagle," Amelia said, thoughts of her own true love causing her insides to ache terribly. "Mei-Ling, you should never let anyone shame you into doing anything you feel is wrong."

"But Bai-Hua is my lord!" Mei-Ling softly repeated.

Amelia glanced down at Bai-Hua, who was now awakening, groaning as he rubbed the bump swelling on his head. "There lies your lord," she said scornfully. "Is he truly worth what you have given up for him? Was it not easy to hit him, to stop him from raping me? He is not worthy of being called a lord! He is not a *da-jen*, a great man. In my eyes, as he should be in yours, he is worthless! A poor excuse for a man!"

Mei-Ling swallowed hard, then slowly nodded. "*Aie yah*, he is," she agreed. "In my eyes he is not even my brother. He has become someone I do not know."

Bai-Hua leaned up on an elbow. He looked blankly around him, then let his gaze move slowly from Amelia to Mei-Ling. He rubbed his head testily. "*Wei!* What happened? Why am I here? Why do you two look at me with such hate in your eyes?"

Amelia and Mei-Ling exchanged quick glances. Amelia wrapped the silk sheet about her, feeling chilled at the memory of what Bai-Hua had done to her. She lifted her chin stubbornly. "*Bi-ni-di-zueh!* Do not act as though you do not know," she hissed. She licked her parched lips, recalling the first taste of opium as the pipe had been forced into her mouth. "I will never forget any of what transpired here this night. Bai-Hua, I shall forever detest you."

Flashes of moments on the bed with Amelia played before Bai-Hua's eyes. His gaze raked over her, seeing how desperately she clung to the sheet that covered her beautiful body. He could recall touching her breasts. He could recall entering her and the pleasure it had given him!

Though he had been drugged, he could remember it all and was glad that he had done it! It was apparent that he would have no opportunity to have her any other way. She would not allow it!

But he could not let her or Mei-Ling believe him capable of such dark, hidden desires! He must pretend as never before!

Humbly lowering his eyes, he rose to his feet and bowed low. "Vona-Lee, I humbly apologize for anything I may have done while under the influence of opium," he said thickly. "Please accept my apologies. It was never my intent to harm you in any way."

Recalling how the opium had made Amelia falsely desire Bai-Hua, and knowing that it was capable of making anyone do that which he would not ordinarily do, Amelia lowered her thick fringe of lashes over her hot cheeks.

Then she raised her eyes and met Bai-Hua's as he looked at her. "Bai-Hua, I will fight to my death before I let you force opium *or* yourself on me again."

She squared her shoulders. "And, Bai-Hua, my name is not Vona-Lee!" she snapped. "It's Amelia! Though you are forcing me to return to China, I shall never behave like a Chinese woman again.''

She glanced over at Mei-Ling. Her mood softened. ''Mei-Ling, please remember to call me Amelia,'' she murmured. ''It is my true name. Using the name Vona-Lee seems a mockery to me somehow.''

Then her eyes flashed as once again she looked at Bai-Hua. ''And remember this, Bai-Hua,'' she said. ''Never will I conform in *any* way in China. And as soon as I can, after we arrive in China, I shall find passage back to Whale Island.''

Bai-Hua clenched his hands into fists at his side. ''I will spread the word to refuse you passage,'' he growled. ''Only I will make decisions where you will travel by ship. Only I!''

Amelia's heart skipped a beat. She now understood the full meaning of this voyage to China. She was Bai-Hua's prisoner! In every sense of the word, no matter how hard she tried to keep him away from her, she was . . . his prisoner. . . .

Soft whimperings drew Gray Wing awake. He sat up, letting the soft glowing embers of the fire light his vision as he glanced around the house. A tiny voice speaking Amelia's name made Gray Wing relax with a smile. His woman was with her sister, comforting her.

Wanting to view the tender scene, he rose to his feet, drew on his breechcloth, then moved quietly to the buckskin curtain that was lowered to the floor. When he peered behind it, something grabbed at his insides. His face paled, for Amelia was not there at all! Only Lorna was there, her eyes wide with fear as she caught him standing there, watching.

One long step took Gray Wing to Lorna's bunk. He knelt down beside it and gently smoothed her fiery hair back from her face. ''White child, you cry for your sister,'' he said guardedly. ''Have you seen her?''

Lorna nodded anxiously. ''She was here with me until

I went to sleep,'' she answered anxiously. "But when I awakened, she was gone."

Lorna wiped a tear from the corner of an eye. She sobbed. "Where is my sister? I need her," she cried. "I'm afraid, Gray Wing. I . . . I have had a horrible dream. I keep seeing Papa. The Haida . . . they are killing him."

She flung herself into Gray Wing's arms. "Papa is dead," she sobbed against his chest. "What if Amelia should die? Would you keep me as your very own? Would you? You aren't like the Haida. You . . . you are so kind. So very, very kind."

"Nothing is going to happen to Amelia," Gray Wing reassured her, yet he feared this very moment that something had. He must search for her. Now! Hopefully she was only down at the beach, taking a nocturnal stroll. "And, white child, do not you know that Gray Wing already looks upon you as his? You are part of the Suquamish life now. You will be happy."

He eased her away from him and framed her tiny face between his hands. He looked down at her, his eyes darkening with worry for Amelia. "But, white child, for now you must sleep," he said hoarsely. "Gray Wing will go and find Amelia and bring her back to you. Try to go back to sleep, little one."

Lorna's eyes were wide with trust. A smile brightened her lovely face. "Yes, I am sleepy," she said. Again she hugged him. "Thank you, Gray Wing," she sighed. "I'm happy my sister loves you. You . . . you are special!"

Gray Wing smiled down at her as he spread a blanket over her tiny form. Then he turned and hurried from the house, tensing when he saw and heard nothing. Only silence. Only an occasional dog barking. Only the steady lapping of the waves upon the shore.

But no signs of Amelia!

"She was taken away," a voice spoke suddenly from behind Gray Wing.

Gray Wing spun around and faced one of his slave prostitutes. His whole body rebelled against the words that she

had spoken . . . spoken calmly . . . spoken as though she
was glad!

Fiercely digging his fingers into the shoulders of the
prostitute slave he had won from Red Eagle during games
between their peoples, Gray Wing glowered down at her.
"Tell me you lie!" he commanded. "Woman, tell me you
lie!"

The slave with sparkling dark eyes and long wavy hair,
dressed skimpily in a plant-fiber skirt and blouse, laughed
huskily. "Now you return to house of prostitutes," she
teased. She placed a hand on his manhood and squeezed.
"Gray Wing cannot do without women. White woman
gone on Chinese ship, so you will use prostitutes again!"

"Chinese . . . ship?" he said in a growl, his lips tightly
pursed. A part of him was dying inside, recalling the ten
long torturous years without Amelia. Was the separation
to be repeated? Could he bear the loss again?

His fingers dug deeper into the woman's flesh, drawing
a cry from the slave. "You saw this and you did not inform
me?"

"White woman evil!" the slave declared, boldly tilting
her chin in defiance. "Haida woman good. It is best white
woman is gone. It is best for everyone!"

So angry he was seeing a white sheen before his eyes,
Gray Wing coiled his fingers into the slave's hair and
yanked until she screamed with pain. With force he
dragged her by the hair into his house.

The slave fell to the floor as Gray Wing released her.
Her eyes became two pools of tears when he picked up a
knife and approached her, leering angrily down at her.

"No!" she cried, inching back away from him on the
floor. "Kill me. Do not humiliate me by cutting my hair.
I would rather die, Gray Wing. Death is much easier than
being ridiculed because of the loss of my hair!"

"That is why I do it!" Gray Wing told her, falling to
his knees beside her. With one hand he held her in place.
With the other he cut her hair, leaving only that which he
could not remove without shaving her head, and he did
not wish to inflict that sort of pain.

Holding the long streamers of hair in one hand, he motioned toward the door with the hand still grasping the knife. "Now go!" he said sternly. "Stand in the middle of the village so that everyone will see you first thing in the morning. You will set an example. You will teach. My people will learn!"

Lorna lay on the bed, trembling. She was too afraid to get up and see what was happening. But she heard it all. She had even heard the slave prostitute say that Amelia was gone!

Tears streamed from her eyes, for she feared and loved Gray Wing at the same time. He was all that she had left in the world, and he had promised to take care of her. Would he? Or would he tire of her and turn her into a slave and one day cut *her* hair for disobeying?

Rolling her body into a tight ball, Lorna forced her eyes shut. She would not think about anything. She would teach herself not to feel!

Life would be much simpler that way. . . .

Sitting beside Mei-Ling in a green sedan chair supported by poles and carried by humble servants, Amelia swung and swayed high above the streets as the procession made its way to the House of Jin. They were now in Canton, the main port of China, the center of Chinese industry and commerce.

Dusk was just breaking. The streets had a peculiar, but not offensive, smell. Mule carts that looked like little houses with coop-shaped blue cloth tops were beginning to fill the very narrow streets. Sleek, fat mules pulled the carts along on large studded wooden wheels. The drivers sat upon the shafts and used the butts of their whips to prod the animals in their most tender parts. Passengers sat cozily, if cramped, inside.

From every axle hung a blue and white porcelain grease bottle and an oiled paper lantern. The rank of the cart's owner was revealed by the color of the cart step—blue for middle class, red for higher rank, yellow for a member of the imperial household.

Amelia tensed when the sedan in which she was traveling made a turn, now going down a different street. "Mei-Ling, must we be carried past the execution ground?" she asked, shivering at the thought. "Why would Bai-Hua want us to see it?"

She looked ahead, anger welling inside her anew when she saw Bai-Hua sitting smugly in his own very fancy sedan, with silk streamers rippling in the breeze. Amelia could never hate anyone as much as she hated him. In time she would give him cause to hate *her*. He would be sorry he had ever decided to claim her as his!

"Bai-Hua is like all men. They enjoy viewing the executions. It makes them feel more powerful, stronger, somehow," Mei-Ling said solemnly, sitting so beautifully beside Amelia in a brilliantly designed orchid silk dress that was similar to Amelia's, only Amelia's was green, to match her eyes.

Their hair was woven into towering edifices atop their heads, their faces were milk white, honey and almond having been used as a base before applying rice powder. They wore only dots of rouge on their cheeks, the tips of their noses, and the lobes of their ears. Golden spools hung from their wrists, a bracelet for each arm.

Amelia clenched her fingers tightly into fists as a small cart, pulled by mules, approached, escorted by soldiers. Several prisoners were crouched on piles of straw in the bed of the cart, each wearing a wooden placard proclaiming his crime.

Amelia grimaced, now passing the execution ground, where the bodies of sixteen pirates lay decapitated. The waiting victims were apathetic and sat silently smoking until the headsman called on them. Amelia's eyes were frozen in place as she watched a pirate kneel down. The headsman, with one cut, parted the head from the body.

Then she jerked her head around, feeling suddenly ill, relieved when the sedan was carried hurriedly onward, away from the death scene.

"Life is cheap in China," Mei-Ling said matter-of-factly.

Amelia nodded her head, then opened her eyes and let her eyes feast on the countryside, now that the city was left behind. Delicate, soft rice paddies stretched across the plain, where beyond, sharp blue hills rose into the heavens.

Villages were huddled and cramped between the paddies, but occasionally Amelia's eyes could single out a big country house with peaked gateways, corner timbers, and russet-tiled roofs.

Where the land rose to a slope, there was always a pagoda, layer on layer of fretted and chromatically painted wood, the roofs built so that they lifted in snub-nosed arches to the sun.

Chinese were wading thigh-deep in the paddies. They were scrabbling in the fields with hoes, or whacking the bony hips of water buffalo, herding pigs and chickens and ducks over the roads. Most of them wore wide-brimmed, high-crowned rattan hats and faded blue cotton clothing.

Women carried small children on their backs. Men strode, stooped with the weight of their carrying poles, buckets or baskets at either end, the tight trousers rucked at the calves where the muscles bulged. Under the hat brims the faces were concave in shadow, and sad, yet calm.

And then a great red-lacquered gate, studded with round brass knobs and guarded by a pair of ancient elms, loomed before Amelia's fearful eyes. To ward off evil the gate faced a blank wall, since the spirits of wind and water, *feng-shui*, could not turn corners.

Amelia was once again at the House of Jin, this time more a prisoner than the last, for this time she had not been bargained over but forced at knifepoint. This time the master, the lord, of the house was not Du-Fu Jin, who until he discovered the pleasure of opium, had treated her kindly.

This time the lord of the house lusted after her body. She was almost powerless, unless she could find a way to escape, and soon!

Yet hadn't Bai-Hua said that he would have her watched? He would not allow her to escape. . . .

Twenty-Six

❧ ❧

Six Months Later

Amelia watched the children at play in the main courtyard of the women's quarters of the House of Jin. She was reminded of her sister, Lorna, and of the news she had overheard just outside Bai-Hua's study when he was entertaining businessmen from Canton. There was an even worse smallpox epidemic than ever before on the islands of the American Northwest. Many had died—men, children, and women alike—because of the disease that had been spread to the land of the Indians by the white man!

"Not even Gray Wing may be spared," Amelia whispered, now pacing. The skirt of her silk dress rustled like paper being wadded. Her hair, dyed coal black again, hung in luscious streamers down her back.

It was not yet the time of day to build her hair delicately upon a framework. She did not wish to do so! She did not like being forced to look Chinese, yet she had no choice. She had no other clothes to wear. And her hair! Oh, how she hated that it had been dyed again. At least while it was woven into the framework she was not reminded of its color. She so wanted to look totally American in defiance of Bai-Hua.

At least I am lucky he has not tried to force himself on me again, she thought. He knows that I would kill him before I would let him take me sexually again. He keeps hoping I will learn to love him. How foolish he is!

She took another lingering look through her window. Peacocks ruffled their rainbow tails and uttered their strange, gutteral cries in the garden. In the far distance a seven-story pagoda, all gilt and chromatic paint, rose slender in the colorless sky. On a wooden trestle, a long porcelain *k'ong* filled with grass orchids was placed where their shadow upon the wall in the glittering northern sunshine would make a picture to gladden the heart.

But nothing would gladden Amelia's heart. It was aching from worry. What if her sister or Gray Wing became ill with the dreaded smallpox? She should be there to nurse them back to health!

Her eyes snapping determinedly, Amelia spun around on her paper-soled shoes and left her room in a flurry. She walked quickly down a long vermilion-lacquered colonnade lined with embroidered satin hangings, and through a series of tiled and severely furnished reception rooms.

When she reached Bai-Hua's private study, she stopped and inhaled a deep breath, trying to steady her nerves. She must be convincing in the lie she was about to tell Bai-Hua. She must also be convincing as to why the voyage to America must be made without him feeling he had the liberty to touch her once she promised to be his wife. She must make him believe that she wished to be a virgin in his eyes until after the elaborate ceremony was performed when they returned again to China.

"A wedding that I shall only promise, not perform!" she whispered, her voice quivering.

If only the fates would grant her the chance to once again be in America, she would never leave again!

Swallowing hard, her courage at its peak, Amelia knocked softly on Bai-Hua's door. She tensed when he, in a low growl, asked who was calling.

"It is I, lord," Amelia said in a voice forced with honey tones. She grimaced at the thought of ever being put in the position of calling him lord! He was not her lord. He never would be!

"Enter!" Bai-Hua half shouted.

Amelia slowly opened the door, immediately seeing Bai-Hua standing behind a great marble-topped desk, his hands tucked within sleeves shaped into flaring cuffs. His hair was drawn back into a neat queue down his back. His robe was styled from embroidered silk, with tiny diamonds glued in the center of the flowers sewn across the robe.

Bai-Hua glared down at Amelia, having long ago given up on her ever marrying him willingly. And he would not beg! He had enough concubines now to keep him happy. While with them, he fantasized about Amelia. That had become a good substitute for the real thing!

"You trouble your lord?" Bai-Hua asked sullenly. "Why do you, Amelia? Do you tire of embroidering? Do you tire of sharing tea and gossip with the other women of my house?"

Amelia felt the utter coldness of his words, as though someone had poured ice water into her veins. Yet she was not to be dissuaded from what she had planned, though she was taking a risk by even suggesting it.

"May I have an audience with you, lord?" Amelia asked softly, fluttering her long eyelashes enticingly up at Bai-Hua. "I have a proposal to offer you. *Ou-nah-nay*, O fortunate one, who can boast of owning so much and who has many lovely concubines to fill your nights with entertainment, let me speak to you of even more that you could have, should you still wish it."

She cast her eyes downward, pretending to humble herself before Bai-Hua; all the while, hate for him was eating away at her insides. "My lord, only a few moments of your time?" she murmured, slowly lifting her eyes upward. "Please?"

Bai-Hua raised an eyebrow quizzically, not trusting Amelia's new humble grace. She was not the sort to humble herself to anyone except for her own scheming purposes. Beneath the fluttering of her eyelashes, he had seen fire . . . spirit! *Wei!* What was on her mind this day?

Bai-Hua could not deny how her presence made his loins stir with a longing that was never going to be satisfied. Oh, how he wished that he had left her in America! At least while she was there, so far from his hungry gaze, he would not be tempted to take her at knifepoint again.

But her murderous threats lay heavy on his heart. She did seem the sort to carry out threats. Perhaps she *would* kill him. Perhaps he should stop toying with her and kill her *first*.

"Speak your mind," Bai-Hua blurted, waving a hand toward a red velveteen high-back chair. "Sit."

Amelia bowed courteously at his request, then eased into the chair as he slowly sat down behind his desk. "Lord, you will listen to my proposal?" she asked, leaning forward, not trusting his silence and questioning eyes. He probably already knew that she was here only on pretense and that what she offered would never happen. Dare she even state the proposal? Was he at the end of his rope as far as she was concerned? He truly no longer needed her for anything!

Bai-Hua placed his fingertips together before him and frowned at Amelia. "*Mei-ya-faza*, nothing to be done but to listen," he grumbled, his almond-shaped eyes squinting. "*Ai*. I will listen. Did I not say that I would? Did I not say to speak your piece?"

Amelia lowered her eyes, again pretending to be humble. "*Ai, ou-nah-nay*, you did," she murmured.

Then her eyes shot anxiously up. She calmed her trembling hands on her lap. "Bai-Hua, I am so worried about my sister, Lorna. All of the time I worry! And now word has spread to China that smallpox runs rampant, more than ever before, in America's Northwest. I must go and see if my sister is all right. Bai-Hua, please take me."

Bai-Hua jerked as though shot. "What servants spread such gossip to you?" he snapped. "Who!"

Amelia swallowed hard. Her eyes widened as she was reminded of just where she had heard the news. She could not tell him that she had been listening at his door, that in a sense she was a *spy*.

"Many speak of what you Chinese call the heavenly flower disease spreading like wildfire on America's shores," she said calmly. "How can they not speak of it so openly? They envy the Americans because they have the disease."

She visibly shuddered, never understanding how the Chinese could consider such a terrible disease *lucky*. But they did. They were even known to deliberately give the disease to many children. Doctors were known to make a serum from pustules of a smallpox patient and blow it up a baby's nostrils. All children who had been exposed to smallpox wore red bands on their heads, partly as a warning to others and partly in celebration of the fact that they were soon to be blessed with the heavenly flower!

No. Amelia would never understand such a strange custom. She dreaded the disease. She *must* get to Whale Island to see if Lorna and Gray Wing were all right!

"And you wish to go and expose yourself to the disease?" Bai-Hua asked, easing his hands down from in front of him to toy with a tiny brass bell on his desk. His eyes twinkled, for he was suddenly seized with an idea. Should he take Amelia to America, and should she contract smallpox, would she not be too ill to make her own decisions? Would she not welcome him as her protector?

Bai-Hua would make sure Gray Wing was not available to protect her. As much as she dreaded smallpox, she would be glad to have someone to look after her . . . care for her. She would welcome Bai-Hua in any capacity then! And once she was well, she would even agree to be his wife!

Amelia grimaced at the thought of contracting the disease herself. "Nay, I do not wish to have the illness," she said in a strained voice. "But if I must expose myself to it to see if my sister is all right, then I must!"

Reaching across the desk, Amelia placed a hand across one of Bai-Hua's. She could feel him tense at her touch. She could see the pulse beat grow more rapid at the hollow of his throat. She was swimming in dangerous waters, for it was imbedded deeply within his eyes just how much he desired her.

"Bai-Hua, if you do this for me," she murmured, her heart pounding, "I will return to China with you. I shall even . . . agree to marry you. You see, taking this voyage to America to see about my sister means the world to me. The world!"

Bai-Hua's spine stiffened and his breathing became shallow; he was not sure he had heard her correctly. She was willing to marry him? She would be this grateful? He knew that she came close to hating him because of his one attack on her body.

Then his insides twisted with hate. "You do not go to America for your sister," he stormed, jerking his hand free of hers. "It is because of the Indian that you return! Is not that the truth, Amelia? It is because of the Indian! You would not marry me. You would not return to China!"

His eyes gleamed as he again thought about how she would humble herself to him once she contracted the disease, smallpox. *Aie*, that was the only answer!

"But *buh-yao-ching*, it does not matter," he said smoothly, smiling. "We will take the journey. Mei-Ling will travel with us. She has not yet been fortunate enough to be exposed to smallpox herself!"

Amelia paled. She eased up from the chair, grabbing the edge of the desk to steady herself. "I cannot believe you want Mei-Ling to get smallpox," she gasped. "Bai-Hua, when people have smallpox, their bodies burn up . . . waste *away* with *fever*. The body becomes one great festering sore! Most . . . most die!"

She began to back away from Bai-Hua, seeing evil deep within his gleaming eyes. "*Nay*, I cannot let you do this," she said, her voice quivering. "I . . . I no longer want to go to America. I will not be responsible for Mei-Ling being exposed to smallpox."

Softly sobbing, Amelia turned and rushed to the door. Her insides grew cold and she stopped with a start when Bai-Hua spoke loudly from behind her.

"It is now March, the month that is hateful with half-promise of spring," he said without feeling. "In April, when the fruit blossoms bloom, we will begin our journey. One month, Amelia. You have one month to prepare for your journey."

Amelia's eyes flashed. She turned and glowered at Bai-Hua, but said nothing. She knew that words were wasted on him. And what was truly on his mind? Surely he was not returning to America without more on his mind than to see that Mei-Ling was exposed to smallpox. He had not even mentioned the proposal of marriage!

As she rushed from the room, Amelia's thoughts were scrambled. She could not trust Bai-Hua. He was scheming. He was evil. What were his true intentions for *her* once they reached America?

Amelia stopped cold in her tracks, her eyes wide. A numbness seized her. Did he also want *her* to contract smallpox? Was that his way of seeking revenge on her for denying herself to him . . . ?

Shaking her head, feeling drained, Amelia went on to her room and stared out the window into space. Had she again made a wrong decision?

Oh, Mei-Ling! What of her . . . ?

The voyage had been a long and arduous one, but Amelia was finally on land again . . . land of the Suquamish Indians. Strange how Bai-Hua had let her leave the ship so easily, Mei-Ling at her side. The Chinese ship had dropped anchor around a bend from Gray Wing's village, hidden from gawking eyes of the "savages," as Bai-Hua still called the Indians. He had remained on the ship, giving Amelia and Mei-Ling freedom to go and do as they pleased on land.

Amelia had not liked the smug look on Bai-Hua's golden face. He surely did plan that both she and Mei-Ling would get smallpox, then come begging him to take them away from this dreaded place festering with disease!

"He is a scheming bastard," Amelia blurted aloud, lifting the skirt of her silk dress as she stumbled on the jutting rocks of the beach. "Mei-Ling, he thinks he sends us to

our doom. We must prove him wrong. We must stay
healthy! Healthy!''

"But he only thinks of our welfare," Mei-Ling murmured, her tiny face lovely with its rouge and white
makeup. Her eyes sparkled, like the eyes of one who was
heading for a celebration. "Bai-Hua wishes us to become
more lovely by being blessed with the heavenly flower
disease." Mei-Ling smiled warmly. "I am happy my
brother cares so much!''

Amelia's eyes widened. "You truly believe that, don't
you?" she murmured, swatting a mosquito that was buzzing around her perspiration-laced brow. The heavy silk
robe was weighing her down. The sun was pressing
through its navy blue coloring, burning her skin. It was
summer; there was snow only on Mount Rainier's cone in
the distance.

"Mei-Ling, don't you think it's strange that Bai-Hua
does not come ashore himself?" Amelia argued, peering
straight ahead, hoping for a glimpse of Gray Wing's village through the leaning madrona trees. She hadn't believed she would ever see him again, and here she was, so
close! "I will wager that he will not expose himself to
smallpox. He was too eager to let us come ashore alone.
Do you not think that a bit odd?"

"He is in command of a great ship," Mei-Ling said,
shrugging. "He must stay aboard to keep the crew in
line.''

"And he trusts us so much?" Amelia sighed, flipping
the long streamers of her hair back from her shoulders,
glancing up at Mei-Ling's framework filled with hair,
looking oppressive in the heat.

"He knows that you will be with Gray Wing," Mei-
Ling said matter-of-factly. "He knows that I will somehow be with Red Eagle. But he also knows that we will
return to the ship. We have promised, have we not?"

"Promises are made to be broken," Amelia said in a
whisper. "I will never go back aboard that ship.''

"Nor will I," Mei-Ling said, giving Amelia a sidewise
glance. She broke into giggles, stopping to throw herself

into Amelia's embrace. "Amelia, are we truly here? Are we truly? I ache to see Red Eagle. I now know that I can never live without him!"

Amelia was thrown off guard by Mei-Ling's sudden change in attitude; then she laughed along with her. Mei-Ling had only pretended to make promises to Bai-Hua. She only pretended to be amenable to his wishes, all along knowing that she would defy him. She had even fooled Amelia!

"Mei-Ling, you are such a tease!" Amelia softly cried, hugging Mei-Ling fiercely. "*Wei!* You had me fooled. I thought you no longer loved Red Eagle. While on the long journey from China you were so solemn . . . so full of thoughts. You seemed so devoted to your brother. I thought perhaps you were no longer my friend." Tears warmed the corners of her eyes. "Oh, Mei-Ling, I am so glad that I was wrong!"

A scattering of rock ahead drew Amelia apart from Mei-Ling. She swung around; then her insides grew mushy warm when she saw Gray Wing standing there, Lorna at his side. In one sweep of the eye Amelia's worst fears were laid to rest. The two people she loved so much in this world of sadness and disappointment were alive and well! And Gray Wing appeared to be treating Lorna like his own child!

"Gray Wing!" Amelia cried, breaking into a run. "I have returned! I have returned!"

Gray Wing was stunned by the discovery. He gawked disbelievingly for a moment, then broke into a mad run and met Amelia's approach. *"La-dida,"* he said hoarsely. "My *la-dida*!"

They flew into each other's arms and fiercely embraced. Lips met in a feverish kiss. . . .

Twenty-Seven

❧❧

Pleasure was spreading through Amelia's body. She was melting beneath the enticing feel of Gray Wing's fingers. She sighed languorously as she eased more comfortably into the pallet of otter furs beside the fire pit in Gray Wing's house, letting him have his way with her, for it was what she also wanted.

"I feel so devilishly wicked," Amelia said, laughing softly as Gray Wing nibbled at her neck, sending electrical currents of ecstasy through her. "Here I am enjoying heaven in your arms while Mei-Ling has to wait until your warriors get her safely by canoe to Red Eagle's island. And Lorna! She must think me cruel sending her off to be kept by one of your Suquamish squaws while we make love in private."

Amelia did not wish to even breathe the words "prostitute slave" aloud. Gray Wing must have surely been having his pleasure with more than one of them in her absence. The thought of him in another woman's arms made Amelia's heart bleed.

But now she had returned to Whale Island. Gray Wing would have no need for other women again, ever!

"*Mah-lie*, forget everything but you and me," Gray Wing murmured, his hands hot against Amelia's breasts. She leaned into him so that she could receive the complete joy of his touch . . . of his sweetness. "We even forget the Chinese lord who stole you away from me. He is *mas-achie*, bad. Wicked! Tomorrow will be soon enough to deal with him."

Amelia tensed. She leaned up on an elbow, her hair spilling sensuously over her shoulders, the nipple of a breast just barely peeking through its silken threads. "I only wish to see him ordered to return to China," she said tightly. "Can you do this peacefully, Gray Wing? He has many Chinese warriors on board the ship with him. He could put up quite a fight to get Mei-Ling and me back."

Gray Wing straddled Amelia, his need of her showing in the strength of his swollen manhood. "He was a fool for returning you and Mei-Ling, if he in truth did not want to," he growled, his gaze raking over Amelia, soaking up the loveliness of her slim, sinuous body that had been denied him these many long months.

He then gazed into Amelia's eyes, cocking an eyebrow. "Why *did* he?" he asked. "I do not understand."

Amelia shook her head solemnly. "Gray Wing, it is something you would never understand," she murmured. "I think I do, but it's almost impossible to fully understand why Bai-Hua does *anything*."

She coiled her arms about Gray Wing's neck and drew his lips close to hers. "But who cares why Bai-Hua does anything?" she whispered. "Now that I am here and see that your island has not been completely devastated by the scourge of smallpox, Bai-Hua's plans will go awry."

Amelia snuggled into his arms as her lips brushed across his. "I am so glad that you and Lorna are all right," she said, trembling with ecstasy as Gray Wing brushed her hair from her breasts and his hands cupped them, his thumbs circling her nipples, causing them to become tautly erect. "If either of you had been ill with smallpox, I do not know what I would have done. As it is, I am so happy."

"Perhaps we should not have allowed my warriors to carry Mei-Ling to the Haida village," Gray Wing said, drawing momentarily away, frowning down at Amelia.

"Why not?" Amelia asked guardedly, fearing to hear the reply. Gray Wing was not the sort to worry aloud about anything. He kept his fears and doubts to himself.

"Many have died from smallpox in Red Eagle's village," he said, dread entering the depths of his eyes. "Mei-Ling was warned, but she did not seem to care. But my warriors are wary. They will let Mei-Ling out on the beach close to Red Eagle's village; then they will return quickly to our island. They do not want to be exposed to the disease any more than they already have."

Amelia paled. "I didn't know!" she gasped.

"You were with Lorna, enjoying being with your sister again, when I informed Mei-Ling of the dangers," Gray Wing said, smoothing a hand over Amelia's face, trying to calm her. "She insisted on going. It was her decision to go."

"It seems that Bai-Hua just might get his way after all," Amelia said dryly. "If Mei-Ling falls ill, Bai-Hua will encourage me to return to China to care for her." She shook her head sorrowfully. "He is clever, that bastard."

"But he will be *gone*," Gray Wing said, chuckling low. "We will send him away tomorrow. He will have no say any longer about anything that you do or that Mei-Ling does."

He drew Amelia into his arms, locking her body against his so that she could feel his ready hardness. "He has lost you to me forever!" he whispered, his lips grazing hers. "You are such a worrier! Do not worry so about Mei-Ling. Red Eagle will make sure she is all right. He loves her almost as much as I love you." He fit his hardness against her thigh and softly probed upward. "Let us make love. It has been too long between embraces!"

Gray Wing kissed Amelia with a fierce heat, entering her with one thrust. She was open and ready for him and moved her hips as he began his easy strokes inside her. She relished the hot, possessive touch of his body, hers growing feverish as currents of passion swept through her. Her hands stroked the flesh of his buttocks. She groaned in a whisper against his lips as he moved slowly within her, then moved faster in quick, sure movements.

"My love . . ." Amelia whispered as Gray Wing lowered his mouth from hers to flick his tongue about her breast. She shivered, she sighed. She locked her legs about his waist, wanting him closer . . . closer . . . closer. . . .

All of Gray Wing's nerve endings were tingling; he was enthralled by her creamy skin, his mouth hot and hungry on her flesh. His fingers explored her body, his breath was becoming short and raspy; he was so filled with need he did not think he could stand another moment without giving in to total release.

But he commanded himself to wait, for he wanted to be sure Amelia experienced total bliss at the exact moment he found it. His passion-heavy lashes draped over his dark gray eyes, he looked down at Amelia. She had the look of one who was peacefully content . . . of one who was experiencing sheer rapture. It was in the haziness of her green eyes and in the blush of her pink cheeks.

When she tightened her arms about his neck and urged his lips once again to hers, Gray Wing kissed her hard and long, his strokes inside her growing more intense.

Amelia felt as though she were running in a field of wild daisies, so carefree . . . so alive! Gray Wing's kisses were the touch of the sun, fiery on her lips. His hands were the wind, caressing . . . caressing! She had never felt so wanted, so beautiful.

Gray Wing was everything to her. Everything. . . .

Clinging to him, Amelia welcomed him as he came to her, thrusting deeply . . . thrusting harder. And then the wondrous feeling of floating enveloped her as she began to climb that peak of ultimate feelings. All at once she was there. Her heart thumped wildly within her chest; her mind began a sensuous spinning. In a brief moment of euphoria she had again reached that magical realm of feelings that were too beautiful to be described. Gray Wing's body shuddered and he thrust almost to the core of her being as he reached the same ultimate pleasure. Amelia cried out softly against his chest, pressing her face against him, smelling him . . . tasting him . . . feeling him as though he had melted into her, become one with her.

Then, too soon, it was over. Gray Wing eased away from Amelia and stretched out on his back beside her. His eyes were closed, his breath trying to catch up with his heartbeat.

"You make lovemaking so beautiful," Amelia murmured, cuddling against Gray Wing. She closed her eyes hard, trying to blot out the remembrances of that one time with Bai-Hua, when opium had made her body do what her heart did not wish to do. If she let herself dwell on that moment in time, she would indeed want to see Bai-Hua dead! He had violated her body, even her *mind*, by forcing the opium on her.

But soon Bai-Hua would see that no matter what he did, he had lost her forever. Gray Wing would make all things right for her. He would!

"You are the reason it is easy for me to pleasure you so," Gray Wing said, turning to face her. He kissed her brow gently. "It is good that you have returned. Twice you have come back to me. Twice your love for me has been proved."

"But still I must prove much more to you," Amelia said, giggling softly. "Gray Wing, still I must display skill at thrusting a harpoon into a whale."

"*Ah-hah*, yes, that is the custom of the Suquamish," Gray Wing said, placing a soft kiss on her lips.

Amelia twined her arms about his neck and lay cheek to cheek with him. She sighed contentedly. "Oh, Gray Wing, I hope Mei-Ling will find such happiness for herself with Red Eagle tonight as I have found with you," she whispered. "She deserves so much happiness."

"And you? You are truly happy?" Gray Wing teased, drawing an invisible circle about her nipple.

"Never happier," Amelia said, shivering sensuously. "I wonder if Mei-Ling *can* be as happy?"

"Red Eagle will treat her like a queen," Gray Wing said, laughing low. "Just as I treat you, my *la-dida*."

Gray Wing's lips devoured Amelia's mouth. His meltingly hot kiss evoked a soft cry of passion from deep within her. Thoughts of Mei-Ling were banished. Gray Wing's hands were caressing her, again lifting her up on a wave of rapture. . . .

Fog was like a gray shroud as darkness fell swiftly over the waters that reached to the Haida village. Mei-Ling sat in the canoe, shivering from the damp chill of the night. Though it was summer, night brought a touch of autumn with it in these waters fed by snow-capped mountains.

Eager to see Red Eagle, to be with him, and to tell him that she would never leave him again, Mei-Ling squinted, trying to see through the fog. But she could see nothing.

The canoe plunged through the water. The Suquamish warriors moved the paddles, stroke by stroke. Mei-Ling sat stiffly in the canoe, now hearing the low monotone of someone wailing. No. It was not one person, but *many*. These wails were accompanied by the incessant drone of drums beating. These sounds, which were morbid and sad, were drawing closer . . . closer . . . closer. . . .

Mei-Ling's body pitched as the canoe in which she was traveling suddenly beached on the shore. A flurry of excitement and hands forcing her from the canoe made Mei-Ling wince. Fear swam through her when she found herself being carried through knee-deep water and then abandoned on the beach while the canoe carrying all of the Suquamish warriors swept back out to sea.

Though she had been warned that she would be abandoned in such a way, it did not make Mei-Ling accept the aloneness any more readily. She was not sure how far she would have to walk to get to Red Eagle's village! Which direction should she travel to get there? In the darkness, nothing was familiar to her. Nothing!

The low drone of the drums and the wailing met Mei-

Ling's ears once again. She slowly turned and looked in the direction from whence this sound was coming. A tremor coursed through her. She had never heard the Haida sound so sad, so distressed, before. What could be the cause?

"Wei!" she whispered. "I must hurry. I must *see.*"

Lifting the tail of her silk dress, the paper-soled shoes she wore not sufficient to carry her painlessly across the rocks on the beach, she emitted low cries of pain as she scampered along, feeling her way through the darkness.

And then suddenly she felt hands on her wrists and a hand thrust over her mouth. Her insides grew cold with fear as she looked up into the fierce eyes of a Haida Indian, tattoos hideously spread across his face and chest.

"You are not wanted on this island," the Haida warrior growled. "You must leave!"

Mei-Ling looked wild-eyed as other warriors stepped out of the darkness, one dragging a canoe. She felt panic rising inside her. Was she going to be forced to go out to sea alone in that canoe? Where was Red Eagle? He would stop this nonsense. He would perhaps even kill these warriors who were treating her so unjustly!

Fearing being put to sea without being able to first talk with Red Eagle, Mei-Ling called upon a reserve of strength she had never known herself to possess. She shoved at the chest of the Indian who was holding her captive, then bit the hand that was held over her mouth.

When the Indian momentarily released her, howling with pain, Mei-Ling began to run, blind to what was ahead or how far she would have to travel to get to Red Eagle. She ran harder . . . harder . . . hearing the Haida warriors gaining on her from behind.

She drew to a quick halt when she found herself suddenly amid Red Eagle's village. When her gaze moved to his wigwam, her eyebrows lifted questioningly, for there were many torches lit about his dwelling and a

shaman was dancing and shaking his rattle at the doorway.

"What is it?" Mei-Ling gasped, covering her mouth
with a hand. "What's happening?"

Mei-Ling cowered, her shoulders hunched, when she
felt herself being surrounded by the Haida. The wailing
had ceased; the drumbeats had faded away. She turned her
back to Red Eagle's dwelling and began to inch backwards, wanting to find peace and solace within its walls,
wanting to find Red Eagle awaiting her with open arms!
She did not like what she was seeing. It was as though
someone had . . . died!

"Oh, no!" Mei-Ling whimpered, seized with the
thought that this someone was Red Eagle. Why else were
his people acting so strangely? Why were torches lit only
in front of his wigwam? Where was *he*?

Voices rang out all about her. "Leave! You are evil!
You and your kind bring evil to our people! Even our chief
suffered long from the malady!"

Mei-Ling's insides aches, her heart was being torn into
shreds. "No," she cried, placing her hands to her throat,
feeling as though there was a constriction there, choking
her.

Turning, she rushed into Red Eagle's wigwam before
anyone had a chance to stop her, but once inside, she felt
a light-headedness sweep through her. Before her very eyes
lay a man wasted away to mere bones and skin, his eyes
two sockets within his face. She scarcely recognized the
man she had fiercely loved! Had smallpox done this to
him? It was a disease treasured by the Chinese! Some died,
true, but never as terribly as this! And this was the man
she *loved*!

The fire's glow made a dim light for Mei-Ling to see
by. She fell to her knees beside Red Eagle who was
shrouded in a cape of otter skins. Reaching a hand to his
cheek, she recoiled and screamed. His body was cold! He
was . . . dead!

Stumbling to her feet, inching back away from Red Eagle, numb from discovery and an aching heart, Mei-Ling

then turned and fled from the wigwam, screaming. She saw no one and nothing except a blackness that was seizing her. She crumpled to the ground unconscious at the feet of a great Haida warrior, the one who had just been appointed the new chief. . . .

Twenty-Eight

❧ ❧

A low rumbling in the earth beneath Amelia awakened her with a start, reminding her that there was always more than a threat of smallpox in this northwestern region of America. There was still the fear of an earthquake. And it seemed imminent now, perhaps closer than ever before. Late last night when Amelia and Gray Wing had decided to take a stroll after lovemaking, they had witnessed strange occurrences, what Gray Wing had said preceded an earthquake. The dogs of the village were barking incessantly, the fish were seen jumping out of the sea, and armies of skunks and minks had swept through the village in mass migration.

But now things were quiet again, calmly peaceful. Amelia turned to Gray Wing who still slept soundly beside her on the pallet of furs before the glowing embers of the fire. She so badly wanted to reach out to touch him, to prove to herself that he was real . . . not a mere figment of her imagination.

But her gaze slowly roving over him proved that, yes, he was real enough. His copper skin and his muscular body spoke of so much that she had shared with him the previous evening, and would again tonight, if all went well with ridding the waters that surrounded Whale Island of Bai-Hua and all the bad that he stood for. Amelia wanted nothing more than to live in peace with Gray Wing, and to make a home for her orphaned sister.

Drawing a fur robe about her shoulders, Amelia looked toward the buckskin curtain where her sister Lorna was sleeping. Amelia grew tense when she heard soft whimperings, but sighed with relief when she had to guess that her sister had been awakened by the earth's rumblings and was only frightened, not ill.

The past evening, after Lorna had returned to Gray Wing's house for the night, she had felt slightly feverish to the cool palm of Amelia's hand. Amelia had tossed and turned throughout the night, worrying about her sister possibly becoming ill with the dreaded smallpox. Though Lorna had been spared thus far the dreaded disease, she was not safe from its evil clutches.

Amelia crept to her feet and tiptoed across the floor to draw back the curtain. Even in the dim light of morning she could see the feverish glaze in her sister's usually brilliant, vivacious eyes. And her face was scarlet; the flush was also induced by the fever.

"No!" Amelia softly cried, going to sit on the bed beside Lorna. She touched Lorna's brow and drew back as though shot. Never had she felt anyone so hot! Even Lorna's lips were parched with fever.

"I'm sick," Lorna cried, her eyes pleading up at Amelia. "I'm *hot*. My head and body hurt, Amelia. Do something."

Amelia was numb with fear. She knew the symptoms of smallpox. Thus far, Lorna had them all but the red spots. They would not appear for another three or four days. Only then could she be absolutely sure.

Gasping, Amelia grabbed for her sister when Lorna began retching. She held on to Lorna as her body spasmed over and over again until there was nothing left inside her to come up.

Amelia tried to lift Lorna up from the tousled bed but

found her too heavy. "Gray Wing!" she cried. "Oh, Gray Wing, help me. My sister . . . she . . . is so ill!"

Gray Wing awakened in jerks. He turned and saw Amelia bending over Lorna. He flinched when he saw that Lorna lay pale and limp within Amelia's arms. Then he saw the red cast to Lorna's face. The disease his people dreaded the most had once again surfaced on his island. Lorna could have nothing else, for he could see it in her eyes and flushed cheeks. He had stood over children of his village as they lay dying with smallpox.

"*An-ah*," Gray Wing said, rushing to his feet. He drew on his breechcloth and ran to Lorna. He lifted her and carried her and placed her on the floor, close beside the fire; Lorna's body was now racked by fitful chills. "There is not much to do for your sister if she has smallpox. Even our shaman is ineffective. We must labor over her . . . keep her comfortable. We must, above all else, keep her isolated from the rest of my people. Only you and I will be exposed, *la-dida*. Only you and I."

Amelia reached for a basin of water and a cloth. She began bathing the vomit from around her sister's mouth. She was torn with feelings . . . worry and grief over her sister being so ill, worry over Gray Wing and that *he* might become ill, and over his people being in danger of the disease. Forever she was made to feel responsible for so many things.

"I am so sorry," she murmured, easing into Gray Wing's embrace as he fell to a knee beside her. "Oh, if you should become ill. If you should . . . die . . ."

Placing a finger to her lips, sealing them of further words, Gray Wing smiled softly down to her. "Worry!" he said thickly. "Never have I seen anyone who worries as much as you. My *la-dida*, let us take each day as it comes. Let us feel blessed for each day that is given us in which we can love."

His eyes wavered as he glanced down at Lorna who had fallen into a restless sleep. He covered her with a blanket of fur. "As for your sister, we will do all that we can. . . ."

• • •

Bai-Hua paced the deck of his ship, looking landward. He had seen the swaying of the trees on shore after hearing the low rumble. Even now he was seeing a strange "earth-light," which was like a curtain of light in the sky and a wall of light on the ground. For a moment he had seen a bright yellow flash and heard a sound like thunder, which seemed to have come from Mount Rainier in the distance. He feared an earthquake, for everything seemed ripe for it in this restless northwest area.

Bai-Hua looked heavenward. He gasped and grew cold inside, for he was seeing sea gulls overhead suddenly flying up into the sky, as though crazed!

Bai-Hua was suddenly *hai-pah*, terrified, and felt the best thing to do was to leave these northwest waters immediately. But how could he? Amelia and Mei-Ling were not aboard the ship! He must go for them! He must get them safely away from this island that seemed filled with restless spirits!

His heavy silk robe rustling ominously, Bai-Hua began shouting orders to his crew. Many longboats filled with Chinese warriors were lowered overboard. Determined not to leave for China without both Amelia and Mei-Ling, Bai-Hua stood at the bow of the lead longboat, his arms folded angrily across his chest, his golden cutlass picking up the shine of the sun in its blade. . . .

Mei-Ling awakened to the slap-slapping of waves, and to aches and pains in her head and limbs. She looked cautiously about her, unable to see anything but the inside of the canoe in which she lay as it swayed and dipped in the waters of the Sound. Panic seized her, now recalling the previous night. After discovering that Red Eagle was dead, she had fainted, but not before she had realized what her fate would be. She was going to be put in a canoe and sent out to sea.

"Aie-yah!" she cried, pulling herself up to look over the sides of the drifting canoe. She blinked her eyes and

looked cautiously about, feeling dead inside because of
the grief that was bearing down upon her. Her beloved.
Red Eagle! He was dead! And he had died without her
having the opportunity to tell him that she loved him more
than life itself!

The fates still proved not to be good to her. Without the
man she loved she did not care to live! Life was worthless
now! Death was easier than having to bear such sorrow!

Yet she did not want to die without first praying to Buddha! And to do that, she must return to her brother's great
Chinese ship!

Willing her arms to move, she picked up a paddle from
the bottom of the canoe and thrust it over the side, into
the water. Viewing land, she let that guide her in which
direction she must go to search for her brother's ship. He
had dropped anchor just around a bend. It should not be
hard to find him. And once there, she would ask for privacy. It would not be all that hard to plunge the knife into
the depths of her chest. . . .

Another rumble of the land beneath her feet drew
Amelia to the door. Stepping through the totem archway,
she was stunned by the strange glare that briefly brightened the sky. It was many colors. It was a blending of
whites, reds, and greens!

"*An-ah*, what is it?" Gray Wing asked, stepping to her
side. "*Kah-ta*, why is the sky so strange in color?"

Then his gaze was drawn elsewhere. Many Chinese
longboats were being beached on the shore. Many warriors with cutlasses were unloading.

Then his gaze was drawn again elsewhere. The earth
was shaking back and forth. Amelia stumbled beside him,
then was thrown to the ground. Sudden gale-force winds
began hurling stones the size of walnuts through the air.
Screams and shouts arose through the village as a white
flash like slow lightning lighted the sky and sparked the
air.

"Gray Wing, Lorna!" Amelia cried, crawling toward
the doorway. "I . . . must . . . get to Lorna!"

A rumbling sound that came from the sky and underground drowned out all other noises. The earth began to shake from side to side, then jerked violently up and down, then again from side to side, as another deep-throated roar issued from deep underground.

"Lord!" Amelia cried, stopping, her gaze now on the beach, watching many Chinese warriors being swallowed into large cracks in the rocky shore.

She then grew numb when she spied Bai-Hua as he was thrown into a wide crack in the earth and was now clinging for his life. "Bai-Hua! Oh, no. Though I detest you, I don't wish you dead!"

Seeing that the land had become calm and that the worst of the earthquake was over, and seeing that the greatest damage had been inflicted on the beach and hearing Amelia's fears for the Chinese lord, Gray Wing saw no other choice but to go to Bai-Hua's rescue.

He glanced at Amelia, then back to Bai-Hua. In the end would he regret such a decision? Would the Chinese lord again take Amelia away from Gray Wing? Was that not why the Chinese warriors had only moments ago arrived with cutlasses?

Gray Wing decided that perhaps it was best to save the crazy Chinese lord, if only to openly challenge him before the surviving warriors. If Bai-Hua was shamed, he would go back to China and never return. He would forget Amelia, realizing that no matter what he did, he could not have her!

Ah-hah, yes. Gray Wing would save Bai-Hua to prove a point once and for all!

He broke into a mad run. When he got to the beach, he dodged the large cracks that had woven across the land in the design of veins on leaves. When he reached one that had split wide and far and was filling with water from the sea, he glared down at Bai-Hua who was clinging for his life to its ledge, his body already mostly immersed in the raging, muddy water. . . .

"Help me!" Bai-Hua pleaded, feeling the water sucking

at his body and lapping just beneath his chin. "*Wei, wei*, help me! I humbly plead with you, Gray Wing. If you save me, I will leave you and Vona-Lee in peace!"

Gray Wing was enjoying the power he had over Bai-Hua. He spread his legs wide apart and folded his arms across his chest as he glowered down at him. "You still call my woman by a wrong name," he growled. "She is not called by a Chinese name. Never again is she!"

"Call her anything," Bai-Hua pleaded, his fingers weakening as they pained so from the steady grasping of the rocks and earth beneath them. "*Buh-yao-ching*, it does not matter. Just save me!"

Gray Wing chuckled and his eyes gleamed as water began splashing into Bai-Hua's mouth and going up his nose. "You will leave? You will no longer torment my woman or Mei-Ling?" he growled.

Bai-Hua's insides splashed cold with hate with the mention of Mei-Ling. He did not want to give up both Vona-Lee and Mei-Ling to the savage Indians! But he now knew that he was in no position to argue. He had lost. Everything!

"Both are yours!" Bai-Hua said, whimpering as he began choking on the water that was closing in on him. "Both! *Ai*, both!"

Realizing that Bai-Hua could hardly hold on much longer, Gray Wing fell to a knee and clasped his hands around both of the Chinese lord's. With sheer force, he began to pull, with one hand grabbing Bai-Hua about the waist until he was safely on shore, his silk robe clinging to him, wet and muddy.

Bai-Hua coughed and choked. He brushed his dark hair back from his eyes, then began bowing. Over and over again he bowed, his hands tucked within the broad cuffs of his robe. "*Hao, hao*, good, good. Thank you! Thank you!"

Not wanting to be in the company of the Chinese lord any longer than he was forced to, Gray Wing pointed toward the few longboats that had not been washed back out to sea. "Go. Take the surviving Chinese warriors and leave and do not look back!" he warned.

Gray Wing glanced over his shoulder at Amelia who had come to stand on the bluff overlooking the beach. He saw something strange in her eyes as she looked down at Bai-Hua, but was glad when she turned and walked back to his village, not wanting to say a farewell aloud to the man who had stood between her and her complete happiness for too long.

"*Kla-how-ya?*" Gray Wing said mockingly. "My woman will not belittle herself by uttering good-bye to you."

Bai-Hua straightened his back. He looked from Amelia to Gray Wing. Hate raged inside him, but this time he would leave and it would be forever. His main regret was not seeing his sister to bid her a farewell.

But perhaps in time Mei-Ling would miss him and China enough to return on another Chinese ship. He would pray to Buddha that she would. Without her, life would be empty, for there was always something special about Mei-Ling, his beloved younger sister. . . .

Downhearted, feeling defeated, Bai-Hua slipped into a dry robe, glad to be aboard his ship. His crew were preparing the ship for departure and Bai-Hua was missing Mei-Ling more by the minute. Soon a large body of water would separate them forever. He was not sure if he could bear it!

Needing to feel close to her, Bai-Hua tied the robe at his waist, then left his cabin to go to Mei-Ling's. Just one look around, to feel her closeness in her personal possessions, and then he would forever turn his back on everything that reminded him of her. She would be the same as dead to him, denied him as though she were!

His feet shuffling heavily on the carpeted flooring of his fancy ship, Bai-Hua opened the door to Mei-Ling's cabin, then was taken aback, shocked at what he saw, and wondering how it could have happened!

"*Aie-yah!* It cannot be!" he shouted, looking at Mei-

Ling's tiny figure lying in a pool of blood before her statue of Buddha. "*Pu-zai-la*, she's dead! She's dead!"

Bai-Hua went to Mei-Ling and cradled her lifeless body within his arms. His tears swam across her pale face as he held her cheek to his, rocking her . . . rocking her. . . .

Twenty-Nine

While Gray Wing was going through his village, calming his people after the earthquake, Amelia was sitting beside the fire pit with Lorna's head resting on her lap. "You're going to be all right," she whispered, smoothing a wet buckskin cloth across her sister's burning brow. "You've . . . *I've* gone through enough. God just can't . . . *won't* let you die."

Lorna slept on, hearing nothing, feeling nothing.

Her back aching from sitting and holding her sister for so long, Amelia had to stand and stretch. Easing Lorna's head back to the fur pallet, she rose quietly and looked toward the door. Perhaps she could be of some help to Gray Wing. So many of his people had panicked during the earthquake, even though hardly any of their homes had been affected. It had been mostly the eerie flashes of light that had frightened them. They had thought it was evil spirits coming to torment them.

Attired in a loosely fitted buckskin dress, stretching her arms above her head, Amelia stepped from the house just in time to bump into Gray Wing as he was rushing angrily toward it. Amelia flinched when he grabbed her by the

286

shoulders, steadying her, his eyes two heated pools of angry fire.

"What . . . is . . . it, Gray Wing?" she murmured, his fingers paining her arms where they dug fiercely into them. "What's . . . happened?"

"It is the crazy Chinese lord!" Gray Wing hissed, glancing over his shoulder in the direction of the sea. "He comes again! I have come to get my arrows tipped in poison. This time I will not waste words on Bai-Hua. I will kill him!"

Amelia's head was spinning with wonder . . . with questions. She looked from Gray Wing to the sea, fear creeping inside her heart when she saw a lone longboat with a lone passenger. There was no mistaking Bai-Hua. But why would he return so shortly after being ordered away? And hadn't he agreed that he would leave peacefully?

Yet wasn't he returning in a peaceful manner? There were no other Chinese with him.

"Why is he returning?" Amelia asked, then turned as Gray Wing fled past her into the house. Her knees grew weak as she recalled his mention of a poison-tipped arrow and what he planned to do with it.

"No!" she cried, running after him into the house. "You can't do that, Gray Wing. Give Bai-Hua a chance to explain why he has returned. There must be a reason. He is not a stupid man. He would not return on the chance that you would kill him. He must have a need to talk." She flailed a hand desperately in the air. "Or *something*."

Flinging his bow across his shoulder and grabbing an arrow, Gray Wing moved on past Amelia through the door, ignoring her.

Frustrated, Amelia glanced down at Lorna, glad that the disturbance hadn't awakened her, then rushed back outside and followed Gray Wing in a half-run as he moved toward the beach.

Placing a hand over her eyes, shielding them from the bright rays of the sun, Amelia studied Bai-Hua in the approaching longboat.

Then her footsteps faltered. At this closer proximity she could see a look of keen grief on Bai-Hua's face. Something terrible had happened. But what . . . ?

Amelia glanced over at Gray Wing who was now at the bluff overlooking the sea. He was raising his bow already notched with the arrow. He was aiming. . . .

Bai-Hua looked up and saw the danger. His insides knotted. He had expected to be met with anger, but not *this*. Panic rising inside him, he saw but one thing to do. Leaning, he lifted Mei-Ling into his arms; then he stood in the longboat and looked up at Gray Wing, then over at Amelia.

"Pu-zai-la!" Bai-Hua shouted, his words reverberating across the water, the beach, and upward. "Vona-Lee . . . Amelia, *pu-zai-la!*"

A dizziness swept through Amelia; she paled. She placed her hands to her throat, feeling a constriction suddenly there at a time when she so badly wanted to scream. Her eyes were riveted on Mei-Ling's lifeless body. Her mind had captured Bai-Hua's words, as though Gray Wing's poison-tipped arrow had been thrust into her heart, slowly claiming her life, inch by inch . . . inch by inch.

Oh, yes, she understood the Chinese words too well! Bai-Hua had said that Mei-Ling was dead!

Gray Wing slowly lowered his bow and arrow, stunned by what he was seeing. Mei-Ling? In Bai-Hua's arms? And she was lifeless! Was . . . she dead? What had the Chinese lord shouted?

Amelia lowered her face into her hands and began softly sobbing. "No," she cried. "Not this also! When will it end? Oh, why? Why?"

Gray Wing dropped his bow and arrow to the ground and went to Amelia. His strong arms engulfed her. He placed his nose into the depths of her hair, cradling her close, rocking with her. "She is dead?" he murmured. "Is that what the Chinese lord said?"

"Yes. Mei-Ling is . . . dead," Amelia cried, clinging desperately to Gray Wing, trying to force herself to recall the Chinese belief that one is never dead but only traveling to a better place in time. How could she believe that Mei-Ling was better off? Mei-Ling would never laugh again . . . would never embrace Amelia again as sisters do! She would never . . . love again!

Jerking free of Gray Wing's embrace, wiping her eyes and nose, Amelia looked up at Gray Wing with a frustrated questioning. "How could this be?" she said, her voice strained. "She was supposed to be with Red Eagle."

"Red Eagle?" Gray Wing said, tilting an eyebrow. "He could not be responsible for her death. Then *who*?"

Both turned and looked at Bai-Hua who still stood with Mei-Ling in his arms, awaiting permission to resume his approach to the island. Gray Wing raised an arm, gesturing to him. "*Chah-ko!*" he shouted. "Come ahead. You and your sister are welcome!"

Amelia's attention was drawn elsewhere. She grabbed for Gray Wing, her spine suddenly stiff when she saw several massive canoes approaching just around the bend. "Gray Wing, look!" she said in a near whisper. "Is not that the Haida? Could it be Red Eagle? Does he know about Mei-Ling?"

"It has been a while since I have met with Red Eagle," Gray Wing said, turning his attention to the approaching Haida warriors. "Because of the smallpox plague on his island I have chosen not to go and have conferences with him." He paused and raised an eyebrow. "But surely he does come because of Mei-Ling. Perhaps the Chinese sent word to him of her death."

The word "death" and its relation to Mei-Ling sent spirals of grief throughout Amelia. She was finding it hard to accept. But she found courage in Gray Wing's nearness. She stood beside him, her chin lifted valiantly, her long streamers of black hair blowing and lifting in the brisk wind, as Bai-Hua reached the shore, seemingly unaware of the approaching Indians behind him. His face tear-streaked, he seemed lost to everything but what he held within his arms as he stepped onto shore, carrying Mei-Ling.

Amelia swallowed back a lump growing in her throat as Bai-Hua made his slow, yet determined approach up the slope of land that led from the sea. She could not pry her eyes from the lifeless form of Mei-Ling. Her friend looked even smaller now in death than she had when alive, as an arm hung limp at her side, her face so ashen in its death mask.

Amelia gasped. With Bai-Hua this close, she could now see the blotch of red . . . the spread of blood on Mei-Ling's blue silk gown. It reached from her lifeless heart down past her waistline. She had died from a knife wound.

But . . . inflicted . . . by whom?

Bai-Hua reached the crest of the hill and stopped before Amelia and Gray Wing. He looked from one to the other, then held Mei-Ling out to Gray Wing. "She is now yours," he said hoarsely.

Amelia's eyes widened, her throat became dry, for she did not understand any of this, Mei-Ling's death *or* Bai-Hua bringing her to Whale Island, offering her to Gray Wing. "Bai-Hua, what happened?" she blurted, so wanting to touch Mei-Ling, caress her smooth, sweet face. Mei-Ling looked so alone in her death!

Bai-Hua ignored Amelia's questions. Again he offered Mei-Ling to Gray Wing. "Take her. *Mei-ya-faza.* I cannot return her to China now. The voyage is too long. Her body would not last the trip. She must remain here. You give her proper burial." He looked over at Amelia, his eyes red-streaked with grief. "Vona-Lee, you will look after her?"

Amelia nodded, choking back the urge to cry. "*Ai*, I shall look after her," she murmured. She took a step closer and dared to touch Mei-Ling's face, then shuddered and drew her hand quickly away when she felt the utter coldness.

"Bai-Hua, how did this happen?" Amelia half shouted, her eyes wild. "Mei-Ling is dead. How?"

She tensed when over Bai-Hua's shoulder she saw the Haida Indians now beaching their canoes. She glanced at Gray Wing as he took Mei-Ling into his arms, seemingly unaware that the Haida were drawing closer. He seemed to be as wrapped up in grief as Amelia over Mei-Ling's death. He was a man of feelings . . . deep, sweet feelings.

"She killed herself," Bai-Hua said, lowering his eyes sadly. "I found her lying before her statue of Buddha. She . . . she must have made peace with herself and Buddha before dying."

Amelia shook her head, feeling ill at the thought of Mei-Ling plunging a knife into her own precious body. "It can't be," she said, choking on the words. "Why would she?"

Her gaze swept downward, her own question fading away on her lips as she watched many Haida warriors now advancing up the slope of land from the sea. She stiffened when she did not see Red Eagle among them. She glanced over at Gray Wing who still stood so gently holding Mei-Ling in his arms. He was defenseless at this time. What if the Haida had come for warring? Without Red Eagle, that was possible.

Then she felt the approach of Suquamish Indian warriors behind her and knew that Gray Wing was never alone and defenseless. His warriors were always there, guarding him.

Now aware of being surrounded by Indians, the Haida at his back, the Suquamish in front of him, Bai-Hua humbly stepped aside, cowering, as Gray Wing took a bold step forward, frowning toward the approaching Haida Indians.

Gray Wing scanned the faces of the Haida, looking for Red Eagle, yet not seeing him among them. Why would his warriors land on Suquamish land without him? Why would they come now when they knew they would not be welcomed? Any among them could be carrying the scent of the dreaded smallpox with them! That was why the Suquamish and Haida had been parted for so long now! One respected the other enough to protect the other!

"Why do you come?" Gray Wing asked, his voice loud and authoritative. "Where is Red Eagle? Did he send you? *Hwah!* Why would he? He always brings his own messages to the chief of the Suquamish!"

Bear's Paw, the new chief of the Haida, glowered down at Mei-Ling, then looked tight-jawed up at Gray Wing. "It is best that she is dead," he said flatly. "For Chief Red Eagle is also dead! I am now chief. Look to me as such, Chief Gray Wing. It is I who will choose either warring or peace for our people."

Amelia's eyes wavered, and something grabbed her at the pit of her stomach when she heard of Red Eagle's death. "He is . . . dead?" she gasped. "How did he die?"

"By diseases brought to my island by such as you and . . . and *her*!" Chief Bear's Paw shouted, motioning toward Mei-Ling. "Red Eagle died of smallpox!"

Amelia was beginning to understand what might have urged Mei-Ling to take her own life. "Did Mei-Ling know of Red Eagle's death?" she asked, meeting the glare in Chief Bear's Paw's eyes with a glare of her own. "Did you . . . by chance send her away from your island after she found out? Were you that cruel?"

Chief Bear's Paw nodded, then eyed Gray Wing with coldness. "If this white woman is to remain with you, possibly even become your wife, you will have to instruct her on how to treat the Haida with respect. Otherwise, peace will be hard to share with you."

Turning on a heel, Chief Bear's Paw lifted a fist into the air and shouted to his warriors, instructing them to return to their canoes and then to his island.

Amelia trembled as she watched his departure. He was nothing at all like Red Eagle. Perhaps peace had just ended between these two tribes of Indians. And again she felt responsible!

Bai-Hua became the focal point of attention again as he went to Mei-Ling and kissed her brow, then her lips, then turned and began to walk heavy-shouldered toward the sea. Amelia choked back a sob. She looked at Gray Wing, then at Mei-Ling, then again at Bai-Hua, then took off running after him. Grabbing him by a hand she stopped him and lunged into his arms, sobbing.

"Bai-Hua, I will take care of Mei-Ling," she cried, clinging to him, even accepting the strength of his arm about her. At this moment she could not recall ever hating him. Pity, grief, took the place of hate. "Return to China and find happiness there among your people. Forget all of your sadness."

She inched from his arms and looked up into the dark pools of his eyes. "Did your people not teach me that when one died she was not dead, but had merely ascended, properly escorted, to the spirit world, where she would continue much the same as on earth?" she murmured. "Did not your people say that one must not grieve too deeply over death, which is only a portal, a stepping stone to the next life? Is not Mei-Ling already there? Only her body remains on this earth."

Bai-Hua's eyes misted with tears. He had always thought that Vona-Lee, Amelia, was special, but at this moment he saw just how much. She had forgiven all the ugly things he was guilty of, to give him encouragement at this time in his life when he felt as though he had nothing left at all. Now his sadness at losing her had increased twofold!

Oh, how could he leave her?

But he must. She and her heart belonged to the Indian.

Drawing her gently into his arms, Bai-Hua embraced Amelia, then swept away from her and hurried to his longboat. Without looking back he was taken out to sea, pride swelling inside him that she did care at least a little for him. She did not totally hate him!

Amelia watched Bai-Hua until he rounded the bend that would lead him to his ship. Then she slowly turned and looked up at Gray Wing. She smiled softly, seeing how he still stood so quietly with Mei-Ling in his arms, awaiting her.

With her chin held firmly high, knowing that she must be strong to make it through the next couple of days of burial rites and of ministering to her ill sister, Amelia went to Gray Wing and accompanied him to his house where Mei-Ling was laid out to be prepared for burying.

As Amelia looked down upon Mei-Ling's body, she kept repeating the Chinese belief to herself, over and over again, or else grief could very well overcome her! At least living in China had given her something she might have never found by being brought up solely in an American household.

She had been taught many ways to have courage. . . .

Thirty

֍ ֎

Three months later

Amelia's heart was filled with warmth, and she was glad
to have the opportunity to sit and braid her sister's hair.
For a while, during Lorna's sickness, it had become
doubtful that she would survive the ordeal of smallpox.

But now only a brown discoloration was left just beneath Lorna's skin due to the blisters that had ravaged her
body. One by one scabs had formed and dropped off.
Slowly the fever had dropped, then left completely. Lorna
was left with a few scars and was still pale and thin, but
she was well. She had been blessed, for most who had
been as ill with smallpox had died. . . .

"Perhaps you are strong enough to go and join the other
children your age today," Amelia said, tying a bow around
the end of Lorna's braid. "But only for a little while. You
don't want to get too worn out. You want to be able to
join the others who will be watching and waiting to see if
I can throw a harpoon, to prove my worth as Gray Wing's
wife."

Amelia turned Lorna around, so their eyes could meet
and hold. She placed her hands on Lorna's pale cheeks.

She bent down and spoke into her face. "I will be thrusting a harpoon into a whale! Isn't that exciting, Lorna?"

Lorna's green eyes sparkled. She smiled widely. "Do you think that one day I may do the same as you?" she asked excitedly, her hands clasped anxiously on her lap. "Do you think I will one day prove my worth as a wife so that I can marry a Suquamish warrior when I am old enough to do so?"

Amelia's eyes misted with tears. Her gaze swept over Lorna, seeing her Indian buckskin dress and beaded moccasins. She had adapted well into the Suquamish tribe. It had been good that she had been allowed to play with Indian children from the time she could walk, for that had helped in the adjustment.

Drawing Lorna into her arms, Amelia sighed. "Yes, perhaps some handsome warrior who is one day to be a chief might want you to be his wife one day," she murmured, stroking her sister's frail back. She then laughed softly. "But you do have a lot of growing up to do, don't you think?"

"I'm glad I am going to grow up," Lorna said, a shudder encasing her. "I was so sick, Amelia. I thought I was going to die."

Lorna leaned away from Amelia. "Did Mei-Ling die because she was sick like me?" she asked, cocking her head. "No one ever says much about her. Do you miss her, Amelia? She was so pretty!"

Amelia's contentment faded, as did her smile, with the mention of Mei-Ling. She doubted if she would ever grow used to her absence. And how could she explain to Lorna that Mei-Ling had taken her own life? That was not acceptable in the Christian teachings.

"Well, uh, sort of," Amelia blurted, deciding it would be best to tell the full truth later, when Lorna was older and not so vulnerable to such truths.

Gray Wing's entrance into the house was very welcome . . . very timely. Amelia smiled up at him when she saw a gleam in his dark gray eyes. As he moved toward her he had a bounce in his steps.

She rose and met his approach, receiving his hug with a sigh. "What are you up to, Gray Wing?" she asked, laughing softly. "You are acting just a mite suspicious."

Stepping back away from him, she grabbed his hands and squeezed them affectionately. "Well? Are you going to tell me?"

Gray Wing pressed a kiss to the tip of Amelia's nose, eased his hands from hers, then went to Lorna and held her at arm's length, eyeing her amusedly. "How would you like a visitor this morning?" he asked, chuckling as he saw her eyes light up. "Someone is just outside the door, asking to see you."

Lorna beamed joyously, already knowing who was there, without asking. A close friend, Little Fox, had visited her quite often of late and had promised to come again this morning. He had said something about a special gift that he was going to bring to her. She was thrilled that he, being a young man two years older than she, would care so much. That she was white made no difference, for everyone in the Suquamish village had already accepted her as one of them.

"Oh, yes, I would love to have company!" Lorna said, lunging into Gray Wing's arms, hugging him fiercely. "May I, Gray Wing? May I?"

"*Ah-hah*," Gray Wing said thickly, brushing a kiss against Lorna's frail cheek. He gave Amelia a nod, silently giving her the signal to invite Little Fox inside. Then he stepped back to watch Lorna's excitement as Little Fox came into the dwelling.

Gray Wing's eyes absorbed the handsome young man, looking like the future warrior he was, in his loincloth and fringed vest. The lad's face was sculpted with Indian features; his eyes were dark gray and flashing. If Gray Wing had no sons, perhaps Little Fox would one day be Gray Wing's choice as next chief in line.

An awkward smile lifted Little Fox's full lips as he stepped up to Lorna and offered her a beautiful necklace of tusks. "*Klas-ka*, yours," he said in a voice verging on manliness. "Do you like?"

Amelia stepped around the two children and went to Gray Wing and slipped an arm through his, to watch with him. It was as though they were watching their very own child, instead of Amelia's sister.

Then Amelia was taken back in time as she watched Lorna accept the gift. Had it truly been so many years ago that Gray Wing had given her the same token of love?

Sad that hers had been destroyed by an angry, jealous father. . . .

Lorna's eyes widened in wonder as Little Fox placed the necklace in her outstretched hands. Never had she been given a gift from the heart. And, oh, wasn't it beautiful? She had already been taught the value of such a necklace! This one was even more valuable, because Little Fox had given it to her!

"Truly? This is mine?" Lorna said with a sigh. "You give this to me to keep, Little Fox?"

"*Ah-hah*, yes," Little Fox said, shifting his moccasined feet nervously. "Do you like it?"

"It is so . . . so very, very pretty," Lorna said, smiling bashfully up at Little Fox. "Can I wear it now?"

Little Fox took a step toward her. He touched the necklace, questioning Lorna with his eyes. "I would like you to wear it always," he said, taking the necklace. "Let me place it around your neck." His face grew solemn. "I so feared for you while you were ill. You were so ill! I had to come and give you this gift to prove how happy I am that you are once again well!"

Amelia's eyes misted with tears. She had to look away from the tender scene, so touching . . . so full of sweet remembrances of when Gray Wing had placed the special necklace about *her* neck. Though Lorna was now only ten and surely did not yet know the true meaning of love—nor did Little Fox, who was only twelve—the gift was innocently sweet and held within it a meaning that perhaps would grow into more as the children matured into adulthood . . . into true passion. . . .

Gray Wing placed an arm about Amelia's waist and drew her to his side, touched deeply by the tender scene, re-

calling the time he had given Amelia his necklace as a
gift. Little had he known at that time just how much they
would share, but he had wanted it all the moment he had
set his eyes upon her. Soon he would have her totally. She
would be his wife. He had faith that she had the strength
to hurl the harpoon skillfully enough. She had many res-
ervoirs of strength. She had proven that, time and time
again. . . .

Lorna's insides quivered as Little Fox gently placed the
necklace about her neck. She looked up into his eyes and
became enmeshed inside with a strange warmth, and wondered at these feelings. Was this what one experienced
when discovering love? Could she at such a young age?
At this moment in time, she truly believed that, yes, all
these things were possible!

The necklace now lying beautifully about her neck,
Lorna looked down at it and touched it meditatively. She
had to give Little Fox a fierce hug!

Throwing herself into his arms, Lorna hugged Little
Fox tightly.

But suddenly she became bashful, realizing that all that
she had done had been done with an audience! Gray Wing
and Amelia had seen her display of affection! Would they
care?

"Thank you, Little Fox," she said, bashfully lowering
her lashes. "I shall always treasure this special gift."

Little Fox was in awe of the hug. He looked awkwardly
over at Gray Wing, then Amelia. A nervous smile played
on his lips. "Can Lorna come outside for a while?" he
blurted. "I will take care of her. I won't let her get too
tired."

Gray Wing smiled softly down at Little Fox, having felt
the young man's embarrassment transfer to him, understanding it. He had been a young man once himself. He
had tasted of a woman's flesh early, as he now understood
that Little Fox would also. The young warrior had much
fire in his blood. He was testing his prowess on Lorna, to
pursue women later, for with them he would learn how to

behave like a man, then know how to perform like a husband when the time came that he would want a wife.

Perhaps even Lorna!

"*Ah-hah*, yes," Gray Wing said, nodding. "Watch her with care, Little Fox. She has only been well enough for playing for a short time now."

Amelia frowned down at Lorna. She pressed a hand to her cheek. "You stay out of the sun," she said. "Your skin is so fair, so tender, after being so ill." She glanced over at Little Fox. "She may come out with you for a walk, but not far. Do you understand?"

Little Fox nodded anxiously, his eyes wide with pride that he was being trusted so much. He knew that Lorna was special. She was special in every way. "She will just walk in the *shade*," he said, thrusting his chest out proudly. "Little Fox will care for her."

"Then be off with you both," Amelia said, patting Lorna on the cheek as Lorna smiled adoringly up at her. "Have fun."

"We will," Lorna murmured, grabbing Little Fox's hand, hurrying from the house.

"I hope we aren't wrong to allow her to become involved with outside activities so soon after her recovery," Amelia worried aloud, aware of the void in the room due to Lorna's absence.

Gray Wing spun Amelia around to face him. "Again you worry!" he said, frowning at her. "My *la-dida*, worrying will be the death of you!"

He drew her into his embrace, his fingers weaving through her waist-length hair, which was showing its fiery red coloring through the black dye. "I can think of much better things to do besides worrying," he said, his breath warm on her cheek as he lowered his mouth to kiss her. "Do you not realize the silence of my dwelling? We are alone, *la-dida*, totally alone. Lorna and Little Fox won't be back for a while. Why not use the time alone in the way we know best? Let us make love. Let us make love *now*."

Amelia's insides began a slow melting as Gray Wing

slipped his hands beneath her skirt. As his fingers moved slowly upward, small fires were set along her flesh. "Gray Wing, dare we?" she murmured, becoming breathless from desire. "Lorna *could* return at any moment. And, Gray Wing, it is broad daylight! Is this not a shameless time of day to make love?"

Gray Wing chuckled as his fingers kneaded and probed between her thighs, aware of her response as she leaned into his hand and began to gyrate her womanwood against it. "Shameless?" he whispered, his tongue weaving its way inside Amelia's ear, tormenting her. "Another word to use when worrying. *La-dida, klose-spose*, let me teach you how easy it is to forget worries!"

"Yes . . . oh, yes . . ." Amelia said in a husky whisper. "I want you. Oh, Lord, how I want you."

Cradling her close, Gray Wing eased Amelia down onto a pallet of furs beside a slow-burning fire in the fire pit. Skillfully he removed her dress and moccasins, then let his tongue and lips awaken her fully to what he wanted from her. While his fingers kneaded her breasts, his tongue made a slow path downward, its heat evoking a sensual moan from deep inside her.

A flood of emotions overwhelmed Amelia as Gray Wing showed her again just how much he loved her. She was thrilled to realize that finally life was going to be good to her. Though she had lost so much, she still possessed Gray Wing's love and would soon be his wife, and her sister had recovered from an illness that could have killed her.

It was a time to relax and enjoy the richness of these blessings. She would love now as never before. She was *free* to love, to *receive* as well as to *give*.

Gray Wing's tongue and lips pleasuring her made Amelia aware of his need of her. She twined her fingers through his shoulder-length hair and drew him closer, enjoying the building euphoria inside her, which Gray Wing was causing. She tossed her head. She bit her lower lip. Perspiration laced her brow, as still he pleasured her in the sensual way he had introduced her to. She could feel his hunger in the hard pressure of his lips on her womanhood and the grasp of his fingers on her breasts. It was a time of cresting passions. . . .

"Please, Gray Wing, fill me with your hardness," Amelia whispered, looking at him with ecstasy. "I am ready. Oh, I am ready!"

Gray Wing had been fighting to go slowly with her, for their times sensually together had been few these past weeks while tending to her ill sister. He wanted to make this moment of pleasure last.

Yet tomorrow would she not prove that she could be his forever? Tomorrow she would ride with him in his canoe. She would throw the harpoon. He would seek and find a whale for her to kill and bring back to his people as a gift to them!

If not tomorrow, the next day . . .

A tremor went through Amelia's body as Gray Wing rose above her and his lips touched hers in a gentle and lingering kiss. His hips moved, and suddenly he was inside her, stroking . . . gently stroking. . . .

Twining her arms about his neck, Amelia met him stroke by stroke, her lips turning to satin beneath his kiss. Molding her close to him, Gray Wing caressed her skin lightly with his fingertips, reveling in the softness of her buttocks beneath his callused fingers.

Then again he sought the swells of her breasts and massaged them, his thumbs circling her nipples, causing them to tighten against his palm.

His breath teased her ear as his mouth left her lips to whisper of his love to her. His eyes burned with passion as he looked down at her, his shaft moving rhythmically within her.

"Send me to paradise," Amelia whispered, now breathless, the sweetness of pleasure spreading, searing her heart . . . her soul. . . .

She clung to his sinewed shoulders as once again he kissed her, his tongue surging audaciously between her teeth. A web of golden magic was now spun between them. With a fierceness they met the ultimate pleasure as their passion crested, then exploded.

Gray Wing eased away from Amelia and cuddled her close. He stroked her cheek with his fingertips, devouring her with his eyes. "Never could I have enough of you," he said huskily. "Never . . ."

Lorna walked slowly beside Little Fox, realizing just how weak her illness had made her. Yet she would not allow Little Fox to know this! Since his first visit to her sickbed after the threat of the exposure to smallpox was over, she had decided she would prove to him that she would never be sickly again once she was back on her feet! After discovering her worth to him, she had begun to feel special. Each day her feelings for him had mounted. Surely he felt the same or why had he bothered with her? Why had he given her such a special gift?

"Let us sit for a while," Little Fox encouraged as he gestured toward a meandering stream deep within the forest. It was a rich land, beautiful and unspoiled, a tangle of vine, maple, alder, and ash. "It is cool and peaceful here. Let us sit and talk."

Feeling shy again, not used to a young man's devoted attention, Lorna only nodded. Suddenly she could not find her voice! Little Fox's presence disturbed her so strangely!

Little Fox plucked a wild rose and offered it to Lorna. "You might like to place this in your hair," he said, admiring the bright red color as he had the first time he had seen her.

It had taken much courage to go that first time to call on her! She had been so ill! How it had hurt him to see her! He had only been offered the right to see her when the danger of his being exposed to the vicious disease was past. Her weakness at the time of his first visit had been due to her being ill for so long! Not from the lingering disease, itself.

Though she was so young, he knew that when she got older there would be much between them. It was their destiny to be together. He had felt it the first time he had seen her, when she was nine and he was eleven.

Their love would be as devoted as that between Gray

Wing and Amelia! He would wait for Lorna forever, if need be, to make this a truth for all to see.

Lorna accepted the rose and placed it in her hair over her ear. She smiled softly at Little Fox. "It's pretty," she murmured. "Thank you."

"Do you know what is going to happen tomorrow?" Little Fox asked, his eyes wide with anxiety.

"Yes. Amelia is going to go with Gray Wing in a massive canoe," Lorna said, turning to face him on her knees. "She is going to prove herself to your people. Then there will be a wedding." She placed her hands on Little Fox's cheeks. "Isn't that exciting? My sister is going to throw a harpoon into a great whale! Oh, how I hope someday to do that to prove myself to the man I love!"

Realizing what she had just said and how her hands were touching Little Fox's cheeks so possessively, Lorna dropped them. Her lashes lowered bashfully. Then her insides quivered strangely as Little Fox took her hands and squeezed them fondly.

"Your sister will prove her worth," he said thickly. "She is courageous. She is strong!" He cleared his throat nervously. "And you will also one day have the ability to prove yourself."

Lorna's eyes moved slowly upward; her face was hot with a blush. "Do you truly think so?" she murmured, thrilled by his faith in her.

"I *know* so," Little Fox said, then drew her to him and held her close, dreaming of that day when she would prove his words true. But *he* must first prove himself worthy of being a Suquamish chief! He would make Gray Wing proud to choose him as the next chief in line.

If he had no sons to bear the title, he worried to himself. If . . .

Thirty-One

The blast of air sounded closer this time, and off to the right. The steersman, crouching in the canoe's stern, used his paddle to guide the craft toward the sound of the whale. For hours Amelia had sat tensely silent in the canoe with Gray Wing and his warrior hunters, stalking a whale as it had dived and surfaced through the gray waters of Puget Sound.

She had been impressed not only by the agility of the hunters but also by the maneuverability of the craft in which they were hunting. It was a special canoe, slim-waisted, with racy lines. The hull had been scorched to remove splinters, then sanded down to a glassy smoothness with sharkskin, to permit the canoe to slip through the water swiftly and noiselessly.

Rain fell in a slow mist over the waters of the Sound, causing a veil of gray to impede the view. Sometimes Amelia saw the twenty-ton giant of a whale. Other times the steersman had relied on the sound of the Whale's blast of air alone as it broke the surface for air.

Amelia brushed a wet strand of hair back from her eyes and wiped rain droplets from her cheeks, huddling beneath a rain shawl made of plant fibers. She trembled inwardly for many reasons. She was thrilled to be on the sea hunt with the man she loved, yet she was worried that in the end, she might lose him because of her inability to do what was required of her today.

Her gaze fell upon the large harpoon resting just only inches away from where Gray Wing sat in front of her, his solid steel back to her. The harpoon was smaller than the one normally used by Gray Wing. This one had a single foreshaft with a long, multiple-barbed bone point. It was made with a detachable foreshaft, the point connected to the foreshaft by a short lanyard, the foreshaft to the shaft by another. The shaft carried a long line to which she would hold fast.

These several joints on this particular harpoon were meant to absorb the impact when the struck quarry lunged, reducing the strain on each individual part of the harpoon and also on the one who would be thrusting it.

Amelia turned her attention back to the sea and the veil of gray through which the canoe was steadily traveling. In all directions nothing but rain and fog met her eyes. But she knew they were close to the whale. Everything was quiet. The warrior hunters who were steadily paddling didn't need to see the steersman's signal for intense quiet. The long, narrow cedar paddles slipped in and out of the water soundlessly, each paddle blade ending in a point, allowing water to drain off silently in a tiny stream.

When Gray Wing turned and suddenly faced Amelia, she flinched. She did not have to be told that this was the moment of trial, for Gray Wing already had his twelve-foot harpoon in hand, a backup for her should she miss *or* hit the target. He would not chance losing the whale, since they had been lucky enough to find one this day to take home to his village.

First Amelia would cast her harpoon into the whale; Gray Wing would follow soon afterward, in kind. Plans were they would return to the village together this day, both triumphant over the largest mammal in the world!

The whale was now in sight, pushing its huge tail flukes

downward to begin a dive. Amelia rushed to her feet and grabbed her harpoon. Her insides mushy with fear, her face pale, she waited as the canoe silently approached the whale from the rear, so that the animal would neither hear nor see it.

Swiftly the canoe came in on the whale's left side, to lie close alongside it, for Amelia's harpoon was heavy. Doing as she had been taught by Gray Wing, she stood with her left foot on the bow thwart, her right foot forward on the gunwale, holding the harpoon crosswise in front of her at about shoulder height.

Breathless, her heart pounding hard, she aimed just behind the cetacean's left flipper, pivoted, and tossed the harpoon, then ducked down into the forward compartment to avoid being struck by the floats or springy coil of line as they paid out. Her eyes were wide as she watched the harpoon hit its target.

"Lord, I *did* it!" she cried, looking anxiously at Gray Wing as his face lighted up into a broad grin. But he said nothing, for his arm was raised to throw his own harpoon.

Amelia flinched when Gray Wing emitted a piercing yell, and she watched breathlessly as his harpoon was hurled into the air and landed alongside hers on the great whale's body. The Suquamish warriors loudly whooped; Amelia emitted a sob of joy. She was glad that Gray Wing's harpoon had landed beside hers.

Then suddenly she realized that, being so caught up in the excitement, she had forgotten that she had, indeed, just proven herself not only to Gray Wing but also his people! She was going to be accepted totally by his people!

She wanted to rush into Gray Wing's arms, to fiercely hug him. She wanted to shout to the world just how much she loved him and how anxious she was to become his wife. She had proved herself worthy! There was no longer any question as to what her status would be in the Suquamish village.

Yet she wanted to hear Gray Wing himself make this declaration aloud, for his crew to hear.

But he and his crew were absorbed in making sure they did not lose the whale she had helped to capture.

Settling down onto the seat of the canoe, Amelia placed her hands on her lap and watched and waited.

As the whale began to roll and thrash about, the canoe sheered off hard to port. This was the most dangerous moment. The whale might turn toward the canoe, smashing it to bits in one of his blind rushes. A crewman might be badly injured by a blow from a float or the rigid line, or even be caught in a bight by the whale and dragged to his death. It was mainly for this moment that the whaler and his crew had practiced long drill sessions to forestall any mishaps at sea.

The canoe followed the whale, running in to drive home more harpoons with short line and floats, until the great creature finally became so weakened by loss of blood, the drag of the floats, and its titanic struggles, that it finally lay quiet in the water as Gray Wing went in for the kill. His eyes dark with pride, Gray Wing turned and faced Amelia. He drew her up to stand beside him as the canoe with its prize swept through the water. The fog was lifting. The rain had stopped. In the distance Whale Island jutted up from the water, shadowed by tall pines and cliffs.

"My *la-dida*, you have made me very proud," Gray Wing said, his chin held high. He looked around at each of his warriors. "Did you all see? Did not my woman hunt today as no woman before her? My warriors, is she not worthy to be my wife?"

Loud shouts of approval followed, causing Amelia's heart to soar with pride. She looked at Gray Wing, choked with emotion.

"*La-dida*, my people will welcome you with much vigor," he said thickly. "With much warmth."

Amelia felt as though in a daze. None of this seemed real. None of it! She had waited forever, it seemed, to find some sort of solace, some sort of happiness, in her life, and finally she had achieved it. From the moment she had seen Gray Wing standing on the shore from her father's ship, something had told her, even then, that the future was theirs! Was it truly happening? Would they truly have no more obstacles to overcome?

"I must help row the canoe to shore," Gray Wing said. He eased Amelia down on the seat, then sat down before her. "It is time for singing!"

In awe of Gray Wing, Amelia clung to the sides of the canoe, listening to him leading his warrior hunters in Suquamish Indian songs. As their voices rang out merrily over the water, sea gulls swept down and eyed them curiously.

Giggling to herself, so enjoying all of this, Amelia then joined in, to hum along with the merriment. The canoe swept smoothly on through the water, the whale carcass following along beside it.

The island drew closer . . . closer.

Yet when they arrived, they could not beach the canoe with its prize catch, as always in the past after each victory over a whale. They must wait for a high tide that would allow them to pull the whale high on the beach for butchering.

But Gray Wing's people came on the beach to see, to stare! They came in flocks. Amelia felt their eyes on her, silently appraising her.

And suddenly songs broke out from sea to shore. Drumbeats were heard in the distance. A great pulsing of orange reflecting in the sky overhead from shore was evidence that a great outdoor fire had been built. There was to be much food shared this night. There was to be a great celebration!

Amelia cast her eyes downward, feeling strangely bashful. Never had she had so much attention as now. . . .

Perfectly, peacefully content, Amelia tucked Lorna into bed, smoothing a buckskin blanket up to her sister's chin. "Did you and Little Fox have fun at the celebration?" she asked in a silken purr.

"Yes, lots of fun," Lorna said, yawning. She grabbed one of Amelia's hands and squeezed it. "Was it fun catching the whale?"

Amelia laughed softly. "Well, I don't know if it is proper to say that I *caught* it," she murmured. "And I don't know if it is proper to call what I did fun. But, yes, I guess you could say that." She leaned close to Lorna's ear. "Can you keep a secret?"

"Oh, yes," Lorna whispered back, her eyes wide. "What secret?"

"I'm very glad it's all over," Amelia sighed. "Never do I wish to do anything like that again. One whale per lifetime is all *I* need."

Lorna placed a hand over her mouth and giggled, then looked seriously up into Amelia's eyes. "I will catch a whale one day, just the same as you," she said determinedly. "When I am older, I am going to prove to Little Fox that I can also be worthy to be a Suquamish wife."

Amelia hugged Lorna. She sighed. "So you plan to marry him?" she whispered, not wanting to remind Lorna that Little Fox was not in line to be chief. Only women who were to marry a *chief* had to prove themselves worthy by casting a harpoon into the great body of a whale!

"Yes. He is so grand!" Lorna said, yawning again. She snuggled down beneath the blanket. "I am so sleepy. So . . . so . . . sleepy."

"I'll tell you a story while you drift into dreamland," Amelia said, stretching out beside Lorna, yet her heart was elsewhere. She knew that Gray Wing was awaiting her arrival by *his* side. Their lovemaking would be special this night. It was the night before they were to become man and wife!

In a soft, soothing voice, Amelia began to tell a tale that came easily for her. She was telling about how she, as a young girl, had found, and had grown to love, a handsome Suquamish warrior.

Lorna fell to sleep with a soft smile on her face. . . .

Amelia's hair spilled over her shoulders as she lay on the pallet of furs. Soon her true color of red would replace the black dye that had been used while she was in China the second time. She looked adoringly up at Gray Wing whose eyes were lit with points of fire as he was straddling her, taking in her nude silkiness. She placed a hand on his smooth bronze face and traced with her fingertips his bold nose, strong chin, and then the slope of his hard jaw.

"Did I do well?" she asked silkily. "Are you truly proud of me, Gray Wing?"

"Did you not see it in my people's eyes when we arrived ashore with the whale, and in its side was your harpoon alongside mine?" he said, smiling down at her. "Did you not feel it in their embraces when they welcomed you as you left the canoe?"

"Yes, I felt all of those things," Amelia murmured, her blood quickening as his hands molded her breasts. "I felt all of those things and even more. I felt a total peace engulf me when I saw the look of love in your eyes as you watched your people accept me as your future wife."

She trembled with aliveness when Gray Wing bent his head to flick his tongue over the taut tip of her breast while his hands now crept lower on her body, seeking all of her pleasure points. "I feel, oh, so much now, Gray Wing," she whispered, closing her eyes with ecstasy. "Oh, how you arouse in me such a passion!"

"Do you see how being with you affects me?" Gray Wing asked, chuckling, his manhood pulsing with need. He reached for her hand and placed it on his hardness. "Pleasure me in this way. Make my mind soar." He guided her hand in an easy up-and-down motion, then stopped and smiled wickedly down at her. "But I can stand only so much and then I must place my hardness inside you."

The sweet pain between Amelia's thighs forewarned of the pleasure she would be receiving very soon. She smiled seductively up at Gray Wing and continued to move her hand on him. She watched his eyes close and his jaw tighten as he groaned and stiffened his muscles. She could see his pulse beat more wildly at the base of his throat and knew that she had been taught the art of pleasuring him well, for he seemed to be imprisoned by the feelings that were raging through him.

Recalling another way of making Gray Wing enjoy her more, Amelia leaned up on an elbow and moved her lips close to his throbbing hardness. She replaced her hand with her tongue. Gray Wing reached out and entwined his fingers in her hair and drew her closer to his point of desire. Slowly he guided her movements, his head spinning with the wondrous feelings the sweetness of her tongue and mouth were creating.

Then, hardly able to bear it any longer, feeling near to exploding, he coaxed her away from him and laid her out beneath him as he drove his hardness deep inside her, plunging deeper . . . deeper . . . deeper. . . .

Amelia's breath was taken away as desire shot through her and she felt his hardness totally filling her. She soared with joy and clung to him. She shot him a look of rapture through her thick lashes as his eyes swept over her, leaving a trail of fire behind the touch of his eyes.

Gray Wing drew her close and kissed her lips, then the soft hollow of her throat, and then the tip of a breast. His hands moved steadily, touching her all over, loving the feel of her, the softness of her. . . .

Amelia felt the ultimate emotion rising within her as the sexual excitement mounted. Suddenly she shuddered and cried out as she arched, as his body also became consumed with wondrous, pleasurable quiverings. They clung, spent. Then Gray Wing rained kisses on her eyelids, her mouth, and hair.

"*La-dida*, my love for you is filled with fire!" Gray Wing said huskily. "Never will I have enough of you."

"I will always be here for you," Amelia said, placing a soft kiss on his brow. "Don't you remember? We will become husband and wife tomorrow."

She leaned up on an elbow, her eyes wide. "I can hardly believe it, Gray Wing," she sighed. "Is it actually going to happen?"

"*Hy-uh*, tomorrow," Gray Wing said, smoothing some locks of hair back from her flushed cheeks. "Tomorrow we will have a potlatch to celebrate our wedding!"

Amelia cocked an eyebrow and tilted her head. She

thought she knew most of the Suquamish customs, yet she had just been introduced to a word that she was not familiar with. "Potlatch?" she questioned, sitting fully upright. "What is a potlatch?"

"You shall see." Gray Wing chuckled, drawing her back down beside him. "You shall see." He enfolded her within his arms. "I do not want to take time explaining it now. Let us make love again, my *la-dida*. I feel the passion once again boiling inside my veins!"

"Gray Wing, you are insatiable," Amelia said, laughing softly. But then her laugh faded into a gurgle of pleasure as Gray Wing swept his lips down across her body and tasted of the sweetness between her thighs.

Once again her senses were beginning to reel with drunken pleasure. . . .

Thirty-Two

❧ ❧

The reflection in the dark heavens was a great pulsing orange from the huge outdoor fire, and the enticing aroma of roasted meat filled the air. The incessant sound of drumming on a hollow box and of dancers turning fast on their heels in a narrow circle, then leaping, had grown somewhat wearisome for Amelia, for this ritual had now been in progress for over two hours.

With Lorna at her side, attired in a beautifully beaded buckskin dress, her hair braided down her back, Amelia was sitting beside Gray Wing on a platform overlooking the celebration ritual.

Amelia and Gray Wing wore the same attire—robes made from the skins of the whistling marmot. These soft-furred hides were equal in value to the sea-otter robes, for hunters climbed high above the timberline to set deadfall traps around the marmot dens. Bone triggers, carved with figures believed to have magical power, were made especially for these traps.

Amelia's hair was drawn back from her face, and the soft down of duckling feathers had been placed above both ears. Gray Wing wore his headdress bearing the carved figure of a whale, painted and inlaid with iridescent shell, spiked with sea lion whiskers, and hung with ermine tails.

Beneath Amelia's robe she wore a white doeskin dress decorated with painted porcupine quills. Under his robe Gray Wing wore only a breechcloth.

Upon arriving at the celebration scene, Amelia had discovered that these rituals were necessary, for while the dancers performed and those who watched chanted, Chief Bear's Paw, his wife, and other Haida warriors and their wives had arrived in the Suquamish village and were now seated about the huge outdoor fire.

Having been forewarned that the Haida chief would come to the wedding celebration, Amelia had not been taken aback any less by it. She still did not know why the Haida should be present for the wedding. Gray Wing had only said that it was necessary for many reasons. . . .

Gray Wing leaned closer to Amelia. "It is almost time for the potlatch to begin," he whispered, his eyes gleaming. "My *la-dida*, soon you will see the importance of the man you are to marry. Chief Bear's Paw will also see!"

The outdoor fire was warm on Amelia's cheeks, but its heat was welcome on the cool autumn evening. She turned her eyes to Gray Wing. His face shone so beautifully bronzed in the light of the fire. His eyes looked pitch black this night instead of gray. But she knew that was due to the building excitement, almost a strong potent flaming of his senses and of hers.

"You still haven't explained what a potlatch is," she persisted softly. "Does the word mean 'marriage'? That is what we are celebrating, is it not?"

Gray Wing chuckled. He took Amelia's hand and squeezed it. "No, it does not mean marriage," he said hoarsely. "*Patshatl*, or potlatch, means 'giving.' "

Amelia's eyes widened. "Oh?" she murmured. "Who gives what?"

Her gaze slowly moved to the great pile of possessions taken from Gray Wing's house. Among them were furs, bark cloth, silver bracelets, zinc wash boilers used in ceremonial exchanges, clothing, blankets, shells, and beads.

Most prominent of them all had come from the beach—his proud, greatly carved canoe, bearing his crest, the *wasgo*, and within it his prized whaling harpoon.

And then her eyes moved to the large piles of fish that Gray Wing had caught early in the day, and to earthenware jars filled with whale blubber!

Amelia had silently watched him assemble these personal possessions, wondering why he was bringing them together, but she had not asked, for he knew ways of eluding her questions when he desired!

Slowly her eyes moved back to Gray Wing. Was he now ready to answer her? It seemed so.

Listening intently, devotedly, Amelia felt herself being drawn more and more into the wondrous customs of the Suquamish Indians, knowing that she would have to learn them all . . . *accept* them all. . . .

"It is with the potlatch that I set myself apart from the rest of my people," Gray Wing began, holding his chin proudly high. "It is important that I impress my people and the neighboring tribes with my wealth, to show my worth as chief, and to show that everyone else is only a commoner. A potlatch this night is not only to celebrate our marriage but also for me to boast of my prestige. To do this I must give away many gifts. I must destroy my most valuable property to demonstrate that I am so powerful and rich that my possessions mean nothing to me."

He gave Chief Bear's Paw a cynical glance. "I must prove much to my rival," he growled. "Bear's Paw is not of the same personality as Red Eagle was. Seems I will always have to prove my worth to him in one way or the other."

Then his eyes grew warm as once again he looked at Amelia. "In wives, even," he said huskily. "My *la-dida*, you will be the loveliest of *all* wives."

Amelia lowered her eyes, suddenly feeling as bashful as she had at age thirteen. She knew that she, as well as Gray Wing and his possessions, was the center of attention this night. In a sense, she was a part of his possessions. And did not mind, for he was also a part of hers.

"It is now time to proceed," Gray Wing said, giving Amelia's hand a final squeeze. He lifted her chin with a forefinger, causing her eyes to meet and hold his. "And do not fret over the loss of my possessions, which soon would also be yours once our hands join in marriage, for, my *la-dida*, soon Chief Bear's Paw will have his own potlatch, in which he will also give me many gifts. He will also want to prove his worth to *me*."

Moving to his feet, swiftly sweeping his robe from around his powerful, muscular shoulders, standing in only his breechcloth and headdress, Gray Wing moved from the platform and reached for a flaming torch that was being handed to him by a young warrior. The drums became silent, the dancers squatted around the fire, their eyes wide and watchful.

Gray Wing smiled smugly as he walked boldly to his canoe and began touching it all over with the flaming torch, setting small fires along its sides. The crowd gasped as the flames hissed and spread. The harpoon that lay inside the canoe soon became a flaming wand; the canoe was soon fully engulfed by fire.

The flames danced and wove into the sky as Gray Wing smiled even more broadly at Chief Bear's Paw, thus far very triumphant in his show of wealth and prestige!

But it was not yet enough! Grabbing blankets and valuable furs, Gray Wing tossed them into the burning canoe. Gasps and whoops erupted through the crowd of onlookers.

Believing enough had been burned to prove his wealth to the Haida and to his own people, Gray Wing nodded toward another young Suquamish warrior to begin the gift-giving. One by one, gifts were laid at the feet of Chief Bear's Paw while he sat, attired in only a loincloth, with his arms folded stiffly across his tattooed chest.

The Haida chief held his chin high. His hair hung down to his waist in one long braid, and he showed no feelings, no emotion, yet within his chest his heart beat soundly. Though Gray Wing was much too brazen, too boisterous, for his liking, it seemed they might be friends after all. I† would be good to have a chief such as Gray Wing to banter with. They were two powerful rivals. They would have many potlatches, many games between their tribes. This was needed to make life interesting . . . worthwhile.

When the last gift was given, Gray Wing went to stand over Chief Bear's Paw. Offering a hand, he was glad when Bear's Paw clasped it and shook it.

But no words were exchanged, only bold, proud looks of admiration.

Then, releasing the Haida chief's hand, Gray Wing sprang around on his heels and emitted a loud shriek, which reverberated into the heavens, bouncing from tree to tree. As he moved back to sit down again beside Amelia, the two tribes of Indians began to sing their tribal songs and perform dances for each other.

Amelia tensed when Little Fox, who was among the dancers, came and stood before Lorna. Attired in a breechcloth, his mantle trimmed with small bells, Little Fox offered Lorna his hands, silently urging her to join him in the dancing. When Lorna implored Amelia with her soft green eyes, Amelia could not help but give her permission. Lorna seemed well enough. In fact, when she was with Little Fox, she seemed never to have been ill at all. He seemed to give her life . . . to give her energy. . . .

Gray Wing slipped an arm about Amelia's waist. He urged her to her feet and led her among the dancers. Alongside Little Fox and Lorna, Amelia and Gray Wing began to sway with the music, looking at each other with heat in their eyes and in their hearts.

Then their bodies touched, their hands intertwined. They spun around together in rhythm to the music and singing; they dipped and again swayed. Amelia's blood was growing hot, she was feeling a euphoria claim her the faster Gray Wing spun her. It was as though she were drugged.

But she was suddenly drawn back to reality when she ⸱ orna out of the corners of her eyes. She looked too, as Little Fox gazed down into her eyes.

Then Little Fox, for a moment, danced by himself, his
eyes holding Lorna spellbound. First he squatted on his
hams, then leapt up and twirled. And then Lorna and Little Fox shared in the dance, Lorna all smiles. . . .

Remembrances of her own young love became vivid in
Amelia's mind and how her body had hungered to be
touched, to be caressed.

Was Lorna experiencing the same? Should it be allowed?

"Let it be," Gray Wing whispered, his breath hot on
her cheeks. He, too, had noticed the intimate scene being
acted out. "It is right. We should have allowed it when
we first met. It was torture having to wait so long after
you were suddenly taken from my life. And who is to say
that something might draw them apart sometime soon and
they would have to spend tormented nights and days alone
also?"

Gray Wing clasped Amelia's buttocks sensually with his
fingers, drawing her into his male strength. "Let it be, my
la-dida. Let it be."

Amelia gasped when Little Fox suddenly swept Lorna
up into his arms and carried her away into the shadows of
the forest. She fought with herself not to cry out. Was this
another custom of the Suquamish that she would have to
learn to accept? That children learned of lovemaking so
early in life? Could Lorna be old enough to understand
the meaning?

"There will only be innocent embraces," Gray Wing
said, chuckling. "Did you think I meant they should make
total love? *La-dida*, even in the Indian culture that waits
until the girl at least begins to shape into a woman. Little
Fox will patiently wait for Lorna to become of proper
age."

Sighing with relief, Amelia smiled awkwardly up at
Gray Wing. "Thank goodness for that," she said, laughing softly. "I had thought—"

"*La-dida*, when we first met, you were budding into a
woman, but yet not totally there," he said hoarsely, gy-
rating his body against hers as the drums beat out th

steady rhythm. "We only kissed and touched. I asked for nothing more. Nor did you."

"As I recall, I felt ashamed to share even that," Amelia said, smiling up at him, feeling feverish as he held her closer, their bodies becoming one.

She glanced all about her, seeing eyes on her and Gray Wing. She looked quickly away, blushing. "I could even admit to feeling a bit of shame *now*," she giggled. "Gray Wing, we are becoming a spectacle! Everyone is watching!"

She glanced about her again, gasping when she realized that everyone else had stopped dancing, leaving only Gray Wing and Amelia to perform by themselves. "Gray Wing, *everyone* is watching now. I feel . . . so awkward."

Low chants began to spread among the throng of Indians, and smiles erupted on their faces when Gray Wing held Amelia close to him and continued to dance. The drumbeats grew louder; rattles clattered. Amelia began to feel as though a great light was centered on her and Gray Wing, causing her to forget everyone else. It seemed meant to be, this moment of frenzied dancing . . . of frenzied music and chants!

Suddenly Gray Wing grabbed Amelia by the waist and stopped her. He gently took her hands and held them up into the air for all to see, his eyes black pits of passion as he looked down at her. Everything grew quiet around them. Amelia's heart seemed to cease to beat as she looked up at Gray Wing, breathless.

"I now make you my wife," Gray Wing blurted, then swept her into his arms. "You are now my *princess*!"

Gray Wing gave Amelia a searing, scorching kiss that stole all reason from her mind. All that she was aware of was that she was now his wife as quickly, as simply, as hands interlocked.

When he swept her fully up into his arms and began to ⌐n with her, leaving the center of the village and all those ⌐now cheered and chanted, she clung to him, her cheek ⌐against his powerfully built chest.

⌐nged, oh, how she belonged!

Carrying her into their house, Gray Wing meditatively removed her clothes before the blazing fire. As he stood with his hands on his hips, she removed his breechcloth, grazing her hand against his hardness, which caused him to tremble and to take a quick breath.

His gaze burned down upon her bare skin. "Now, my *la-dida*," he said huskily, lowering her to the pallet of furs beside the fire. "No preliminaries are needed. Let us make love. Let us make love as husband and wife."

The word "wife" thrilled Amelia. She lifted her hips and accepted his hardness as he plunged his readiness inside her. His hands twined through her hair; his lips were trembling as he kissed her long and sweetly, their bodies working, each drawing from the other the wondrous joy offered.

Amelia's breath quickened as Gray Wing's hands went to her breasts and began to knead them. She felt that she was spinning; the fact that she was his wife made everything more sensual . . . more free!

"Oh, how I do love you," Amelia whispered, caressing his back with the tips of her fingers. "Always I will love and cherish you."

"Did I not promise you long ago that I would make you my princess?" Gray Wing murmured, pausing to take in her total loveliness.

"Yes, your princess," Amelia sighed, smiling up at him, adoring him.

"It is now the autumn mating season," he said, his eyes gleaming. "It is the season of the mad moon."

Amelia drifted toward him and twined her arms about his neck, their bodies touching, fusing into one. "Then love me with a gentle passion," she whispered, having gone to hell and back, it seemed, for this moment. "It is *our* season of the mad moon. Only ours."

Bestselling author

CASSIE EDWARDS

Sensual and captivating tales of "Indian lore and undaunted love – Cassie Edwards captivates!"

—Karen Harper, bestselling author of *One Fervent Fire*

"Cassie Edwards is a shining talent!"

—*Romantic Times*

___SAVAGE EDEN   1-55773-007-5/$3.95
___SAVAGE SURRENDER   0-441-05384-X/$3.95
___SAVAGE SPLENDOR   1-55773-094-6/$3.95

<u>Check book(s). Fill out coupon. Send to:</u>

BERKLEY PUBLISHING GROUP
390 Murray Hill Pkwy., Dept. B
East Rutherford, NJ 07073

NAME_____

ADDRESS_____

CITY_____

STATE_____ZIP_____

**PLEASE ALLOW 6 WEEKS FOR DELIVERY.
PRICES ARE SUBJECT TO CHANGE
WITHOUT NOTICE.**

POSTAGE AND HANDLING:
$1.00 for one book, 25¢ for each additional. Do not exceed $3.50.

BOOK TOTAL $ _____

POSTAGE & HANDLING $ _____

APPLICABLE SALES TAX $ _____
(CA, NJ, NY, PA)

TOTAL AMOUNT DUE $ _____

PAYABLE IN US FUNDS.
(No cash orders accepted.)

218

"Superb!" —*New York Times*

"Charming and engaging!"
—*Atlanta Journal-Constitution*

Eugenia Price's

Sweeping <u>New York Times</u> *bestselling*

saga of the Old South

___SAVANNAH	0-515-10486-8/$5.50
___TO SEE YOUR FACE AGAIN	0-425-09203-8/$4.95
___BEFORE THE DARKNESS FALLS	0-425-11092-3/$5.50
___STRANGER IN SAVANNAH	0-515-10344-6/$5.95

Check book(s). Fill out coupon. Send to:

BERKLEY PUBLISHING GROUP
390 Murray Hill Pkwy., Dept. B
East Rutherford, NJ 07073

NAME_____

ADDRESS_____

CITY_____

STATE_____ZIP_____

**PLEASE ALLOW 6 WEEKS FOR DELIVERY.
PRICES ARE SUBJECT TO CHANGE
WITHOUT NOTICE.**

POSTAGE AND HANDLING:
$1.00 for one book, 25¢ for each additional. Do not exceed $3.50.

BOOK TOTAL	$____
POSTAGE & HANDLING	$____
APPLICABLE SALES TAX
(CA, NJ, NY, PA)	$____
TOTAL AMOUNT DUE	$____

PAYABLE IN US FUNDS.
(No cash orders accepted.)

214a